Fiction

A HarperCollins Pocket Anthology

R. S. Gwynn
Lamar University

HarperCollins *CollegePublishers*

Acquisitions Editor: Lisa Moore
Cover Design: Lucy Krikorian
Production Administrator: Kewal Sharma
Compositors: Pearl Klein & Mark Gerrard
Printer and Binder: R. R. Donnelley & Sons Company
Cover Printer: The Lehigh Press, Inc.

ISBN: 0-06-501461-8
94 95 96 9 8 7 6 5

Contents

A Collection of Short Fiction

Alphabetical Listing of Authors

Foreword

✧

✧

✧

The **HarperCollins Pocket Anthology** series was born of a need we hear almost daily for brief, inexpensive anthologies. Professors tell us they are concerned that anthologies seem to grow larger and larger, and that their students feel cheated when less than a third of the selections are actually taught in the course. To meet this demand, we have published three new titles: *FICTION: A HarperCollins Pocket Anthology*; *POETRY: A HarperCollins Pocket Anthology;* and *DRAMA: A HarperCollins Pocket Anthology*. The three can be used together in an introductory literature class as a replacement for the big textbook anthology that covers all three genres, or they can be used individually for courses that focus specifically on one of the genres. They are easy to supplement with novels or collections of works by single authors as well.

These brief, inexpensive anthologies can easily be carried to class and offer students real value at a reasonable price. They are designed to offer the most teachable blend of classic and contemporary selections with only the most essential information on each genre so that choice is provided but more of the book is actually used. To determine which selections to include—and whether this idea would hit a responsive chord among professors—we surveyed numerous professors to ask what they want in an anthology. Our survey helped us determine which stories professors want to teach; we therefore include traditional favorites like "A Rose For Emily" by William Faulkner and "Young Goodman Brown" by Nathaniel Hawthorne, alongside contemporary classics like "Everyday Use" by Alice Walker and "Rape Fantasies" by Margaret Atwood. We have made a special effort to broaden the canon: Fifty percent of our selections are by women, and newly appreciated voices, like Chinua Achebe, Louise Erdrich, and Denise Chávez, are included as well. The suggestions from those professors we surveyed were critical in determining the final shape of the contents, with its range of classic and modern—and, particularly, multicultural writers, women writers, and writers from around the world.

It is our hope that these books respond to the needs of students and professors who are looking for comprehensive, but affordable, alternatives to the big-book anthology. We particularly want to thank R.S. Gwynn, whose teaching experience and knowledge of literature are the foundation for the **HarperCollins Pocket Anthology** series. We are also grateful to all those fiction and introductory literature professors whose advice guided us in making selections and putting together the essential introductory material that their students would find useful for *FICTION: A HarperCollins Pocket Anthology*: L.L. Agosta, California State University at Sacramento; Stephen Arch, Michigan State University; Tom Bailey, Western Michigan University; James Cagnacci, City College of San Francisco; Betty Cochen, Beaufort County Community College; Robert Correale, Wright State University; James Davis, Denison University; Wil Gehne, State University of New York, Binghamton; Sally Harrold, Southwestern Oregon Community College; Thomas J. Hatton, Southern Illinois University at Carbondale; Douglas Hesse, Illinois State University; Harold Hurley, Roberts Wesleyan College; Donald B. Johns, University of California at Davis; Kate Kiefer, Colorado State University; Carrie Krantz-Fischer, Washtenaw Community College; Janet Madden, El Camino College; Daniel McAfee, Navarro College; Milla McConnell-Tuite, College of San Mateo; Alan L. McLeod, Rider College; Richard Priebe, Virginia Commonwealth University; Meme Riordan, City College of San Francisco; Don Ross, University of Minnesota; Linda Schwartz, Coastal Carolina College; Richard Spilman, Marshall University; Isabel B. Stanley, East Tennessee State; David Thomas, West Liberty State College; T. A. Whalen, Saint Mary's University; and Margaret E. Whitt, University of Denver.

Lisa Moore
Literature Editor

Introduction

✧

✧

✧

The Telling of the Tale

The memory begins with a scene like this: the circle contains about thirty boys and girls, all in their pre-teen years and dressed identically in khaki shorts and t-shirts, who sit on sections of logs around a leaping fire. The sun has just dropped beneath the summit of a nearby mountain, and a hint of damp chill steals into the August woods. It is the last night of camp, and the youngsters have gathered to sing songs and receive awards. Now one of the counselors, a college student who could pass as an older brother of any of the campers, puts away his guitar and nods to his colleague, a young woman who steps into the firelight and begins to speak. "Many, many years ago," she begins, her solemn voice describing three characters—a brave warrior, a maiden with a beautiful laugh, a wolf cub raised as a pet—"on a night not unlike tonight . . . " The surrounding woods seem to grow darker as the campers lean forward toward the rise and fall of her voice and the blaze of the flames. Caught in the spell of her words, they have momentarily left television and Walkmans behind, enacting one of the human race's oldest rituals as they respond to the simple magic of the storyteller's art.

Before we can begin to examine the elements of literary fiction we must bear in mind that literature in its written form is historically a recent innovation; indeed, its two most common modern forms, the short story and the novel, have been in existence for little more than two centuries. Yet long before the invention of writing, ancient peoples developed complex **oral traditions** of literature. These primitive stories, dealing with the creation of the cosmos and the origins of gods and goddesses, formed a body of **myths**, supernatural narratives widely believed to be true by the people of a given culture, and **legends**, popular stories about characters and events which may contain elements of historical truth. Even in modern societies elements of this primitive **folklore** survive in regional and ethnic tales passed on through the generations, most often taking the written form of **folk tales** collected by literary scholars; **fairy tales,** like Charles Perrault's (1628-1703) "Beauty and the Beast" and Hans Christian Andersen's (1805-1875) "The Little Mermaid"; **beast fables**, like those of Aesop (c. 550 B.C.) and Joel Chandler Harris (1848-1908); or **parables** like those in the Gospels. Many of these, especially the last two types, are to some degree **didactic**, with the narrative events illustrating a **moral** that is either stated or implied.

Even in modern societies other ancient forms of oral literature still enjoy a good state of health. These include **anecdotes**, accounts of single incidents usually involving a well-known person, and **riddles** and **jokes** of all types, which often seem to spring into circulation overnight and often unwittingly mirror the situations and humor of venerable **fabliaux**—short, realistic tales that often turn on a bawdy situation. Recently, much attention has been given to what folklorist Jan Brunvand calls **urban legends**, short narratives involving grotesque incidents that are widely accepted as true. The title of one of Dr. Brunvand's collections, *The Vanishing Hitchhiker*, refers to a ghost tale that virtually every American has heard in one of its many versions.

When myths and legends are assembled around the exploits of a great hero, the result is the **folk epic**, a long narrative in elevated style that is generally considered a starting point for any culture's literary history. Like most types of oral folk literature, epics were originally composed in verse for the sake of memorization, but they otherwise contain the same elements as modern literary forms like the short story and novel. For example, the individual **episodes** of Homer's *Odyssey*—Odysseus's outwitting of the Cyclops or his adventures with the sorceress Circe—can stand alone as exciting tales and can also fit into the larger structure of the epic, like chapters in a novel. Later authors, living in societies that had invented writing, consciously imitated the style of folk epics in composing **literary epics**. The *Aeneid* by Virgil (70-19 B.C.) and *The Divine Comedy* by Dante (1265-1321) are two famous examples.

In the Middle Ages, **romances**, written in both poetry and prose, gained great popularity among all classes. These tales of chivalry involving a knightly hero and a series of exciting, if improbable, adventures were ridiculed by Cervantes (1547-1616) in *Don Quixote*, a realistic account of an impoverished Spanish gentleman driven mad by reading too many romances. The eventual form that Cervantes gave Don Quixote's adventures was perhaps influenced by **picaresque novels** like the anonymous *Lazarillo of Tormes* (c. 1450), which involved a young orphan (or *pícaro*, Spanish for "rascal") in a series of loosely connected adventures. These picaresque tales are rightly considered the ancestors of modern fiction. Many novels, from Mark Twain's *The*

Adventures of Huckleberry Finn to J. D. Salinger's *The Catcher in the Rye,* borrow their structure from the picaresque novel, and the modern short story is indebted to its often stark level of realism.

The Short Story Genre

There is no agreement on the precise origins of the modern short story. One important influence in its development was the Italian **novella** of the late Middle Ages and Renaissance. The most famous collection of these realistic prose narratives is *The Decameron* by Boccaccio (1313-1375). In translation these tales were popular in other countries and widely imitated. In writing his plays Shakespeare frequently borrowed from Italian writers; his tragedy *Othello* takes its plot from a novella by Giraldi Cinthio. We still use the term "novella" for short stories that are long enough (usually over 15,000 words) to be published separately in book form. Ernest Hemingway's *The Old Man and the Sea* is one of the best-known examples from modern American literature.

The first half of the nineteenth century was the great period of the growth of the short story as a distinct **literary genre**, or type, and its rise took place in many countries at roughly the same time. Many explanations for this rapid development can be put forth, but perhaps the most important is the literary market established at that time by newspapers and magazines aimed at middle-class audiences. The United States, with its high rate of literacy and expanding middle class, led the way in this period; Washington Irving's tales, for example "Rip Van Winkle" and "The Legend of Sleepy Hollow," were among the first American writings to attain international popularity. Edgar Allan Poe, the first great theorist of the short story and one of its notable practitioners in this period, supported himself primarily as a magazine editor and contributor and thus had a large personal stake in promoting short fiction. Poe's influential review in 1842 of Nathaniel Hawthorne's *Twice-Told Tales* first stated the theory that a short story ought to be a unified artistic creation, as carefully shaped as a sonnet.

> A skillful literary artist has constructed a tale. If wise, he has not fashioned his thoughts to accommodate his incidents; but having conceived, with deliberate care, a certain unique or single *effect* to be wrought out, he then invents such incidents—he then combines such events as may best aid him in establishing this preconceived effect. If his very initial sequence tend not to the outbringing of this effect, then he has failed in his first step. In the whole composition there should be no word written, of which the tendency, direct or indirect, is not to the one pre-established design. And by such means, with such care and skill, a picture is at length painted which leaves in the mind

of him who contemplates it with a kindred art, a sense of the fullest satisfaction.

This idea of the *single effect* is perhaps Poe's most important contribution to the development of the short story as a serious literary genre.

Most of Hawthorne's and Poe's stories are perhaps more properly termed tales, if by that term we mean narratives which contain elements that are exotic or supernatural and which to some degree depart from the level of ordinary experience. Poe himself established many of the conventions of the horror, science fiction, and detective tales still being written and read today; **formula stories**, which rigidly follow the clichés and conventions of a particular genre, are sometimes half-affectionately called **pulp fiction**, a reminder of the low grade of paper once used in inexpensive magazines. Still, the tale remains a lively tradition among serious artists as well. Among the stories collected in this volume, selections by Shirley Jackson, William Faulkner, Joyce Carol Oates, and others show their debt to the tradition of the tale.

The short story in its present form, on the other hand, developed somewhat later, and its evolution was part of the larger literary movement of **realism**, which profoundly influenced the arts in the middle of the nineteenth century with its "slice-of-life" approach to subject matter which, in early centuries, would have been deemed inappropriate for serious treatment. It has been rightly noted that realism simply represents the effect of democracy on literary history. Celebrating its appearance as early as 1837, Ralph Waldo Emerson noted, "The literature of the poor, the feelings of the child, the philosophy of the street, the meaning of household life, are the topics of the time." **Naturalism**, an outgrowth of realism, emerged in the second half of the century and also proved influential, for it joined realistic treatment of everyday life with understanding of human behavior drawn from the new sciences of psychology and sociology. A story like Willa Cather's "Paul's Case" reveals in its title (with its overtones of "case study") this almost clinical approach to fictional characters. Both realism and naturalism remain vital currents in contemporary short fiction, as stories here by Raymond Carver, Alice Walker, and Bobbie Ann Mason attest.

The present century has seen the short story rise to its highest level of popularity and just as rapidly decline in its influence as a literary form. During the first half of the century, when magazines like *Collier's* and the *Saturday Evening Post* paid large sums for short stories by important authors, the genre flourished. F. Scott Fitzgerald kept a meticulous ledger in which he noted, in one six-month period in 1922-23, that he earned over $15,000 from magazine sales alone. A decade later, in the depths of the Depression, Fitzgerald complained that stories that earlier would have sold for prices in excess of $4,000 now commanded only $2,500. If these amounts seem exorbitant, remember that we are talking about times when a new automobile sold for under $1,000 and a gallon of gasoline cost a dime! Today, when virtually every college in the country employs one or more writers-in-residence whose primary income comes from teaching, we tend perhaps to underestimate the impact that economic realities have had on the history of literature.

In the second half of this century many of the established magazines that regularly ran serious fiction ceased publication. Search a typical supermarket magazine rack and you will find only one weekly magazine, the *New Yorker*, and a handful of monthlies containing short stories. Reading tastes have changed, and increased competition from television and other forms of entertainment have made the writing of short stories an expensive pastime for writers. Still, the pages of little magazines and literary quarterlies continue to provide outlets for publication, and new writers seem undeterred by the prospect of being paid little more that what one writer has called "two copies of what I've already got." Almost every writer of short fiction prominent today first appeared in small-circulation periodicals of this type, and many have continued to publish in magazines that can offer only prestige and a discriminating readership numbering in the hundreds. Indeed, the little magazines have traditionally been hospitable to many kinds of **experimental fiction** that editors of commercial magazines would never have considered. If the quantity of contemporary short fiction being published has shrunk from what it was in prior decades, the quality, one might argue, has remained the same or even improved. When we look at lists of recent winners of the Pulitzer or Nobel prizes, we discover many writers who have counted the short story as their first home.

Reading and Analyzing Short Fiction

We read for many reasons. In our daily lives most of our reading is strictly utilitarian—it is part of our jobs or education—or informational, as we scan the headlines of a daily newspaper for current events, business trends, or sports scores. We also read short stories and other types of fiction for various reasons. Sometimes our motive is simply to be entertained and to pass the time. Reading matter of this type is usually termed **escapist literature** and includes such popular categories as romance and detective novels, science fiction tales, and westerns. On the other hand, we might consciously choose to read "inspirational" fiction that is obviously didactic and contains "messages" or moral lessons with application to our own lives. Literary reading, though, occupies a position between the two extremes. Serious literature should certainly entertain us, but on a deeper level than, say, a half-hour episode of a television situation comedy show. Similarly, it may also contain an ethical theme with which we can identify, even if it does not try to "preach" its moral message to the reader. A short story that we can treat as a serious work of art will not yield all of its subtlety at first glance; to understand and appreciate its author's achievement fully we may have to examine its components—its plot, characterization, point of view, theme, setting, and style—noting how each part contributes to the story's overall effect. With that purpose in mind, let us read a very brief example by a modern American master of the genre.

John Cheever (1912-1982)

For most of Cheever's creative life he was associated with the *New Yorker*, the magazine that first published most of his short stories. Cheever's examinations of the tensions of life in white-collar suburbia take many forms—from naturalism to outright fantasy—but virtually all of his fiction is suffused with a melancholy that is often fueled by marital tensions, failed social aspirations, and what one story aptly calls "the sorrows of gin." Born in Quincy, Massachusetts, Cheever was expelled from Thayer Academy at seventeen, an event that formed the subject of his first published story, and worked almost exclusively as a writer of fiction for the rest of his life, with occasional periods spent teaching at universities and writing for television. His most original writing is arguably in his short stories, but novels like the National Book Award-winning *The Wapshot Chronicle* (1957), *The Wapshot Scandal* (1964), *Bullet Park* (1969), and *Falconer* (1977) brought him to the attention of large audiences. *The Stories of John Cheever* won the Pulitzer Prize in 1979. In recent years his daughter Susan Cheever has published a memoir, *Home Before Dark*, and an edition of her father's journals, both of which chronicle Cheever's long struggles with alcoholism and questions of sexual identity.

Reunion

The last time I saw my father was in Grand Central Station. I was going from my grandmother's in the Adirondacks to a cottage on the Cape that my mother had rented, and I wrote my father that I would be in New York between trains for an hour and a half, and asked if we could have lunch together. His secretary wrote to say that he would meet me at the information booth at noon, and at twelve o'clock sharp I saw him coming through the crowd. He was a stranger to me—my mother divorced him three years ago and I hadn't been with him since—but as soon as I saw him I felt that he was my father, my flesh and blood, my future and my doom. I knew that when I was grown I would be something like him; I would have to plan my campaigns within his limitations. He was a big, good-looking man, and I was terribly happy to see him again. He struck me on the back and shook my hand. "Hi, Charlie," he said. "Hi, boy. I'd like to take you up to my club, but it's in the Sixties, and if you have to catch an early train I guess we'd better get something to eat around here." He put his arm around me, and I smelled my father the way my mother sniffs a rose. It was a rich compound of whiskey, after-shave lotion, shoe polish, woolens, and the rankness of a mature male. I hoped that someone would see us together. I wished that we could be photographed. I wanted some record of our having been together.

We went out of the station and up a side street to a restaurant. It was still early, and the place was empty. The bartender was quarreling with a delivery boy, and there was one very old waiter in a red coat down by the kitchen door. We sat down, and my father hailed the waiter in a loud voice. *"Kellner!"* he shouted. *"Garçon! Cameriere! You!"* His boisterousness in the empty restaurant seemed out of place. "Could we have a little service here!" he shouted. "Chop-chop." Then he clapped his hands. This caught the waiter's attention, and he shuffled over to our table.

"Were you clapping your hands at me?" he asked.

"Calm down, calm down, *sommelier,"* my father said. "If it isn't too much to ask of you—if it wouldn't be too much above and beyond the call of duty, we would like a couple of Beefeater Gibsons."

"I don't like to be clapped at," the waiter said.

"I should have brought my whistle," my father said. "I have a whistle that is audible only to the ears of old waiters. Now, take out your little pad and your little pencil and see if you can get this straight: two Beefeater Gibsons. Repeat after me: two Beefeater Gibsons."

"I think you'd better go somewhere else," the waiter said quietly.

"That," said my father, "is one of the most brilliant suggestions I have ever heard. Come on, Charlie, let's get the hell out of here."

I followed my father out of that restaurant into another. He was not so boisterous this time. Our drinks came, and he cross-questioned me about the baseball season. He then struck the edge of his empty glass with his knife and began shouting again. *"Garçon! Kellner! Cameriere! You!* Could we trouble you to bring us two more of the same."

"How old is the boy?" the waiter asked.

"That," my father said, "is none of your God-damned business."

"I'm sorry, sir," the waiter said, "but I won't serve the boy another drink."

"Well, I have some news for you," my father said. "I have some very interesting news for you. This doesn't happen to be the only restaurant in New York. They've opened another on the corner. Come on, Charlie."

He paid the bill, and I followed him out of that restaurant into another. Here the waiters wore pink jackets like hunting coats, and there was a lot of horse tack on the walls. We sat down, and my father began to shout again. "Master of the hounds! Tallyhoo and all that sort of thing. We'd like a little something in the way of a stirrup cup. Namely, two Bibson Geefeaters."

"Two Bibson Geefeaters?" the waiter asked, smiling.

"You know damned well what I want," my father said angrily. "I want two Beefeater Gibsons, and make it snappy. Things have changed in jolly old England. So my friend the duke tells me. Let's see what England can produce in the way of a cocktail."

"This isn't England," the waiter said.

"Don't argue with me," my father said. "Just do as you're told."

"I just thought you might like to know where you are," the waiter said.

"If there is one thing I cannot tolerate," my father said, "it is an impudent domestic. Come on, Charlie."

The fourth place we went to was Italian. *"Buon giorno,"* my father said. *"Per favore, possiamo avere due cocktail americani, forti, forti. Molto gin, poco vermut."*

"I don't understand Italian," the waiter said.

"Oh, come off it," my father said. "You understand Italian, and you know damned well you do. *Vogliamo due cocktail americani. Subito."*

The waiter left us and spoke with the captain, who came over to our table and said, "I'm sorry, sir, but this table is reserved."

"All right," my father said. "Get us another table."

"All the tables are reserved," the captain said.

"I get it," my father said. "You don't desire our patronage. Is that it? Well, the hell with you. *Vada all' inferno.* Let's go, Charlie."

"I have to get my train," I said.

"I'm sorry, sonny," my father said. "I'm terribly sorry." He put his arm around me and pressed me against him. "I'll walk you back to the station. If there had only been time to go up to my club."

"That's all right, Daddy," I said.

"I'll get you a paper," he said. "I'll get you a paper to read on the train."

The he went up to a newsstand and said, "Kind sir, will you be good enough to favor me with one of your God-damned, no-good, ten-cent afternoon papers?" The clerk turned away from him and stared at a magazine cover. "Is it asking too much, kind sir," my father said, "is it asking too much for you to sell me one of your disgusting specimens of yellow journalism?"

"I have to go, Daddy," I said. "It's late."

"Now, just wait a second, sonny," he said. "Just wait a second. I want to get a rise our of this chap."

"Goodbye, Daddy," I said, and I went down the stairs and got my train, and that was the last time I saw my father.

—1962

Plot

In his discussion of tragedy in the *Poetics*, Aristotle (384-322 B.C.) gives first priority to **plot** as an element of a play, and most readers would probably agree that it holds a similar position in a work of fiction. Indeed, if we tell a friend about a short story we have enjoyed we will probably give a **synopsis** or brief summary of its incidents. In the case of a very brief story like "Reunion," this synopsis is only a few sentences long:

> In "Reunion" the narrator, a teenaged boy, meets his estranged father between trains in New York City. Over the course of an hour and a half the father's alcoholism and abusive personality are revealed. The story ends with the narrator boarding his train, indicating that this was the last time he saw his father, possibly by choice.

Plot may be defined as a story's sequence of incidents, arranged in dramatic order. One is tempted to insert the word "chronological," but doing so would exclude many stories that depart from this strict ordering of events. Though its use is more characteristic in longer works like novels, many stories employ the **flashback** to narrate incidents in the past. William Faulkner's "A Rose for Emily" begins with the funeral of the title character and then goes back in time to relate events that occurred as long as fifty years earlier. In opposite fashion, writers sometimes use **foreshadowing** to provide hints of future action in the story; an effective use of foreshadowing prevents a story's outcome from seeming haphazard or contrived. Of course, the manner in which stories handle time is largely illusory. During scenes with dialogue and action, time is slowed down by descriptive and explanatory phrases. On the other hand, stories cover gaps in chronology or leap over uneventful periods with transitional phrases and passages; the opening sentence of the second paragraph of "Reunion" compresses into a second or two an action that in reality would have taken at least several minutes. Even though "Reunion" does not take serious liberties with chronological time as we experience it, the ninety minutes of action in the story are compressed into about ten minutes of the reader's time. A plot like this, in which the action is more or less continuous within a single day, is called a **unified plot**; one that stretches over weeks or even longer periods, and thus consists of isolated scenes connected by a thin tissue of transitional devices, is called an **episodic plot**.

When we speak of the **dramatic structure** of a story, we refer to the exact way in which our emotional involvement in its plot is increased and relaxed. As Janet Burroway in *Writing Fiction* observes of the short story, "*Only* trouble is interesting." If we are not quickly engaged by the situation of a story we pronounce the cruellest of all critical verdicts on it by setting the story aside unfinished. The first part of this dramatic structure is the **exposition**, which provides the reader with essential information—who, what, when, where—he or she needs to know before continuing. While writers of sophisticated fiction may try to disguise the fact, they often begin their stories with a variation of the "Once upon a time" opening common to fairy tales. A variation on this type of beginning, called the ***in medias res*** ("in the middle of things") opening after the conventions of the old epic poems, may actually open with a "blind" bit of action before supplying its context.

The exposition of "Reunion" is fairly straightforward; in the first paragraph we learn who (Charlie and his father), what (a lunchtime meeting between trains), when (noon to 1:30 P.M.), and where (in and near Grand Central Station in New York City). Cheever might have begun the story with a slightly more "dramatic" sentence ("At twelve o'clock sharp I saw him coming through the crowd"), but he would have to have provided the essential contextual information in short order to avoid unnecessarily confusing the reader. Exposition usually describes a stable situation, even if it is not an entirely happy one. Charlie tells us that his parents divorced three years before and that he has not seen his father in that time. If he had not taken the step of writing the letter arranging the "reunion," that state of affairs might have gone on indefinitely.

The appearance of "trouble," some circumstance or event that shakes up the stable situation, constitutes the second part of a plot, the **complication**. This begins the **rising action** of the story. Complication in a story may be either external or internal, or a combination of the two. A fateful blow such as illness or an accident that affects a character is a typical example of an external complication, a problem that the characters cannot turn away from. An internal complication, on the other hand, might not be immediately apparent, the result of a character's deep-seated uncertainties, dissatisfactions, and fears. The external complication in "Reunion" is the father's series of confrontations with waiters; the internal complication is Charlie's growing sense of pity and revulsion. Typically, the complication of a plot is heightened by **conflict** between two characters who have different personalities and goals. At the beginning of the story, Charlie is overjoyed to see his father, but despite his knowledge that he will grow up to "be something like him," he is more than eager to escape his father's company at the end, even if he is unconsciously trying to run away from his own "future and . . . doom."

The rising action usually consists of a number of scenes containing action and dialogue that build to **moments of crisis** as a resolution of the complication momentarily seems at hand but quickly disappears. Aristotle uses the term **peripety** for these moments of reversal, as the hopes of the characters rise and fall. Thus, in "Reunion" all that needs to be resolved, at least on the surface, is for the characters to order lunch, eat, and return in time for the departing train. The father's increasingly obnoxious behavior, however, keeps postponing this resolution until the reunion has turned from a happy occasion to something very different. Unlike most stories, "Reunion" has a rising action as rigidly structured as a joke, with four similar restaurant scenes gradually escalating in absurdity as the father's senseless rage increases.

The central moment of crisis in a plot is the **climax**, or moment of greatest tension, which inaugurates the **falling action** of the story, in which the built-up tension is finally released. Some stories, particularly those that depend heavily on the use of suspense, have a steep "dramatic curve," and the writer uses all of his or her skills to impel the reader toward the final confrontation. Among writers included here, Edgar Allan Poe is the master of this kind of plot construction. Often one encounters the **trick ending** (also called the **O. Henry ending**, after its chief popularizer). A climax like this depends on a quick reversal of the situation from an unexpected source; its success is always relative to the degree to which the reader is surprised when it occurs. More typically, modern short stories rely on climactic devices that are somewhat subtler than unexpected plot twists. Many modern writers have followed James Joyce's lead in building not to a physical confrontation but to a moment of spiritual insight or revelation, what Joyce termed an **epiphany**. In the hands of a melodramatic writer insistent on sentimental happy endings, "Reunion" might have concluded with Charlie delivering a "tough love" sermon to his father, who would then fall to his knees and beg his son's forgiveness, having seen "the error of his ways." Cheever's more realistic method of climax in this case avoids the confrontation altogether as Charlie escapes to his train.

The final part of a plot is the **dénouement** or **resolution**. The French term refers literally to the untying of a knot, and we might compare the emotional release of a story's ending to a piece of cloth that has been twisted tighter and tighter and is then untwisted as the action winds down. The dénouement returns the characters to another stable situation. Just as a fairy tale traditionally ends with "And they lived happily ever after," many stories conclude with an indication of what the future holds for the characters. In the case of "Reunion" we return to the estrangement between Charlie and his father that existed at the beginning of the story, though this time all indications are that it will be a permanent one. The dénouement may be either closed or open. A

closed dénouement ties up everything neatly and explains all unanswered questions the reader might have; a typical example is the "Elementary, my dear Watson" that Sherlock Holmes provides in the final paragraph of Arthur Conan Doyle's famous tales to explain any remaining mysteries. On the other hand, an **open dénouement** leaves us with a few tantalizing loose ends; the last phrase of "Reunion," which consciously mirrors the story's opening sentence, does not explicitly state *why* Charlie never sees his father again. Was it strictly his own choice? Did the father die soon after their meeting? Or were other factors involved? We do not know, of course, and such an ending invites us to speculate.

One final word about plot: The fledgling writer attempting to invent a totally original plot is doomed to failure, and it is no exaggeration to say that there is nothing new under the sun where plots of short stories are concerned. These plots often draw upon what psychologist Carl Jung called **archetypes**, universal types of characters and situations that all human beings carry in their subconscious minds. Plots deriving from these archetypes may be found in ancient myths, fairy tales, and even in contemporary fiction. Among a few of the most familiar are the triangle plot, a love story involving three people; the quest plot, which is unified around a group of characters on a journey; and the transformation plot, in which a weak or physically unattractive character changes radically in the course of the story. "Reunion" is an example of one of the most widely used of all archetypal plots, the **initiation story**. In a plot of this type the main character, usually a child or adolescent, undergoes an experience (or "rite of passage") that prepares him or her for adulthood. In this book such stories as John Updike's "A & P" and Joyce Carol Oates's "Where Are You Going, Where Have You Been?" share the initiation archetype, though they differ in almost every other respect.

Characterization

Every story hinges on the actions undertaken by its main character, or **protagonist** (literally "first debater"), a term drawn from ancient tragedy. This term is more useful in discussions of fiction than such misleading ones as hero and heroine. Additionally, stories may contain an opposing character, or **antagonist**, with whom the protagonist is drawn into conflict. In many modern stories there is little in any traditional sense that is heroic about the protagonist; it may be more accurate to use a negative term, **antihero**, to designate one who occupies center stage but otherwise seems incapable of fitting the traditional heroic mold. Indeed, modern writers have often been so reluctant to seem didactic in presenting characters that are "moral beacons" that they have gone to the opposite extreme in presenting protagonists whom we regard with pity or even disgust instead of with admiration.

Characters in short stories are often described as **flat characters** or **round characters**, depending on the depth of detail the writer lavishes on them. In "Reunion" the father is essentially a flat character, rendered with a few quick strokes of the pen and reduced to a single personality trait, his alcoholic rudeness. Flat minor characters in stories are often **stock characters**, stereotypes who may be necessary to advance the plot but otherwise deserve no more than the barest outlines of description. Round characters, on the other hand, are given more than one trait, some of which may even seem contradictory, and are explored in depth as the author delves into the character's past and even into his or her unconscious mind. Characters of this type, usually the protagonists of stories, begin to approach the level of complexity that we associate with real human beings.

Development and **motivation** are also important in any consideration of a story's characters. Characters can be termed either **static** or **dynamic** depending on the degree to which they change in the course of the story. In "Reunion" the father is a static character. His personality was fixed long before the story opens, and Cheever holds out no likelihood that he will ever alter his course. Charlie, on the other hand, does attain some understanding in the course of the story, even if it is at the cost of his own disillusionment with what he wants his father to be. If development in a character is usually clear, motivation, the reasons the reader is given for a character's actions, may not be so obvious. In many cases an author will simply tell us what is going on in a character's mind, but in others we are denied access to this level of understanding. Although we can speculate, playing the amateur psychiatrist, about Charlie's father's strange behavior, we are not given any direct insight into the father's own view of his actions. In some stories writers may try to plug directly into a character's thoughts by using **interior monologue**, a direct presentation of thought something like a soliloquy in drama, or **stream of consciousness**, an attempt to duplicate raw sensory information in the same disordered state that the mind receives it. As useful as these devices can be in explaining motivation, they sometimes place excessive demands on readers and are thus comparatively rare.

Description of characters also helps us understand the author's intent. In real life we are told from an early age not to judge people by external appearance, but in fiction the opposite is more often the case: physical description is invariably a sign of what lurks beneath the surface. Given the brevity of most short stories, these physical details may be minimal but revealing in their lack of particulars. Cheever has Charlie describe his father at first as only "a big, good-looking man." Remarkably, the author here uses his protagonist's sense of smell to make the character vivid: Charlie breathes in "a rich compound of whiskey, after-shave lotion, shoe polish, woolens, and the rankness of a mature male." In that burst of imagery we may momentarily overlook the most important item in the list, the evidence that Charlie's father has been drinking in the morning.

Other elements may add to our understanding of a story's characters. Many writers take particular care in naming their characters in such a way as to draw attention to aspects of their personalities. This device (**characternym** is a term coined for it) is sometimes obvious, as is the case with Hawthorne's Young Goodman Brown, and sometimes not: in one of her stories Flannery O'Connor calls an unscrupulous seducer Manley Pointer, a name that a moment's thought reveals as an outrageous pun. Similarly, speech patterns and mannerisms may also disclose personality traits. A character's misuse of grammar or stilted vocabulary can *show* us a great deal more about background and self-image than a whole page of background information or analysis. Charlie's father's gestures and loud attempts at ordering in various foreign languages grow more embarrassing until his request for two "Bibson Geefeaters" comes as the punchline to a grotesque joke on himself.

Point of View

When we speak of a politician's **point of view** on an issue we mean his or her attitude toward it, pro or con. In fiction, however, the term "point of view" is employed in a specialized sense, referring to the question of ***authority*** in the story. Every story has a **narrator**, a voice or character that provides the reader with information about and insight into characters and incidents, but in some cases the identity of this voice of authority is not immediately apparent. Being too literal-minded about the matter of point of view is usually a mistake, and we usually have to accept certain **narrative conventions** without questioning them too seriously if we are to enjoy reading stories. Thus, when we finish reading a detective story narrated by the sleuth himself, we should not worry ourselves too much about when such a busy character found time to jot down the events of the story. Similarly, we accept as a convention the fact that a narrator may suddenly jump from simply recording a conversation to telling us what one of its participants is thinking. Very early in our lives we learn how stories are told, just as we do not think twice while watching a movie when our perspective shifts in the blink of an eye from one man's frightened stare, to the flashing barrel of a gun, to a hand clutching a chest, to another man's sneer of triumph.

Almost all narrative points of view can be classified as either first person or third person. In **first-person narration**, the narrator is a **participant** in the action. He or she may be either a major character (e.g., Charlie in "Reunion") or a minor character, and may be close to the event in time or distant from it. Though it is never directly stated, it seems clear that the adult Charlie is narrating an account of something that happened years before; thus, his repeated phrase about the last time he saw his father has a finality about it that goes far beyond a simple statement like "The last time I saw my father was a week ago in Grand Central Station." In general, first-person stories seem more immediate than third-person stories, but they are limited by the simple fact that the narrator must be present at all times and must also have some knowledge of what is going on. If, for example, an attempt had been made to tell "Reunion" from the point of view of one of the waiters, the narrator might have to resort to eavesdropping on Charlie and his father to report their circumstances. The ability of the narrator to tell the story accurately is also important. An **unreliable narrator**, either through naïveté, ignorance, or impaired mental processes, relates events in such a distorted manner that the reader, who has been tipped off, has literally to turn the narrator's reporting on its head to make sense of it. Imagine how we would read "Reunion" if it had been told from the boozy, self-deluded point of view of Charlie's father.

Third-person narration, by definition, employs a **nonparticipant** narrator, a voice of authority that never reveals its source and is capable of moving from place to place to describe action and report dialogue. In third-person stories the question of reliability is rarely an issue, but the matter of **omniscience**, the degree to which the "all-knowing" narrator can reveal the thoughts of characters, is. **Total omniscience** means just that—the narrator knows everything about the characters and their lives, even their futures, and may reveal the thoughts of anyone in the story. An **editorial point of view** goes even farther, allowing the godlike author to comment directly on the action (also called **authorial intrusion**).

Most contemporary authors avoid total omniscience in short fiction, perhaps sensing that a story's strength is dissipated if more than one perspective is used. Instead, they employ **limited omniscience**, also called **selective omniscience** or the **method of central intelligence**, limiting themselves to the thoughts and perceptions of a single character. This point of view is perhaps the most flexible of all since it allows the writer to compromise between the immediacy of first-person narration and the mobility of third-person. A further departure from omniscience is the **dramatic point of view** (also called the **objective point of view**). Here the narrator simply reports dialogue and action with minimal interpretation and no delving into the characters' minds. The dramatic point of view, as the name implies, approaches the method of plays, where readers are provided only with set descriptions, stage directions, and dialogue, and thus must supply motivations based solely on this external evidence.

Technically, other points of view are possible, though they are rarely used. Stories have been told in the second person ("You lie face down in the mud while rain pelts your back") and first-person plural (William Faulkner's "A Rose for Emily" is one example), but such points of view are difficult to sustain and may quickly prove distracting to readers. Also, there is an unwritten rule that point of view should be consistent throughout a story, although occasionally a writer may utilize multiple perspectives to illustrate how the "truth" of any incident is relative to the way in which it is witnessed.

Theme

We have already discussed the manner in which fables and other types of didactic literature make their purposes clear by explicitly stating an interpretation or moral at the end of the story. Literary fiction, however, is usually much more subtle in revealing its **theme**, the overall meaning the reader derives from the story. Most of the reading we did as children probably fell into two distinct categories—sheer escape or overt didacticism—with very little middle ground. Thus many readers coming to serious fiction for the first time, want either to avoid the search for "hidden meanings" or to complain, "If the writer was trying to say that then why didn't she just come right out and say it!" To further complicate matters, the manner in which we analyze stories and the preconceptions we bring to bear on them may result in multiple interpretations of meaning. No single statement of theme is likely to be the "correct" one, though some seem more likely than others.

What, then, is the theme of a story like "Reunion"? A reader insistent on a moral might denounce Charlie's father, inveighing against "demon rum" and its destructive effect on "family values." Another reader, slightly more charitable, might recognize alcoholism as a disease and feel considerable sympathy for the father. Yet another, perhaps entirely too self-righteous, might fault Charlie for running away from his father, interpreting the older man's actions as a "cry for help." If we investigate Cheever's own troubled biography and note his own serious problems with parents and alcohol, we may read the story as a psychological confession, with Cheever himself simultaneously standing for father and son. With so many possibilities before us, it is often best to state a story's theme as broadly as possible. "Reunion," like most initiation stories, is about growth through loss of innocence: "Children have to learn, often through painful experience, that they are not responsible for their parents' well-being, and sometimes they must distance themselves from their parents in order to survive." Such a statement does not encompass every possible nuance of the story's theme, but it does at least provide us with a starting point for arguing about the author's intended meaning.

All this is not to say that modern stories are always reticent in revealing their themes. A moralist like Flannery O'Connor judges characters according to her Roman Catholic moral standards. William Faulkner's moderate racial views made him something of an outcast in his native Mississippi in the turbulent 1950s. Margaret Atwood's feminism is rarely hidden in her stories and poems. Many modern stories are in fact **allegorical tales**, in which the literal events point to a parallel sequence of symbolic ideas. In many of O'Connor's stories the literal setting of the story, a doctor's waiting room or a crowded city bus, is a **microcosm**, a "small world" that reflects the tensions of the larger world outside, and the author often uses **traditional symbols** drawn from religion to make her point. Thus, despite their outward sophistication, many of the stories included here reveal their debt to the ancient ethical functions of fables and parables.

Setting

Novelists can lavish pages of prose on setting, just as they can describe characters down to such minutiae as the contents of their pockets. But short story writers, hemmed in by limitations of space, rarely have such luxury and must ordinarily limit themselves to very selective descriptions of time and place. When a writer like Edgar Allan Poe goes into great detail in his descriptions it is likely that **atmosphere**, the emotional aura surrounding a certain setting, is more important to him than the actual locale.

Setting is simply the time and place of a story. In most cases the details of the setting are given to the reader directly by the narrator. A story may employ multiple locations in its different scenes, and its time frame may encompass a few hours or many years. "Reunion" is a story with relatively few details of setting. Because Cheever wrote his stories almost exclusively for the *New Yorker*, it is not necessary for him to describe the interior of Grand Central Station to an audience doubtless familiar with it, nor would we feel at much of a loss if we were not. Similarly, he spends no more than a sentence or two describing each of the restaurants: one has "a lot of horse tack on the walls," one is "Italian," and the other two are not described at all. The time is also relatively unimportant here. We know that the action is taking place during the lunch hour on a weekday, probably in the summer, but as far as a more specific time is concerned we know little or nothing. "Reunion" could take place in 1992 or fifty years ago or, for that matter, twenty years from now.

Some stories, however, depend on their **locale** or time setting much more heavily and thus demand fuller exposition of setting. **Historical fiction** usually requires great attention to the altered landscapes and customs of bygone eras. A writer who carelessly mentions an alarm clock ringing in a story set in the early 1800s has committed an anachronism that may be only slightly more obvious than another writer's use of contemporary slang in the same setting. **Local color fiction** depends heavily on the unique characteristics of a particular area, usually a rural one that is off the beaten path. Such places have become increasingly rare in contemporary America, but the Deep South and Alaska (if popular television shows are any indication) still provide locales that possess intrinsic interest. Some writers establish reputations as practitioners of **regionalism**, setting most of their work in one particular area or country. A recent American writer like Bobbie Ann Mason shows, in virtually every one of the stories in her first collection, her deep roots in her native Kentucky. A South American writer like Gabriel García Márquez continually draws us into the strange world of Colombian villages cut off from the contemporary world, places where past and present, natural and supernatural, seamlessly join in what has been called "magical realism."

Stories contain both specific and general settings. The specific setting is the precise time and place where the action takes place. The general setting of a story, what is called its **enveloping action**, is its sense of the "times" and how its characters interact with events and social currents going on in the larger world. We have already mentioned how the specific setting of a story is often a microcosm that reflects the doings of society at large. It is impossible to read stories by Flannery O'Connor or Alice Walker and not become aware of the social changes that have transformed the rural South in the last thirty years. Stories sometimes depend on the reader's ability to bring his or her knowledge of history and culture to bear on the events taking place. For example, reading Ralph Ellison's "Flying Home," younger readers may be unaware of the curious circumstances under which black aviators trained and served during World War II.

Style

Style in fiction refers equally to the characteristics of language in a particular story and to the same characteristics in a writer's complete works. The more idiosyncratic a writer's style is, the easier it is to write a **parody**, or satirical imitation, of it, as the well-publicized annual Faux Faulkner and International Imitation Hemingway contests attests. A detailed analysis of style in an individual story might include attention to such matters as diction, sentence structure, punctuation (or lack thereof), and figurative language. In English we usually make a distinction between the differing qualities of words—standard versus slang usage, Latinate versus Germanic vocabulary, abstract versus concrete diction, and so on. While such matters are most meaningful only in the context of an individual story, there is obviously a difference between one character who says, "I have profited to a great degree from the educational benefits of the realm of experience," and another who says, "I graduated from the school of hard knocks." The style of "Reunion" is for the most part straightforward, with few flourishes of vocabulary (if we except the foreign phrases) or sentence structure. The only significant departure from this plain style is in the opening paragraph, where Charlie momentarily rises to a slightly elevated rhetorical plateau: " . . . As soon as I saw him I felt that he was my father, my flesh and blood, my future and my doom." In analyzing style, however, we must be sensitive to the literary fashions of periods other than our own; it is senseless to fault Poe for "flowery diction" when we compare his use of language to that of his contemporaries. The prevailing fashion in fiction today is the unadorned starkness of writers like Bobbie Ann Mason and Raymond Carver, what has been called "K-Mart realism" by one critic, but one should not be surprised if a decade from now writers are trying to outdo Faulkner at his most ornate.

The **tone** of the story, that is, what we can indirectly determine about the author's own feelings about its events, is also carefully controlled. Cheever avoids the twin pitfalls of sentimentality on the one hand and cynicism on the other by deftly walking an emotional tightrope. After the opening paragraph, at no point does Charlie tell us how he feels, instead letting his father's actions speak for themselves. There are points in "Reunion" where we may laugh, but it is an uncomfortable laugh at which we probably feel guilty. The range of tones available in any given story runs through the whole range of human emotions, from outright comedy to pathos of the most wrenching sort. An unwary reader may fail to appreciate the keen edge of Flannery O'Connor's satire, for example, but this failure should not be laid at the feet of the writer, who has taken great pains to make her own attitudes clear.

Writing About Short Fiction

Writing assignments differ greatly, and your teacher's instructions may range from general ("Discuss characterization in one of the short stories we have read") to very specific ("Contrast, in no fewer than five hundred words, the major differences in the plot, characterization, and setting between Joyce Carol Oates's short story "Where Are You Going, Where Have You Been?' and Joyce Chopra's *Smooth Talk*, the 1985 film version of the story"). Such practices as choosing, limiting, and developing a topic; "brainstorming" by taking notes on random ideas and refining those ideas further through group discussion or conferences with your instructor; using the library, if required, to locate supporting critical materials; and revising a first draft in light of critical remarks are undoubtedly techniques you have used in other composition classes. Basic types of organizational schemes learned in "theme-writing" courses can also be applied to writing about fiction.

Typical writing assignments on short stories fall into three main categories: explication or close reading, analysis, and comparison-contrast. An explication assignment is perhaps the most demanding of the three since it requires the closest attention to the precise nuances of a writer's language. Typically, an explication (literally an "unfolding") might ask you to focus carefully on a key passage, explaining how it contains some key element upon which the whole story hinges and without which the story could not succeed. Suppose, for example, that you are asked to explicate the opening paragraph of "Reunion" and are explicitly requested to focus on what the paragraph conveys beyond obvious expository information. After reading the paragraph carefully several times, you might decide it contains ample foreshadowing of the disastrous events that are about to occur. In particular you might cite such telltale phrases as "His secretary wrote to say" or "My mother divorced him" as Cheever's way dropping subtle hints about the father's unsavory personality. Then you might go on to mention Charlie's forebodings of his own "doom," all leading up to the aroma of pre-lunch cocktails that Charlie notices when they embrace. Any explication demands that you quote extensively from the text, explaining why certain choices of words and details are important and speculating about why the writer made these choices. If you are asked to support your explication with secondary critical sources, you might consult indexes like *Short Story Criticism* or *Twentieth Century Short Story Explication* before you search the card catalogue or other more general indexes like the *MLA Index.*

Analysis assignments typically turn on definition and illustration, focusing on only one or two of the main elements of the story, such as plot or theme. For example, you might be asked to explain what a "rites of passage" story is and demonstrate that "Reunion" has most of the characteristics of the genre. Here you might want to first define the initiation story, using your lecture notes and your familiarity with other stories from popular sources like fairy tales or motion pictures. After demonstrating that this type of story is indeed well established and describing its attributes, you might then focus on such matters from "Reunion" as Charlie's age, his naïve expectations, his disillusioning experience, and his eventual "passage" out of his father's life at the end of the story. Again, critical sources may be useful. In particular, general studies of the short genre may help you establish the critical vocabulary to use.

Comparison-and-contrast assignments are also popular, especially for longer writing projects. Generally, comparison seeks out common ground between two subjects while contrast finds differences; most papers of this type do both, pointing out the similarities first before going on to demonstrate how each story represents a variation on the theme. Comparison-contrast may focus on a single story, asking you to examine two characters' approaches to a similar situation or even a single character's "before and after" view of another character or event. If you are examining a single author in depth, you might be required to find other stories by him or her that deal with similar themes. Since Cheever writes extensively about alcoholism, family tensions, and divorce you might find several of his stories that illuminate the basic themes of "Reunion." Even more demanding might be a topic asking you to find stories (or even poems or plays) by other authors to compare or contrast. Among the stories in this book, there are several examples of initiation stories and others that deal with tensions between parents and children. Comparison and contrast assignments require careful selection and planning, and it is essential to find significant examples of both similarities and differences to support your thesis.

It is always necessary to support the statements you make about a story, either by quoting directly from the story or, if you are required, by using secondary sources for additional critical opinion. The *MLA Handbook*, which you will find in the reference section of almost any library, contains formats that most instructors consider standard for bibliographies and manuscripts; indeed, many of the handbooks of grammar and usage commonly used in college courses follow MLA style. If you have doubts, however, ask your instructor about what format he or she prefers. The type of parenthetical citation used today to indicate the source of quotations is simple to learn and dispenses with such time-consuming and repetitive chores as footnotes and endnotes. In using parenthetical citations remember that your goal is to direct your reader from the quoted passage in the paper to its source in your bibliography and from there, if necessary, to the book or periodical from which the quote is taken. A good parenthetical citation gives only the ***minimal*** information needed to accomplish this. Here are a few examples from student papers on "Reunion":

> As soon as father and son enter the first restaurant, Charlie's father begins to act strangely: "We sat down, and my father hailed the waiter in a loud voice. '<u>Kellner!</u>' he shouted. '<u>Garcon! Cameriere! You!</u>' His boisterousness in the empty restaurant seemed out of place" (518).

Here you should note a couple of conventions of writing about fiction. One is that the present tense is used in speaking of the events of the story; in general, use the present tense throughout your critical writing except when you are giving biographical or historical information. Second, note the use of single and double quotation marks. Double quotation marks from the story are changed to single quotation marks here since they appear within the writer's own quotation marks. The parenthetical citation lists only a page number since earlier in this paper the writer has mentioned Cheever by name and only one work by him appears in the bibliography. If several works by Cheever had been listed among the works cited, the parenthetical citation would clarify which one was being referred to by adding a shortened form of the book's title: (*Stories* 518). The reader finds the following entry among the sources:

Cheever, John. The Stories of John Cheever. New York: Knopf, 1978.

Similarly, quotations and paraphrases from secondary critical sources should follow the same rules of common sense.

Cheever's daughter Susan, in her candid memoir of her father, remarks that the author's alcoholism followed a familiar pattern. She notes that "there were bottles hidden all over the house, and even outside in the privet hedge and the garden shed. Drink was his crucible, his personal hell" (43).

In this case, the author of the quotation is identified, so only the page number is included in the parenthetical citation. The reader knows where to look among the sources:

Cheever, Susan. Home Before Dark. Boston: Houghton, 1984.

To simplify the whole matter of parenthetical citation, it is recommended that quotations from secondary sources be introduced, whenever possible, in a manner that identifies the author so that only the page number of the quotation is needed inside parentheses.

Of course, different types of sources—reference book entries, articles in periodicals, newspaper reviews of plays—require different bibliographical information, so be sure to check the *MLA Handbook* if you have questions. The following are a few more of the most commonly used bibliographical formats.

Book with author and editor:

Cheever, John. The Letters of John Cheever. Ed. Benjamin Cheever. New York: Simon, 1988.

Casebook or collection of critical essays:

Collins, R. G., ed. Critical Essays on John Cheever. Boston: Hall, 1982.

Story reprinted in an anthology or textbook:

Cheever, John. "The Enormous Radio." The Story and Its Writer: An Introduction to Short Fiction. Ed. Ann Charters. New York: St. Martin's, 1983. 858-66

Article in a reference book:

Seymour-Smith, Martin "Cheever, John." Who's Who in Twentieth Century Literature. New York: McGraw, 1976.

Article in a scholarly journal:

Kendle, Burton. "Cheever's Use of Mythology in 'The Enormous Radio.'" Studies in Short Fiction 4 (1968): 262-64.

Book review in a periodical:

Oberbeck, S. K. "Curdled Camelot." Rev. of The World of Apples, by John Cheever. Newsweek 21 May 1973: 97, 99.

Interview:

Cheever, John. Interview. "John Cheever: The Art of Fiction 62." By Annette Grant. Paris Review 17 (1976): 39-66.

✧ ✧ ✧

Nathaniel Hawthorne
(1804-1864)

Young Goodman Brown

Hawthorne was born in Salem, Massachusetts, and could trace his heritage back to the earliest settlers of New England. He attended Bowdoin College, where his schoolmates included Henry Wadsworth Longfellow and future president Franklin Pierce, for whom Hawthorne later wrote an official campaign biography. For twelve years after his 1825 graduation Hawthorne lived at his parents' home, devoting himself solely to learning the craft of writing. An early novel, *Fanshawe* (1828), attracted no attention, but a collection of short stories, *Twice-Told Tales* (1837), was the subject of an enthusiastic review by Edgar Allan Poe (see the introduction to this text). Hawthorne traveled in Europe in his later years and served as American consul at Liverpool during the Pierce administration. Unlike his friend Ralph Waldo Emerson, whose optimism was a constant in his transcendentalist credo, Hawthorne was a moralist who did not shrink from depicting the dark side of human nature, and his often painful examinations of American history and conscience have set the tone for many subsequent generations of writers. His ambivalent attitude toward his Puritan ancestors' religious beliefs (one of his forebears, John Hathorne, was a magistrate who assisted the prosecution during the infamous Salem witch trials) supplied material for his novel *The Scarlet Letter* (1850) and many of his short stories, including "Young Goodman Brown," which is set roughly in the same period as the trials.

Young Goodman Brown came forth, at sunset, into the street at Salem village, but put his head back, after crossing the threshold, to exchange a parting kiss with his young wife. And Faith, as the wife was aptly named, thrust her pretty head into the street, letting the wind play with the pink ribbons of her cap while she called to Goodman Brown.

2 "Dearest heart," whispered she, softly and rather sadly, when her lips were close to his ear, "prithee put off your journey until sunrise and sleep in your

own bed to-night. A lone woman is troubled with such dreams and such thoughts that she's afeared of herself sometimes. Pray tarry with me this night, dear husband, of all nights in the year."

3 "My love and my Faith," replied young Goodman Brown, "of all nights in the year, this one night must I tarry away from thee. My journey, as thou callest it, forth and back again, must needs be done 'twixt now and sunrise. What, my sweet, pretty wife, dost thou doubt me already, and we but three months married?"

4 "Then God bless you!" said Faith, with the pink ribbons; "and may you find all well when you come back."

5 "Amen!" cried Goodman Brown. "Say thy prayers, dear Faith, and go to bed at dusk, and no harm will come to thee."

6 So they parted; and the young man pursued his way until, being about to the corner by the meeting-house, he looked back and saw the head of Faith peeping after him with a melancholy air, in spite of her pink ribbons.

7 "Poor little Faith!" thought he, for his heart smote him. "What a wretch am I to leave her on such an errand! She talks of dreams, too. Methought as she spoke there was trouble in her face, as if a dream had warned her what work is to be done to-night. But no, no; 'twould kill her to think it. Well, she's a blessed angel on earth and after this one night, I'll cling to her skirts and follow her to heaven."

8 With this excellent resolve for the future, Goodman Brown felt himself justified in making more haste on his present evil purpose. He had taken a dreary road, darkened by all the gloomiest trees of the forest, which barely stood aside to let the narrow path creep through, and closed immediately behind. It was all as lonely as could be; and there is this peculiarity in such a solitude, that the traveller knows not who may be concealed by the innumerable trunks and the thick boughs overhead; so that with lonely footsteps he may yet be passing through an unseen multitude.

9 "There may be a devilish Indian behind every tree," said Goodman Brown to himself and he glanced fearfully behind him as he added, "What if the devil himself should be at my very elbow!"

10 His head being turned back, he passed a crook of the road, and, looking forward again, beheld the figure of a man, in grave and decent attire, seated at the foot of an old tree. He arose at Goodman Brown's approach and walked onward side by side with him.

11 "You are late, Goodman Brown," said he. "The clock of the Old South was striking as I came through Boston, and that is full fifteen minutes agone."

12 "Faith kept me back a while," replied the young man, with a tremor in his voice, caused by the sudden appearance of his companion, though not wholly unexpected.

13 It was now deep dusk in the forest, and deepest in that part of it where these two were journeying. As nearly as could be discerned, the second traveller was about fifty years old, apparently in the same rank of life as Goodman Brown, and bearing a considerable resemblance to him, though perhaps more in expression than features. Still they might have been taken for father and son. And yet, though the elder person was as simply clad as the younger, and as simple in manner too, he had an indescribable air of one who knew the world, and who would not have felt abashed at the governor's dinner table, or in King William's court, were it possible that his affairs should call him thither. But the only thing about him that could be fixed upon as remarkable was his staff, which bore the likeness of a great black snake, so curiously wrought that it might almost be seen to twist and wriggle itself like a living serpent. This, of course, must have been an ocular deception, assisted by uncertain light.

14 "Come, Goodman Brown," cried his fellow-traveller, "this is a dull pace for the beginning of a journey. Take my staff, if you are so soon weary."

15 "Friend," said the other, exchanging his slow pace for a full stop, "having kept covenant by meeting thee here, it is my purpose now to return whence I came. I have scruples touching the matter thou wot'st of."

16 "Sayest thou so?" replied he of the serpent, smiling apart. "Let us walk on, nevertheless, reasoning as we go; and if I convince thee not thou shalt turn back. We are but a little way in the forest yet."

17 "Too far! too far!" exclaimed the goodman, unconsciously resuming his walk. "My father never went into the woods on such an errand, nor his father before him. We have been a race of honest men and good Christians since the days of the martyrs; and shall I be the first of the name of Brown that ever took this path and kept—"

18 "Such company, thou wouldst say," observed the elder person, interpreting his pause. "Well said, Goodman Brown! I have been as well acquainted with your family as with ever a one among the Puritans; and that's no trifle to say. I helped your grandfather, the constable, when he lashed the Quaker woman so smartly through the streets of Salem; and it was I that brought your father a pitch-pine knot, kindled at my own hearth, to set fire to an Indian village, in King Philip's war. They were my good friends, both; and many a pleasant walk have we had along this path, and returned merrily after midnight. I would fain be friends with you for their sake."

19 "If it be as thou sayest," replied Goodman Brown, "I marvel they never spoke of these matters, or, verily, I marvel not, seeing that the least rumor of the sort would have driven them from New England. We are a people of prayer, and good works to boot, and abide no such wickedness."

20 "Wickedness or not," said the traveller with the twisted staff, "I have a very general acquaintance here in New England. The deacons of many a church have drunk the communion wine with me; the selectmen of divers towns make me

their chairman; and a majority of the Great and General Court are firm supporters of my interest. The governor and I, too—But these are state secrets."

21 "Can this be so!" cried Goodman Brown, with a stare of amazement at his undisturbed companion. "Howbeit, I have nothing to do with the governor and council; they have their own ways, and are no rule for a simple husbandman like me. But, were I to go on with thee, how should I meet the eye of that good old man, our minister, at Salem village? Oh, his voice would make me tremble both Sabbath day and lecture day!"

22 Thus far the elder traveller had listened with due gravity; but now burst into a fit of irrepressible mirth, shaking himself so violently that his snake-like staff actually seemed to wriggle in sympathy.

23 "Ha! ha! ha!" shouted he again and again; then composing himself, "Well, go on, Goodman Brown, go on; but, prithee, don't kill me with laughing."

24 "Well, then, to end the matter at once," said Goodman Brown, considerably nettled, "there is my wife, Faith. It would break her dear little heart; and I'd rather break my own."

25 "Nay, if that be the case," answered the other, "e'en go thy ways, Goodman Brown. I would not for twenty old women like the one hobbling before us that Faith should come to any harm."

26 As he spoke he pointed his staff at a female figure on the path, in whom Goodman Brown recognized a very pious and exemplary dame, who had taught him his catechism in youth, and was still his moral and spiritual adviser, jointly with the minister and Deacon Gookin.

27 "A marvel, truly, that Goody Cloyse should be so far in the wilderness at night fall," said he. "But with your leave, friend, I shall take a cut through the woods until we have left this Christian woman behind. Being a stranger to you, she might ask whom I was consorting with and whither I was going."

28 "Be it so," said his fellow-traveller. "Betake you the woods, and let me keep the path."

29 Accordingly the young man turned aside, but took care to watch his companion, who advanced softly along the road until he had come within a staff's length of the old dame. She, meanwhile, was making the best of her way, with singular speed for so aged a woman, and mumbling some indistinct words—a prayer, doubtless—as she went. The traveller put forth his staff and touched her withered neck with what seemed the serpent's tail.

30 "The devil!" screamed the pious old lady.

31 "Then Goody Cloyse knows her old friend?" observed the traveller, confronting her and leaning on his writhing stick.

32 "Ah, forsooth, and is it your worship indeed?" cried the good dame. "Yea, truly is it, and in the very image of my old gossip, Goodman Brown, the grandfather of the silly fellow that now is. But—would your worship believe it?—my broomstick hath strangely disappeared, stolen, as I suspect, by that unhanged

witch, Goody Cory and that, too, when I was all anointed with the juice of smallage and cinquefoil and wolf's bane—"

33 "Mingled with fine wheat and the fat of a new-born babe," said the shape of old Goodman Brown.

34 "Ah, your worship knows the recipe," cried the old lady, cackling aloud. "So, as I was saying, being all ready for the meeting, and no horse to ride on, I made up my mind to foot it; for they tell me there is a nice young man to be taken into communion to-night. But now your good worship will lend me your arm, and we shall be there in a twinkling."

35 "That can hardly be," answered her friend. "I may not spare you my arm, Goody Cloyse; but here is my staff, if you will."

36 So saying, he threw it down at her feet, where, perhaps, it assumed life, being one of the rods which its owner had formerly lent to the Egyptian magi. Of this fact, however, Goodman Brown could not take cognizance. He had cast up his eyes in astonishment, and, looking down again, beheld neither Goody Cloyse nor the serpentine staff but his fellow-traveller alone, who waited for him as calmly as if nothing had happened.

37 "That old woman taught me my catechism," said the young man; and there was a world of meaning in this simple comment.

38 They continued to walk onward, while the elder traveller exhorted his companion to make good speed and persevere in the path, discoursing so aptly that his arguments seemed rather to spring up in the bosom of his auditor than to be suggested by himself. As they went, he plucked a branch of maple to serve for a walking-stick, and began to strip it of the twigs and little boughs, which were wet with evening dew. The moment his fingers touched them they became strangely withered and dried up as with a week's sunshine. Thus the pair proceeded, at a good free pace, until suddenly, in a gloomy hollow of the road, Goodman Brown sat himself down on the stump of a tree and refused to go any farther.

39 "Friend," said he, stubbornly, "my mind is made up. Not another step will I budge on this errand. What if a wretched old woman do choose to go to the devil when I thought she was going to heaven: is that any reason why I should quit my dear Faith and go after her?"

40 "You will think better of this by and by," said his acquaintance, composedly. "Sit here and rest yourself a while; and when you feel like moving again, there is my staff to help you along."

41 Without more words, he threw his companion the maple stick, and was as speedily out of sight as if he had vanished into the deepening gloom. The young man sat a few moments by the roadside, applauding himself greatly, and thinking with how clear a conscience he should meet the minister in his morning walk, nor shrink from the eye of good old Deacon Gookin. And what calm sleep would be his that very night, which was to have been spent so wickedly, but

so purely and sweetly now, in the arms of Faith! Amidst these pleasant and praiseworthy meditations, Goodman Brown heard the tramp of horses along the road, and deemed it advisable to conceal himself within the verge of the forest, conscious of the guilty purpose that had brought him thither, though now so happily turned from it.

42 On came the hoof-tramps and the voices of the riders, two grave old voices, conversing soberly as they drew near. These mingled sounds appeared to pass along the road, within a few yards of the young man's hiding-place; but, owing doubtless to the depth of the gloom at that particular spot, neither the travellers nor their steeds were visible. Though their figures brushed the small boughs by the wayside, it could not be seen that they intercepted, even for a moment, the faint gleam from the strip of bright sky athwart which they must have passed. Goodman Brown alternately crouched and stood on tiptoe, pulling aside the branches and thrusting forth his head as far as he durst without discerning so much as a shadow. It vexed him the more, because he could have sworn, were such a thing possible, that he recognized the voices of the minister and Deacon Gookin, jogging along quietly, as they were wont to do, when bound to some ordination or ecclesiastical council. While yet within hearing, one of the riders stopped to pluck a switch.

43 "Of the two, reverend sir," said the voice like the deacon's, "I had rather miss an ordination dinner than to-night's meeting. They tell me that some of our community are to be here from Falmouth and beyond, and others from Connecticut and Rhode Island, besides several of the Indian powwows, who, after their fashion, know almost as much deviltry as the best of us. Moreover, there is a goodly young woman to be taken into communion."

44 "Mighty well, Deacon Gookin!" replied the solemn old tones of the minister. "Spur up, or we shall be late. Nothing can be done, you know, until I get on the ground."

45 The hoofs clattered again; and the voices, talking so strangely in the empty air, passed on through the forest, where no church had ever been gathered or solitary Christian prayed. Whither, then, could these holy men be journeying so deep into the heathen wilderness? Young Goodman Brown caught hold of a tree for support, being ready to sink down on the ground, faint and overburdened with the heavy sickness of his heart. He looked up to the sky, doubting whether there really was a heaven above him. Yet, there was the blue arch, and the stars brightening in

46 "With heaven above, and Faith below, I will yet stand firm against the devil," cried Goodman Brown.

47 While he still gazed upward into the deep arch of the firmament and had lifted his hands to pray, a cloud, though no wind was stirring, hurried across the zenith and hid the brightening stars. The blue sky was still visible, except directly overhead, where this black mass of cloud was sweeping swiftly north-

ward. Aloft in the air, as if from the depths of the cloud, came a confused and doubtful sound of voices. Once the listener fancied that he could distinguish the accents of towns-people of his own, men and women, both pious and ungodly, many of whom he had met at the communion table, and had seen others rioting at the tavern. The next moment, so indistinct were the sounds, he doubted whether he had heard aught but the murmur of the old forest, whispering without a wind. Then came a stronger swell of those familiar tones, heard daily in the sunshine at Salem village, but never until now from a cloud of night. There was one voice, of a young woman, uttering lamentations, yet with an uncertain sorrow, and entreating for some favor, which, perhaps it would grieve her to obtain; and all the unseen multitude, both saints and sinners seemed to encourage her onward.

48 "Faith!" shouted Goodman Brown, in a voice of agony and desperation; and the echoes of the forest mocked him, crying, "Faith! Faith!" as if bewildered wretches were seeking her all through the wilderness.

49 The cry of grief, rage, and terror was yet piercing the night, when the unhappy husband held his breath for a response. There was a scream, drowned immediately in a louder murmur of voices, fading into far-off laughter, as the dark cloud swept away, leaving the clear and silent sky above Goodman Brown. But something fluttered lightly down through the air and caught on the branch of a tree. The young man seized it, and beheld a pink ribbon.

50 "My Faith is gone!" cried he, after one stupefied moment. "There is no good on earth; and sin is but a name. Come, devil; for to thee is this world given."

51 And, maddened with despair, so that he laughed loud and long, did Goodman Brown grasp his staff and set forth again, at such a rate that he seemed to fly along the forest path, rather than to walk or run. The road grew wilder and drearier and more faintly traced, and vanished at length, leaving him in the heart of the dark wilderness, still rushing onward with the instinct that guides mortal man to evil. The whole forest was peopled with frightful sounds—the creaking of the trees, the howling of wild beasts, and the yell of Indians; while sometimes the wind tolled like a distant church bell, and sometimes gave a broad roar around the traveller, as if all Nature were laughing him to scorn. But he was himself the chief horror of the scene, and shrank not from its other horrors.

52 "Ha! ha! ha!" roared Goodman Brown when the wind laughed at him. "Let us hear which will laugh loudest! Think not to frighten me with your deviltry! Come witch, come wizard, come Indian powwow, come devil himself, and here comes Goodman Brown. You may as well fear him as he fear you!"

53 In truth, all through the haunted forest there could be nothing more frightful than the figure of Goodman Brown. On he flew among the black pines, brandishing his staff with frenzied gestures, now giving vent to an

inspiration of horrid blasphemy, and now shouting forth such laughter as set all the echoes of the forest laughing like demons around him. The fiend in his own shape is less hideous than when he rages in the breast of man. Thus sped the demoniac on his course, until, quivering among the trees, he saw a red light before him, as when the felled trunks and branches of a clearing have been set on fire, and throw up their lurid blaze against the sky, at the hour of midnight. He paused, in a lull of the tempest that had driven him onward, and heard the swell of what seemed a hymn, rolling solemnly from a distance with the weight of many voices. He knew the tune; it was a familiar one in the choir of the village meeting-house. The verse died heavily away, and was lengthened by a chorus, not of human voices, but of all the sounds of the benighted wilderness pealing in awful harmony together. Goodman Brown cried out; and his cry was lost to his own ear by its unison with the cry of the desert.

54 In the interval of silence he stole forward until the light glared full upon his eyes. At one extremity of an open space, hemmed in by the dark wall of the forest, arose a rock, bearing some rude, natural resemblance either to an altar or a pulpit, and surrounded by four blazing pines, their tops aflame, their stems untouched, like candles at an evening meeting. The mass of foliage that had overgrown the summit of the rock was all on fire, blazing high into the night and fitfully illuminating the whole field. Each pendent twig and leafy festoon was in a blaze. As the red light arose and fell, a numerous congregation alternately shone forth, then disappeared in shadow, and again grew, as it were, out of the darkness, peopling the heart of the solitary woods at once.

55 "A grave and dark-clad company," quoth Goodman Brown.

56 In truth, they were such. Among them, quivering to-and-fro between gloom and splendor, appeared faces that would be seen next day at the council board of the province, and others which, Sabbath after Sabbath, looked devoutly heavenward, and benignantly over the crowded pews, from the holiest pulpits in the land. Some affirm that the lady of the governor was there. At least there were high dames well known to her, and wives of honored husbands, and widows, a great multitude, and ancient maidens, all of excellent repute, and fair young girls, who trembled lest their mothers should espy them. Either the sudden gleams of light flashing over the obscure field bedazzled Goodman Brown, or he recognized a score of the church-members of Salem village famous for their especial sanctity. Good old Deacon Gookin had arrived, and waited at the skirts of that venerable saint, his revered pastor. But, irreverently consorting with these grave, reputable, and pious people, these elders of the church, these chaste dames and dewy virgins, there were men of dissolute lives and women of spotted fame, wretches given over to all mean and filthy vice, and suspected even of horrid crimes. It was strange to see, that the good shrank not from the wicked, nor were the sinners abashed by the saints. Scattered also among their pale-faced

enemies were the Indian priests, or powwows, who had often scared their native forest with more hideous incantations than any known to English witchcraft.

57 "But, where is Faith?" thought Goodman Brown; and, as hope came into his heart, he trembled.

58 Another verse of the hymn arose, a slow and mournful strain, such as the pious love, but joined to words which expressed all that our nature can conceive of sin, and darkly hinted at far more. Unfathomable to mere mortals is the lore of fiends. Verse after verse was sung; and still the chorus of the desert swelled between, like the deepest tone of a mighty organ; and, with the final peal of that dreadful anthem there came a sound, as if the roaring wind, the rushing streams, the howling beasts, and every other voice of the unconcerted wilderness were mingling and according with the voice of guilty man in homage to the prince of all. The four blazing pines threw up a loftier flame, and obscurely discovered shapes and visages of horror on the smoke wreaths above the impious assembly. At the same moment the fire on the rock shot redly forth and formed a glowing arch above its base, where now appeared a figure. With reverence be it spoken, the figure bore no slight similitude, both in garb and manner, to some grave divine of the New England church

59 "Bring forth the converts!" cried a voice that echoed through the field and rolled into the forest.

60 At the word, Goodman Brown stepped forth from the shadow of the trees and approached the congregation, with whom he felt a loathful brotherhood by the sympathy of all that was wicked in his heart. He could have well nigh sworn that the shape of his own dead father beckoned him to advance, looking downward from a smoke wreath, while a woman, with dim features of despair, threw out her hand to warn him back. Was it his mother? But he had no power to retreat one step, nor to resist, even in thought, when the minister and good old Deacon Gookin seized his arms and led him to the blazing rock. Thither came also the slender form of a veiled female, led between Goody Cloyse, that pious teacher of the catechism, and Martha Carrier, who had received the devil's promise to be queen of hell. A rampant hag was she. And there stood the proselytes beneath the canopy of fire.

61 "Welcome, my children," said the dark figure, "to the communion of your race. Ye have found thus young your nature and your destiny. My children, look behind you!"

62 They turned; and flashing forth, as it were, in a sheet of flame, the fiend worshippers were seen; the smile of welcome gleamed darkly on every visage.

63 "There," resumed the sable form, "are all whom ye have reverenced from youth. Ye deemed them holier than yourselves, and shrank from your own sin, contrasting it with their lives of righteousness and prayerful aspirations heavenward. Yet here are they all in my worshipping assembly. This night it shall be granted you to know their secret deeds: how hoary-bearded elders of the

church have whispered wanton words to the young maids of their households; how many a woman, eager for widow's weeds, has given her husband a drink at bedtime, and let him sleep his last sleep in her bosom; how beardless youths have made haste to inherit their fathers' wealth; and how fair damsels—blush not, sweet ones—have dug little graves in the garden, and bidden me, the sole guest, to an infant's funeral. By the sympathy of your human hearts for sin ye shall scent out all the places—whether in church, bed-chamber, street, field, or forest—where crime has been committed, and shall exult to behold the whole earth one stain of guilt, one mighty blood spot. Far more than this. It shall be yours to penetrate, in every bosom, the deep mystery of sin, the fountain of all wicked arts, and which inexhaustibly supplies more evil impulses than human power—than my power at its utmost—can make manifest in deeds. And now, my, children, look upon each other."

64 They did so; and, by the blaze of the hell-kindled torches, the wretched man beheld his Faith, and the wife her husband, trembling before that unhallowed altar.

65 "Lo, there ye stand, my children," said the figure, in a deep and solemn tone, almost sad with its despairing awfulness, as if his once angelic nature could yet mourn for our miserable race. "Depending upon one another's hearts, ye had still hoped that virtue were not all a dream. Now are ye undeceived. Evil is the nature of mankind. Evil must be your only happiness. Welcome, again, my children, to the communion of your race."

66 "Welcome," repeated the fiend worshippers, in one cry of despair and triumph.

67 And there they stood, the only pair, as it seemed, who were yet hesitating on the verge of wickedness in this dark world. A basin was hollowed, naturally, in the rock. Did it contain water, reddened by the lurid light? or was it blood? or, perchance, a liquid flame? Herein did the shape of evil dip his hand and prepare to lay the mark of baptism upon their foreheads, that they might be partakers of the mystery of sin, more conscious of the secret guilt of others, both in deed and thought, than they could now be of their own. The husband cast one look at his pale wife, and Faith at him. What polluted wretches would the next glance show them to each other, shuddering alike at what they disclosed and what they saw!

68 "Faith! Faith!" cried the husband, "look up to heaven, and resist the wicked one."

69 Whether Faith obeyed he knew not. Hardly had he spoken when he found himself amid calm night and solitude, listening to a roar of the wind which died heavily away through the forest. He staggered against the rock, and felt it chill and damp; while a hanging twig, that had been all on fire, besprinkled his cheek with the coldest dew.

70 The next morning young Goodman Brown came slowly into the street of Salem village, staring around him like a bewildered man. The good old minister was taking a walk along the graveyard to get an appetite for breakfast and meditate his sermon, and bestowed a blessing, as he passed, on Goodman Brown. He shrank from the venerable saint as if to avoid an anathema. Old Deacon Gookin was at domestic worship, and the holy words of his prayer were heard through the open window. "What God doth the wizard pray to?" quoth Goodman Brown. Goody Cloyse, that excellent old Christian, stood in the early sunshine at her own lattice, catechizing a little girl who had brought her a pint of morning's milk. Goodman Brown snatched away the child as from the grasp of the fiend himself. Turning the corner by the meeting-house, he spied the head of Faith, with the pink ribbons, gazing anxiously forth, and bursting into such joy at sight of him that she skipped along the street and almost kissed her husband before the whole village. But Goodman Brown looked sternly and sadly into her face, and passed on without a greeting.

71 Had Goodman Brown fallen asleep in the forest and only dreamed a wild dream of a witch-meeting?

72 Be it so, if you will; but, alas! it was a dream of evil omen for young Goodman Brown. A stern, a sad, a darkly meditative, a distrustful, if not a desperate man did he become from the night of that fearful dream. On the Sabbath day, when the congregation were singing a holy psalm, he could not listen because an anthem of sin rushed loudly upon his ear and drowned all the blessed strain. When the minister spoke from the pulpit with power and fervid eloquence, and, with his hand on the open Bible, of the sacred truths of our religion, and of saint-like lives and triumphant deaths, and of future bliss or misery unutterable, then did Goodman Brown turn pale, dreading lest the roof should thunder down upon the gray blasphemer and his hearers. Often, awakening suddenly at midnight, he shrank from the bosom of Faith; and at morning or eventide, when the family knelt down at prayer, he scowled and muttered to himself, and gazed sternly at his wife, and turned away. And when he had lived long, and was borne to his grave a hoary corpse, followed by Faith, an aged woman, and children and grandchildren, a goodly procession, besides neighbors, not a few, they carved no hopeful verse upon his tombstone, for his dying hour was gloom.

—1835

Edgar Allan Poe
(1809-1849)

The Masque of the Red Death

Poe has become so much the captive of his own legend that his name summons up visions of a mad genius who has little in common with the meticulous craftsman of criticism, fiction, and poetry whose influence on world literature has been immense. Born in Boston, Poe was the child of actors and orphaned at two but nevertheless lived a privileged childhood as the ward of John Allan, a wealthy Richmond, Virginia, merchant who gave Poe his middle name. After a profligate year at the University of Virginia, successful military service (under an assumed name), and an abortive stay at West Point, Poe broke with his foster father, married his young cousin, and set about a literary career, succeeding as editor of several prominent magazines. However, his irregular habits and a drinking problem, which grew more pronounced following the death of his wife in 1847, led to his mysterious death in Baltimore at the age of thirty-nine. Poe's poetry and short fiction have influenced writers as diverse as Charles Baudelaire and Stephen King; genres like the horror tale and the detective story must list contributions by Poe such as "The Fall of the House of Usher" and "The Murders in the Rue Morgue" among their earliest important examples. "The Masque of the Red Death," a Gothic allegory that may have been influenced by an 1831 cholera outbreak in Baltimore, has lost little of its power in a world threatened by epidemics of ever more terrifying proportions.

The "Red Death" had long devastated the country. No pestilence had ever been so fatal, or so hideous. Blood was its Avatar and its seal—the redness and the horror of blood. There were sharp pains, and sudden dizziness, and then profuse bleeding at the pores, with dissolution. The scarlet stains upon the body and especially upon the face of the victim, were the pest ban which shut him out from the aid and from the sympathy of his fellow-men. And the whole seizure, progress, and termination of the disease, were the incidents of half an hour.

2 But the Prince Prospero was happy and dauntless and sagacious. When his dominions were half depopulated, he summoned to his presence a thousand hale and light-hearted friends from among the knights and dames of his court, and with these retired to the deep seclusion of one of his castellated abbeys. This was an extensive and magnificent structure, the creation of the prince's own eccentric yet august taste. A strong and lofty wall girdled it in. This wall had gates of iron. The courtiers, having entered, brought furnaces and massy hammers and welded the bolts. They resolved to leave means neither of ingress nor egress to the sudden impulses of despair or of frenzy from within. The abbey was amply provisioned. With such precautions the courtiers might bid defiance to contagion. The external world could take care of itself. In the meantime it was folly to grieve, or to think. The prince had provided all the appliances of pleasure. There were buffoons, there were in improvisatori, there were ballet-dancers, there were musicians, there was Beauty, there was wine. All these and security were within. Without was the "Red Death."

3 It was toward the close of the fifth or sixth month of his seclusion, and while the pestilence raged most furiously abroad, that the Prince Prospero entertained his thousand friends at a masked ball of the most unusual magnificence.

4 It was a voluptuous scene, that masquerade. But first let me tell of the rooms in which it was held. There were seven—an imperial suite. In many palaces, however, such suites form a long and straight vista, while the folding doors slide back nearly to the walls on either hand, so that the view of the whole extent is scarcely impeded. Here the case was very different: as might have been expected from the duke's love of the *bizarre.* The apartments were so irregularly disposed that the vision embraced but little more than one at a time. There was a sharp turn at every twenty or thirty yards, and at each turn a novel effect. To the right and left, in the middle of each wall, a tall and narrow Gothic window looked out upon a closed corridor which pursued the windings of the suite. These windows were of stained glass whose color varied in accordance with the prevailing hue of the decorations of the chamber into which it opened. That at the eastern extremity was hung, for example, in blue—and vividly blue were its windows. The second chamber was purple in its ornaments and tapestries, and here the panes were purple. The third was green throughout, and so were the casements. The fourth was furnished and lighted with orange—the fifth with white—the sixth with violet. The seventh apartment was closely shrouded in black velvet tapestries that hung all over the ceiling and down the walls, falling in heavy folds upon a carpet of the same material and hue. But in this chamber only, the color of the windows failed to correspond with the decorations. The panes here were scarlet—a deep blood color. Now in no one of the seven apartments was there any lamp or candelabrum, amid the profusion of golden ornaments that lay scattered to and

fro or depended from the roof. There was no light of any kind emanating from lamp or candle within the suite of chambers. But in the corridors that followed the suite, there stood, opposite to each window, a heavy tripod, bearing a brazier of fire, that projected its rays through the tinted glass and so glaringly illumined the room. And thus were produced a multitude of gaudy and fantastic appearances. But in the western or black chamber the effect of the firelight that streamed upon the dark hangings through the blood-tinted panes was ghastly in the extreme, and produced so wild a look upon the countenances of those who entered, that there were few of the company bold enough to set foot within its precincts at all.

5 It was in this apartment, also, that there stood against the western wall, a gigantic clock of ebony. Its pendulum swung to and fro with a dull, heavy, monotonous clang; and when the minute-hand made the circuit of the face, and the hour was to be stricken, there came from the brazen lungs of the clock a sound which was clear and loud and deep and exceedingly musical, but of so peculiar a note and emphasis that, at each lapse of an hour, the musicians of the orchestra were constrained to pause, momentarily, in their performance, to hearken to the sound; and thus the waltzers perforce ceased their evolutions; and there was a brief disconcert of the whole gay company; and, while the chimes of the clock yet rang, it was observed that the giddiest grew pale, and the more aged and sedate passed their hands over their brows as if in confused revery or meditation. But when the echoes had fully ceased, a light laughter at once pervaded the assembly; the musicians looked at each other and smiled as if at their own nervousness and folly, and made whispering vows, each to the other, that the next chiming of the clock should produce in them no similar emotion; and then, after the lapse of sixty minutes (which embrace three thousand and six hundred seconds of the Time that flies), there came yet another chiming of the clock, and then were the same disconcert and tremulousness and meditation as before.

6 But, in spite of these things, it was a gay and magnificent revel. The tastes of the duke were peculiar. He had a fine eye for colors and effects. He disregarded the *decora* of mere fashion. His plans were bold and fiery, and his conceptions glowed with barbaric lustre. There are some who would have thought him mad. His followers felt that he was not. It was necessary to hear and see and touch him to be *sure* that he was not.

7 He had directed, in great part, the movable embellishments of the seven chambers, upon occasion of this great fête, and it was his own guiding taste which had given character to the masqueraders. Be sure they were grotesque. There were much glare and glitter and piquancy and phantasm—much of what has been since seen in "Hernani." There were arabesque figures with unsuited limbs and appointments. There were delirious fancies such as the madman fashions. There were much of the beautiful, much of the wanton, much of the

bizarre, something of the terrible, and not a little of that which might have excited disgust. To and fro in the seven chambers there stalked, in fact, a multitude of dreams. And these—the dreams—writhed in and about, taking hue from the rooms, and causing the wild music of the orchestra to seem as the echo of their steps. And, anon, there strikes the ebony clock which stands in the hall of the velvet. And then, for a moment, all is still, and all is silent save the voice of the clock. The dreams are stiff-frozen as they stand. But the echoes of the chime die away—they have endured but an instant—and a light, half-subdued laughter floats after them as they depart. And now again the music swells, and the dreams live, and writhe to and fro more merrily than ever, taking hue from the many-tinted windows through which stream the rays from the tripods. But to the chamber which lies most westwardly of the seven there are now none of the maskers who venture; for the night is waning away; and there flows a ruddier light through the blood-colored panes; and the blackness of the sable drapery appalls; and to him whose foot falls upon the sable carpet, there comes from the near clock of ebony a muffled peal more solemnly emphatic than any which reaches *their* ears who indulge in the more remote gaieties of the other apartments.

8 But these other apartments were densely crowded, and in them beat feverishly the heart of life. And the revel went whirlingly on, until at length there commenced the sounding of midnight upon the clock. And then the music ceased, as I have told; and the evolutions of the waltzers were quieted; and there was an uneasy cessation of all things as before. But now there were twelve strokes to be sounded by the bell of the clock; and thus it happened, perhaps that more of thought crept, with more of time, into the meditations of the thoughtful among those who revelled. And thus too, it happened, perhaps, that before the last echoes of the last chime had utterly sunk into silence, there were many individuals in the crowd who had found leisure to become aware of the presence of a masked figure which had arrested the attention of no single individual before. And the rumor of this new presence having spread itself whisperingly around, there arose at length from the whole company a buzz, or murmur, expressive of disapprobation and surprise—then, finally, of terror, of horror, and of disgust.

9 In an assembly of phantasms such as I have painted, it may well be supposed that no ordinary appearance could have excited such sensation. In truth the masquerade license of the night was nearly unlimited; but the figure in question had out-Heroded Herod, and gone beyond the bounds of even the prince's indefinite decorum. There are chords in the hearts of the most reckless which cannot be touched without emotion. Even with the utterly lost, to whom life and death are equally jests, there are matters of which no jest can be made. The whole company, indeed, seemed now deeply to feel that in the costume and bearing of the stranger neither wit nor propriety existed. The figure was tall and

gaunt, and shrouded from head to foot in the habiliments of the grave. The mask which concealed the visage was made so nearly to resemble the countenance of a stiffened corpse that the closest scrutiny must have had difficulty in detecting the cheat. And yet all this might have been endured, if not approved, by the mad revellers around. But the mummer had gone so far as to assume the type of the Red Death. His vesture was dabbled in *blood*—and his broad brow, with all the features of the face, was besprinkled with the scarlet horror.

10 When the eyes of Prince Prospero fell upon this spectral image (which, with a slow and solemn movement, as if more fully to sustain its *rôle*, stalked to and fro among the waltzers) he was seen to be convulsed, in the first moment with a strong shudder either of terror or distaste; but, in the next, his brow reddened with rage.

11 "Who dares"—he demanded hoarsely of the courtiers who stood near him—"who dares insult us with this blasphemous mockery. Seize him and unmask him—that we may know whom we have to hang, at sunrise, from the battlements!"

12 It was in the eastern or blue chamber in which stood the Prince Prospero as he uttered these words. They rang throughout the seven rooms loudly and clearly, for the prince was a bold and robust man, and the music had become hushed at the waving of his hand.

13 It was in the blue room where stood the prince, with a group of pale courtiers by his side. At first, as he spoke, there was a slight rushing movement of this group in the direction of the intruder, who, at the moment was also near at hand, and now, with deliberate and stately step, made closer approach to the speaker. But from a certain nameless awe with which the mad assumptions of the mummer had inspired the whole party, there were found none who put forth hand to seize him; so that, unimpeded, he passed within a yard of the prince's person; and, while the vast assembly, as if with one impulse, shrank from the centres of the rooms to the walls, he made his way uninterruptedly, but with the same solemn and measured step which had distinguished him from the first, through the blue chamber to the purple—through the purple to the green—through the green to the orange—through this again to the white—and even thence to the violet, ere a decided movement had been made to arrest him. It was then, however, that the Prince Prospero, maddening with rage and the shame of his own momentary cowardice, rushed hurriedly through the six chambers, while none followed him on account of a deadly terror that had seized upon all. He bore aloft a drawn dagger, and had approached, in rapid impetuosity, to within three or four feet of the retreating figure, when the latter, having attained the extremity of the velvet apartment, turned suddenly and confronted his pursuer. There was a sharp cry—and the dagger dropped gleaming upon the sable carpet, upon which, instantly afterward, fell prostrate in death the Prince

Prospero. Then, summoning the wild courage of despair, a throng of the revellers at once threw themselves into the black apartment, and, seizing the mummer, whose tall figure stood erect and motionless within the shadow of the ebony clock, gasped in unutterable horror at finding the grave cerements and corpse-like mask, which they handled with so violent a rudeness, untenanted by any tangible form.

14 And now was acknowledged the presence of the Red Death. He had come like a thief in the night. And one by one dropped the revellers in the blood-bedewed halls of their revel, and died each in the despairing posture of his fall. And the life of the ebony clock went out with that of the last of the gay. And the flames of the tripods expired. And Darkness and Decay and the Red Death held illimitable dominion over all.

—1842

Guy de Maupassant
(1850-1893)

The Necklace

Maupassant did not consider a literary career until he was almost thirty. After military service he worked as a French government clerk until 1882. The great influence on his development as a writer was the novelist Gustave Flaubert, who introduced him to other Parisian literary figures, including Emile Zola, the leader of the naturalists. "Boule-de-suif," the story of a prostitute (the title, literally "greaseball," is her nickname) whose generosity is gratefully accepted by a group of war refugees until they reach safety and revert to their former contempt, made Maupassant a celebrity when it was published in 1880 in a collection of stories about the Franco-Prussian War. Maupassant died young, a victim of a self-destructive lifestyle that led to syphilis, attempted suicide, and madness, but during his most productive decade (1880-1890) he produced over three hundred stories, six novels, poetry, travel writing, and a play. Like his American contemporary O. Henry (William Sidney Porter), Maupassant first reached a large popular audience through mass-circulation

---

Translated by Marjorie Laurie

magazines. Maupassant's focus on the unglamorous realities of both rural and urban life mark him as one of the masters of literary naturalism, and his careful plot construction and attention to detail set high standards for later writers of short fiction. "The Necklace," with its brilliant economy and wrenching ultimate irony, typifies his strengths.

She was one of those pretty and charming girls who are sometimes, as if by a mistake of destiny, born in a family of clerks. She had no dowry, no expectations, no means of being known, understood, loved, wedded by any rich and distinguished man; and she let herself be married to a little clerk at the Ministry of Public Instruction.

2 She dressed plainly because she could not dress well, but she was as unhappy as though she had really fallen from her proper station, since with women there is neither caste nor rank: and beauty, grace and charm act instead of family and birth. Natural fineness, instinct for what is elegant, suppleness of wit, are the sole hierarchy, and make from women of the people the equals of the very greatest ladies.

3 She suffered ceaselessly, feeling herself born for all the delicacies and all the luxuries. She suffered from the poverty of her dwelling, from the wretched look of the walls, from the worn-out chairs, from the ugliness of the curtains. All those things, of which another woman of her rank would never even have been conscious, tortured her and made her angry. The sight of the little Breton peasant who did her humble housework aroused in her regrets which were despairing, and distracted dreams. She thought of the silent antechambers hung with Oriental tapestry, lit by tall bronze candelabra, and of the two great footmen in knee breeches who sleep in the big armchairs, made drowsy by the heavy warmth of the hot-air stove. She thought of the long *salons*° fitted up with ancient silk, of the delicate furniture carrying priceless curiosities, and of the coquettish perfumed boudoirs made for talks at five o'clock with intimate friends, with men famous and sought after, whom all women envy and whose attention they all desire.

4 When she sat down to dinner, before the round table covered with a tablecloth three days old, opposite her husband, who uncovered the soup tureen and declared with an enchanted air, "Ah, the good *pot-au-feu*°! I don't know anything better than that," she thought of dainty dinners, of shining silverware, of tapestry which peopled the walls with ancient personages and with strange birds flying in the midst of a fairy forest; and she thought of delicious dishes served

---

salons drawing-rooms
pot-au-feu stew

on marvelous plates, and of the whispered gallantries which you listen to with a sphinxlike smile, while you are eating the pink flesh of a trout or the wings of a quail.

5 She had no dresses, no jewels, nothing. And she loved nothing but that; she felt made for that. She would so have liked to please, to be envied, to be charming, to be sought after.

6 She had a friend, a former schoolmate at the convent, who was rich, and whom she did not like to go and see any more, because she suffered so much when she came back.

7 But one evening, her husband returned home with a triumphant air, and holding a large envelope in his hand.

8 "There," said he. "Here is something for you."

9 She tore the paper sharply, and drew out a printed card which bore these words:

10 "The Minister of Public Instruction and Mme. Georges Ramponneau request the honor of M. and Mme. Loisel's company at the palace of the Ministry on Monday evening, January eighteenth."

11 Instead of being delighted, as her husband hoped, she threw the invitation on the table with disdain, murmuring:

12 "What do you want me to do with that?"

13 "But, my dear, I thought you would be glad. You never go out, and this is such a fine opportunity. I had awful trouble to get it. Everyone wants to go; it is very select, and they are not giving many invitations to clerks. The whole official world will be there."

14 She looked at him with an irritated glance, and said, impatiently:

15 "And what do you want me to put on my back?"

16 He had not thought of that; he stammered:

17 "Why, the dress you go to the theater in. It looks very well, to me."

18 He stopped, distracted, seeing his wife was crying. Two great tears descended slowly from the corners of her eyes toward the corners of her mouth. He stuttered:

19 "What's the matter? What's the matter?"

20 But, by violent effort, she had conquered her grief, and she replied, with a calm voice, while she wiped her wet cheeks:

21 "Nothing. Only I have no dress and therefore I can't go to this ball. Give your card to some colleague whose wife is better equipped than I."

22 He was in despair. He resumed:

23 "Come, let us see, Mathilde. How much would it cost, a suitable dress, which you could use on other occasions, something very simple?"

24 She reflected several seconds, making her calculations and wondering also what sum she could ask without drawing on herself an immediate refusal and a frightened exclamation from the economical clerk.

25 Finally, she replied, hesitatingly:

26 "I don't know exactly, but I think I could manage it with four hundred francs."

27 He had grown a little pale, because he was laying aside just that amount to buy a gun and treat himself to a little shooting next summer on the plain of Nanterre, with several friends who went to shoot larks down there, of a Sunday.

28 But he said:

29 "All right. I will give you four hundred francs. And try to have a pretty dress."

30 The day of the ball drew near, and Mme. Loisel seemed sad, uneasy, anxious. Her dress was ready, however. Her husband said to her one evening:

31 "What is the matter? Come, you've been so queer these last three days."

32 And she answered:

33 "It annoys me not to have a single jewel, not a single stone, nothing to put on. I shall look like distress. I should almost rather not go at all."

34 He resumed:

35 "You might wear natural flowers. It's very stylish at this time of the year. For ten francs you can get two or three magnificent roses."

36 She was not convinced.

37 "No; there's nothing more humiliating than to look poor among other women who are rich."

38 But her husband cried:

39 "How stupid you are! Go look up your friend Mme. Forestier, and ask her to lend you some jewels. You're quite thick enough with her to do that."

40 She uttered a cry of joy:

41 "It's true. I never thought of it."

42 The next day she went to her friend and told of her distress.

43 Mme. Forestier went to a wardrobe with a glass door, took out a large jewel-box, brought it back, opened it, and said to Mme. Loisel:

44 "Choose, my dear."

45 She saw first of all some bracelets, then a pearl necklace, then a Venetian cross, gold and precious stones of admirable workmanship. She tried on the ornaments before the glass, hesitated, could not make up her mind to part with them, to give them back. She kept asking:

46 "Haven't you any more?"

47 "Why, yes. Look. I don't know what you like."

48 All of a sudden she discovered, in a black satin box, a superb necklace of diamonds, and her heart began to beat with an immoderate desire. Her hands trembled as she took it. She fastened it around her throat, outside her high-necked dress, and remained lost in ecstasy at the sight of herself.

49 Then she asked, hesitating, filled with anguish:

50 "Can you lend me that, only that?"

51 "Why, yes, certainly."

52 She sprang upon the neck of her friend, kissed her passionately, then fled with her treasure.

53 The day of the ball arrived. Mme. Loisel made a great success. She was prettier than them all, elegant, gracious, smiling, and crazy with joy. All the men looked at her, asked her name, endeavored to be introduced. All the attachés of the Cabinet wanted to waltz with her. She was remarked by the minister himself.

54 She danced with intoxication, with passion, made drunk by pleasure, forgetting all, in the triumph of her beauty, in the glory of her success, in a sort of cloud of happiness composed of all this homage, of all this admiration, of all these awakened desires, and of that sense of complete victory which is so sweet to a woman's heart.

55 She went away about four o'clock in the morning. Her husband had been sleeping since midnight, in a little deserted anteroom, with three other gentlemen whose wives were having a very good time. He threw over her shoulders the wraps which he had brought, modest wraps of common life, whose poverty contrasted with the elegance of the ball dress. She felt this, and wanted to escape so as not to be remarked by the other women, who were enveloping themselves in costly furs.

56 Loisel held her back.

57 "Wait a bit. You will catch cold outside. I will go and call a cab."

58 But she did not listen to him, and rapidly descended the stairs. When they were in the street they did not find a carriage; and they began to look for one, shouting after the cabmen whom they saw passing by at a distance.

59 They went down toward the Seine, in despair, shivering with cold. At last they found on the quay one of those ancient noctambulant coupés which, exactly as if they were ashamed to show their misery during the day, are never seen round Paris until after nightfall.

60 It took them to their door in the Rue des Martyrs, and once more, sadly, they climbed up homeward. All was ended, for her. And as to him, he reflected that he must he at the Ministry at ten o'clock.

61 She removed the wraps which covered her shoulders, before the glass, so as once more to see herself in all her glory. But suddenly she uttered a cry. She no longer had the necklace around her neck!

62 Her husband, already half undressed, demanded:

63 "What is the matter with you?"

64 She turned madly towards him:

65 "I have—I have—I've lost Mme. Forestier's necklace."

66 He stood up, distracted.

67 "What!—how?—impossible!"

68 And they looked in the folds of her dress, in the folds of her cloak, in her pockets, everywhere. They did not find it.

69 He asked:

70 "You're sure you had it on when you left the ball?"

71 "Yes, I felt it in the vestibule of the palace."

72 "But if you had lost it in the street we should have heard it fall. It must be in the cab."

73 "Yes. Probably. Did you take his number?"

74 "No. And you, didn't you notice it?"

75 "No. "

76 They looked, thunderstruck, at one another. At last Loisel put on his clothes.

77 "I shall go back on foot," said he, "over the whole route which we have taken to see if I can find it."

78 And he went out. She sat waiting on a chair in her ball dress, without strength to go to bed, overwhelmed, without fire, without a thought.

79 Her husband came back about seven o'clock. He had found nothing.

80 He went to Police Headquarters, to the newspaper offices, to offer a reward: he went to the cab companies—everywhere, in fact, whither he was urged by the least suspicion of hope.

81 She waited all day, in the same condition of mad fear before this terrible calamity.

82 Loisel returned at night with a hollow, pale face; he had discovered nothing.

83 "You must write to your friend," said he, "that you have broken the clasp of her necklace and that you are having it mended. That will give us time to turn round."

84 She wrote at his dictation.

85 At the end of a week they had lost all hope.

86 And Loisel, who had aged five years, declared:

87 "We must consider how to replace that ornament."

88 The next day they took the box which had contained it, and they went to the jeweler whose name was found within. He consulted his books.

89 "It was not I, madame, who sold that necklace; I must simply have furnished the case."

90 Then they went from jeweler to jeweler, searching for a necklace like the other, consulting their memories, sick both of them with chagrin and anguish.

91 They found, in a shop at the Palais Royal, a string of diamonds which seemed to them exactly like the one they looked for. It was worth forty thousand francs. They could have it for thirty-six.

92 So they begged the jeweler not to sell it for three days yet. And they made a bargain that he should buy it back for thirty-four thousand francs, in case they found the other one before the end of February.

93 Loisel possessed eighteen thousand francs which his father had left him. He would borrow the rest.

94 He did borrow, asking a thousand francs of one, five hundred of another, five louis here, three louis there. He gave notes, took up ruinous obligations, dealt with usurers and all the race of lenders. He compromised all the rest of his life, risked his signature without even knowing if he could meet it; and, frightened by the pains yet to come, by the black misery which was about to fall upon him, by the prospect of all the physical privation and of all the moral tortures which he was to suffer, he went to get the new necklace, putting down upon the merchant's counter thirty-six thousand francs.

95 When Mme. Loisel took back the necklace, Mme. Forestier said to her, with a chilly manner:

96 "You should have returned it sooner; I might have needed it."

97 She did not open the case, as her friend had so much feared. If she had detected the substitution, what would she have thought, what would she have said? Would she not have taken Mme. Loisel for a thief?

98 Mme. Loisel now knew the horrible existence of the needy. She took her part, moreover, all of a sudden, with heroism. That dreadful debt must be paid. She would pay it. They dismissed their servant; they changed their lodgings; they rented a garret under the roof.

99 She came to know what heavy housework meant and the odious cares of the kitchen. She washed the dishes, using her rosy nails on the greasy pots and pans. She washed the dirty linen, the shirts, and the dishcloths, which she dried upon a line; she carried the slops down to the street every morning, and carried up the water, stopping for breath at every landing. And, dressed like a woman of the people, she went to the fruiterer, the grocer, the butcher, her basket on her arm, bargaining, insulted, defending her miserable money sou by sou.

100 Each month they had to meet some notes, renew others, obtain more time.

101 Her husband worked in the evening making a fair copy of some tradesman's accounts, and late at night he often copied manuscript for five sous a page.

102 And this life lasted for ten years.

103 At the end of ten years, they had paid everything, everything, with the rates of usury, and the accumulations of the compound interest.

104 Mme. Loisel looked old now. She had become the woman of impoverished households—strong and hard and rough. With frowsy hair, skirts askew, and red hands, she talked loud while washing the floor with great swishes of water. But sometimes, when her husband was at the office, she sat down near the window, and she thought of that gay evening of long ago, of the ball where she had been so beautiful and so fêted.

105 What would have happened if she had not lost that necklace? Who knows? Who knows? How life is strange and changeful! How little a thing is needed for us to be lost or to be saved!

106 But, one Sunday, having gone to take a walk in the Champs Elysées to refresh herself from the labor of the week, she suddenly perceived a woman who was leading a child. It was Mme. Forestier, still young, still beautiful, still charming.

107 Mme. Loisel felt moved. Was she going to speak to her? Yes, certainly. And now that she had paid, she was going to tell her all about it. Why not?

108 She went up.

109 "Good day, Jeanne."

110 The other, astonished to be familiarly addressed by this plain goodwife, did not recognize her at all, and stammered:

111 "But—madam!—I do not know—You must be mistaken."

112 "No. I am Mathilde Loisel."

113 Her friend uttered a cry.

114 "Oh, my poor Mathilde! How you are changed!"

115 "Yes, I have had days hard enough, since I have seen you, days wretched enough—and that because of you!"

116 "Of me! How so?"

117 "Do you remember that diamond necklace which you lent me to wear at the ministerial ball?"

118 "Yes. Well?"

119 "Well, I lost it."

120 "What do you mean? You brought it back."

121 "I brought you back another just like it. And for this we have been ten years paying. You can understand that it was not easy for us, us who had nothing. At last it is ended, and I am very glad."

122 Mme. Forestier had stopped.

123 "You say that you bought a necklace of diamonds to replace mine?"

124 "Yes. You never noticed it, then! They were very like."

125 And she smiled with a joy which was proud and naïve at once.

126 Mme. Forestier, strongly moved, took her two hands.

127 "Oh, my poor Mathilde! Why, my necklace was paste. It was worth at most five hundred francs!"

—1884

✧ ✧ ✧

Kate Chopin
(1851-1904)

The Storm

Virtually forgotten for most of this century, Chopin was rarely mentioned in histories of American literature and was remembered primarily as a chronicler of life among the Louisiana Creoles and Cajuns. Her works had long been out of print when they were rediscovered in recent decades, initially by feminist critics and subsequently by general readers. Her most important novel, *The Awakening* (1899), today appears frequently on college reading lists and was filmed in 1992 as *Grand Isle*. Born in St. Louis, Missouri, Chopin spent the 1870s in rural Louisiana, the wife of Oscar Chopin, a cotton broker from New Orleans. Later she lived with her husband on a plantation near Natchitoches, Louisiana, an area that later provided the setting of "The Storm" and other stories collected in *Bayou Folk* (1894) and *A Night in Arcadie* (1897) and from which she absorbed a rich mixture of French and black cultures. After her husband's death in 1883, Chopin returned to St. Louis with her six children and began her literary career, placing stories and regional pieces in popular magazines. Much of her later work is remarkable for its frank depiction of women's sexuality, a subject rarely broached in the literature of the era, and Chopin became the subject of controversy after the appearance of *The Awakening*. The negative reception of that work caused Chopin to suffer social ostracism and effectively ended her active career as a writer; "The Storm" remained unpublished at her death.

I

The leaves were so still that even Bibi thought it was going to rain. Bobinôt, who was accustomed to converse on terms of perfect equality with his little son, called the child's attention to certain sombre clouds that were rolling with sinister intention from the west, accompanied by a sullen, threatening roar. They were at Friedheimer's store and decided to remain there till the storm had passed. They sat within the door on two empty kegs. Bibi was four years old and looked very wise.

2 "Mama'll be 'fraid, yes," he suggested with blinking eyes.

3 "She'll shut the house. Maybe she got Sylvie helpin' her this evenin'," Bobinôt responded reassuringly.

4 "No; she ent got Sylvie. Sylvie was helpin' her yistiday," piped Bibi.

5 Bobinôt arose and going across to the counter purchased a can of shrimps, of which Calixta was very fond. Then he returned to his perch on the keg and sat stolidly holding the can of shrimps while the storm burst. It shook the wooden store and seemed to be ripping great furrows in the distant field. Bibi laid his little hand on his father's knee and was not afraid.

II

6 Calixta, at home, felt no uneasiness for their safety. She sat at a side window sewing furiously on a sewing machine. She was greatly occupied and did not notice the approaching storm. But she felt very warm and often stopped to mop her face on which the perspiration gathered in beads. She unfastened her white sacque at the throat. It began to grow dark, and suddenly realizing the situation she got up hurriedly and went about closing windows and doors.

7 Out on the small front gallery she had hung Bobinôt's Sunday clothes to air and she hastened out to gather them before the rain fell. As she stepped outside, Alcée Laballière rode in at the gate. She had not seen him very often since her marriage, and never alone. She stood there with Bobinôt's coat in her hands, and the big rain drops began to fall. Alcée rode his horse under the shelter of a side projection where the chickens had huddled and there were plows and a harrow piled up in the corner.

8 "May I come and wait in your gallery till the storm is over, Calixta?" he asked.

9 "Come 'long in, M'sieur Alcée."

10 His voice and her own startled her as if from a trance, and she seized Bobinôt's vest. Alcée, mounting to the porch, grabbed the trousers and snatched Bibi's braided jacket that was about to be carried away by a sudden gust of wind. He expressed an intention to remain outside, but it was soon apparent that he might as well have been out in the open: the water beat in upon the boards in driving sheets, and he went inside, closing the door after him. It was even necessary to put something beneath the door to keep the water out.

11 "My! what a rain! It's good two years sence it rain like that," exclaimed Calixta as she rolled up a piece of bagging and Alcée helped her to thrust it beneath the crack.

12 She was a little fuller of figure than five years before when she married; but she had lost nothing of her vivacity. Her blue eyes still retained their melt-

ing quality; and her yellow hair, dishevelled by the wind and rain, kinked more stubbornly than ever about her ears and temples.

13 The rain beat upon the low, shingled roof with a force and clatter that threatened to break an entrance and deluge them there. They were in the dining room—the sitting room—the general utility room. Adjoining was her bedroom, with Bibi's couch along side her own. The door stood open, and the room with its white, monumental bed, its closed shutters, looked dim and mysterious.

14 Alcée flung himself into a rocker and Calixta nervously began to gather up from the floor the lengths of a cotton sheet which she had been sewing.

15 "If this keeps up, *Dieu sait*° if the levees goin' to stan' it!" she exclaimed.

16 "What have you got to do with the levees?"

17 "I got enough to do! An' there's Bobinôt with Bibi out in that storm—if only he didn' left Friedheimer's!"

18 "Let us hope, Calixta, that Bobinôt's got sense enough to come in out of a cyclone."

19 She went and stood at the window with a greatly disturbed look on her face. She wiped the frame that was clouded with moisture. It was stiflingly hot. Alcée got up and joined her at the window, looking over her shoulder. The rain was coming down in sheets obscuring the view of far-off cabins and enveloping the distant wood in a gray mist. The playing of the lightning was incessant. A bolt struck a tall chinaberry tree at the edge of the field. It filled all visible space with a blinding glare and the crash seemed to invade the very boards they stood upon.

20 Calixta put her hands to her eyes, and with a cry, staggered backward. Alcée's arm encircled her, and for an instant he drew her close and spasmodically to him.

21 *"Bonté!"*° she cried, releasing herself from his encircling arm and retreating from the window, "the house'll go next! If I only knew w'ere Bibi was!" She would not compose herself; she would not be seated. Alcée clasped her shoulders and looked into her face. The contact of her warm, palpitating body when he had unthinkingly drawn her into his arms, had aroused all the old-time infatuation and desire for her flesh.

22 "Calixta," he said, "don't be frightened. Nothing can happen. The house is too low to be struck, with so many tall trees standing about. There! aren't you going to be quiet? say, aren't you?" He pushed her hair back from her face that was warm and steaming. Her lips were as red and moist as pomegranate seed. Her white neck and a glimpse of her full, firm bosom disturbed him power-

---

Dieu sait God knows
Bonté! Heavens!

fully. As she glanced up at him the fear in her liquid blue eyes had given place to a drowsy gleam that unconsciously betrayed a sensuous desire. He looked down into her eyes and there was nothing for him to do but gather her lips in a kiss. It reminded him of Assumption.

23 "Do you remember—in Assumption, Calixta?" he asked in a low voice broken by passion. Oh! she remembered; for in Assumption he had kissed her and kissed and kissed her; until his senses would well nigh fail, and to save her he would resort to a desperate flight. If she was not an immaculate dove in those days, she was still inviolate; a passionate creature whose very defenselessness had made her defense, against which his honor forbade him to prevail. Now—well, now—her lips seemed in a manner free to be tasted, as well as her round, white throat and her whiter breasts.

24 They did not heed the crashing torrents, and the roar of the elements made her laugh as she lay in his arms. She was a revelation in that dim, mysterious chamber; as white as the couch she lay upon. Her firm, elastic flesh that was knowing for the first time its birthright, was like a creamy lily that the sun invites to contribute its breath and perfume to the undying life of the world.

25 The generous abundance of her passion, without guile or trickery, was like a white flame which penetrated and found response in depths of his own sensuous nature that had never yet been reached.

26 When he touched her breasts they gave themselves up in quivering ecstasy, inviting his lips. Her mouth was a fountain of delight. And when he possessed her, they seemed to swoon together at the very borderland of life's mystery.

27 He stayed cushioned upon her, breathless, dazed, enervated, with his heart beating like a hammer upon her. With one hand she clasped his head, her lips lightly touching his forehead. The other hand stroked with a soothing rhythm his muscular shoulders.

28 The growl of the thunder was distant and passing away. The rain beat softly upon the shingles, inviting them to drowsiness and sleep. But they dared not yield.

29 The rain was over; and the sun was turning the glistening green world into a palace of gems. Calixta, on the gallery, watched Alcée ride away. He turned and smiled at her with a beaming face; and she lifted her pretty chin in the air and laughed aloud.

III

30 Bobinôt and Bibi, trudging home, stopped without at the cistern to make themselves presentable.

31 "My! Bibi, w'at will yo' mama say! You ought to be ashame'. You oughtn' put on those good pants. Look at 'em! An' that mud on yo' collar! How you got that mud on yo' collar, Bibi? I never saw such a boy!" Bibi was the picture of

pathetic resignation. Bobinôt was the embodiment of serious solicitude as he strove to remove from his own person and his son's the signs of their tramp over heavy roads and through wet fields. He scraped the mud off Bibi's bare legs and feet with a stick and carefully removed all traces from his heavy brogans. Then, prepared for the worst—the meeting with an over-scrupulous housewife, they entered cautiously at the back door.

32 Calixta was preparing supper. She had set the table and was dripping coffee at the hearth. She sprang up as they came in.

33 "Oh, Bobinôt! You back! My! but I was uneasy. W'ere you been during the rain? An' Bibi? he ain't wet? he ain't hurt?" She had clasped Bibi and was kissing him effusively. Bobinôt's explanations and apologies which he had been composing all along the way, died on his lips as Calixta felt him to see if he were dry, and seemed to express nothing but satisfaction at their safe return.

34 "I brought you some shrimps, Calixta," offered Bobinôt, hauling the can from his ample side pocket and laying it on the table.

35 "Shrimps! Oh, Bobinôt! you too good fo' anything!" and she gave him a smacking kiss on the cheek that resounded. *"J'vous réponds,*° we'll have a feas' tonight! umph-umph!"

36 Bobinôt and Bibi began to relax and enjoy themselves, and when the three seated themselves at table they laughed much and so loud that anyone might have heard them as far away as Laballière's.

IV

37 Alcée Laballière wrote to his wife, Clarisse, that night. It was a loving letter, full of tender solicitude. He told her not to hurry back, but if she and the babies liked it at Biloxi, to stay a month longer. He was getting on nicely; and though he missed them, he was willing to bear the separation a while longer—realizing that their health and pleasure were the first things to be considered.

V

38 As for Clarisse, she was charmed upon receiving her husband's letter. She and the babies were doing well. The society was agreeable; many of her old friends and acquaintances were at the bay. And the first free breath since her marriage seemed to restore the pleasant liberty of her maiden days. Devoted as she was to her husband, their intimate conjugal life was something which she was more than willing to forego for a while.

39 So the storm passed and everyone was happy.

—1898

J'vous réponds Take my word

Anton Chekhov
(1860-1904)

The Lady with the Pet Dog

Chekhov was the grandchild of Russian serfs but showed great understanding of and sympathy for upper-class characters, like those in his masterpiece *The Cherry Orchard* (1904), who could see their world ending in the decades before the Russian Revolution. After an early education in his native town of Taganrog, Chekhov entered the University of Moscow, where he took a medical degree in 1884. Except for occasional service during epidemics he practiced only rarely, preferring to earn his living as a regular contributor of stories to humor magazines. His first play, *Ivanov*, was produced in 1887, beginning a career as a dramatist that flourished in the last decade of his life when he allied himself with the Moscow Art Theatre and its influential director, Konstantin Stanislavsky. Chekhov's early stories are primarily comic, but those of his mature period, like his plays, are remarkable for their emotional depth. Chekhov's objectivity and realism, qualities that he perhaps gained from his medical studies, continue to make him one of the most modern of nineteenth century authors; rarely are there unabmiguous moral resolutions in his works. "The Lady with the Pet Dog," written in 1898, seems even more remarkable when we consider the author's lack of condemnation of his characters' illicit affair. The "unheroic heroes" whom he depicts with sympathy and gentle irony embody many of the key literary themes of our times.

I

A new person, it was said, had appeared on the esplanade: a lady with a pet dog. Dmitry Dmitrich Gurov, who had spent a fortnight at Yalta and had got

---

Translated by Avrahm Yarmolinsky

used to the place, had also begun to take an interest in new arrivals. As he sat in Vernet's confectionery shop, he saw, walking on the esplanade, a fair-haired young woman of medium height, wearing a beret; a white Pomeranian was trotting behind her.

2 And afterwards he met her in the public garden and in the square several times a day. She walked alone, always wearing the same beret and always with the white dog; no one knew who she was and everyone called her simply "the lady with the pet dog."

3 "If she is here alone without husband or friends," Gurov reflected, "it wouldn't be a bad thing to make her acquaintance."

4 He was under forty, but he already had a daughter twelve years old, and two sons at school. They had found a wife for him when he was very young, a student in his second year, and by now she seemed half as old again as he. She was a tall, erect woman with dark eyebrows, stately and dignified and, as she said of herself, intellectual. She read a great deal, used simplified spelling in her letters, called her husband, not Dmitry, but Dimitry, while he privately considered her of limited intelligence, narrow-minded, dowdy, was afraid of her, and did not like to be at home. He had begun being unfaithful to her long ago—had been unfaithful to her often and, probably for that reason, almost always spoke ill of women, and when they were talked of in his presence used to call them "the inferior race."

5 It seemed to him that he had been sufficiently tutored by bitter experience to call them what he pleased, and yet he could not have lived without "the inferior race" for two days together. In the company of men he was bored and ill at ease, he was chilly and uncommunicative with them; but when he was among women he felt free, and knew what to speak to them about and how to comport himself; and even to be silent with them was no strain on him. In his appearance, in his character, in his whole make-up there was something attractive and elusive that disposed women in his favor and allured them. He knew that, and some force seemed to draw him to them, too.

6 Oft-repeated and really bitter experience had taught him long ago that with decent people—particularly Moscow people—who are irresolute and slow to move, every affair which at first seems a light and charming adventure inevitably grows into a whole problem of extreme complexity, and in the end a painful situation is created. But at every new meeting with an interesting woman this lesson of experience seemed to slip from his memory, and he was eager for life, and everything seemed so simple and diverting.

7 One evening while he was dining in the public garden the lady in the beret walked up without haste to take the next table. Her expression, her gait, her dress, and the way she did her hair told him that she belonged to the upper

class, that she was married, that she was in Yalta for the first time and alone, and that she was bored there. The stories told of the immorality in Yalta are to a great extent untrue; he despised them, and knew that such stories were made up for the most part by persons who would have been glad to sin themselves if they had had the chance; but when the lady sat down at the next table three paces from him, he recalled these stories of easy conquests, of trips to the mountains, and the tempting thought of a swift, fleeting liaison, a romance with an unknown woman of whose very name he was ignorant suddenly took hold of him.

8 He beckoned invitingly to the Pomeranian, and when the dog approached him, shook his finger at it. The Pomeranian growled; Gurov threatened it again.

9 The lady glanced at him and at once dropped her eyes.

10 "He doesn't bite," she said and blushed.

11 "May I give him a bone?" he asked; and when she nodded he inquired affably, "Have you been in Yalta long?"

12 "About five days."

13 "And I am dragging out the second week here."

14 There was a short silence.

15 "Time passes quickly, and yet it is so dull here!" she said, not looking at him.

16 "It's only the fashion to say it's dull here. A provincial will live in Belyov or Zhizdra and not be bored, but when he comes here it's 'Oh, the dullness! Oh, the dust!' One would think he came from Granada."

17 She laughed. Then both continued eating in silence, like strangers, but after dinner they walked together and there sprang up between them the light banter of people who are free and contented, to whom it does not matter where they go or what they talk about. They walked and talked of the strange light on the sea: the water was a soft, warm, lilac color, and there was a golden band of moonlight upon it. They talked of how sultry it was after a hot day. Gurov told her that he was a native of Moscow, that he had studied languages and literature at the university, but had a post in a bank; that at one time he had trained to become an opera singer but had given it up, that he owned two houses in Moscow. And he learned from her that she had grown up in Petersburg, but had lived in S_______ since her marriage two years previously, that she was going to stay in Yalta for about another month, and that her husband, who needed a rest, too, might perhaps come to fetch her. She was not certain whether her husband was a member of a Government Board or served on a Zemstvo Council, and this amused her. And Gurov learned that her name was Anna Sergeyevna.

18 Afterwards in his room at the hotel he thought about her—and was certain that he would meet her the next day. It was bound to happen. Getting into bed he

recalled that she had been a schoolgirl only recently, doing lessons like his own daughter; he thought how much timidity and angularity there was still in her laugh and her manner of talking with a stranger. It must have been the first time in her life that she was alone in a setting in which she was followed, looked at, and spoken to for one secret purpose alone, which she could hardly fail to guess. He thought of her slim, delicate throat, her lovely gray eyes.

19 "There's something pathetic about her, though," he thought, and dropped off.

II

20 A week had passed since they had struck up an acquaintance. It was a holiday. It was close indoors, while in the street the wind whirled the dust about and blew people's hats off. One was thirsty all day, and Gurov often went into the restaurant and offered Anna Sergeyevna a soft drink or ice cream. One did not know what to do with oneself.

21 In the evening when the wind had abated they went out on the pier to watch the steamer come in. There were a great many people walking about the dock; they had come to welcome someone and they were carrying bunches of flowers. And two peculiarities of a festive Yalta crowd stood out: the elderly ladies were dressed like young ones and there were many generals.

22 Owing to the choppy sea, the steamer arrived late, after sunset, and it was a long time tacking about before it put in at the pier. Anna Sergeyevna peered at the steamer and the passengers through her lorgnette as though looking for acquaintances, and whenever she turned to Gurov her eyes were shining. She talked a great deal and asked questions jerkily, forgetting the next moment what she had asked; then she lost her lorgnette in the crush.

23 The festive crowd began to disperse; it was now too dark to see people's faces; there was no wind any more, but Gurov and Anna Sergeyevna still stood as though waiting to see someone else come off the steamer. Anna Sergeyevna was silent now, and sniffed her flowers without looking at Gurov.

24 "The weather has improved this evening," he said. "Where shall we go now? Shall we drive somewhere?"

25 She did not reply.

26 Then he looked at her intently, and suddenly embraced her and kissed her on the lips, and the moist fragrance of her flowers enveloped him; and at once he looked round him anxiously, wondering if anyone had seen them.

27 "Let us go to your place," he said softly. And they walked off together rapidly.

28 The air in her room was close and there was the smell of the perfume she had bought at the Japanese shop. Looking at her, Gurov thought: "What encounters life offers!" From the past he preserved the memory of carefree, good-natured women whom love made gay and who were grateful to him for the happiness he gave them, however brief it might be; and of women like his wife who loved without sincerity, with too many words, affectedly, hysterically, with an expression that it was not love or passion that engaged them but something more significant; and of two or three others, very beautiful, frigid women, across whose faces would suddenly flit a rapacious expression—an obstinate desire to take from life more than it could give, and these were women no longer young, capricious, unreflecting, domineering, unintelligent, and when Gurov grew cold to them their beauty aroused his hatred, and the lace on their lingerie seemed to him to resemble scales.

29 But here there was the timidity, the angularity of inexperienced youth, a feeling of awkwardness; and there was a sense of embarrassment, as though someone had suddenly knocked at the door. Anna Sergeyevna, "the lady with the pet dog," treated what had happened in a peculiar way, very seriously, as though it were her fall—so it seemed, and this was odd and inappropriate. Her features drooped and faded, and her long hair hung down sadly on either side of her face; she grew pensive and her dejected pose was that of a Magdalene in a picture by an old master.

30 "It's not right," she said. "You don't respect me now, you first of all."

31 There was a watermelon on the table. Gurov cut himself a slice and began eating it without haste. They were silent for at least half an hour.

32 There was something touching about Anna Sergeyevna; she had the purity of a well bred, naïve woman who has seen little of life. The single candle burning on the table barely illuminated her face, yet it was clear that she was unhappy.

33 "Why should I stop respecting you, darling?" asked Gurov. "You don't know what you're saying."

34 "God forgive me," she said, and her eyes filled with tears. "It's terrible."

35 "It's as though you were trying to exonerate yourself."

36 "How can I exonerate myself? No. I am a bad, low woman; I despise myself and I have no thought of exonerating myself. It's not my husband but myself I have deceived. And not only just now; I have been deceiving myself for a long time. My husband may be a good, honest man, but he is a flunkey! I don't know what he does, what his work is, but I know he is a flunkey! I was twenty when I married him. I was tormented by curiosity; I wanted something better. 'There must be a different sort of life,' I said to myself. I wanted to live! To live, to live! Curiosity kept eating at me—you don't understand, but I swear to

God I could no longer control myself; something was going on in me; I could not be held back. I told my husband I was ill, and came here. And here I have been walking about as though in a daze, as though I were mad; and now I have become a vulgar, vile woman whom anyone may despise."

37 Gurov was already bored with her; he was irritated by her naïve tone, by her repentance, so unexpected and so out of place, but for the tears in her eyes he might have thought she was joking or play-acting.

38 "I don't understand, my dear," he said softly. "What do you want?"

39 She hid her face on his breast and pressed close to him.

40 "Believe me, believe me, I beg you," she said, "I love honesty and purity, and sin is loathsome to me; I don't know what I'm doing. Simple people say, 'The Evil One has led me astray.' And I may say of myself now that the Evil One has led me astray."

41 "Quiet, quiet," he murmured.

42 He looked into her fixed, frightened eyes, kissed her, spoke to her softly and affectionately, and by degrees she calmed down, and her gaiety returned; both began laughing.

43 Afterwards when they went out there was not a soul on the esplanade. The town with its cypresses looked quite dead, but the sea was still sounding as it broke upon the beach; a single launch was rocking on the waves and on it a lantern was blinking sleepily.

44 They found a cab and drove to Oreanda.

45 "I found out your surname in the hall just now; it was written on the board—von Dideritz," said Gurov. "Is your husband German?"

46 "No; I believe his grandfather was German, but he is Greek Orthodox himself."

47 At Oreanda they sat on a bench not far from the church, looked down at the sea, and were silent. Yalta was barely visible through the morning mist; white clouds rested motionlessly on the mountaintops. The leaves did not stir on the trees, cicadas twanged, and the monotonous muffled sound of the sea that rose from below spoke of the peace, the eternal sleep awaiting us. So it rumbled below when there was no Yalta, no Oreanda here; so it rumbles now, and it will rumble as indifferently and as hollowly when we are no more. And in this constancy, in this complete indifference to the life and death of each of us, there lies, perhaps, a pledge of our eternal salvation, of the unceasing advance of life upon earth, of unceasing movement towards perfection. Sitting beside a young woman who in the dawn seemed so lovely, Gurov, soothed and spellbound by these magical surroundings—the sea, the mountains, the clouds, the wide sky—thought how everything is really beautiful in this world when one reflects:

everything except what we think or do ourselves when we forget the higher aims of life and our own human dignity.

48 A man strolled up to them—probably a guard—looked at them and walked away. And this detail, too, seemed so mysterious and beautiful. They saw a steamer arrive from Feodosia, its lights extinguished in the glow of dawn.

49 "There is dew on the grass," said Anna Sergeyevna, after a silence.

50 "Yes, it's time to go home."

51 They returned to the city.

52 Then they met every day at twelve o'clock on the esplanade, lunched and dined together, took walks, admired the sea. She complained that she slept badly, that she had palpitations, asked the same questions, troubled now by jealousy and now by the fear that he did not respect her sufficiently. And often in the square or the public garden, when there was no one near them, he suddenly drew her to him and kissed her passionately. Complete idleness, these kisses in broad daylight exchanged furtively in dread of someone's seeing them, the heat, the smell of the sea, and the continual flitting before his eyes of idle, well-dressed, well-fed people, worked a complete change in him; he kept telling Anna Sergeyevna how beautiful she was, how seductive, was urgently passionate; he would not move a step away from her, while she was often pensive and continually pressed him to confess that he did not respect her, did not love her in the least, and saw in her nothing but a common woman. Almost every evening rather late they drove somewhere out of town, to Oreanda or to the waterfall; and the excursion was always a success, the scenery invariably impressed them as beautiful and magnificent.

53 They were expecting her husband, but a letter came from him saying that he had eye-trouble, and begging his wife to return home as soon as possible. Anna Sergeyevna made haste to go.

54 "It's a good thing I am leaving," she said to Gurov. "It's the hand of Fate!"

55 She took a carriage to the railway station, and he went with her. They were driving the whole day. When she had taken her place in the express, and when the second bell had rung, she said, "Let me look at you once more—let me look at you again. Like this."

56 She was not crying but was so sad that she seemed ill and her face was quivering.

57 "I shall be thinking of you—remembering you," she said. "God bless you; be happy. Don't remember evil against me. We are parting forever—it has to be, for we ought never to have met. Well, God bless you."

58 The train moved off rapidly, its lights soon vanished, and a minute later there was no sound of it, as though everything had conspired to end as quickly as possible that sweet trance, that madness. Left alone on the platform, and gazing

into the dark distance, Gurov listened to the twang of the grasshoppers and the hum of the telegraph wires, feeling as though he had just waked up. And he reflected, musing, that there had now been another episode or adventure in his life, and it, too, was at an end, and nothing was left of it but a memory. He was moved, sad, and slightly remorseful: this young woman whom he would never meet again had not been happy with him; he had been warm and affectionate with her, but yet in his manner, his tone, and his caresses there had been a shade of light irony, the slightly coarse arrogance of a happy male who was, besides, almost twice her age. She had constantly called him kind, exceptional, high-minded; obviously he had seemed to her different from what he really was, so he had involuntarily deceived her.

59 Here at the station there was already a scent of autumn in the air; it was a chilly evening.

60 "It is time for me to go north, too," thought Gurov as he left the platform. "High time!"

III

61 At home in Moscow the winter routine was already established; the stoves were heated, and in the morning it was still dark when the children were having breakfast and getting ready for school, and the nurse would light the lamp for a short time. There were frosts already. When the first snow falls, on the first day the sleighs are out, it is pleasant to see the white earth, the white roofs; one draws easy, delicious breaths, and the season brings back the days of one's youth. The old limes and birches, white with hoar-frost, have a good natured look; they are closer to one's heart than cypresses and palms, and near them one no longer wants to think of mountains and the sea.

62 Gurov, a native of Moscow, arrived there on a fine frosty day, and when he put on his fur coat and warm gloves and took a walk along Petrovka, and when on Saturday night he heard the bells ringing, his recent trip and the places he had visited lost all charm for him. Little by little he became immersed in Moscow life, greedily read three newspapers a day, and declared that he did not read the Moscow papers on principle. He already felt a longing for restaurants, clubs, formal dinners, anniversary celebrations, and it flattered him to entertain distinguished lawyers and actors, and to play cards with a professor at the physicians' club. He could eat a whole portion of meat stewed with pickled cabbage and served in a pan, Moscow style.

63 A month or so would pass and the image of Anna Sergeyevna, it seemed to him, would become misty in his memory, and only from time to time he would dream of her with her touching smile as he dreamed of others. But more than a

month went by, winter came into its own, and everything was still clear in his memory as though he had parted from Anna Sergeyevna only yesterday. And his memories glowed more and more vividly. When in the evening stillness the voices of his children preparing their lessons reached his study, or when he listened to a song or to an organ playing in a restaurant, or when the storm howled in the chimney, suddenly everything would rise up in his memory; what had happened on the pier and the early morning with the mist on the mountains, and the steamer coming from Feodosia, and the kisses. He would pace about his room a long time, remembering and smiling; then his memories passed into reveries, and in his imagination the past would mingle with what was to come. He did not dream of Anna Sergeyevna, but she followed him about everywhere and watched him. When he shut his eyes he saw her before him as though she were there in the flesh, and she seemed to him lovelier, younger, tenderer than she had been, and he imagined himself a finer man than he had been in Yalta. Of evenings she peered out at him from the bookcase, from the fireplace, from the corner—he heard her breathing, the caressing rustle of her clothes. In the street he followed the women with his eyes, looking for someone who resembled her.

64 Already he was tormented by a strong desire to share his memories with someone. But in his home it was impossible to talk of his love, and he had no one to talk to outside; certainly he could not confide in his tenants or in anyone at the bank. And what was there to talk about? He hadn't loved her then, had he? Had there been anything beautiful, poetical, edifying, or simply interesting in his relations with Anna Sergeyevna? And he was forced to talk vaguely of love, of women, and no one guessed what he meant; only his wife would twitch her black eyebrows and say, "The part of a philanderer does not suit you at all, Dimitry."

65 One evening, coming out of the physicians' club with an official with whom he had been playing cards, he could not resist saying:

66 "If you only knew what a fascinating woman I became acquainted with at Yalta!"

67 The official got into his sledge and was driving away, but turned suddenly and shouted:

68 "Dmitry Dmitrich!"

69 "What is it?"

70 "You were right this evening: the sturgeon was a bit high."

71 These words, so commonplace, for some reason moved Gurov to indignation, and struck him as degrading and unclean. What savage manners, what mugs! What stupid nights, what dull, humdrum days! Frenzied gambling, gluttony, drunkenness, continual talk always about the same thing! Futile pursuits and

conversations always about the same topics take up the better part of one's time, the better part of one's strength, and in the end there is left a life clipped and wingless, an absurd mess, and there is no escaping or getting away from it—just as though one were in a madhouse or a prison.

72 Gurov, boiling with indignation, did not sleep all night. And he had a headache all the next day. And the following nights too he slept badly; he sat up in bed, thinking, or paced up and down his room. He was fed up with his children, fed up with the bank; he had no desire to go anywhere or to talk of anything.

73 In December during the holidays he prepared to take a trip and told his wife he was going to Petersburg to do what he could for a young friend—and he set off for S________. What for? He did not know, himself. He wanted to see Anna Sergeyevna and talk with her, to arrange a rendezvous if possible.

74 He arrived at S________ in the morning, and at the hotel took the best room, in which the floor was covered with gray army cloth, and on the table there was an inkstand, gray with dust and topped by a figure on horseback, its hat in its raised hand and its head broken off. The porter gave him the necessary information: von Dideritz lived in a house of his own on Staro-Goncharnaya Street, not far from the hotel: he was rich and lived well and kept his own horses; everyone in the town knew him. The porter pronounced the name: "Dridiritz."

75 Without haste Gurov made his way to Staro-Goncharnaya Street and found the house. Directly opposite the house stretched a long gray fence studded with nails.

76 "A fence like that would make one run away," thought Gurov, looking now at the fence, now at the windows of the house.

77 He reflected: this was a holiday, and the husband was apt to be at home. And in any case, it would be tactless to go into the house and disturb her. If he were to send her a note, it might fall into her husband's hands, and that might spoil everything. The best thing was to rely on chance. And he kept walking up and down the street and along the fence, waiting for the chance. He saw a beggar go in at the gate and heard the dogs attack him; then an hour later he heard a piano, and the sound came to him faintly and indistinctly. Probably it was Anna Sergeyevna playing. The front door opened suddenly, and an old woman came out, followed by the familiar white Pomeranian. Gurov was on the point of calling to the dog, but his heart began beating violently, and in his excitement he could not remember the Pomeranian's name.

78 He kept walking up and down, and hated the gray fence more and more, and by now he thought irritably that Anna Sergeyevna had forgotten him, and was perhaps already diverting herself with another man, and that that was very

natural in a young woman who from morning till night had to look at that damn fence. He went back to his hotel room and sat on the couch for a long while, not knowing what to do, then he had dinner and a long nap.

79 "How stupid and annoying all this is!" he thought when he woke and looked at the dark windows: it was already evening. "Here I've had a good sleep for some reason. What am I going to do at night?"

80 He sat on the bed, which was covered with a cheap gray blanket of the kind seen in hospitals, and he twitted himself in his vexation:

81 "So there's your lady with the pet dog. There's your adventure. A nice place to cool your heels in."

82 That morning at the station a playbill in large letters had caught his eye. *The Geisha* was to be given for the first time. He thought of this and drove to the theater.

83 "It's quite possible that she goes to first nights," he thought.

84 The theater was full. As in all provincial theaters, there was a haze above the chandelier, the gallery was noisy and restless; in the front row, before the beginning of the performance the local dandies were standing with their hands clasped behind their backs; in the Governor's box the Governor's daughter, wearing a boa, occupied the front seat, while the Governor himself hid modestly behind the portiere and only his hands were visible; the curtain swayed; the orchestra was a long time tuning up. While the audience was coming in and taking their seats, Gurov scanned the faces eagerly.

85 Anna Sergeyevna, too, came in. She sat down in the third row, and when Gurov looked at her his heart contracted, and he understood clearly that in the whole world there was no human being so near, so precious, and so important to him; she, this little, undistinguished woman, lost in a provincial crowd, with a vulgar lorgnette in her hand, filled his whole life now, was his sorrow and his joy, the only happiness that he now desired for himself, and to the sounds of the bad orchestra, of the miserable local violins, he thought how lovely she was. He thought and dreamed.

86 A young man with small side-whiskers, very tall and stooped, came in with Anna Sergeyevna and sat down beside her; he nodded his head at every step and seemed to be bowing continually. Probably this was the husband whom at Yalta, in an access of bitter feeling, she had called a flunkey. And there really was in his lanky figure, his side-whiskers, his small bald patch, something of a flunkey's retiring manner; his smile was mawkish, and in his buttonhole there was an academic badge like a waiter's number.

87 During the first intermission the husband went out to have a smoke; she remained in her seat. Gurov, who was also sitting in the orchestra, went up to her and said in a shaky voice, with a forced smile:

88 "Good evening!"

89 She glanced at him and turned pale, then looked at him again in horror, unable to believe her eyes, and gripped the fan and the lorgnette tightly together in her hands, evidently trying to keep herself from fainting. Both were silent. She was sitting, he was standing, frightened by her distress and not daring to take a seat beside her. The violins and the flute that were being tuned up sang out. He suddenly felt frightened: it seemed as if all the people in the boxes were looking at them. She got up and went hurriedly to the exit; he followed her, and both of them walked blindly along the corridors and up and down stairs, and figures in the uniforms prescribed for magistrates, teachers, and officials of the Department of Crown Lands, all wearing badges, flitted before their eyes, as did also ladies, and fur coats on hangers; they were conscious of drafts and the smell of stale tobacco. And Gurov, whose heart was beating violently, thought:

90 "Oh, Lord! Why are these people here and this orchestra!"

91 And at that instant he suddenly recalled how when he had seen Anna Sergeyevna off at the station he had said to himself that all was over between them and that they would never meet again. But how distant the end still was!

92 On the narrow, gloomy staircase over which it said "To the Amphitheatre," she stopped.

93 "How you frightened me!" she said, breathing hard, still pale and stunned. "Oh, how you frightened me! I am barely alive. Why did you come? Why?"

94 "But do understand, Anna, do understand—" he said hurriedly, under his breath. "I implore you, do understand—"

95 She looked at him with fear, with entreaty, with love; she looked at him intently, to keep his features more distinctly in her memory.

96 "I suffer so," she went on, not listening to him. "All this time I have been thinking of nothing but you; I live only by the thought of you. And I wanted to forget, to forget; but why, oh, why have you come?"

97 On the landing above them two high school boys were looking down and smoking, but it was all the same to Gurov; he drew Anna Sergeyevna to him and began kissing her face and hands.

98 "What are you doing, what are you doing!" she was saying in horror, pushing him away. "We have lost our senses. Go away today; go away at once—I conjure you by all that is sacred, I implore you—People are coming this way!"

99 Someone was walking up the stairs.

100 "You must leave," Anna Sergeyevna went on in a whisper. "Do you hear, Dmitry Dmitrich? I will come and see you in Moscow. I have never been happy; I am unhappy now, and I never, never shall be happy, never! So don't make

me suffer still more! I swear I'll come to Moscow. But now let us part. My dear, good, precious one, let us part!"

101 She pressed his hand and walked rapidly downstairs, turning to look round at him, and from her eyes he could see that she really was unhappy. Gurov stood for a while, listening, then when all grew quiet, he found his coat and left the theater.

IV

102 And Anna Sergeyevna began coming to see him in Moscow. Once every two or three months she left S_______ telling her husband that she was going to consult a doctor about a woman's ailment from which she was suffering—and her husband did and did not believe her. When she arrived in Moscow she would stop at the Slavyansky Bazar Hotel, and at once send a man in a red cap to Gurov. Gurov came to see her, and no one in Moscow knew of it.

103 Once he was going to see her in this way on a winter morning (the messenger had come the evening before and not found him in). With him walked his daughter, whom he wanted to take to school; it was on the way. Snow was coming down in big wet flakes.

104 "It's three degrees above zero, and yet it's snowing," Gurov was saying to his daughter. "But this temperature prevails only on the surface of the earth; in the upper layers of the atmosphere there is quite a different temperature."

105 "And why doesn't it thunder in winter, papa?"

106 He explained that, too. He talked, thinking all the while that he was on his way to a rendezvous, and no living soul knew of it, and probably no one would ever know. He had two lives, an open one, seen and known by all who needed to know it, full of conventional truth and conventional falsehood, exactly like the lives of his friends and acquaintances; and another life that went on in secret. And through some strange, perhaps accidental, combination of circumstances, everything that was of interest and importance to him, everything that was essential to him, everything about which he felt sincerely and did not deceive himself, everything that constituted the core of his life, was going on concealed from others; while all that was false, the shell in which he hid to cover the truth—his work at the bank, for instance, his discussions at the club, his references to the "inferior race," his appearances at anniversary celebrations with his wife—all that went on in the open. Judging others by himself, he did not believe what he saw, and always fancied that every man led his real, most interesting life under cover of secrecy as under cover of night. The personal life of every individual is based on secrecy, and perhaps it is partly for that

reason that civilized man is so nervously anxious that personal privacy should be respected.

107 Having taken his daughter to school, Gurov went on to the Slavyansky Bazar Hotel. He took off his fur coat in the lobby, went upstairs, and knocked gently at the door. Anna Sergeyevna, wearing his favorite gray dress, exhausted by the journey and by waiting, had been expecting him since the previous evening. She was pale, and looked at him without a smile, and had hardly entered when she flung herself on his breast. That kiss was a long, lingering one, as though they had not seen one another for two years.

108 "Well, darling, how are you getting on there?" he asked. "What news?"

109 "Wait; I'll tell you in a moment—I can't speak."

110 She could not speak; she was crying. She turned away from him, and pressed her handkerchief to her eyes.

111 "Let her have her cry; meanwhile I'll sit down," he thought, and he seated himself in an armchair.

112 Then he rang and ordered tea, and while he was having his tea she remained standing at the window with her back to him. She was crying out of sheer agitation, in the sorrowful consciousness that their life was so sad; that they could only see each other in secret and had to hide from people like thieves! Was it not a broken life?

113 "Come, stop now, dear!" he said.

114 It was plain to him that this love of theirs would not be over soon, that the end of it was not in sight. Anna Sergeyevna was growing more and more attached to him. She adored him, and it was unthinkable to tell her that their love was bound to come to an end some day; besides, she would not have believed it!

115 He went up to her and took her by the shoulders, to fondle her and say something diverting, and at that moment he caught sight of himself in the mirror.

116 His hair was already beginning to turn gray. And it seemed odd to him that he had grown so much older in the last few years, and lost his looks. The shoulders on which his hands rested were warm and heaving. He felt compassion for this life, still so warm and lovely, but probably already about to begin to fade and wither like his own. Why did she love him so much? He always seemed to women different from what he was, and they loved in him not himself, but the man whom their imagination created and whom they had been eagerly seeking all their lives; and afterwards, when they saw their mistake, they loved him nevertheless. And not one of them had been happy with him. In the past he had met women, come together with them, parted from them, but he had never once loved; it was anything you please, but not love. And only now when

his head was gray he had fallen in love, really, truly—for the first time in his life.

117 Anna Sergeyevna and he loved each other as people do who are very close and intimate, like man and wife, like tender friends; it seemed to them that Fate itself had meant them for one another, and they could not understand why he had a wife and she a husband; and it was as though they were a pair of migratory birds, male and female, caught and forced to live in different cages. They forgave each other what they were ashamed of in their past, they forgave everything in the present, and felt that this love of theirs had altered them both.

118 Formerly in moments of sadness he had soothed himself with whatever logical arguments came into his head, but now he no longer cared for logic; he felt profound compassion, he wanted to be sincere and tender.

119 "Give it up now, my darling," he said. "You've had your cry; that's enough. Let us have a talk now, we'll think up something."

120 Then they spent a long time taking counsel together, they talked of how to avoid the necessity for secrecy, for deception, for living in different cities, and not seeing one another for long stretches of time. How could they free themselves from these intolerable fetters?

121 "How? How?" he asked, clutching his head. "How?"

122 And it seemed as though in a little while the solution would be found, and then a new and glorious life would begin; and it was clear to both of them that at the end was still far off, and that what was to be most complicated and difficult for them was only just beginning.

—1899

✧ ✧ ✧

Edith Wharton
(1862-1937)

Roman Fever

Wharton, a child of wealth and status, was for many years America's best-known woman writer, the confidante of Henry James and other Europeanized American intellectuals. Born in New York City to a socially prominent family that listed a Revolutionary War general among its forebears, Wharton was educated by tutors and traveled extensively in Europe in her youth. She married Edward Wharton, a banker, in 1885; the unhappy marriage, plagued by his slow descent into insanity, ended in divorce in 1913, after which Wharton lived in France. Her first published book was a co-authored work on interior decorating, but she soon began to place stories with prestigious periodicals like *Scribner's Magazine*. Her second novel, *The House of Mirth* (1905), was a best seller and was successfully adapted for the stage by Clyde Fitch. "Roman Fever," like much of Wharton's fiction, accurately captures the lifestyle of the upper classes of the era, but in other works she shows considerable knowledge of different levels of society, as is evident especially in *Ethan Frome* (1911), a novella about a tragic love triangle in rural New England. Wharton received many honors in her later life, among them the French Legion of Honor and a doctorate from Yale University, the first awarded to a woman. Her novel *The Age of Innocence* (1920) was awarded a Pulitzer prize for fiction, and an adaptation of one of her novels, *The Old Maid*, won the drama prize in 1935. *The Writing of Fiction* (1925) remains an effective manual for writers.

I

From the table at which they had been lunching two American ladies of ripe but well-cared-for middle age moved across the lofty terrace of the Roman restaurant and, leaning on its parapet, looked first at each other, and then down on the outspread glories of the Palatine and the Forum, with the same expression of vague but benevolent approval.

2 As they leaned there a girlish voice echoed up gaily from the stairs leading to the court below. "Well, come along, then," it cried, not to them but to an invisible companion, "and let's leave the young things to their knitting"; and a voice as fresh laughed back: "Oh, look here, Babs, not actually *knitting*—" "Well, I mean figuratively," rejoined the first. "After all, we haven't left our poor parents much else to do . . . " and at that point the turn of the stairs engulfed the dialogue.

3 The two ladies looked at each other again, this time with a tinge of smiling embarrassment, and the smaller and paler one shook her head and colored slightly.

4 "Barbara!" she murmured, sending an unheard rebuke after the mocking voice in the stairway.

5 The other lady, who was fuller, and higher in color, with a small determined nose supported by vigorous black eyebrows, gave a good-humored laugh. "That's what our daughters think of us!"

6 Her companion replied by a deprecating gesture. "Not of us individually. We must remember that. It's just the collective modern idea of Mothers. And you see—" Half guiltily she drew from her handsomely mounted black hand-bag a twist of crimson silk run through by two fine knitting needles. "One never knows," she murmured. "The new system has certainly given us a good deal of time to kill; and sometimes I get tired just looking—even at this." Her gesture was now addressed to the stupendous scene at their feet.

7 The dark lady laughed again, and they both relapsed upon the view, contemplating it in silence, with a sort of diffused serenity which might have been borrowed from the spring effulgence of the Roman skies. The luncheon-hour was long past, and the two had their end of the vast terrace to themselves. At this opposite extremity a few groups, detained by a lingering look at the outspread city, were gathering up guide-books and fumbling for tips. The last of them scattered, and the two ladies were alone on the air-washed height.

8 "Well, I don't see why we shouldn't just stay here," said Mrs. Slade, the lady of the high color and energetic brows. Two derelict basket-chairs stood near, and she pushed them into the angle of the parapet, and settled herself in one, her gaze upon the Palatine. "After all, it's still the most beautiful view in the world."

9 "It always will be, to me," assented her friend Mrs. Ansley, with so slight a stress on the "me" that Mrs. Slade, though she noticed it, wondered if it were not merely accidental, like the random underlinings of old-fashioned letter-writers.

10 "Grace Ansley was always old-fashioned," she thought; and added aloud, with a retrospective smile: "It's a view we've both been familiar with for a good many years. When we first met here we were younger than our girls are now. You remember?"

11 "Oh, yes, I remember," murmured Mrs. Ansley, with the same undefinable stress.—"There's that head-waiter wondering," she interpolated. She was evidently far less sure than her companion of herself and of her rights in the world.

12 "I'll cure him of wondering," said Mrs. Slade, stretching her hand toward a bag as discreetly opulent looking as Mrs. Ansley's. Signing to the head-waiter, she explained that she and her friend were old lovers of Rome, and would like to spend the end of the afternoon looking down on the view—that is, if it did not disturb the service? The head-waiter, bowing over her gratuity, assured her that the ladies were most welcome, and would be still more so if they would condescend to remain for dinner. A full moon night, they would remember . . .

13 Mrs. Slade's black brows drew together, as though references to the moon were out-of-place and even unwelcome. But she smiled away her frown as the head-waiter retreated. "Well, why not? We might do worse. There's no know-

ing, I suppose, when the girls will be back. Do you even know back from *where?* I don't!"

14 Mrs. Ansley again colored slightly. "I think those young Italian aviators we met at the Embassy invited them to fly to Tarquinia for tea. I suppose they'll want to wait and fly back by moonlight."

15 "Moonlight—moonlight! What a part it still plays. Do you suppose they're as sentimental as we were?"

16 "I've come to the conclusion that I don't in the least know what they are," said Mrs. Ansley. "And perhaps we didn't know much more about each other."

17 "No; perhaps we didn't."

18 Her friend gave her a shy glance. "I never should have supposed you were sentimental, Alida."

19 "Well, perhaps I wasn't." Mrs. Slade drew her lids together in retrospect; and for a few moments the two ladies, who had been intimate since childhood, reflected how little they knew each other. Each one, of course, had a label ready to attach to the other's name; Mrs. Delphin Slade, for instance, would have told herself, or any one who asked her, that Mrs. Horace Ansley, twenty-five years ago, had been exquisitely lovely—no, you wouldn't believe it, would you? . . . though, of course, still charming, distinguished . . . Well, as a girl she had been exquisite; far more beautiful than her daughter Barbara, though certainly Babs, according to the new standards at any rate, was more effective—had more edge, as they say. Funny where she got it, with those two nullities as parents. Yes; Horace Ansley was—well, just the duplicate of his wife. Museum specimens of old New York. Good-looking, irreproachable, exemplary. Mrs. Slade and Mrs. Ansley had lived opposite each other—actually as well as figuratively—for years. When the drawing-room curtains in No. 20 East 73rd Street were renewed, No. 23, across the way, was always aware of it. And of all the movings, buyings, travels, anniversaries, illnesses—the tame chronicle of an estimable pair. Little of it escaped Mrs. Slade. But she had grown bored with it by the time her husband made his big *coup* in Wall Street, and when they bought in upper Park Avenue had already begun to think: "I'd rather live opposite a speak-easy for a change; at least one might see it raided." The idea of seeing Grace raided was so amusing that (before the move) she launched it at a woman's lunch. It made a hit, and went the rounds—she sometimes wondered if it had crossed the street, and reached Mrs. Ansley. She hoped not, but didn't much mind. Those were the days when respectability was at a discount, and it did the irreproachable no harm to laugh at them a little.

20 A few years later, and not many months apart, both ladies lost their husbands. There was an appropriate exchange of wreaths and condolences, and a brief renewal of intimacy in the half shadow of their mourning; and now, after another interval, they had run across each other in Rome, at the same hotel, each of them the modest appendage of a salient daughter. The similarity of their lot

had again drawn them together, lending itself to mild jokes, and the mutual confession that, if in old days it must have been tiring to "keep up" with daughters, it was now, at times, a little dull not to.

21 No doubt, Mrs. Slade reflected, she felt her unemployment more than poor Grace ever would. It was a big drop from being the wife of Delphin Slade to being his widow. She had always regarded herself (with a certain conjugal pride) as his equal in social gifts, as contributing her full share to the making of the exceptional couple they were: but the difference after his death was irremediable. As the wife of the famous corporation lawyer, always with an international case or two on hand, every day brought its exciting and unexpected obligation: the impromptu entertaining of eminent colleagues from abroad, the hurried dashes on legal business to London, Paris or Rome, where the entertaining was so handsomely reciprocated; the amusement of hearing in her wake: "What, that handsome woman with the good clothes and eyes is Mrs. Slade—*the* Slade's wife? Really? Generally the wives of celebrities are such trumps."

22 Yes; being *the* Slade's widow was a dullish business after that. In living up to such a husband all her faculties had been engaged; now she had only her daughter to live up to, for the son who seemed to have inherited his father's gifts had died suddenly in boyhood. She had fought through that agony because her husband was there, to be helped and to help; now, after the father's death, the thought of the boy had become unbearable. There was nothing left but to mother her daughter; and dear Jenny was such a perfect daughter that she needed no excessive mothering. "Now with Babs Ansley I don't know that I *should* be so quiet," Mrs. Slade sometimes half-enviously reflected; but Jenny, who was younger than her brilliant friend, was that rare accident, an extremely pretty girl who somehow made youth and prettiness seem as safe as their absence. It was all perplexing—and to Mrs. Slade a little boring. She wished that Jenny would fall in love—with the wrong man, even; that she might have to be watched, outmaneuvered, rescued. And instead, it was Jenny who watched her mother, kept her out of draughts, made sure that she had taken her tonic . . .

23 Mrs. Ansley was much less articulate than her friend, and her mental portrait of Mrs. Slade was slighter, and drawn with fainter touches. "Alida Slade's awfully brilliant; but not as brilliant as she thinks," would have summed it up; though she would have added, for the enlightenment of strangers, that Mrs. Slade had been an extremely dashing girl; much more so than her daughter, who was pretty, of course, and clever in a way, but had none of her mother's—well, "vividness," some one had once called it. Mrs. Ansley would take up current words like this, and cite them in quotation marks, as unheard-of audacities. No; Jenny was not like her mother. Sometimes Mrs. Ansley thought Alida Slade was disappointed; on the whole she had had a sad life. Full of failures and mistakes; Mrs. Ansley had always been rather sorry for her . . .

24 So these two ladies visualized each other, each through the wrong end of her little telescope.

II

25 For a long time they continued to sit side by side without speaking. It seemed as though, to both, there was a relief in laying down their somewhat futile activities in the presence of the vast *Memento Mori* which faced them. Mrs. Slade sat quite still, her eyes fixed on the golden slope of the Palace of the Caesars, and after a while Mrs. Ansley ceased to fidget with her bag, and she too sank into meditation. Like many intimate friends, the two ladies had never before had occasion to be silent together, and Mrs. Ansley was slightly embarrassed by what seemed, after so many years, a new stage in their intimacy, and one with which she did not yet know how to deal.

26 Suddenly the air was full of that deep clangor of bells which periodically covers Rome with a roof of silver. Mrs. Slade glanced at her wrist-watch. "Five o'clock already," she said, as though surprised.

27 Mrs. Ansley suggested interrogatively: "There's bridge at the Embassy at five." For a long time Mrs. Slade did not answer. She appeared to be lost in contemplation, and Mrs. Ansley thought the remark had escaped her. But after a while she said, as if speaking out of a dream: "Bridge, did you say? Not unless you want to . . . But I don't think I will, you know."

28 "Oh, no," Mrs. Ansley hastened to assure her. "I don't care to at all. It's so lovely here; and so full of old memories, as you say." She settled herself in her chair, and almost furtively drew forth her knitting. Mrs. Slade took sideways note of this activity, but her own beautifully cared-for hands remained motionless on her knee.

29 "I was just thinking," she said slowly, "what different things Rome stands for to each generation of travelers. To our grandmothers, Roman fever; to our mothers, sentimental dangers—how we used to be guarded!—to our daughters, no more dangers than the middle of Main Street. They don't know it—but how much they're missing!"

30 The long golden light was beginning to pale, and Mrs. Ansley lifted her knitting a little closer to her eyes. "Yes; how we were guarded!"

31 "I always used to think," Mrs. Slade continued,"that our mothers had a much more difficult job than our grandmothers. When Roman fever stalked the streets it must have been comparatively easy to gather in the girls at the danger hour; but when you and I were young, with such beauty calling us, and the spice of disobedience thrown in, and no worse risk than catching cold during the cool hour after sunset, the mothers used to be put to it to keep us in—didn't they?"

32 She turned again toward Mrs. Ansley, but the latter had reached a delicate point in her knitting. "One, two, three—slip two; yes, they must have been," she assented, without looking up.

33 Mrs. Slade's eyes rested on her with a deepened attention. "She can knit—in the face of *this!* How like her . . . "

34 Mrs. Slade leaned back, brooding, her eyes ranging from the ruins which faced her to the long green hollow of the Forum, the fading glow of the church fronts beyond it, and the outlying immensity of the Colosseum. Suddenly she thought: "It's all very well to say that our girls have done away with sentiment and moonlight. But if Babs Ansley isn't out to catch that young aviator—the one who's a Marchese—then I don't know anything. And Jenny has no chance beside her. I know that too. I wonder if that's why Grace Ansley likes the two girls to go everywhere together? My poor Jenny as a foil—!" Mrs. Slade gave a hardly audible laugh, and at the sound Mrs. Ansley dropped her knitting.

35 "Yes—?"

36 "I—oh, nothing. I was only thinking how your Babs carries everything before her. That Campolieri boy is one of the best matches in Rome. Don't look so innocent, my dear—you know he is. And I was wondering, ever so respectfully, you understand . . . wondering how two such exemplary characters as you and Horace had managed to produce anything quite so dynamic." Mrs. Slade laughed again, with a touch of asperity.

37 Mrs. Ansley's hands lay inert across her needles. She looked straight out at the great accumulated wreckage of passion and splendor at her feet. But her small profile was almost expressionless. At length she said: "I think you overrate Babs, my dear."

38 Mrs. Slade's tone grew easier. "No; I don't. I appreciate her. And perhaps envy you. Oh, my girl's perfect; if I were a chronic invalid I'd—well, I think I'd rather be in Jenny's hands. There must be times . . . but there! I always wanted a brilliant daughter . . . and never quite understood why I got an angel instead."

39 Mrs. Ansley echoed her laugh in a faint murmur. "Babs is an angel too."

40 "Of course—of course! But she's got rainbow wings. Well, they're wandering by the sea with their young men; and here we sit . . . and it all brings back the past a little too acutely."

41 Mrs. Ansley had resumed her knitting. One might almost have imagined (if one had known her less well, Mrs. Slade reflected) that, for her also, too many memories rose from the lengthening shadows of those august ruins. But no; she was simply absorbed in her work. What was there for her to worry about? She knew that Babs would almost certainly come back engaged to the extremely eligible Campolieri. "And she'll sell the New York house, and settle down near them in Rome, and never be in their way . . . she's much too tactful. But she'll have an excellent cook, and just the right people in for bridge and cocktails . . . and a perfectly peaceful old age among her grandchildren."

42 Mrs. Slade broke off this prophetic flight with a recoil of self-disgust. There was no one of whom she had less right to think unkindly than of Grace Ansley. Would she never cure herself of envying her? Perhaps she had begun too long ago.

43 She stood up and leaned against the parapet, filling her troubled eyes with the tranquilizing magic of the hour. But instead of tranquilizing her the sight seemed to increase her exasperation. Her gaze turned toward the Colosseum. Already its golden flank was drowned in purple shadow, and above it the sky curved crystal clear, without light or color. It was the moment when the afternoon and evening hang balanced in mid-heaven.

44 Mrs. Slade turned back and laid her hand on her friend's arm. The gesture was so abrupt that Mrs. Ansley looked up, startled.

45 "The sun's set. You're not afraid, my dear?"

46 "Afraid—?"

47 "Of Roman fever or pneumonia? I remember how ill you were that winter. As a girl you had a very delicate throat, hadn't you?"

48 "Oh, we're all right up here. Down below, in the Forum, it does get deathly cold, all of a sudden . . . but not here."

49 "Ah, of course you know because you had to be careful." Mrs. Slade turned back to the parapet. She thought: "I must make one more effort not to hate her." Aloud she said: "Whenever I look at the Forum from up here, I remember that story about a great-aunt of yours, wasn't she? A dreadfully wicked great-aunt?"

50 "Oh, yes; Great-aunt Harriet. The one who was supposed to have sent her young sister out to the Forum after sunset to gather a night-blooming flower for her album. All our great-aunts and grandmothers used to have albums of dried flowers."

51 Mrs. Slade nodded. "But she really sent her because they were in love with the same man—"

52 "Well, that was the family tradition. They said Aunt Harriet confessed it years afterward. At any rate, the poor little sister caught the fever and died. Mother used to frighten us with the story when we were children."

53 "And you frightened *me* with it, that winter when you and I were here as girls. The winter I was engaged to Delphin."

54 Mrs. Ansley gave a faint laugh. "Oh, did I? Really frightened you? I don't believe you're easily frightened."

55 "Not often; but I was then. I was easily frightened because I was too happy. I wonder if you know what that means?"

56 "I—yes . . . " Mrs. Ansley faltered.

57 "Well, I suppose that was why the story of your wicked aunt made such an impression on me. And I thought: 'There's no more Roman fever, but the Forum is deathly cold after sunset—especially after a hot day. And the Colosseum's even colder and damper.'"

58 "The Colosseum—?"

59 "Yes. It wasn't easy to get in, after the gates were locked for the night. Far from easy. Still, in those days it could be managed; it was managed, often. Lovers met there who couldn't meet elsewhere. You knew that?"

60 "I—I daresay. I don't remember."

61 "You don't remember? You don't remember going to visit some ruins or other one evening, just after dark, and catching a bad chill? You were supposed to have gone to see the moon rise. People always said that expedition was what caused your illness."

62 There was a moment's silence; then Mrs. Ansley rejoined: "Did they? It was all so long ago."

63 "Yes. And you got well again—so it didn't matter. But I suppose it struck your friends—the reason given for your illness, I mean—because everybody knew you were so prudent on account of your throat, and your mother took such care of you . . . You *had* been out late sightseeing, hadn't you, that night?"

64 "Perhaps I had. The most prudent girls aren't always prudent. What made you think of it now?"

65 Mrs. Slade seemed to have no answer ready. But after a moment she broke out: "Because I simply can't bear it any longer—!"

66 Mrs. Ansley lifted her head quickly. Her eyes were wide and very pale. "Can't bear what?"

67 "Why—your not knowing that I've always known why you went."

68 "Why I went?"

69 "Yes. You think I'm bluffing, don't you? Well, you went to meet the man I was engaged to—and I can repeat every word of the letter that you took there."

70 While Mrs. Slade spoke Mrs. Ansley had risen unsteadily to her feet. Her bag, her knitting and gloves, slid in a panic-stricken heap to the ground. She looked at Mrs. Slade as though she were looking at a ghost.

71 "No, no—don't," she faltered out.

72 "Why not? Listen, if you don't believe me. 'My one darling, things can't go on like this. I must see you alone. Come to the Colosseum immediately after dark tomorrow. There will be somebody to let you in. No one whom you need fear will suspect'—but perhaps you've forgotten what the letter said?"

73 Mrs. Ansley met the challenge with an unexpected composure. Steadying herself against the chair she looked at her friend, and replied: "No, I know it by heart too."

74 "And the signature? 'Only *your* D.S.' Was that it? I'm right, am I? That was the letter that took you out that evening after dark?"

75 Mrs. Ansley was still looking at her. It seemed to Mrs. Slade that a slow struggle was going on behind the voluntarily controlled mask of her small quiet face. "I shouldn't have thought she had herself so well in hand," Mrs.

Slade reflected, almost resentfully. But at this moment Mrs. Ansley spoke. "I don't know how you knew. I burnt that letter at once."

76 "Yes; you would, naturally—you're so prudent!" The sneer was open now. "And if you burnt the letter you're wondering how on earth I know what was in it. That's it, isn't it?"

77 Mrs. Slade waited, but Mrs. Ansley did not speak.

78 "Well, my dear, I know what was in that letter because I wrote it!"

79 "You wrote it?"

80 "Yes."

81 The two women stood for a minute staring at each other in the last, golden light. Then Mrs. Ansley dropped back into her chair. "Oh," she murmured, and covered her face with her hands.

82 Mrs. Slade waited nervously for another word or movement. None came, and at length she broke out: "I horrify you."

83 Mrs. Ansley's hands dropped to her knee. The face they uncovered was streaked with tears. "I wasn't thinking of you. I was thinking—it was the only letter I ever had from him!"

84 "And I wrote it. Yes; I wrote it! But I was the girl he was engaged to. Did you happen to remember that?"

85 Mrs. Ansley's head dropped again. "I'm not trying to excuse myself . . . I remembered . . . "

86 "And still you went?"

87 "Still I went."

88 Mrs. Slade stood looking down on the small bowed figure at her side. The flame of her wrath had already sunk, and she wondered why she had ever thought there would be any satisfaction in inflicting so purposeless a wound on her friend. But she had to justify herself.

89 "You do understand? I found out—and I hated you, hated you. I knew you were in love with Delphin—and I was afraid; afraid of you, of your quiet ways, your sweetness . . . your . . . well, I wanted you out of the way, that's all. Just for a few weeks; just till I was sure of him. So in a blind fury I wrote that letter . . . I don't know why I'm telling you now."

90 "I suppose," said Mrs. Ansley slowly, "it's because you've always gone on hating me."

91 "Perhaps. Or because I wanted to get the whole thing off my mind." She paused. "I'm glad you destroyed the letter. Of course I never thought you'd die."

92 Mrs. Ansley relapsed into silence, and Mrs. Slade, leaning above her, was conscious of a strange sense of isolation, of being cut off from the warm current of human communion. "You think me a monster!"

93 "I don't know . . . It was the only letter I had, and you say he didn't write it?"

94 "Ah, how you care for him still!"

95 "I cared for that memory," said Mrs. Ansley.

96 Mrs. Slade continued to look down on her. She seemed physically reduced by the blow—as if, when she got up, the wind might scatter her like a puff of dust. Mrs. Slade's jealousy suddenly leapt up again at the sight. All these years the woman had been living on that letter. How she must have loved him, to treasure the mere memory of its ashes! The letter of the man her friend was engaged to. Wasn't it she who was the monster?

97 "You tried your best to get him away from me, didn't you? But you failed; and I kept him. That's all."

98 "Yes. That's all."

99 "I wish now I hadn't told you. I'd no idea you'd feel about it as you do; I thought you'd be amused. It all happened so long ago, as you say; and you must do me the justice to remember that I had no reason to think you'd ever taken it seriously. How could I, when you were married to Horace Ansley two months afterward? As soon as you could get out of bed your mother rushed you off to Florence and married you. People were rather surprised—they wondered at its being done so quickly; but I thought I knew. I had an idea you did it out of *pique*—to be able to say you'd got ahead of Delphin and me. Girls have such silly reasons for doing the most serious things. And your marrying so soon convinced me that you'd never really cared."

100 "Yes, I suppose it would," Mrs. Ansley assented.

101 The clear heaven overhead was emptied of all its gold. Dusk spread over it, abruptly darkening the Seven Hills. Here and there lights began to twinkle through the foliage at their feet. Steps were coming and going on the deserted terrace—waiters looking out of the doorway at the head of the stairs, then reappearing with trays and napkins and flasks of wine. Tables were moved, chairs straightened. A feeble string of electric lights flickered out. Some vases of faded flowers were carried away, and brought back replenished. A stout lady in a dustcoat suddenly appeared, asking in broken Italian if any one had seen the elastic band which held together her tattered Baedeker. She poked with her stick under the table at which she had lunched, the waiters assisting.

102 The corner where Mrs. Slade and Mrs. Ansley sat was still shadowy and deserted. For a long time neither of them spoke. At length Mrs. Slade began again: "I suppose I did it as a sort of joke—"

103 "A joke?"

104 "Well, girls are ferocious sometimes, you know. Girls in love especially. And I remember laughing to myself all that evening at the idea that you were waiting around there in the dark, dodging out of sight, listening for every sound, trying to get in—. Of course I was upset when I heard you were so ill afterward."

105 Mrs. Ansley had not moved for a long time. But now she turned slowly toward her companion. "But I didn't wait. He'd arranged everything. He was there. We were let in at once," she said.

106 Mrs. Slade sprang up from her leaning position. "Delphin there? They let you in?—Ah, now you're lying!" she burst out with violence.

107 Mrs. Ansley's voice grew clearer, and full of surprise. "But of course he was there. Naturally he came—"

108 "Came? How did he know he'd find you there? You must be raving!"

109 Mrs. Ansley hesitated, as though reflecting. "But I answered the letter. I told him I'd be there. So he came."

110 Mrs. Slade flung her hands up to her face. "Oh, God—you answered! I never thought of your answering . . . "

111 "It's odd you never thought of it, if you wrote the letter."

112 "Yes. I was blind with rage."

113 Mrs. Ansley rose, and drew her fur scarf about her. "It is cold here. We'd better go . . . I'm sorry for you," she said, as she clasped the fur about her throat.

114 The unexpected words sent a pang through Mrs. Slade. "Yes; we'd better go." She gathered up her bag and cloak. "I don't know why you should be sorry for me," she muttered.

115 Mrs. Ansley stood looking away from her toward the dusky secret mass of the Colosseum. "Well—because I didn't have to wait that night."

116 Mrs. Slade gave an unquiet laugh. "Yes; I was beaten there. But I oughtn't to begrudge it to you, I suppose. At the end of all these years. After all, I had everything; I had him for twenty-five years. And you had nothing but that one letter he didn't write."

117 Mrs. Ansley was again silent. At length she turned toward the door of the terrace. She took a step, and turned back, facing her companion.

118 "I had Barbara," she said, and began to move ahead of Mrs. Slade toward the stairway.

—1936

Willa Cather
(1876-1947)

Paul's Case

Cather was born in rural Virginia but moved in childhood to the Nebraska farmlands. After graduating from the University of Nebraska she lived for a time in Pittsburgh (the hometown of the title character in "Paul's Case"), where she moved so that she, like Paul, could attend the theater and concerts. After some years as a drama critic for the Pittsburgh *Daily Leader* and a brief term as a high school English teacher, she moved to New York, where she eventually became managing editor of *McClure's Magazine*, a position she held from 1906-1912. Her novels about the settling of the Nebraska farmlands, *O Pioneers!* (1913) and *My Antonía* (1918), proved successful, and for the rest of her life Cather devoted her full energies to writing fiction. In her later years she ranged further for her subjects—New Mexico for the setting of *Death Comes to the Archbishop* (1927) and Quebec for *Shadows on the Rock* (1931). "Paul's Case," one of the stories that helped her obtain a position with *McClure's*, casts an almost clinical eye on heredity and environment as influences on the protagonist's personality. This deterministic view of character and Paul's desperate attempt to escape the dreary trap of his hometown reflect important themes of naturalism, a literary movement with which Cather would later express dissatisfaction but that dominated much fiction written near the turn of the century.

It was Paul's afternoon to appear before the faculty of the Pittsburgh High School to account for his various misdemeanors. He had been suspended a week ago, and his father had called at the Principal's office and confessed his perplexity about his son. Paul entered the faculty room suave and smiling. His clothes were a trifle outgrown and the tan velvet on the collar of his open overcoat was frayed and worn; but for all that there was something of the dandy about him, and he wore an opal pin in his neatly knotted black four-in-hand, and a red carnation in his buttonhole. This latter adornment the faculty somehow felt was not properly significant of the contrite spirit befitting a boy under the ban of suspension.

2 Paul was tall for his age and very thin, with high, cramped shoulders and a narrow chest. His eyes were remarkable for a certain hysterical brilliancy and he continually used them in a conscious, theatrical sort of way, peculiarly offensive in a boy. The pupils were abnormally large, as though he were addicted to belladonna, but there was a glassy glitter about them which that drug does not produce.

3 When questioned by the Principal as to why he was there, Paul stated, politely enough, that he wanted to come back to school. This was a lie, but Paul was quite accustomed to lying; found it, indeed, indispensable for overcoming friction. His teachers were asked to state their respective charges against him, which they did with such a rancor and aggrievedness as evinced that this was not a usual case. Disorder and impertinence were among the offenses named, yet each of his instructors felt that it was scarcely possible to put into words the real cause of the trouble, which lay in a sort of hysterically defiant manner of the boy's; in the contempt which they all knew he felt for them, and which he seemingly made not the least effort to conceal. Once, when he had been making a synopsis of a paragraph at the blackboard, his English teacher had stepped to his side and attempted to guide his hand. Paul had started back with a shudder and thrust his hands violently behind him. The astonished woman could scarcely have been more hurt and embarrassed had he struck at her. The insult was so involuntary and definitely personal as to be unforgettable. In one way and another, he had made all his teachers, men and women alike, conscious of the same feeling of physical aversion. In one class he habitually sat with his hand shading his eyes; in another he always looked out of the window during the recitation; in another he made a running commentary on the lecture, with humorous intention.

4 His teachers felt this afternoon that his whole attitude was symbolized by his shrug and his flippantly red carnation flower, and they fell upon him without mercy, his English teacher leading the pack. He stood through it smiling, his pale lips parted over his white teeth. (His lips were continually twitching, and he had a habit of raising his eyebrows that was contemptuous and irritating to the last degree.) Older boys than Paul had broken down and shed tears under that baptism of fire, but his set smile did not once desert him, and his only sign of discomfort was the nervous trembling of the fingers that toyed with the buttons of his overcoat, and an occasional jerking of the other hand that held his hat. Paul was always smiling, always glancing about him, seeming to feel that people might be watching him and trying to detect something. This conscious expression, since it was as far as possible from boyish mirthfulness, was usually attributed to insolence or "smartness."

5 As the inquisition proceeded, one of his instructors repeated an impertinent remark of the boy's, and the Principal asked him whether he thought that a courteous speech to have made a woman. Paul shrugged his shoulders slightly and his eyebrows twitched.

6 "I don't know," he replied. "I didn't mean to be polite or impolite, either. I guess it's a sort of way I have of saying things regardless."

7 The Principal, who was a sympathetic man, asked him whether he didn't think that a way it would be well to get rid of. Paul grinned and said he guessed so. When he was told that he could go, he bowed gracefully and went out. His bow was but a repetition of the scandalous red carnation.

8 His teachers were in despair, and his drawing master voiced the feeling of them all when he declared there was something about the boy which none of them understood. He added: "I don't really believe that smile of his comes altogether from insolence; there's something sort of haunted about it. The boy is not strong, for one thing. I happen to know that he was born in Colorado, only a few months before his mother died out there of a long illness. There is something wrong about the fellow."

9 The drawing master had come to realize that, in looking at Paul, one saw only his white teeth and the forced animation of his eyes. One warm afternoon the boy had gone to sleep at his drawing-board, and his master had noted with amazement what a white, blue-veined face it was; drawn and wrinkled like an old man's about the eyes, the lips twitching even in his sleep, and stiff with a nervous tension that drew them back from his teeth.

10 His teachers left the building dissatisfied and unhappy; humiliated to have felt so vindictive toward a mere boy, to have uttered this feeling in cutting terms, and to have set each other on, as it were, in the gruesome game of intemperate reproach. Some of them remembered having seen a miserable street cat set at bay by a ring of tormentors.

11 As for Paul, he ran down the hill whistling the Soldiers' Chorus from *Faust* looking wildly behind him now and then to see whether some of his teachers were not there to writhe under his light-heartedness. As it was now late in the afternoon and Paul was on duty that evening as usher at Carnegie Hall, he decided that he would not go home to supper. When he reached the concert hall the doors were not yet open and, as it was chilly outside, he decided to go up into the picture gallery—always deserted at this hour—where there were some of Raffaelli's gay studies of Paris streets and an airy blue Venetian scene or two that always exhilarated him. He was delighted to find no one in the gallery but the old guard, who sat in one corner, a newspaper on his knee, a black patch over one eye and the other closed. Paul possessed himself of the place and walked confidently up and down, whistling under his breath. After a while he sat down before a blue Rico and lost himself. When he bethought him to look at his watch, it was after seven o'clock, and he rose with a start and ran downstairs,

making a face at Augustus, peering out from the cast-room, and an evil gesture at the Venus of Milo as he passed her on the stairway.

12 When Paul reached the ushers' dressing-room half-a-dozen boys were there already, and he began excitedly to tumble into his uniform. It was one of the few that at all approached fitting, and Paul thought it very becoming—though he knew that the tight, straight coat accentuated his narrow chest, about which he was exceedingly sensitive. He was always considerably excited while he dressed, twanging all over to the tuning of the strings and the preliminary flourishes of the horns in the music-room; but tonight he seemed quite beside himself, and he teased and plagued the boys until, telling him that he was crazy, they put him down on the floor and sat on him.

13 Somewhat calmed by his suppression, Paul dashed out to the front of the house to seat the early comers. He was a model usher; gracious and smiling he ran up and down the aisles; nothing was too much trouble for him; he carried messages and brought programmes as though it were his greatest pleasure in life, and all the people in his section thought him a charming boy, feeling that he remembered and admired them. As the house filled, he grew more and more vivacious and animated, and the color came to his cheeks and lips. It was very much as though this were a great reception and Paul were the host. Just as the musicians came out to take their places, his English teacher arrived with checks for the seats which a prominent manufacturer had taken for the season. She betrayed some embarrassment when she handed Paul the tickets, and a *hauteur* which subsequently made her feel very foolish. Paul was startled for a moment, and had the feeling of wanting to put her out; what business had she here among all these fine people and gay colors? He looked her over and decided that she was not appropriately dressed and must be a fool to sit downstairs in such togs. The tickets had probably been sent her out of kindness, he reflected as he put down a seat for her, and she had about as much right to sit there as he had.

14 When the symphony began Paul sank into one of the rear seats with a long sigh of relief, and lost himself as he had done before the Rico. It was not that symphonies, as such, meant anything in particular to Paul, but the first sigh of the instruments seemed to free some hilarious and potent spirit within him; something that struggled there like the Genius in the bottle found by the Arab fisherman. He felt a sudden zest of life; the lights danced before his eyes and the concert hall blazed into unimaginable splendor. When the soprano soloist came on, Paul forgot even the nastiness of his teacher's being there and gave himself up to the peculiar stimulus such personages always had for him. The soloist chanced to be a German woman, by no means in her first youth, and the mother of many children; but she wore an elaborate gown and a tiara, and above all she had that indefinable air of achievement, that world-shine upon her, which, in Paul's eyes, made her a veritable queen of Romance.

15 After a concert was over Paul was always irritable and wretched until he got to sleep, and tonight he was even more than usually restless. He had the feeling of not being able to let down, of its being impossible to give up this delicious excitement which was the only thing that could be called living at all. During the last number he withdrew and, after hastily changing his clothes in the dressing-room, slipped out to the side door where the soprano's carriage stood. Here he began pacing rapidly up and down the walk, waiting to see her come out.

16 Over yonder the Schenley, in its vacant stretch, loomed big and square through the fine rain, the windows of its twelve stories glowing like those of a lighted cardboard house under a Christmas tree. All the actors and singers of the better class stayed there when they were in the city, and a number of the big manufacturers of the place lived there in the winter. Paul had often hung about the hotel, watching the people go in and out, longing to enter and leave schoolmasters and dull care behind him forever.

17 At last the singer came out, accompanied by the conductor, who helped her into her carriage and closed the door with a cordial *auf wiedersehen* which set Paul to wondering whether she were not an old sweetheart of his. Paul followed the carriage over to the hotel, walking so rapidly as not to be far from the entrance when the singer alighted and disappeared behind the swinging glass doors that were opened by a negro in a tall hat and a long coat. In the moment that the door was ajar it seemed to Paul that he, too, entered. He seemed to feel himself go after her up the steps, into the warm, lighted building, into an exotic, a tropical world of shiny, glistening surfaces and basking ease. He reflected upon the mysterious dishes that were brought into the dining-room, the green bottles in buckets of ice, as he had seen them in the supper party pictures of the *Sunday World* supplement. A quick gust of wind brought the rain down with sudden vehemence, and Paul was startled to find that he was still outside in the slush of the gravel driveway; that his boots were letting in the water and his scanty overcoat was clinging wet about him; that the lights in front of the concert hall were out, and that the rain was driving in sheets between him and the orange glow of the windows above him. There it was, what he wanted—tangibly before him, like the fairy world of a Christmas pantomime, but mocking spirits stood guard at the doors, and, as the rain beat in his face, Paul wondered whether he were destined always to shiver in the black night outside, looking up at it.

18 He turned and walked reluctantly toward the car tracks. The end had to come sometime; his father in his night-clothes at the top of the stairs, explanations that did not explain, hastily improvised fictions that were forever tripping him up, his upstairs room and its horrible yellow wall-paper, the creaking bureau with the greasy plush collar-box, and over his painted wooden

bed the pictures of George Washington and John Calvin, and the framed motto, "Feed my Lambs," which had been worked in red worsted by his mother.

19 Half an hour later, Paul alighted from his car and went slowly down one of the side streets off the main thoroughfare. It was a highly respectable street, where all the houses were exactly alike, and where businessmen of moderate means begot and reared large families of children, all of whom went to Sabbath-school and learned the shorter catechism, and were interested in arithmetic; all of whom were as exactly alike as their homes, and of a piece with the monotony in which they lived. Paul never went up Cordelia Street without a shudder of loathing. His home was next to the house of the Cumberland minister. He approached it tonight with the nerveless sense of defeat, the hopeless feeling of sinking back forever into ugliness and commonness that he had always had when he came home. The moment he turned into Cordelia Street he felt the waters close above his head. After each of these orgies of living, he experienced all the physical depression which follows a debauch; the loathing of respectable beds, of common food, of a house penetrated by kitchen odors; a shuddering repulsion for the flavorless, colorless mass of everyday existence; a morbid desire for cool things and soft lights and fresh flowers.

20 The nearer he approached the house, the more absolutely unequal Paul felt to the sight of it all; his ugly sleeping chamber; the cold bathroom with the grimy zinc tub, the cracked mirror, the dripping spigots; his father, at the top of the stairs, his hairy legs sticking out from his night-shirt, his feet thrust into carpet slippers. He was so much later than usual that there would certainly be inquiries and reproaches. Paul stopped short before the door. He felt that he could not be accosted by his father tonight; that he could not toss again on that miserable bed. He would not go in. He would tell his father that he had no car fare, and it was raining so hard he had gone home with one of the boys and stayed all night.

21 Meanwhile, he was wet and cold. He went around to the back of the house and tried one of the basement windows, found it open, raised it cautiously, and scrambled down the cellar wall to the floor. There he stood, holding his breath, terrified by the noise he had made, but the floor above him was silent, and there was no creak on the stairs. He found a soap-box, and carried it over to the soft ring of light that streamed from the furnace door, and sat down. He was horribly afraid of rats, so he did not try to sleep, but sat looking distrustfully at the dark, still terrified lest he might have awakened his father. In such reactions, after one of the experiences which made days and nights out of the dreary blanks of the calendar, when his senses were deadened, Paul's head was always singularly clear. Suppose his father had heard him getting in at the window and had come down and shot him for a burglar? Then, again, suppose his father had come down, pistol in hand, and he had cried out in time to save himself, and his father had been horrified to think how nearly he had killed him? Then, again,

suppose a day should come when his father would remember that night, and wish there had been no warning cry to stay his hand? With this last supposition Paul entertained himself until daybreak.

22 The following Sunday was fine; the sodden November chill was broken by the last flash of autumnal summer. In the morning Paul had to go to church and Sabbath-school, as always. On seasonable Sunday afternoons the burghers of Cordelia Street always sat out on their front "stoops," and talked to their neighbors on the next stoop, or called to those across the street in neighborly fashion. The men usually sat on gay cushions placed upon the steps that led down to the sidewalk, while the women, in their Sunday "waists," sat in rockers on the cramped porches, pretending to be greatly at their ease. The children played in the streets; there were so many of them that the place resembled the recreation grounds of a kindergarten. The men on the steps—all in their shirt sleeves, their vests unbuttoned—sat with their legs well apart, their stomachs comfortably protruding, and talked of the prices of things, or told anecdotes of the sagacity of their various chiefs and overlords. They occasionally looked over the multitude of squabbling children, listened affectionately to their high-pitched, nasal voices, smiling to see their own proclivities reproduced in their offspring, and interspersed their legends of the iron kings with remarks about their sons' progress at school, their grades in arithmetic, and the amounts they had saved in their toy banks.

23 On this last Sunday of November, Paul sat all the afternoon on the lowest step of his "stoop," staring into the street, while his sisters, in their rockers, were talking to the minister's daughters next door about how many shirt-waists they had made in the last week, and how many waffles some one had eaten at the last church supper. When the weather was warm, and his father was in a particularly jovial frame of mind, the girls made lemonade, which was always brought out in a red-glass pitcher, ornamented with forget-me-nots in blue enamel. This the girls thought very fine, and the neighbors always joked about the suspicious color of the pitcher.

24 Today Paul's father sat on the top step, talking to a young man who shifted a restless baby from knee to knee. He happened to be the young man who was daily held up to Paul as a model, and after whom it was his father's dearest hope that he would pattern. This young man was of a ruddy complexion, with a compressed, red mouth, and faded, near-sighted eyes, over which he wore thick spectacles, with gold bows that curved about his ears. He was clerk to one of the magnates of a great steel corporation, and was looked upon in Cordelia Street as a young man with a future. There was a story that, some five years ago—he was now barely twenty-six—he had been a trifle dissipated but in order to curb his appetites and save the loss of time and strength that a sowing of wild oats might have entailed, he had taken his chief's advice, oft reiterated to his employees, and at twenty-one had married the first woman whom he could persuade to share

his fortunes. She happened to be an angular schoolmistress, much older than he, who also wore thick glasses, and who had now borne him four children, all near-sighted, like herself.

25 The young man was relating how his chief, now cruising in the Mediterranean, kept in touch with all the details of the business, arranging his office hours on his yacht just as though he were at home, and "knocking off work enough to keep two stenographers busy." His father told, in turn, the plan his corporation was considering, of putting in an electric railway plant at Cairo. Paul snapped his teeth; he had an awful apprehension that they might spoil it all before he got there. Yet he rather liked to hear these legends of the iron kings, that were told and retold on Sundays and holidays; these stories of palaces in Venice, yachts on the Mediterranean, and high play at Monte Carlo appealed to his fancy, and he was interested in the triumphs of these cash boys who had become famous, though he had no mind for the cash-boy stage.

26 After supper was over, and he had helped to dry the dishes, Paul nervously asked his father whether he could go to George's to get some help in his geometry, and still more nervously asked for car fare. This latter request he had to repeat, as his father, on principle, did not like to hear requests for money, whether much or little. He asked Paul whether he could not go to some boy who lived nearer, and told him that he ought not to leave his school work until Sunday; but he gave him the dime. He was not a poor man, but he had a worthy ambition to come up in the world. His only reason for allowing Paul to usher was, that he thought a boy ought to be earning a little.

27 Paul bounded upstairs, scrubbed the greasy odor of the dish-water from his hands with the ill-smelling soap he hated, and then shook over his fingers a few drops of violet water from the bottle he kept hidden in his drawer. He left the house with his geometry conspicuously under his arm, and the moment he got out of Cordelia Street and boarded a downtown car, he shook off the lethargy of two deadening days, and began to live again.

28 The leading juvenile of the permanent stock company which played at one of the downtown theatres was an acquaintance of Paul's, and the boy had been invited to drop in at the Sunday-night rehearsals whenever he could. For more than a year Paul had spent every available moment loitering about Charley Edwards's dressing-room. He had won a place among Edwards's following not only because the young actor, who could not afford to employ a dresser, often found him useful, but because he recognized in Paul something akin to what churchmen term "vocation."

29 It was at the theatre and at Carnegie Hall that Paul really lived; the rest was but a sleep and a forgetting. This was Paul's fairy tale, and it had for him all the allurement of a secret love. The moment he inhaled the gassy, painty, dusty odor behind the scenes, he breathed like a prisoner set free, and felt within him the possibility of doing or saying splendid, brilliant, poetic things. The

moment the cracked orchestra beat out the overture from *Martha*, or jerked at the serenade from *Rigoletto*, all stupid and ugly things slid from him, and his senses were deliciously, yet delicately fired.

30 Perhaps it was because, in Paul's world, the natural nearly always wore the guise of ugliness, that a certain element of artificiality seemed to him necessary in beauty. Perhaps it was because his experience of life elsewhere was so full of Sabbath-school picnics, petty economies, wholesome advice as to how to succeed in life, and the unescapable odors of cooking, that he found this existence so alluring, these smartly-clad men and women so attractive, that he was so moved by these starry apple orchards that bloomed perennially under the limelight.

31 It would be difficult to put it strongly enough how convincingly the stage entrance of that theatre was for Paul the actual portal of Romance. Certainly none of the company ever suspected it, least of all Charley Edwards. It was very like the old stories that used to float about London of fabulously rich Jews, who had subterranean halls there, with palms, and fountains, and soft lamps and richly apparelled women who never saw the disenchanting light of London day. So, in the midst of that smoke-palled city, enamored of figures and grimy toil, Paul had his secret temple, his wishing carpet, his bit of blue-and-white Mediterranean shore bathed in perpetual sunshine.

32 Several of Paul's teachers had a theory that his imagination had been perverted by garish fiction, but the truth was that he scarcely ever read at all. The books at home were not such as would either tempt or corrupt a youthful mind, and as for reading the novels that some of his friends urged upon him—well, he got what he wanted much more quickly from music; any sort of music, from an orchestra to a barrel organ. He needed only the spark, the indescribable thrill that made his imagination master of his senses, and he could make plots and pictures enough of his own. It was equally true that he was not stage struck—not, at any rate, in the usual acceptation of that expression. He had no desire to become an actor, any more than he had to become a musician. He felt no necessity to do any of these things; what he wanted was to see, to be in the atmosphere, float on the wave of it, to be carried out, blue league after blue league, away from everything.

33 After a night behind the scenes, Paul found the school room more than ever repulsive; the bare floors and naked walls; the prosy men who never wore frock coats, or violets in their buttonholes; the women with their dull gowns, shrill voices, and pitiful seriousness about prepositions that govern the dative. He could not bear to have the other pupils think, for a moment, that he took these people seriously; he must convey to them that he considered it all trivial, and was there only by way of a jest, anyway. He had autographed pictures of all the members of the stock company which he showed his classmates, telling them the most incredible stories of his familiarity with these people, of his acquaintance with the soloists who came to Carnegie Hall, his suppers with them and

the flowers he sent them. When these stories lost their effect, and his audience grew listless, he became desperate and would bid all the boys good-bye, announcing that he was going to travel for a while; going to Naples, to Venice, to Egypt. Then, next Monday, he would slip back, conscious and nervously smiling; his sister was ill, and he should have to defer his voyage until spring.

34 Matters went steadily worse with Paul at school. In the itch to let his instructors know how heartily he despised them and their homilies, and how thoroughly he was appreciated elsewhere, he mentioned once or twice that he had no time to fool with theorems; adding—with a twitch of the eyebrows and a touch of that nervous bravado which so perplexed them—that he was helping the people down at the stock company; they were old friends of his.

35 The upshot of the matter was that the Principal went to Paul's father, and Paul was taken out of school and put to work. The manager at Carnegie Hall was told to get another usher in his stead; the door-keeper at the theatre was warned not to admit him to the house; and Charley Edwards remorsefully promised the boy's father not to see him again.

36 The members of the stock company were vastly amused when some of Paul's stories reached them—especially the women. They were hardworking women, most of them supporting indigent husbands or brothers, and they laughed rather bitterly at having stirred the boy to such fervid and florid inventions. They agreed with the faculty and with his father that Paul's was a bad case.

37 The east-bound train was ploughing through a January snow-storm; the dull dawn was beginning to show grey when the engine whistled a mile out of Newark. Paul started up from the seat where he had lain curled in uneasy slumber, rubbed the breath-misted window glass with his hand, and peered out. The snow was whirling in curling eddies above the white bottom lands, and the drifts lay already deep in the fields and along the fences, while here and there the long dead grass and dried weed stalks protruded black above it. Lights shone from the scattered houses, and a gang of laborers who stood beside the track waved their lanterns.

38 Paul had slept very little, and he felt grimy and uncomfortable. He had made the all-night journey in a day coach, partly because he was ashamed, dressed as he was, to go into a Pullman, and partly because he was afraid of being seen there by some Pittsburgh businessman, who might have noticed him in Denny & Carson's office. When the whistle awoke him, he clutched quickly at his breast pocket, glancing about him with an uncertain smile. But the little, clay-bespattered Italians were still sleeping, the slatternly women across the aisle were in open-mouthed oblivion, and even the crumby, crying babies were for the nonce stilled. Paul settled back to struggle with his impatience as best as he could.

39 When he arrived at the Jersey City station, he hurried through his breakfast manifestly ill at ease and keeping a sharp eye about him. After he reached the Twenty-third Street station, he consulted a cabman, and had himself driven to a men's furnishing establishment that was just opening for the day. He spent upward of two hours there, buying with endless reconsidering and great care. His new street suit he put on in the fitting-room; the frock coat and dress clothes he had bundled into the cab with his linen. Then he drove to a hatter's and a shoe house. His next errand was at Tiffany's, where he selected his silver and a new scarf-pin. He would not wait to have his silver marked, he said. Lastly, he stopped at a trunk shop on Broadway, and had his purchases packed into various travelling bags.

40 It was a little after one o'clock when he drove up to the Waldorf, and after settling with the cabman, went into the office. He registered from Washington; said his mother and father had been abroad, and that he had come down to await the arrival of their steamer. He told his story plausibly and had no trouble, since he volunteered to pay for them in advance, in engaging his rooms; a sleeping-room, sitting-room and bath.

41 Not once, but a hundred times Paul had planned this entry into New York. He had gone over every detail of it with Charley Edwards, and in his scrap book at home there were pages of description about New York hotels, cut from the Sunday papers. When he was shown to his sitting-room on the eighth floor, he saw at a glance that everything was as it should be; there was but one detail in his mental picture that the place did not realize, so he rang for the bell boy and sent him down for flowers. He moved about nervously until the boy returned, putting away his new linen and fingering it delightedly as he did so. When the flowers came, he put them hastily into water, and then tumbled into a hot bath. Presently he came out of his white bathroom, resplendent in his new silk underwear, and playing with the tassels of his red robe. The snow was whirling so fiercely outside his windows that he could scarcely see across the street, but within the air was deliciously soft and fragrant. He put the violets and jonquils on the taboret beside the couch, and threw himself down, with a long sigh, covering himself with a Roman blanket. He was thoroughly tired; he had been in such haste, he had stood up to such a strain, covered so much ground in the last twenty-four hours, that he wanted to think how it had all come about. Lulled by the sound of the wind, the warm air, and the cool fragrance of the flowers, he sank into deep, drowsy retrospection.

42 It had been wonderfully simple; when they had shut him out of the theatre and concert hall, when they had taken away his bone, the whole thing was virtually determined. The rest was a mere matter of opportunity. The only thing that at all surprised him was his own courage—for he realized well enough that he had always been tormented by fear, a sort of apprehensive dread that, of late years, as the meshes of the lies he had told closed about him, had been

pulling the muscles of his body tighter and tighter. Until now, he could not remember the time when he had not been dreading something. Even when he was a little boy, it was always there—behind him, or before, or on either side. There had always been the shadowed corner, the dark place into which he dared not look, but from which something seemed always to be watching him—and Paul had done things that were not pretty to watch, he knew.

43 But now he had a curious sense of relief, as though he had at last thrown down the gauntlet to the thing in the corner.

44 Yet it was but a day since he had been sulking in the traces; but yesterday afternoon that he had been sent to the bank with Denny & Carson's deposit, as usual—but this time he was instructed to leave the book to be balanced. There was above two thousand dollars in checks, and nearly a thousand in the bank notes which he had taken from the book and quietly transferred to his pocket. At the bank he had made out a new deposit slip. His nerves had been steady enough to permit of his returning to the office, where he had finished his work and asked for a full day's holiday tomorrow, Saturday, giving a perfectly reasonable pretext. The bank book, he knew, would not be returned before Monday or Tuesday, and his father would be out of town for the next week. From the time he slipped the bank notes into his pocket until he boarded the night train for New York, he had not known a moment's hesitation. It was not the first time Paul had steered through treacherous waters.

45 How astonishingly easy it had all been; here he was, the thing done; and this time there would be no awakening, no figure at the top of the stairs. He watched the snow flakes whirling by his window until he fell asleep.

46 When he awoke, it was three o'clock in the afternoon. He bounded up with a start; half of one of his precious days gone already! He spent more than an hour in dressing, watching every stage of his toilet carefully in the mirror. Everything was quite perfect; he was exactly the kind of boy he had always wanted to be.

47 When he went downstairs, Paul took a carriage and drove up Fifth Avenue toward the Park. The snow had somewhat abated; carriages and tradesmen's wagons were hurrying soundlessly to and fro in the winter twilight; boys in woollen mufflers were shovelling off the doorsteps; the avenue stages made fine spots of color against the white street. Here and there on the corners were stands, with whole flower gardens blooming under glass cases, against the sides of which the snow flakes stuck and melted; violets, roses, carnations, lilies of the valley—somewhat vastly more lovely and alluring that they blossomed thus unnaturally in the snow. The Park itself was a wonderful stage winterpiece.

48 When he returned, the pause of the twilight had ceased, and the tune of the streets had changed. The snow was falling faster, lights streamed from the hotels that reared their dozen stories fearlessly up into the storm, defying the raging Atlantic winds. A long, black stream of carriages poured down the

avenue, intersected here and there by other streams, tending horizontally. There were a score of cabs about the entrance of his hotel, and his driver had to wait. Boys in livery were running in and out of the awning stretched across the sidewalk, up and down the red velvet carpet laid from the door to the street. Above, about, within it all was the rumble and roar, the hurry and toss of thousands of human beings as hot for pleasure as himself, and on every side of him towered the glaring affirmation of the omnipotence of wealth.

49 The boy set his teeth and drew his shoulders together in a spasm of realization: the plot of all dramas, the text of all romances, the nerve-stuff of all sensations was whirling about him like the snow flakes. He burnt like a faggot in a tempest.

50 When Paul went down to dinner, the music of the orchestra came floating up the elevator shaft to greet him. His head whirled as he stepped into the thronged corridor, and he sank back into one of the chairs against the wall to get his breath. The lights, the chatter, the perfumes, the bewildering medley of color—he had, for a moment, the feeling of not being able to stand it. But only for a moment; these were his own people, he told himself. He went slowly about the corridors, through the writing-rooms, smoking-rooms, reception-rooms, as though he were exploring the chambers of an enchanted palace, built and peopled for him alone.

51 When he reached the dining-room he sat down at a table near a window. The flowers, the white linen, the many-colored wine glasses, the gay toilettes of the women, the low popping of corks, the undulating repetitions of the *Blue Danube* from the orchestra, all flooded Paul's dream with bewildering radiance. When the roseate tinge of his champagne was added—that cold, precious, bubbling stuff that creamed and foamed in his glass—Paul wondered that there were honest men in the world at all. This was what all the world was fighting for, he reflected; this was what all the struggle was about. He doubted the reality of his past. Had he ever known a place called Cordelia Street, a place where fagged-looking businessmen got on the early car; mere rivets in a machine they seemed to Paul—sickening men, with combings of children's hair always hanging to their coats, and the smell of cooking in their clothes. Cordelia Street—Ah! that belonged to another time and country; had he not always been thus, had he not sat here night after night, from as far back as he could remember, looking pensively over just such shimmering textures, and slowly twirling the stem of a glass like this one between his thumb and middle finger? He rather thought he had.

52 He was not in the least abashed or lonely. He had no especial desire to meet or to know any of these people; all he demanded was the right to look on and conjecture, to watch the pageant. The mere stage properties were all he contended for. Nor was he lonely later in the evening, in his loge at the Metropolitan. He was now entirely rid of his nervous misgivings, of his

forced aggressiveness, of the imperative desire to show himself different from his surroundings. He felt now that his surroundings explained him. Nobody questioned the purple; he had only to wear it passively. He had only to glance down at his attire to reassure himself that here it would be impossible for anyone to humiliate him.

53 He found it hard to leave his beautiful sitting-room to go to bed that night, and sat long watching the raging storm from his turret window. When he went to sleep it was with the lights turned on in his bedroom; partly because of his old timidity, and partly so that, if he should wake in the night, there would be no wretched moment of doubt, no horrible suspicion of yellow wallpaper, or of Washington and Calvin above his bed.

54 Sunday morning the city was practically snowbound. Paul breakfasted late, and in the afternoon he fell in with a wild San Francisco boy, a freshman at Yale, who said he had run down for a "little flyer" over Sunday. The young man offered to show Paul the night side of the town, and the two boys went out together after dinner, not returning to the hotel until seven o'clock the next morning. They had started out in the confiding warmth of a champagne friendship, but their parting in the elevator was singularly cool. The freshman pulled himself together to make his train, and Paul went to bed. He awoke at two o'clock in the afternoon, very thirsty and dizzy, and rang for ice-water, coffee, and the Pittsburgh papers.

55 On the part of the hotel management, Paul excited no suspicion. There was this to be said for him, that he wore his spoils with dignity and in no way made himself conspicuous. Even under the glow of his wine he was never boisterous, though he found the stuff like a magician's wand for wonder-building. His chief greediness lay in his ears and eyes, and his excesses were not offensive ones. His dearest pleasures were the grey winter twilights in his sitting-room; his quiet enjoyment of his flowers, his clothes, his wide divan, his cigarette, and his sense of power. He could not remember a time when he had felt so at peace with himself. The mere release from the necessity of petty lying, lying every day and every day, restored his self-respect. He had never lied for pleasure, even at school; but to be noticed and admired, to assert his difference from other Cordelia Street boys; and he felt a good deal more manly, more honest, even, now that he had no need for boastful pretensions, now that he could, as his actor friends used to say, "dress the part." It was characteristic that remorse did not occur to him. His golden days went by without a shadow, and he made each as perfect as he could.

56 On the the eighth day after his arrival in New York, he found the whole affair exploited in the Pittsburgh papers, exploited with a wealth of detail which indicated that local news of a sensational nature was at a low ebb. The firm of Denny & Carson announced that the boy's father had refunded the full amount of the theft, and that they had no intention of prosecuting. The

Cumberland minister had been interviewed, and expressed his hope of yet reclaiming the motherless lad, and his Sabbath-school teacher declared that she would spare no effort to that end. The rumor had reached Pittsburgh that the boy had been seen in a New York hotel, and his father had gone East to find him and bring him home.

57 Paul had just come in to dress for dinner; he sank into a chair, weak to the knees, and clasped his head in his hands. It was to be worse than jail, even; the tepid waters of Cordelia Street were to close over him finally and forever. The grey monotony stretched before him in hopeless, unrelieved years; Sabbath-school, Young People's Meeting, the yellow-papered room, the damp dish-towels; it all rushed back upon him with a sickening vividness. He had the old feeling that the orchestra had suddenly stopped, the sinking sensation that the play was over. The sweat broke out on his face, and he sprang to his feet, looked about him with his white, conscious smile, and winked at himself in the mirror. With something of the old childish belief in miracles with which he had so often gone to class, all his lessons unlearned, Paul dressed and dashed whistling down the corridor to the elevator.

58 He had no sooner entered the dining-room and caught the measure of the music than his remembrance was lightened by his old elastic power of claiming the moment, mounting with it, and finding it all sufficient. The glare and glitter about him, the mere scenic accessories had again, and for the last time, their old potency. He would show himself that he was game, he would finish the thing splendidly. He doubted, more than ever, the existence of Cordelia Street, and for the first time he drank his wine recklessly. Was he not, after all, one of those fortunate beings born to the purple, was he not still himself and in his own place? He drummed a nervous accompaniment to the Pagliacci music and looked about him, telling himself over and over that it had paid.

59 He reflected drowsily, to the swell of the music and the chill sweetness of his wine, that he might have done it more wisely. He might have caught an outboard steamer and been well out of their clutches before now. But the other side of the world had seemed too far away and too uncertain then; he could not have waited for it; his need had been too sharp. If he had to choose over again, he would do the same thing tomorrow. He looked affectionately about the dining-room, now gilded with a soft mist. Ah, it had paid indeed!

60 Paul was awakened next morning by a painful throbbing in his head and feet. He had thrown himself across the bed without undressing, and had slept with his shoes on. His limbs and hands were lead heavy, and his tongue and throat were parched and burnt. There came upon him one of those fateful attacks of clearheadedness that never occurred except when he was physically exhausted and his nerves hung loose. He lay still and closed his eyes and let the tide of things wash over him.

61 His father was in New York; "stopping at some joint or other," he told himself. The memory of successive summers on the front stoop fell upon him like a weight of black water. He had not a hundred dollars left; and he knew now, more than ever, that money was everything, the wall that stood between all he loathed and all he wanted. The thing was winding itself up; he had thought of that on his first glorious day in New York, and had even provided a way to snap the thread. It lay on his dressing-table now; he had got it out last night when he came blindly up from dinner, but the shiny metal hurt his eyes, and he disliked the looks of it.

62 He rose and moved about with a painful effort, succumbing now and again to attacks of nausea. It was the old depression exaggerated; all the world had become Cordelia Street. Yet somehow he was not afraid of anything, was absolutely calm; perhaps because he had looked into the dark corner at last and knew. It was bad enough, what he saw there, but somehow not so bad as his long fear of it had been. He saw everything clearly now. He had a feeling that he had made the best of it, that he had lived the sort of life he was meant to live, and for half an hour he sat staring at the revolver. But he told himself that was not the way, so he went downstairs and took a cab to the ferry.

63 When Paul arrived at Newark, he got off the train and took another cab, directing the driver to follow the Pennsylvania tracks out of the town. The snow lay heavy on the roadways and had drifted deep in the open fields. Only here and there the dead grass or dried weed stalks projected, singularly black, above it. Once well into the country, Paul dismissed the carriage and walked, floundering along the tracks, his mind a medley of irrelevant things. He seemed to hold in his brain an actual picture of everything he had seen that morning. He remembered every feature of both his drivers, of the toothless old woman from whom he had bought the red flowers in his coat, the agent from whom he had got his ticket, and all of his fellow-passengers on the ferry. His mind, unable to cope with vital matters near at hand, worked feverishly and deftly at sorting and grouping these images. They made for him a part of the ugliness of the world, of the ache in his head, and the bitter burning on his tongue. He stooped and put a handful of snow into his mouth as he walked, but that, too, seemed hot. When he reached a little hillside, where the tracks ran through a cut some twenty feet below him, he stopped and sat down.

64 The carnations in his coat were drooping with the cold, he noticed; their red glory all over. It occurred to him that all the flowers he had seen in the glass cases that first night must have gone the same way, long before this. It was only one splendid breath they had, in spite of their brave mockery at the winter outside the glass; and it was a losing game in the end, it seemed, this revolt against the homilies by which the world is run. Paul took one of the blossoms carefully from his coat and scooped a little hole in the snow, where he covered

it up. Then he dozed a while, from his weak condition, seemingly insensible to the cold.

65 The sound of an approaching train awoke him, and he started to his feet, remembering only his resolution, and afraid lest he should be too late. He stood watching the approaching locomotive, his teeth chattering, his lips drawn away from them in a frightened smile; once or twice he glanced nervously sidewise, as though he were being watched. When the right moment came, he jumped. As he fell, the folly of his haste occurred to him with merciless clearness, the vastness of what he had left undone. There flashed through his brain, clearer than ever before, the blue of Adriatic water, the yellow of Algerian sands.

66 He felt something strike his chest, and that his body was being thrown swiftly through the air, on and on, immeasurably far and fast, while his limbs were gently relaxed. Then, because the picture-making mechanism was crushed, the disturbing visions flashed into black, and Paul dropped back into the immense design of things.

—1904

James Joyce
(1882-1941)

The Dead

Joyce's masterpiece is *Ulysses*, the difficult novel of a single day in the life of Dublin, that shortly after its appearance in 1922 became both a modern classic and the subject of a landmark censorship case, which its publishers eventually won. Joyce's lifelong quarrel with the provincial concerns of Irish religious, cultural, and literary life (all touched on in "The Dead") led him to permanent self-exile in Zurich and Paris. Most readers associate Joyce with his pioneering of experimental techniques such as the fragmentary observations found in his early *Epiphanies* (posthumously published in 1956), his use of interior monologue and stream of consciousness, and the complicated linguistic games of *Finnegan's Wake* (1939), forgetting that his earlier works lie squarely in the realm of traditional fiction. *Dubliners* (1914), his collection of short stories of life in his native city, remains an imposing achievement, as does his autobiographical novel

A Portrait of the Artist as a Young Man (1916). "The Dead," the last story in *Dubliners*, touches many themes—marital love, family duties, and Joyce's own ambivalence toward his homeland—and is without doubt one of the triumphs of the realistic tradition of the short story. A film version of "The Dead," the final project of director John Huston, appeared in 1987.

Lily, the caretaker's daughter, was literally run off her feet. Hardly had she brought one gentleman into the little pantry behind the office on the ground floor and helped him off with his overcoat than the wheezy hall-door bell clanged again and she had to scamper along the bare hallway to let in another guest. It was well for her she had not to attend to the ladies also. But Miss Kate and Miss Julia had thought of that and had converted the bathroom upstairs into a ladies' dressing-room. Miss Kate and Miss Julia were there, gossiping and laughing and fussing, walking after each other to the head of the stairs, peering down over the banisters and calling down to Lily to ask her who had come.

2 It was always a great affair, the Misses Morkan's annual dance. Everybody who knew them came to it, members of the family, old friends of the family, the members of Julia's choir, any of Kate's pupils that were grown up enough and even some of Mary Jane's pupils too. Never once had it fallen flat. For years and years it had gone off in splendid style as long as anyone could remember; ever since Kate and Julia, after the death of their brother Pat, had left the house in Stoney Batter and taken Mary Jane, their only niece, to live with them in the dark gaunt house on Usher's Island, the upper part of which they had rented from Mr Fulham, the corn-factor on the ground floor. That was a good thirty years ago if it was a day. Mary Jane, who was then a little girl in short clothes, was now the main prop of the household for she had the organ in Haddington Road. She had been through the Academy and gave a pupils' concert every year in the upper room of the Antient Concert Rooms. Many of her pupils belonged to better-class families on the Kingstown and Dalkey line. Old as they were, her aunts also did their share. Julia, though she was quite grey, was still the leading soprano in Adam and Eve's,° and Kate, being too feeble to go about much, gave music lessons to beginners on the old square piano in the back room. Lily, the caretaker's daughter, did house-maid's work for them. Though their life was modest they believed in eating well; the best of everything; diamond-bone sirloins, three-shilling tea and the best bottled stout. But Lily seldom made a mistake in the orders so that she got on well with her three

---

Adam and Eve's a church in Dublin

mistresses. They were fussy, that was all. But the only thing they would not stand was back answers.

3 Of course they had good reason to be fussy on such a night. And then it was long after ten o'clock and yet there was no sign of Gabriel and his wife. Besides they were dreadfully afraid that Freddy Malins might turn up screwed. They would not wish for worlds that any of Mary Jane's pupils should see him under the influence; and when he was like that it was sometimes very hard to manage him. Freddy Malins always came late but they wondered what could be keeping Gabriel: and that was what brought them every two minutes to the banisters to ask Lily had Gabriel or Freddy come.

4 —O, Mr Conroy, said Lily to Gabriel when she opened the door for him, Miss Kate and Miss Julia thought you were never coming. Good-night, Mrs Conroy.

5 —I'll engage they did, said Gabriel, but they forget that my wife here takes three mortal hours to dress herself.

6 He stood on the mat, scraping the snow from his goloshes, while Lily led his wife to the foot of the stairs and called out:

7 —Miss Kate, here's Mrs Conroy.

8 Kate and Julia came toddling down the dark stairs at once. Both of them kissed Gabriel's wife, said she must be perished alive and asked was Gabriel with her.

9 —Here I am as right as the mail, Aunt Kate! Go on up. I'll follow, called out Gabriel from the dark.

10 He continued scraping his feet vigorously while the three women went upstairs, laughing, to the ladies' dressing-room. A light fringe of snow lay like a cape on the shoulders of his overcoat and like toecaps on the toes of his goloshes; and, as the buttons of his overcoat slipped with a squeaking noise through the snow-stiffened frieze, a cold fragrant air from out-of-doors escaped from crevices and folds.

11 —Is it snowing again, Mr Conroy? asked Lily.

12 She had preceded him into the pantry to help him off with his overcoat. Gabriel smiled at the three syllables she had given his surname and glanced at her. She was a slim, growing girl, pale in complexion and with hay-coloured hair. The gas in the pantry made her look still paler. Gabriel had known her when she was a child and used to sit on the lowest step nursing a rag doll.

13 —Yes, Lily, he answered, and I think we're in for a night of it.

14 He looked up at the pantry ceiling, which was shaking with the stamping and shuffling of feet on the floor above, listened for a moment to the piano and then glanced at the girl, who was folding his overcoat carefully at the end of a shelf.

15 —Tell me, Lily, he said in a friendly tone, do you still go to school?

16 —O no, sir, she answered. I'd done schooling this year and more.

17 —O, then, said Gabriel gaily, I suppose we'll be going to your wedding one of these fine days with your young man, eh?

18 The girl glanced back at him over her shoulder and said with great bitterness:

19 —The men that is now is only all palaver and what they can get out of you.

20 Gabriel coloured as if he felt he had made a mistake and, without looking at her, kicked off his goloshes and flicked actively with his muffler at his patent-leather shoes.

21 He was a stout tallish young man. The high colour of his cheeks pushed upwards even to his forehead where it scattered itself in a few formless patches of pale red; and on his hairless face there scintillated restlessly the polished lenses and the bright gilt rims of the glasses which screened his delicate and restless eyes. His glossy black hair was parted in the middle and brushed in a long curve behind his ears where it curled slightly beneath the groove left by his hat.

22 When he had flicked lustre into his shoes he stood up and pulled his waistcoat down more tightly on his plump body. Then he took a coin rapidly from his pocket.

23 —O Lily, he said, thrusting it into her hands, it's Christmas-time, isn't it? Just . . . here's a little . . .

24 He walked rapidly towards the door.

25 —O no, sir! cried the girl, following him. Really, sir, I wouldn't take it.

26 —Christmas-time! Christmas-time! said Gabriel, almost trotting to the stairs and waving his hand to her in deprecation.

27 The girl, seeing that he had gained the stairs, called out after him:

28 —Well, thank you, sir.

29 He waited outside the drawing-room door until the waltz should finish, listening to the skirts that swept against it and to the shuffling of feet. He was still discomposed by the girl's bitter and sudden retort. It had cast a gloom over him which he tried to dispel by arranging his cuffs and the bows of his tie. Then he took from his waistcoat pocket a little paper and glanced at the headings he had made for his speech. He was undecided about the lines from Robert Browning for he feared they would be above the heads of his hearers. Some quotation that they could recognise from Shakespeare or from the Melodies would be better. The indelicate clacking of the men's heels and the shuffling of their soles reminded him that their grade of culture differed from his. He would only make himself ridiculous by quoting poetry to them which they could not understand. They would think that he was airing his superior education. He would fail with them just as he had failed with the girl in the pantry.

He had taken up a wrong tone. His whole speech was a mistake from first to last, an utter failure.

30 Just then his aunts and his wife came out of the ladies' dressing-room. His aunts were two small plainly dressed old women. Aunt Julia was an inch or so the taller. Her hair, drawn low over the tops of her ears, was grey; and grey also, with darker shadows, was her large flaccid face. Though she was stout in build and stood erect her slow eyes and parted lips gave her the appearance of a woman who did not know where she was or where she was going. Aunt Kate was more vivacious. Her face, healthier than her sister's, was all puckers and creases, like a shrivelled red apple, and her hair, braided in the same old-fashioned way, had not lost its ripe nut colour.

31 They both kissed Gabriel frankly. He was their favourite nephew, the son of their dead elder sister, Ellen, who had married T. J. Conroy of the Port and Docks.

32 —Gretta tells me you're not going to take a cab back to Monkstown to-night, Gabriel, said Aunt Kate.

33 —No, said Gabriel, turning to his wife, we had quite enough of that last year, hadn't we? Don't you remember, Aunt Kate, what a cold Gretta got out of it? Cab windows rattling all the way, and the east wind blowing in after we passed Merrion. Very jolly it was. Gretta caught a dreadful cold.

34 Aunt Kate frowned severely and nodded her head at every word.

35 —Quite right, Gabriel, quite right, she said. You can't be too careful.

36 —But as for Gretta there, said Gabriel, she'd walk home in the snow if she were let.

37 Mrs Conroy laughed.

38 —Don't mind him, Aunt Kate, she said. He's really an awful bother, what with green shades for Tom's eyes at night and making him do the dumb-bells, and forcing Eva to eat the stirabout. The poor child! And she simply hates the sight of it! . . . O, but you'll never guess what he makes me wear now!

39 She broke out into a peal of laughter and glanced at her husband, whose admiring and happy eyes had been wandering from her dress to her face and hair. The two aunts laughed heartily too, for Gabriel's solicitude was a standing joke with them.

40 —Goloshes! said Mrs Conroy. That's the latest. Whenever it's wet underfoot I must put on my goloshes. To-night even he wanted me to put them on, but I wouldn't. The next thing he'll buy me will be a diving suit.

41 Gabriel laughed nervously and patted his tie reassuringly while Aunt Kate nearly doubled herself, so heartily did she enjoy the joke. The smile soon faded from Aunt Julia's face and her mirthless eyes were directed towards her nephew's face. After a pause she asked:

42 —And what are goloshes, Gabriel?

43 —Goloshes, Julia! exclaimed her sister. Goodness me, don't you know what goloshes are? You wear them over your . . . over your boots, Gretta, isn't it?

44 —Yes, said Mrs Conroy. Guttapercha° things. We both have a pair now. Gabriel says everyone wears them on the continent.

45 —O, on the continent, murmured Aunt Julia, nodding her head slowly.

46 Gabriel knitted his brows and said, as if he were slightly angered:

47 —It's nothing very wonderful but Gretta thinks it very funny because she says the word reminds her of Christy Minstrels.

48 —But tell me, Gabriel, said Aunt Kate, with brisk tact. Of course, you've seen about the room. Gretta was saying . . .

49 —O, the room is all right, replied Gabriel. I've taken one in the Gresham.

50 —To be sure, said Aunt Kate, by far the best thing to do. And the children, Gretta, you're not anxious about them?

51 —O, for one night, said Mrs Conroy. Besides, Bessie will look after them.

52 —To be sure, said Aunt Kate again. What a comfort it is to have a girl like that, one you can depend on! There's that Lily, I'm sure I don't know what has come over her lately. She's not the girl she was at all.

53 Gabriel was about to ask his aunt some questions on this point but she broke off suddenly to gaze after her sister who had wandered down the stairs and was craning her neck over the banisters.

54 —Now, I ask you, she said, almost testily, where is Julia going? Julia! Julia! Where are you going?

55 Julia, who had gone halfway down one flight, came back and announced blandly:

56 —Here's Freddy.

57 At the same moment a clapping of hands and a final flourish of the pianist told that the waltz had ended. The drawing-room door was opened from within and some couples came out. Aunt Kate drew Gabriel aside hurriedly and whispered into his ear:

58 —Slip down, Gabriel, like a good fellow and see if he's all right, and don't let him up if he's screwed. I'm sure he's screwed. I'm sure he is.

59 Gabriel went to the stairs and listened over the banisters. He could hear two persons talking in the pantry. Then he recognised Freddy Malins' laugh. He went down the stairs noisily.

60 —It's such a relief, said Aunt Kate to Mrs Conroy, that Gabriel is here. I always feel easier in my mind when he's here . . . Julia, there's Miss Daly and

---

Guttapercha a rubberlike substance

Miss Power will take some refreshment. Thanks for your beautiful waltz, Miss Daly. It made lovely time.

61 A tall wizen-faced man, with a stiff grizzled moustache and swarthy skin, who was passing out with his partner said:

62 —And may we have some refreshment, too, Miss Morkan?

63 —Julia, said Aunt Kate summarily, and here's Mr Browne and Miss Furlong. Take them in, Julia, with Miss Daly and Miss Power.

64 —I'm the man for the ladies, said Mr Browne, pursing his lips until his moustache bristled and smiling in all his wrinkles. You know, Miss Morkan, the reason they are so fond of me is—

65 He did not finish his sentence, but, seeing that Aunt Kate was out of earshot, at once led the three young ladies into the back room. The middle of the room was occupied by two square tables placed end to end, and on these Aunt Julia and the caretaker were straightening and smoothing a large cloth. On the sideboard were arrayed dishes and plates, and glasses and bundles of knives and forks and spoons. The top of the closed square piano served also as a sideboard for viands and sweets. At a smaller sideboard in one corner two young men were standing, drinking hop-bitters.

66 Mr Browne led his charges thither and invited them all, in jest, to some ladies' punch, hot, strong and sweet. As they said they never took anything strong he opened three bottles of lemonade for them. Then he asked one of the young men to move aside, and, taking hold of the decanter, filled out for himself a goodly measure of whisky. The young men eyed him respectfully while he took a trial sip.

67 —God help me, he said, smiling, it's the doctor's orders.

68 His wizened face broke into a broader smile, and the three young ladies laughed in musical echo to his pleasantry, swaying their bodies to and fro, with nervous jerks of their shoulders. The boldest said:

69 —O, now, Mr Browne, I'm sure the doctor never ordered anything of the kind.

70 Mr Browne took another sip of his whisky and said, with sidling mimicry:

71 —Well, you see, I'm like the famous Mrs Cassidy, who is reported to have said: *Now, Mary Grimes, if I don't take it, make me take it, for I feel I want it.*

72 His hot face had leaned forward a little too confidentially and he had assumed a very low Dublin accent so that the young ladies, with one instinct, received his speech in silence. Miss Furlong, who was one of Mary Jane's pupils, asked Miss Daly what was the name of the pretty waltz she had played; and Mr Browne, seeing that he was ignored, turned promptly to the two young men who were more appreciative.

73 A red-faced young woman, dressed in pansy, came into the room, excitedly clapping her hands and crying:

74 —Quadrilles! Quadrilles!

75 Close on her heels came Aunt Kate, crying:

76 —Two gentlemen and three ladies, Mary Jane!

77 —O, here's Mr Bergin and Mr Kerrigan, said Mary Jane. Mr Kerrigan, will you take Miss Power? Miss Furlong, may I get you a partner, Mr Bergin. O, that'll just do now.

78 —Three ladies, Mary Jane, said Aunt Kate.

79 The two young gentlemen asked the ladies if they might have the pleasure, and Mary Jane turned to Miss Daly.

80 —O, Miss Daly, you're really awfully good, after playing for the last two dances, but really we're so short of ladies to-night.

81 —I don't mind in the least, Miss Morkan.

82 —But I've a nice partner for you, Mr Bartell D'Arcy, the tenor. I'll get him to sing later on. All Dublin is raving about him.

83 —Lovely voice, lovely voice! said Aunt Kate.

84 As the piano had twice begun the prelude to the first figure Mary Jane led her recruits quickly from the room. They had hardly gone when Aunt Julia wandered slowly into the room, looking behind her at something.

85 —What is the matter, Julia? asked Aunt Kate anxiously. Who is it?

86 Julia, who was carrying in a column of table-napkins, turned to her sister and said, simply, as if the question had surprised her:

87 —It's only Freddy, Kate, and Gabriel with him.

88 In fact right behind her Gabriel could be seen piloting Freddy Malins across the landing. The latter, a young man of about forty, was of Gabriel's size and build, with very round shoulders. His face was fleshy and pallid, touched with colour only at the thick hanging lobes of his ears and at the wide wings of his nose. He had coarse features, a blunt nose, a convex and receding brow, tumid and protruding lips. His heavy-lidded eyes and the disorder of his scanty hair made him look sleepy. He was laughing heartily in a high key at a story which he had been telling Gabriel on the stairs and at the same time rubbing the knuckles of his left fist backwards and forwards into his left eye.

89 —Good-evening, Freddy, said Aunt Julia.

90 Freddy Malins bade the Misses Morkan good-evening in what seemed an off-hand fashion by reason of the habitual catch in his voice and then, seeing that Mr Browne was grinning at him from the sideboard, crossed the room on rather shaky legs and began to repeat in an undertone the story he had just told to Gabriel.

91 —He's not so bad, is he? said Aunt Kate to Gabriel.

92 Gabriel's brows were dark but he raised them quickly and answered:

93 —O no, hardly noticeable.

94 —Now, isn't he a terrible fellow! she said. And his poor mother made him take the pledge on New Year's Eve. But come on, Gabriel, into the drawing-room.

95 Before leaving the room with Gabriel she signalled to Mr Browne by frowning and shaking her forefinger in warning to and fro. Mr Browne nodded in answer and, when she had gone, said to Freddy Malins:

96 —Now, then, Teddy, I'm going to fill you out a good glass of lemonade just to buck you up.

97 Freddy Malins, who was nearing the climax of his story, waved the offer aside impatiently but Mr Browne, having first called Freddy Malins' attention to a disarray in his dress, filled out and handed him a full glass of lemonade. Freddy Malins' left hand accepted the glass mechanically, his right hand being engaged in the mechanical readjustment of his dress. Mr Browne, whose face was once more wrinkling with mirth, poured out for himself a glass of whisky while Freddy Malins exploded, before he had well reached the climax of his story, in a kink of high-pitched bronchitic laughter and, setting down his untasted and overflowing glass, began to rub the knuckles of his left fist backwards and forwards into his left eye, repeating words of his last phrase as well as his fit of laughter would allow him.

98 Gabriel could not listen while Mary Jane was playing her Academy piece, full of runs and difficult passages, to the hushed drawing-room. He liked music but the piece she was playing had no melody for him and he doubted whether it had any melody for the other listeners, though they had begged Mary Jane to play something. Four young men, who had come from the refreshment-room to stand in the doorway at the sound of the piano, had gone away quietly in couples after a few minutes. The only persons who seemed to follow the music were Mary Jane herself, her hands racing along the keyboard or lifted from it at the pauses like those of a priestess in momentary imprecation, and Aunt Kate standing at her elbow to turn the page.

99 Gabriel's eye, irritated by the floor, which glittered with beeswax under the heavy chandelier, wandered to the wall above the piano. A picture of the balcony scene in *Romeo and Juliet* hung there and beside it was a picture of the two murdered princes in the Tower which Aunt Julia had worked in red, blue and brown wools when she was a girl. Probably in the school they had gone to as girls that kind of work had been taught, for one year his mother had worked for him as a birthday present a waistcoat of purple tabinet, with little foxes' heads upon it, lined with brown satin and having round mulberry buttons. It was strange that his mother had had no musical talent though Aunt Kate used to call her the brains carrier of the Morkan family. Both she and Julia had always

seemed a little proud of their serious and matronly sister. Her photograph stood before the pierglass. She held an open book on her knees and was pointing out something in it to Constantine who, dressed in a man-o'-war suit, lay at her feet. It was she who had chosen the names for her sons for she was very sensible of the dignity of family life. Thanks to her, Constantine was now senior curate in Balbriggan and, thanks to her, Gabriel himself had taken his degree in the Royal University. A shadow passed over his face as he remembered her sullen opposition to his marriage. Some slighting phrases she had used still rankled in his memory; she had once spoken of Gretta as being country cute and that was not true of Gretta at all. It was Gretta who had nursed her during all her last long illness in their house at Monkstown.

100 He knew that Mary Jane must be near the end of her piece for she was playing again the opening melody with runs of scales after every bar and while he waited for the end the resentment died down in his heart. The piece ended with a trill of octaves in the treble and a final deep octave in the bass. Great applause greeted Mary Jane as, blushing and rolling up her music nervously, she escaped from the room. The most vigorous clapping came from the four young men in the doorway who had gone away to the refreshment-room at the beginning of the piece but had come back when the piano had stopped.

101 Lancers were arranged. Gabriel found himself partnered with Miss Ivors. She was a frank-mannered talkative young lady, with a freckled face and prominent brown eyes. She did not wear a low cut bodice and the large brooch which was fixed in the front of her collar bore on it an Irish device.

102 When they had taken their places she said abruptly:

103 —I have a crow to pluck with you.

104 —With me? said Gabriel.

105 She nodded her head gravely.

106 —What is it? asked Gabriel, smiling at her solemn manner.

107 —Who is G. C.? answered Miss Ivors, turning her eyes upon him.

108 Gabriel coloured and was about to knit his brows, as if he did not understand, when she said bluntly:

109 —O, innocent Amy! I have found out that you write for *The Daily Express*. Now, aren't you ashamed of yourself?

110 —Why should I be ashamed of myself? asked Gabriel, blinking his eyes and trying to smile.

111 —Well, I'm ashamed of you, said Miss Ivors frankly. To say you'd write for a rag like that. I didn't think you were a West Briton.

112 A look of perplexity appeared on Gabriel's face. It was true that he wrote a literary column every Wednesday in *The Daily Express*, for which he was paid fifteen shillings. But that did not make him a West Briton surely. The books he received for review were almost more welcome than the paltry cheque.

He loved to feel the covers and turn over the pages of newly printed books. Nearly every day when his teaching in the college was ended he used to wander down the quays to the second-hand booksellers, to Hickey's on Bachelor's Walk, to Webb's or Massey's on Aston's Quay, or to O'Clohissey's in the by-street. He did not know how to meet her charge. He wanted to say that literature was above politics. But they were friends of many years' standing and their careers had been parallel, first at the University and then as teachers: he could not risk a grandiose phrase with her. He continued blinking his eyes and trying to smile and murmured lamely that he saw nothing political in writing reviews of books.

113 When their turn to cross had come he was still perplexed and inattentive. Miss Ivors promptly took his hand in a warm grasp and said in a soft friendly tone:

114 —Of course, I was only joking. Come, we cross now.

115 When they were together again she spoke of the University question and Gabriel felt more at ease. A friend of hers had shown her his review of Browning's poems. That was how she had found out the secret: but she liked the review immensely. Then she said suddenly:

116 —O, Mr Conroy, will you come for an excursion to the Aran Isles this summer? We're going to stay there a whole month. It will be splendid out in the Atlantic. You ought to come. Mr Clancy is coming, and Mr Kilkelly and Kathleen Kearney. It would be splendid for Gretta too if she'd come. She's from Connacht, isn't she?

117 —Her people are, said Gabriel shortly.

118 —But you will come, won't you? said Miss Ivors, laying her warm hand eagerly on his arm.

119 —The fact is, said Gabriel, I have already arranged to go—

120 —Go where? asked Miss Ivors.

121 —Well, you know, every year I go for a cycling tour with some fellows and so—

122 —But where? asked Miss Ivors.

123 —Well, we usually go to France or Belgium or perhaps Germany, said Gabriel awkwardly.

124 —And why do you go to France and Belgium, said Miss Ivors, instead of visiting your own land?

125 —Well, said Gabriel, it's partly to keep in touch with the languages and partly for a change.

126 —And haven't you your own language to keep in touch with—Irish? asked Miss Ivors.

127 —Well, said Gabriel, if it comes to that, you know, Irish is not my language.

128 Their neighbours had turned to listen to the cross-examination. Gabriel glanced right and left nervously and tried to keep his good humour under the ordeal which was making a blush invade his forehead.

129 —And haven't you your own land to visit, continued Miss Ivors, that you know nothing of, your own people, and your own country?

130 —O, to tell you the truth, retorted Gabriel suddenly, I'm sick of my own country, sick of it!

131 —Why? asked Miss Ivors.

132 Gabriel did not answer for his retort had heated him.

133 —Why? repeated Miss Ivors.

134 They had to go visiting together and, as he had not answered her, Miss Ivors said warmly:

135 —Of course, you've no answer.

136 Gabriel tried to cover his agitation by taking part in the dance with great energy. He avoided her eyes for he had seen a sour expression on her face. But when they met in the long chain he was surprised to feel his hand firmly pressed. She looked at him from under her brows for a moment quizzically until he smiled. Then, just as the chain was about to start again, she stood on tiptoe and whispered into his ear:

137 —West Briton!

138 When the lancers were over Gabriel went away to a remote corner of the room where Freddy Malins' mother was sitting. She was a stout feeble old woman with white hair. Her voice had a catch in it like her son's and she stuttered slightly. She had been told that Freddy had come and that he was nearly all right. Gabriel asked her whether she had had a good crossing. She lived with her married daughter in Glasgow and came to Dublin on a visit once a year. She answered placidly that she had had a beautiful crossing and that the captain had been most attentive to her. She spoke also of the beautiful house her daughter kept in Glasgow, and of all the nice friends they had there. While her tongue rambled on Gabriel tried to banish from his mind all memory of the unpleasant incident with Miss Ivors. Of course the girl or woman, or whatever she was, was an enthusiast but there was a time for all things. Perhaps he ought not to have answered her like that. But she had no right to call him a West Briton before people, even in joke. She had tried to make him ridiculous before people, heckling him and staring at him with her rabbit's eyes.

139 He saw his wife making her way towards him through the waltzing couples. When she reached him she said into his ear:

140 —Gabriel, Aunt Kate wants to know won't you carve the goose as usual. Miss Daly will carve the ham and I'll do the pudding.

141 —All right, said Gabriel.

142 —She's sending in the younger ones first as soon as this waltz is over so that we'll have the tables to ourselves.

143 —Were you dancing? asked Gabriel.

144 —Of course I was. Didn't you see me? What words had you with Molly Ivors?

145 —No words. Why? Did she say so?

146 —Something like that. I'm trying to get that Mr D'Arcy to sing. He's full of conceit, I think.

147 —There were no words, said Gabriel moodily, only she wanted me to go for a trip to the west of Ireland and I said I wouldn't.

148 His wife clasped her hands excitedly and gave a little jump.

149 —O, do go, Gabriel, she cried. I'd love to see Galway again.

150 —You can go if you like, said Gabriel coldly.

151 She looked at him for a moment, then turned to Mrs Malins and said:

152 —There's a nice husband for you, Mrs Malins.

153 While she was threading her way back across the room Mrs Malins, without adverting to the interruption, went on to tell Gabriel what beautiful places there were in Scotland and beautiful scenery. Her son-in-law brought them every year to the lakes and they used to go fishing. Her son-in-law was a splendid fisher. One day he caught a fish, a beautiful big big fish, and the man in the hotel boiled it for their dinner.

154 Gabriel hardly heard what she said. Now that supper was coming near he began to think again about his speech and about the quotation. When he saw Freddy Malins coming across the room to visit his mother Gabriel left the chair free for him and retired into the embrasure of the window. The room had already cleared and from the back room came the clatter of plates and knives. Those who still remained in the drawing-room seemed tired of dancing and were conversing quietly in little groups. Gabriel's warm trembling fingers tapped the cold pane of the window. How cool it must be outside! How pleasant it would be to walk out alone, first along by the river and then through the park! The snow would be lying on the branches of the trees and forming a bright cap on the top of the Wellington Monument. How much more pleasant it would be there than at the supper-table!

155 He ran over the headings of his speech: Irish hospitality, sad memories, the Three Graces, Paris, the quotation from Browning. He repeated to himself a phrase he had written in his review: *One feels that one is listening to a thought-tormented music.* Miss Ivors had praised the review. Was she sincere? Had she really any life of her own behind all her propagandism. There had never been any ill-feeling between them until that night. It unnerved him to think that she would be at the supper-table, looking up at him while he spoke with her critical quizzing eyes. Perhaps she would not be sorry to see him fail

in his speech. An idea came into his mind and gave him courage. He would say, alluding to Aunt Kate and Aunt Julia: *Ladies and Gentlemen, the generation which is now on the wane among us may have had its faults but for my part I think it had certain qualities of hospitality, of humour, of humanity, which the new and very serious and hypereducated generation that is growing up around us seems to me to lack.* Very good: that was one for Miss Ivors. What did he care that his aunts were only two ignorant old women

156 A murmur in the room attracted his attention. Mr Browne was advancing from the door, gallantly escorting Aunt Julia, who leaned upon his arm, smiling and hanging her head. An irregular musketry of applause escorted her also as far as the piano and then, as Mary Jane seated herself on the stool, and Aunt Julia, no longer smiling, half turned so as to pitch her voice fairly into the room, gradually ceased. Gabriel recognised the prelude. It was that of an old song of Aunt Julia's—*Arrayed for the Bridal.* Her voice, strong and clear in tone, attacked with great spirit the runs which embellish the air and though she sang very rapidly she did not miss even the smallest of the grace notes. To follow the voice, without looking at the singer's face, was to feel and share the excitement of swift and secure flight. Gabriel applauded loudly with all the others at the close of the song and loud applause was borne in from the invisible supper-table. It sounded so genuine that a little colour struggled into Aunt Julia's face as she bent to replace in the music-stand the old leather-bound songbook that had her initials on the cover. Freddy Malins, who had listened with his head perched sideways to hear her better, was still applauding when everyone else had ceased and talking animatedly to his mother who nodded her head gravely and slowly in acquiescence. At last, when he could clap no more, he stood up suddenly and hurried across the room to Aunt Julia whose hand he seized and held in both his hands, shaking it when words failed him or the catch in his voice proved too much for him.

157 —I was just telling my mother, he said, I never heard you sing so well, never. No, I never heard your voice so good as it is to-night. Now! Would you believe that now! That's the truth. Upon my word and honour that's the truth. I never heard your voice sound so fresh and so . . . so clear and fresh, never.

158 Aunt Julia smiled broadly and murmured something about compliments as she released her hand from his grasp. Mr Browne extended his open hand towards her and said to those who were near him in the manner of a showman introducing a prodigy to an audience:

159 —Miss Julia Morkan, my latest discovery!

160 He was laughing very heartily at this himself when Freddy Malins turned to him and said:

161 —Well, Browne, if you're serious you might make a worse discovery. All I can say is I never heard her sing half so well as long as I am coming here. And that's the honest truth.

162 —Neither did I, said Mr Browne. I think her voice has greatly improved.

163 Aunt Julia shrugged her shoulders and said with meek pride:

164 —Thirty years ago I hadn't a bad voice as voices go.

165 —I often told Julia, said Aunt Kate emphatically, that she was simply thrown away in that choir. But she never would be said by me.

166 She turned as if to appeal to the good sense of the others against a refractory child while Aunt Julia gazed in front of her, a vague smile of reminiscence playing on her face.

167 —No, continued Aunt Kate, she wouldn't be said or led by anyone, slaving there in that choir night and day, night and day. Six o'clock on Christmas morning! And all for what?

168 —Well, isn't it for the honour of God, Aunt Kate? asked Mary Jane, twisting round on the piano-stool and smiling.

169 Aunt Kate turned fiercely on her niece and said:

170 —I know all about the honour of God, Mary Jane, but I think it's not at all honourable for the pope to turn out the women out of the choirs that have slaved there all their lives and put little whipper-snappers of boys over their heads. I suppose it is for the good of the Church if the pope does it. But it's not just, Mary Jane, and it's not right.

171 She had worked herself into a passion and would have continued in defence of her sister for it was a sore subject with her but Mary Jane, seeing that all the dancers had come back, intervened pacifically:

172 —Now, Aunt Kate, you're giving scandal to Mr Browne who is of the other persuasion.

173 Aunt Kate turned to Mr Browne, who was grinning at this allusion to his religion, and said hastily:

174 —O, I don't question the pope's being right. I'm only a stupid old woman and I wouldn't presume to do such a thing. But there's such a thing as common everyday politeness and gratitude. And if I were in Julia's place I'd tell that Father Healy straight up to his face . . .

175 —And besides, Aunt Kate, said Mary Jane, we really are all hungry and when we are hungry we are all very quarrelsome.

176 —And when we are thirsty we are also quarrelsome, added Mr Browne.

177 —So that we had better go to supper, said Mary Jane, and finish the discussion afterwards.

178 On the landing outside the drawing-room Gabriel found his wife and Mary Jane trying to persuade Miss Ivors to stay for supper. But Miss Ivors, who

had put on her hat and was buttoning her cloak, would not stay. She did not feel in the least hungry and she had already overstayed her time.

179 —But only for ten minutes, Molly, said Mrs Conroy. That won't delay you.

180 —To take a pick itself, said Mary Jane, after all your dancing.

181 —I really couldn't, said Miss Ivors.

182 —I am afraid you didn't enjoy yourself at all, said Mary Jane hopelessly.

183 —Ever so much, I assure you, said Miss Ivors, but you really must let me run off now.

184 —But how can you get home? asked Mrs Conroy.

185 —O, it's only two steps up the quay.

186 Gabriel hesitated a moment and said:

187 —If you will allow me, Miss Ivors, I'll see you home if you really are obliged to go.

188 But Miss Ivors broke away from them.

189 —I won't hear of it, she cried. For goodness sake go in to your suppers and don't mind me. I'm quite well able to take care of myself.

190 —Well, you're the comical girl, Molly, said Mrs Conroy frankly.

191 —*Beannacht libh,*° cried Miss Ivors, with a laugh, as she ran down the staircase.

192 Mary Jane gazed after her, a moody puzzled expression on her face, while Mrs Conroy leaned over the banisters to listen for the hall-door. Gabriel asked himself was he the cause of her abrupt departure. But she did not seem to be in ill humour: she had gone away laughing. He stared blankly down the staircase.

193 At that moment Aunt Kate came toddling out of the supper-room, almost wringing her hands in despair.

194 —Where is Gabriel? she cried. Where on earth is Gabriel? There's everyone waiting in there, stage to let, and nobody to carve the goose!

195 —Here I am, Aunt Kate! cried Gabriel, with sudden animation, ready to carve a flock of geese, if necessary.

196 A fat brown goose lay at one end of the table and at the other end, on a bed of creased paper strewn with sprigs of parsley, lay a great ham, stripped of its outer skin and peppered over with crust crumbs, a neat paper frill round its shin and beside this was a round of spiced beef. Between these rival ends ran parallel lines of side-dishes: two little minsters of jelly, red and yellow; a shallow dish full of blocks of blancmange and red jam, a large green leaf-shaped dish with a stalk-shaped handle, on which lay bunches of purple raisins and peeled almonds, a companion dish on which lay a solid rectangle of Smyrna figs, a dish of custard topped with grated nutmeg, a small bowl full of chocolates and

---

Beannacht libh A blessing on you

sweets wrapped in gold and silver papers and a glass vase in which stood some tall celery stalks. In the centre of the table there stood, as sentries to a fruit-stand which upheld a pyramid of oranges and American apples, two squat old-fashioned decanters of cut glass, one containing port and the other dark sherry. On the closed square piano a pudding in a huge yellow dish lay in waiting and behind it were three squads of bottles of stout and ale and minerals, drawn up according to the colours of their uniforms, the first two black, with brown and red labels, the third and smallest squad white, with transverse green sashes.

197 Gabriel took his seat boldly at the head of the table and, having looked to the edge of the carver, plunged his fork firmly into the goose. He felt quite at ease now for he was an expert carver and liked nothing better than to find himself at the head of a well-laden table.

198 —Miss Furlong, what shall I send you? he asked. A wing or a slice of the breast?

199 —Just a small slice of the breast.

200 —Miss Higgins, what for you?

201 —O, anything at all, Mr Conroy.

202 While Gabriel and Miss Daly exchanged plates of goose and plates of ham and spiced beef Lily went from guest to guest with a dish of hot floury potatoes wrapped in a white napkin. This was Mary Jane's idea and she had also suggested apple sauce for the goose but Aunt Kate had said that plain roast goose without apple sauce had always been good enough for her and she hoped she might never eat worse. Mary Jane waited on her pupils and saw that they got the best slices and Aunt Kate and Aunt Julia opened and carried across from the piano bottles of stout and ale for the gentlemen and bottles of minerals for the ladies. There was a great deal of confusion and laughter and noise, the noise of orders and counter-orders, of knives and forks, of corks and glass-stoppers. Gabriel began to carve second helpings as soon as he had finished the first round without serving himself. Everyone protested loudly so that he compromised by taking a long draught of stout for he had found the carving hot work. Mary Jane settled down quietly to her supper but Aunt Kate and Aunt Julia were still toddling round the table, walking on each other's heels, getting in each other's way and giving each other unheeded orders. Mr Browne begged of them to sit down and eat their suppers and so did Gabriel but they said there was time enough so that, at last, Freddy Malins stood up and, capturing Aunt Kate, plumped her down on her chair amid general laughter.

203 When everyone had been well served Gabriel said, smiling:

204 —Now, if anyone wants a little more of what vulgar people call stuffing let him or her speak.

205 A chorus of voices invited him to begin his own supper and Lily came forward with three potatoes which she had reserved for him.

206 —Very well, said Gabriel amiably, as he took another preparatory draught, kindly forget my existence, ladies and gentlemen, for a few minutes.

207 He set to his supper and took no part in the conversation with which the table covered Lily's removal of the plates. The subject of talk was the opera company which was then at the Theatre Royal. Mr Bartell D'Arcy, the tenor, a dark-complexioned young man with a smart moustache, praised very highly the leading contralto of the company but Miss Furlong thought she had a rather vulgar style of production. Freddy Malins said there was a negro chieftain singing in the second part of the Gaiety pantomime who had one of the finest tenor voices he had ever heard.

208 —Have you heard him? he asked Mr Bartell D'Arcy across the table.

209 —No, answered Mr Bartell D'Arcy carelessly.

210 —Because, Freddy Malins explained, now I'd be curious to hear your opinion of him. I think he has a grand voice.

211 —It takes Teddy to find out the really good things, said Mr Browne familiarly to the table.

212 —And why couldn't he have a voice too? asked Freddy Malins sharply. Is it because he's only a black?

213 Nobody answered this question and Mary Jane led the table back to the legitimate opera. One of her pupils had given her a pass for *Mignon.* Of course it was very fine, she said, but it made her think of poor Georgina Burns. Mr Browne could go back farther still, to the old Italian companies that used to come to Dublin—Tietjens, Ilma de Murzka, Campanini, the great Trebelli, Giuglini, Ravelli, Aramburo. Those were the days, he said, when there was something like singing to be heard in Dublin. He told too of how the top gallery of the old Royal used to be packed night after night, of how one night an Italian tenor had sung five encores to *Let Me Like A Soldier Fall,* introducing a high C every time, and of how the gallery boys would sometimes in their enthusiasm unyoke the horses from the carriage of some great *prima donna* and pull her themselves through the streets to her hotel. Why did they never play the grand old operas now, he asked, *Dinorah, Lucrezia Borgia?* Because they could not get the voices to sing them: that was why.

214 —O, well, said Mr Bartell D'Arcy, I presume there are as good singers today as there were then.

215 —Where are they? asked Mr Browne defiantly.

216 —In London, Paris, Milan, said Mr Bartell D'Arcy warmly. I suppose Caruso, for example, is quite as good, if not better than any of the men you have mentioned.

217 —Maybe so, said Mr Browne. But I may tell you I doubt it strongly.

218 —O, I'd give anything to hear Caruso sing, said Mary Jane.

219 —For me, said Aunt Kate, who had been picking a bone, there was only one tenor. To please me, I mean. But I suppose none of you ever heard of him.

220 —Who was he, Miss Morkan? asked Mr Bartell D'Arcy politely.

221 —His name, said Aunt Kate, was Parkinson. I heard him when he was in his prime and I think he had then the purest tenor voice that was ever put into a man's throat.

222 —Strange, said Mr Bartell D'Arcy. I never even heard of him.

223 —Yes, yes, Miss Morkan is right, said Mr Browne. I remember hearing of old Parkinson but he's too far back for me.

224 —A beautiful pure sweet mellow English tenor, said Aunt Kate with enthusiasm.

225 Gabriel having finished, the huge pudding was transferred to the table. The clatter of forks and spoons began again. Gabriel's wife served out spoonfuls of the pudding and passed the plates down the table. Midway down they were held up by Mary Jane, who replenished them with raspberry or orange jelly or with blancmange and jam. The pudding was of Aunt Julia's making and she received praises for it from all quarters. She herself said that it was not quite brown enough.

226 —Well, I hope, Miss Morkan, said Mr Browne, that I'm brown enough for you because, you know, I'm all brown.

227 All the gentlemen, except Gabriel, ate some of the pudding out of compliment to Aunt Julia. As Gabriel never ate sweets the celery had been left for him. Freddy Malins also took a stalk of celery and ate it with his pudding. He had been told that celery was a capital thing for the blood and he was just then under the doctor's care. Mrs Malins, who had been silent all through the supper, said that her son was going down to Mount Melleray in a week or so. The table then spoke of Mount Melleray, how bracing the air was down there, how hospitable the monks were and how they never asked for a penny-piece from their guests.

228 —And do you mean to say, asked Mr Browne incredulously, that a chap can go down there and put up there as if it were a hotel and live on the fat of the land and then come away without paying a farthing?

229 —O, most people give some donation to the monastery when they leave, said Mary Jane.

230 —I wish we had an institution like that in our Church, said Mr Browne candidly.

231 He was astonished to hear that the monks never spoke, got up at two in the morning and slept in their coffins. He asked what they did it for.

232 —That's the rule of the order, said Aunt Kate firmly.

233 —Yes, but why? asked Mr Browne.

234 Aunt Kate repeated that it was the rule, that was all. Mr Browne still seemed not to understand. Freddy Malins explained to him, as best he could, that the monks were trying to make up for the sins committed by all the sinners in the outside world. The explanation was not very clear for Mr Browne grinned and said:

235 —I like that idea very much but wouldn't a comfortable spring bed do them as well as a coffin?

236 —The coffin, said Mary Jane, is to remind them of their last end.

237 As the subject had grown lugubrious it was buried in a silence of the table during which Mrs Malins could be heard saying to her neighbour in an indistinct undertone:

238 —They are very good men, the monks, very pious men.

239 The raisins and almonds and figs and apples and oranges and chocolates and sweets were now passed about the table and Aunt Julia invited all the guests to have either port or sherry. At first Mr Bartell D'Arcy refused to take either but one of his neighbours nudged him and whispered something to him upon which he allowed his glass to be filled. Gradually as the last glasses were being filled the conversation ceased. A pause followed, broken only by the noise of the wine and by unsettlings of chairs. The Misses Morkan, all three, looked down at the tablecloth. Someone coughed once or twice and then a few gentlemen patted the table gently as a signal for silence. The silence came and Gabriel pushed back his chair and stood up.

240 The patting at once grew louder in encouragement and then ceased altogether. Gabriel leaned his ten trembling fingers on the tablecloth and smiled nervously at the company. Meeting a row of upturned faces he raised his eyes to the chandelier. The piano was playing a waltz tune and he could hear the skirts sweeping against the drawing-room door. People, perhaps, were standing in the snow on the quay outside, gazing up at the lighted windows and listening to the waltz music. The air was pure there. In the distance lay the park where the trees were weighted with snow. The Wellington Monument wore a gleaming cap of snow that flashed westward over the white field of Fifteen Acres.

241 He began:

242 —Ladies and Gentlemen.

243 —It has fallen to my lot this evening, as in years past, to perform a very pleasing task but a task for which I am afraid my poor powers as a speaker are all too inadequate.

244 —No, no! said Mr Browne.

245 —But, however that may be, I can only ask you to-night to take the will for the deed and to lend me your attention for a few moments while I endeavour to express to you in words what my feelings are on this occasion.

246 —Ladies and Gentlemen. It is not the first time that we have gathered together under this hospitable roof, around this hospitable board. It is not the first time that we have been the recipients—or perhaps, I had better say, the victims—of the hospitality of certain good ladies.

247 He made a circle in the air with his arm and paused. Everyone laughed or smiled at Aunt Kate and Aunt Julia and Mary Jane who all turned crimson with pleasure. Gabriel went on more boldly:

248 —I feel more strongly with every recurring year that our country has no tradition which does it so much honour and which it should guard so jealously as that of its hospitality. It is a tradition that is unique as far as my experience goes (and I have visited not a few places abroad) among the modern nations. Some would say, perhaps, that with us it is rather a failing than anything to be boasted of. But granted even that, it is, to my mind, a princely failing, and one that I trust will long be cultivated among us. Of one thing, at least, I am sure. As long as this one roof shelters the good ladies aforesaid—and I wish from my heart it may do so for many and many a long year to come—the tradition of genuine warm-hearted courteous Irish hospitality, which our forefathers have handed down to us and which we in turn must hand down to our descendants, is still alive among us.

249 A hearty murmur of assent ran round the table. It shot through Gabriel's mind that Miss Ivors was not there and that she had gone away discourteously: and he said with confidence in himself:

250 —Ladies and Gentlemen.

251 —A new generation is growing up in our midst, a generation actuated by new ideas and new principles. It is serious and enthusiastic for these new ideas and its enthusiasm, even when it is misdirected, is, I believe, in the main sincere. But we are living in a skeptical and, if I may use the phrase, a thought-tormented age: and sometimes I fear that this new generation, educated or hypereducated as it is, will lack those qualities of humanity, of hospitality, of kindly humour which belonged to an older day. Listening tonight to the names of all those great singers of the past it seemed to me, I must confess, that we were living in a less spacious age. Those days might, without exaggeration, be called spacious days: and if they are gone beyond recall let us hope, at least, that in gatherings such as this we shall still speak of them with pride and affection, still cherish in our hearts the memory of those dead and gone great ones whose fame the world will not willingly let die.

252 —Hear, hear! said Mr Browne loudly.

253 —But yet, continued Gabriel, his voice falling into a softer inflection, there are always in gatherings such as this sadder thoughts that will recur to our minds: thoughts of the past, of youth, of changes, of absent faces that we miss here to-night. Our path through life is strewn with many such sad memories:

and were we to brood upon them always we could not find the heart to go on bravely with our work among the living. We have all of us living duties and living affections which claim, and rightly claim, our strenuous endeavours.

254 —Therefore, I will not linger on the past. I will not let any gloomy moralising intrude upon us here to-night. Here we are gathered together for a brief moment from the bustle and rush of our everyday routine. We are met here as friends, in the spirit of good-fellowship, as colleagues, also to a certain extent, in the true spirit of *camaraderie*, and as the guests of—what shall I call them?—the Three Graces of the Dublin musical world.

255 The table burst into applause and laughter at this sally. Aunt Julia vainly asked each of her neighbours in turn to tell her what Gabriel had said.

256 —He says we are the Three Graces, Aunt Julia, said Mary Jane.

257 Aunt Julia did not understand but she looked up, smiling, at Gabriel, who continued in the same vein:

258 —Ladies and Gentlemen.

259 —I will not attempt to play to-night the part that Paris played on another occasion. I will not attempt to choose between them. The task would be an invidious one and one beyond my poor powers. For when I view them in turn, whether it be our chief hostess herself, whose good heart, whose too good heart, has become a byword with all who know her, or her sister, who seems to be gifted with perennial youth and whose singing must have been a surprise and a revelation to us all tonight, or, last but not least, when I consider our youngest hostess, talented, cheerful, hard-working and the best of nieces, I confess, Ladies and Gentlemen, that I do not know to which of them I should award the prize.

260 Gabriel glanced down at his aunts and, seeing the large smile on Aunt Julia's face and the tears which had risen to Aunt Kate's eyes, hastened to close. He raised his glass of port gallantly, while every member of the company fingered a glass expectantly, and said loudly:

261 —Let us toast them all three together. Let us drink to their health, wealth, long life, happiness and prosperity and may they long continue to hold the proud and self-won position which they hold in their profession and the position of honour and affection which they hold in our hearts.

262 All the guests stood up, glass in hand, and, turning towards the three seated ladies, sang in unison, with Mr Browne as leader:

263 *For they are jolly gay fellows,*
For they are jolly gay fellows,
For they are jolly gay fellows,
Which nobody can deny.

264 Aunt Kate was making frank use of her handkerchief and even Aunt Julia seemed moved. Freddy Malins beat time with his pudding-fork and the singers turned towards one another, as if in melodious conference, while they sang, with emphasis:

265 *Unless he tells a lie,*
Unless he tells a lie.

266 Then, turning once more towards their hostesses, they sang:

267 *For they are jolly gay fellows,*
For they are jolly gay fellows,
For they are jolly gay fellows,
Which nobody can deny.

268 The acclamation which followed was taken up beyond the door of the supper-room by many of the other guests and renewed time after time, Freddy Malins acting as officer with his fork on high.

269 The piercing morning air came into the hall where they were standing so that Aunt Kate said:

270 —Close the door, somebody. Mrs Malins will get her death of cold.

271 —Browne is out there, Aunt Kate, said Mary Jane.

272 —Browne is everywhere, said Aunt Kate, lowering her voice.

273 Mary Jane laughed at her tone.

274 —Really, she said archly, he is very attentive.

275 —He has been laid on here like the gas, said Aunt Kate in the same tone, all during the Christmas.

276 She laughed herself this time good-humouredly and then added quickly:

277 —But tell him to come in, Mary Jane, and close the door. I hope to goodness he didn't hear me.

278 At that moment the hall-door was opened and Mr Browne came in from the doorstep, laughing as if his heart would break. He was dressed in a long green overcoat with mock astrakhan cuffs and collar and wore on his head an oval fur cap. He pointed down the snow-covered quay from where the sound of shrill prolonged whistling was borne in.

279 —Teddy will have all the cabs in Dublin out, he said.

280 Gabriel advanced from the little pantry behind the office, struggling into his overcoat and, looking round the hall, said:

281 —Gretta not down yet?

282 —She's getting on her things, Gabriel, said Aunt Kate.

283 —Who's playing up there? asked Gabriel.

284 —Nobody. They're all gone.

285 —O no, Aunt Kate, said Mary Jane. Bartell D'Arcy and Miss O'Callaghan aren't gone yet.

286 —Someone is strumming at the piano, anyhow, said Gabriel.

287 Mary Jane glanced at Gabriel and Mr Browne and said with a shiver:

288 —It makes me feel cold to look at you two gentlemen muffled up like that. I wouldn't like to face your journey home at this hour.

289 —I'd like nothing better this minute, said Mr Browne stoutly, than a rattling fine walk in the country or a fast drive with a good spanking goer between the shafts.

290 —We used to have a very good horse and trap at home, said Aunt Julia sadly.

291 —The never-to-be-forgotten Johnny, said Mary Jane, laughing.

292 Aunt Kate and Gabriel laughed too.

293 —Why, what was wonderful about Johnny? asked Mr Browne.

294 —The late lamented Patrick Morkan, our grandfather, that is, explained Gabriel, commonly known in his later years as the old gentleman, was a glue boiler.

295 —O, now, Gabriel, said Aunt Kate, laughing, he had a starch mill.

296 —Well, glue or starch, said Gabriel, the old gentleman had a horse by the name of Johnny. And Johnny used to work in the old gentleman's mill, walking round and round in order to drive the mill. That was all very well; but now comes the tragic part about Johnny. One fine day the old gentleman thought he'd like to drive out with the quality to a military review in the park.

297 —The Lord have mercy on his soul, said Aunt Kate compassionately.

298 —Amen, said Gabriel. So the old gentleman, as I said, harnessed Johnny and put on his very best tall hat and his very best stock collar and drove out in grand style from his ancestral mansion somewhere near Back Lane, I think.

299 Everyone laughed, even Mrs Malins, at Gabriel's manner and Aunt Kate said:

300 —O now, Gabriel, he didn't live in Back Lane, really. Only the mill was there.

301 —Out from the mansion of his forefathers, continued Gabriel, he drove with Johnny. And everything went on beautifully until Johnny came in sight of King Billy's statue: and whether he fell in love with the horse King Billy sits on or whether he thought he was back again in the mill, anyhow he began to walk round the statue.

302 Gabriel paced in a circle round the hall in his goloshes amid the laughter of the others.

303 —Round and round he went, said Gabriel, and the old gentleman, who was a very pompous old gentleman, was highly indignant. *Go on, sir! What do you mean, sir? Johnny! Johnny! Most extraordinary conduct! Can't understand the horse!*

304 The peals of laughter which followed Gabriel's imitation of the incident were interrupted by a resounding knock at the hall-door. Mary Jane ran to open it and let in Freddy Malins. Freddy Malins, with his hat well back on his head and his shoulders humped with cold, was puffing and steaming after his exertions.

305 —I could only get one cab, he said.

306 —O, we'll find another along the quay, said Gabriel.

307 —Yes, said Aunt Kate. Better not keep Mrs Malins standing in the draught.

308 Mrs Malins was helped down the front steps by her son and Mr Browne and, after many manœuvres, hoisted into the cab. Freddy Malins clambered in after her and spent a long time settling her on the seat, Mr Browne helping him with advice. At last she was settled comfortably and Freddy Malins invited Mr Browne into the cab. There was a good deal of confused talk, and then Mr Browne got into the cab. The cabman settled his rug over his knees, and bent down for the address. The confusion grew greater and the cabman was directed differently by Freddy Malins and Mr Browne, each of whom had his head out through a window of the cab. The difficulty was to know where to drop Mr Browne along the route and Aunt Kate, Aunt Julia and Mary Jane helped the discussion from the doorstep with cross-directions and contradictions and abundance of laughter. As for Freddy Malins he was speechless with laughter. He popped his head in and out of the window every moment, to the great danger of his hat, and told his mother how the discussion was progressing till at last Mr Browne shouted to the bewildered cabman above the din of everybody's laughter:

309 —Do you know Trinity College?

310 —Yes, sir, said the cabman.

311 —Well, drive bang up against Trinity College gates, said Mr Browne, and then we'll tell you where to go. You understand now?

312 —Yes, sir, said the cabman.

313 —Make like a bird for Trinity College.

314 —Right, sir, cried the cabman.

315 The horse was whipped up and the cab rattled off along the quay amid a chorus of laughter and adieus.

316 Gabriel had not gone to the door with the others. He was in a dark part of the hall gazing up the staircase. A woman was standing near the top of the first flight, in the shadow also. He could not see her face but he could see the terra-

cotta and salmonpink panels of her skirt which the shadow made appear black and white. It was his wife. She was leaning on the banisters, listening to something. Gabriel was surprised at her stillness and strained his ear to listen also. But he could hear little save the noise of laughter and dispute on the front steps, a few chords struck on the piano and a few notes of a man's voice singing.

317 He stood still in the gloom of the hall, trying to catch the air that the voice was singing and gazing up at his wife. There was grace and mystery in her attitude as if she were a symbol of something. He asked himself what is a woman standing on the stairs in the shadow, listening to distant music, a symbol of. If he were a painter he would paint her in that attitude. Her blue felt hat would show off the bronze of her hair against the darkness and the dark panels of her skirt would show off the light ones. *Distant Music* he would call the picture if he were a painter.

318 The hall-door closed; and Aunt Kate, Aunt Julia and Mary Jane came down the hall, still laughing.

319 —Well, isn't Freddy terrible? said Mary Jane. He's really terrible.

320 Gabriel said nothing but pointed up the stairs towards where his wife was standing. Now that the hall-door was closed the voice and the piano could be heard more clearly. Gabriel held up his hand for them to be silent. The song seemed to be in the old Irish tonality and the singer seemed uncertain both of his words and of his voice. The voice, made plaintive by distance and by the singer's hoarseness, faintly illuminated the cadence of the air with words expressing grief:

321 *O, the rain falls on my heavy locks*
And the dew wets my skin,
My babe lies cold . . .

322 —O, exclaimed Mary Jane. It's Bartell D'Arcy singing and he wouldn't sing all the night. O, I'll get him to sing a song before he goes.

323 —O do, Mary Jane, said Aunt Kate.

324 Mary Jane brushed past the others and ran to the staircase but before she reached it the singing stopped and the piano was closed abruptly.

325 —O, what a pity! she cried. Is he coming down, Gretta?

326 Gabriel heard his wife answer yes and saw her come down towards them. A few steps behind her were Mr Bartell D'Arcy and Miss O'Callaghan.

327 —O, Mr D'Arcy, cried Mary Jane, it's downright mean of you to break off like that when we were all in raptures listening to you.

328 —I have been at him all the evening, said Miss O'Callaghan, and Mrs Conroy too and he told us he had a dreadful cold and couldn't sing.

329 —O, Mr D'Arcy, said Aunt Kate, now that was a great fib to tell.

330 —Can't you see that I'm as hoarse as a crow? said Mr D'Arcy roughly.

331 He went into the pantry hastily and put on his overcoat. The others, taken aback by his rude speech, could find nothing to say. Aunt Kate wrinkled her brows and made signs to the others to drop the subject. Mr D'Arcy stood swathing his neck carefully and frowning.

332 —It's the weather, said Aunt Julia, after a pause.

333 —Yes, everybody has colds, said Aunt Kate readily, everybody.

334 —They say, said Mary Jane, we haven't had snow like it for thirty years; and I read this morning in the newspapers that the snow is general all over Ireland.

335 —I love the look of snow, said Aunt Julia sadly.

336 —So do I, said Miss O'Callaghan. I think Christmas is never really Christmas unless we have the snow on the ground.

337 —But poor Mr D'Arcy doesn't like the snow, said Aunt Kate, smiling.

338 Mr D'Arcy came from the pantry, fully swathed and buttoned, and in a repentant tone told them the history of the cold. Everyone gave him advice and said it was a great pity and urged him to be very careful of his throat in the night air. Gabriel watched his wife, who did not join in the conversation. She was standing right under the dusty fanlight and the flame of the gas lit up the rich bronze of her hair which he had seen her drying at the fire a few days before. She was in the same attitude and seemed unaware of the talk about her. At last she turned towards them and Gabriel saw that there was colour on her cheeks and that her eyes were shining. A sudden tide of joy went leaping out of his heart.

339 —Mr D'Arcy, she said, what is the name of that song you were singing?

340 —It's called *The Lass of Aughrim,* said Mr D'Arcy, but I couldn't remember it properly. Why? Do you know it?

341 —*The Lass of Aughrim,* she repeated. I couldn't think of the name.

342 —It's a very nice air, said Mary Jane. I'm sorry you were not in voice tonight.

343 —Now, Mary Jane, said Aunt Kate, don't annoy Mr D'Arcy. I won't have him annoyed.

344 Seeing that all were ready to start she shepherded them to the door where good-night was said:

345 —Well, good-night, Aunt Kate, and thanks for the pleasant evening.

346 —Good-night, Gabriel. Good-night, Gretta!

347 —Good-night, Aunt Kate, and thanks ever so much. Good-night, Aunt Julia.

348 —O, good-night Gretta, I didn't see you.

349 —Good-night, Mr D'Arcy. Good-night, Miss O'Callaghan.

350 —Good-night, Miss Morkan.

351 —Good-night, again.

352 —Good-night, all. Safe home.

353 —Good-night. Good-night.

354 The morning was still dark. A dull yellow light brooded over the houses and the river; and the sky seemed to be descending. It was slushy underfoot; and only streaks and patches of snow lay on the roofs, on the parapets of the quay and on the area railings. The lamps were still burning redly in the murky air and, across the river, the palace of the Four Courts stood out menacingly against the heavy sky.

355 She was walking on before him with Mr Bartell D'Arcy, her shoes in a brown parcel tucked under one arm and her hands holding her skirt up from the slush. She had no longer any grace of attitude but Gabriel's eyes were still bright with happiness. The blood went bounding along his veins; and the thoughts were rioting through his brain, proud, joyful, tender, valorous.

356 She was walking on before him so lightly and so erect that he longed to run after her noiselessly, catch her by the shoulders and say something foolish and affectionate into her ear. She seemed to him so frail that he longed to defend her against something and then to be alone with her. Moments of their secret life together burst like stars upon his memory. A heliotrope envelope was lying beside his breakfast-cup and he was caressing it with his hand. Birds were twittering in the ivy and the sunny web of the curtain was shimmering along the floor: he could not eat for happiness. They were standing on the crowded platform and he was placing a ticket inside the warm palm of her glove. He was standing with her in the cold, looking in through a grated window at a man making bottles in a roaring furnace. It was very cold. Her face, fragrant in the cold air, was quite close to his; and suddenly she called out to the man at the furnace.

357 —Is the fire hot, sir?

358 But the man could not hear her with the noise of the furnace. It was just as well. He might have answered rudely.

359 A wave of yet more tender joy escaped from his heart and went coursing in warm flood along his arteries. Like the tender fires of stars moments of their life together, that no one knew of or would ever know of, broke upon and illumined his memory. He longed to recall to her those moments, to make her forget the years of their dull existence together and remember only their moments of ecstasy. For the years, he felt, had not quenched his soul or hers. Their children, his writing, her household cares had not quenched their souls' tender fire. In one letter that he had written to her then he had said: *Why is it that words like these seem to me so dull and cold? Is it because there is no word tender enough to be your name?*

360 Like distant music these words that he had written years before were borne towards him from the past. He longed to be alone with her. When the others had gone away, when he and she were in their room in the hotel, then they would be alone together. He would call her softly:

361 —Gretta!

362 Perhaps she would not hear at once: she would be undressing. Then something in his voice would strike her. She would turn and look at him . . .

363 At the corner of Winetavern Street they met a cab. He was glad of its rattling noise as it saved him from conversation. She was looking out of the window and seemed tired. The others spoke only a few words, pointing out some building or street. The horse galloped along wearily under the murky morning sky, dragging his old rattling box after his heels, galloping to their honeymoon.

364 As the cab drove across O'Connell Bridge Miss O'Callaghan said:

365 —They say you never cross O'Connell Bridge without seeing a white horse.

366 —I see a white man this time, said Gabriel.

367 —Where? asked Mr Bartell D'Arcy.

368 Gabriel pointed to the statue, on which lay patches of snow. Then he nodded familiarly to it and waved his hand.

369 —Good-night, Dan, he said gaily.

370 When the cab drew up before the hotel Gabriel jumped out and, in spite of Mr Bartell D'Arcy's protest, paid the driver. He gave the man a shilling over his fare. The man saluted and said:

371 —A prosperous New Year to you, sir.

372 —The same to you, said Gabriel cordially.

373 She leaned for a moment on his arm in getting out of the cab and while standing at the curbstone, bidding the others good-night. She leaned lightly on his arm, as lightly as when she had danced with him a few hours before. He had felt proud and happy then, happy that she was his, proud of her grace and wifely carriage. But now, after the kindling again of so many memories, the first touch of her body, musical and strange and perfumed, sent through him a keen pang of lust. Under cover of her silence he pressed her arm closely to his side; and, as they stood at the hotel door, he felt that they had escaped from their lives and duties, escaped from home and friends and run away together with wild and radiant hearts to a new adventure.

374 An old man was dozing in a great hooded chair in the hall. He lit a candle in the office and went before them to the stairs. They followed him in silence, their feet falling in soft thuds on the thickly carpeted stairs. She mounted the stairs behind the porter, her head bowed in the ascent, her frail shoulders curved as with a burden, her skirt girt tightly about her. He could

have flung his arms about her hips and held her still for his arms were trembling with desire to seize her and only the stress of his nails against the palms of his hands held the wild impulse of his body in check. The porter halted on the stairs to settle his guttering candle. They halted too on the steps below him. In the silence Gabriel could hear the falling of the molten wax into the tray and the thumping of his own heart against his ribs.

375 The porter led them along a corridor and opened a door. Then he set his unstable candle down on a toilet-table and asked at what hour they were to be called in the morning.

376 —Eight, said Gabriel.

377 The porter pointed to the tap of the electric-light and began a muttered apology but Gabriel cut him short.

378 —We don't want any light. We have enough light from the street. And I say, he added, pointing to the candle, you might remove that handsome article, like a good man.

379 The porter took up his candle again, but slowly for he was surprised by such a novel idea. Then he mumbled good-night and went out. Gabriel shot the lock to.

380 A ghostly light from the street lamp lay in a long shaft from one window to the door. Gabriel threw his overcoat and hat on a couch and crossed the room towards the window. He looked down into the street in order that his emotion might calm a little. Then he turned and leaned against a chest of drawers with his back to the light. She had taken off her hat and cloak and was standing before a large swinging mirror, unhooking her waist. Gabriel paused for a few moments, watching her, and then said:

381 —Gretta!

382 She turned away from the mirror slowly and walked along the shaft of light towards him. Her face looked so serious and weary that the words would not pass Gabriel's lips. No, it was not the moment yet.

383 —You look tired, he said.

384 —I am a little, she answered.

385 —You don't feel ill or weak?

386 —No, tired; that's all.

387 She went on to the window and stood there, looking out. Gabriel waited again and then, fearing that diffidence was about to conquer him, he said abruptly:

388 —By the way, Gretta!

389 —What is it?

390 —You know that poor fellow Malins? he said quickly.

391 —Yes. What about him?

392 —Well, poor fellow, he's a decent sort of chap after all, continued Gabriel in a false voice. He gave me back that sovereign I lent him and I didn't expect it really. It's a pity he wouldn't keep away from that Browne, because he's not a bad fellow at heart.

393 He was trembling now with annoyance. Why did she seem so abstracted? He did not know how he could begin. Was she annoyed, too, about something? If she would only turn to him or come to him of her own accord! To take her as she was would be brutal. No, he must see some ardour in her eyes first. He longed to be master of her strange mood.

394 —When did you lend him the pound? she asked, after a pause.

395 Gabriel strove to restrain himself from breaking out into brutal language about the sottish Malins and his pound. He longed to cry to her from his soul, to crush her body against his, to overmaster her. But he said:

396 —O, at Christmas, when he opened that little Christmas-card shop in Henry Street.

397 He was in such a fever of rage and desire that he did not hear her come from the window. She stood before him for an instant, looking at him strangely. Then, suddenly raising herself on tiptoe and resting her hands lightly on his shoulders, she kissed him.

398 —You are a very generous person, Gabriel, she said.

399 Gabriel, trembling with delight at her sudden kiss and at the quaintness of her phrase, put his hands on her hair and began smoothing it back, scarcely touching it with his fingers. The washing had made it fine and brilliant. His heart was brimming over with happiness. Just when he was wishing for it she had come to him of her own accord. Perhaps her thoughts had been running with his. Perhaps she had felt the impetuous desire that was in him and then the yielding mood had come upon her. Now that she had fallen to him so easily he wondered why he had been so diffident.

400 He stood, holding her head between his hands. Then, slipping one arm swiftly about her body and drawing her towards him, he said softly:

401 —Gretta, dear, what are you thinking about?

402 She did not answer nor yield wholly to his arm. He said again, softly:

403 —Tell me what it is, Gretta. I think I know what is the matter. Do I know?

404 She did not answer at once. Then she said in an outburst of tears:

405 —O, I am thinking about that song, *The Lass of Aughrim.*

406 She broke loose from him and ran to the bed and, throwing her arms across the bed-rail, hid her face. Gabriel stood stock-still for a moment in astonishment and then followed her. As he passed in the way of the cheval-glass he caught sight of himself in full length, his broad, well-filled shirt-front, the

face whose expression always puzzled him when he saw it in a mirror and his glimmering gilt-rimmed eye glasses. He halted a few paces from her and said:

407 —What about the song? Why does that make you cry?

408 She raised her head from her arms and dried her eyes with the back of her hand like a child. A kinder note than he had intended went into his voice.

409 —Why, Gretta? he asked.

410 —I am thinking about a person long ago who used to sing that song.

411 —And who was the person long ago? asked Gabriel, smiling.

412 —It was a person I used to know in Galway when I was living with my grandmother, she said.

413 The smile passed away from Gabriel's face. A dull anger began to gather again at the back of his mind and the dull fires of his lust began to glow angrily in his veins.

414 —Someone you were in love with? he asked ironically.

415 —It was a young boy I used to know, she answered, named Michael Furey. He used to sing that song, *The Lass of Aughrim.* He was very delicate.

416 Gabriel was silent. He did not wish her to think that he was interested in this delicate boy.

417 —I can see him so plainly, she said after a moment. Such eyes as he had: big dark eyes! And such an expression in them—an expression!

418 —O then, you were in love with him? said Gabriel.

419 —I used to go out walking with him, she said, when I was in Galway.

420 A thought flew across Gabriel's mind.

421 —Perhaps that was why you wanted to go to Galway with that Ivors girl? he said coldly.

422 She looked at him and asked in surprise:

423 —What for?

424 Her eyes made Gabriel feel awkward. He shrugged his shoulders and said:

425 —How do I know? To see him perhaps.

426 She looked away from him along the shaft of light towards the window in silence.

427 —He is dead, she said at length. He died when he was only seventeen. Isn't that a terrible thing to die so young as that?

428 —What was he? asked Gabriel, still ironically.

429 —He was in the gasworks, she said.

430 Gabriel felt humiliated by the failure of his irony and by the evocation of this figure from the dead, a boy in the gasworks. While he had been full of memories of their secret life together, full of tenderness and joy and desire, she had been comparing him in her mind with another. A shameful consciousness of his own person assailed him. He saw himself as a ludicrous figure, acting as a pennyboy for his aunts, a nervous well-meaning sentimentalist, orating to

vulgarians and idealising his own clownish lusts, the pitiable fatuous fellow he had caught a glimpse of in the mirror. Instinctively he turned his back more to the light lest she might see the shame that burned upon his forehead.

431 He tried to keep up his tone of cold interrogation but his voice when he spoke was humble and indifferent.

432 —I suppose you were in love with this Michael Furey, Gretta, he said.

433 —I was great with him at that time, she said.

434 Her voice was veiled and sad. Gabriel, feeling now how vain it would be to try to lead her whither he had purposed, caressed one of her hands and said, also sadly:

435 —And what did he die of so young, Gretta? Consumption, was it?

436 —I think he died for me, she answered.

437 A vague terror seized Gabriel at this answer as if, at that hour when he had hoped to triumph, some impalpable and vindictive being was coming against him, gathering forces against him in its vague world. But he shook himself free of it with an effort of reason and continued to caress her hand. He did not question her again for he felt that she would tell him of herself. Her hand was warm and moist: it did not respond to his touch but he continued to caress it just as he had caressed her first letter to him that spring morning.

438 —It was in the winter, she said, about the beginning of the winter when I was going to leave my grandmother's and come up here to the convent. And he was ill at the time in his lodgings in Galway and wouldn't be let out and his people in Oughterard were written to. He was in decline, they said, or something like that. I never knew rightly.

439 She paused for a moment and sighed.

440 —Poor fellow, she said. He was very fond of me and he was such a gentle boy. We used to go out together, walking, you know, Gabriel, like they way they do in the country. He was going to study singing only for his health. He had a very good voice, poor Michael Furey.

441 —Well; and then? asked Gabriel.

442 —And then when it came to the time for me to leave Galway and come up to the convent he was much worse and I wouldn't be let see him so I wrote a letter saying I was going up to Dublin and would be back in the summer and hoping he would be better then.

443 She paused for a moment to get her voice under control and then went on:

444 —Then the night before I left I was in my grandmother's house in Nuns' Island, packing up, and I heard gravel thrown up against the window. The window was so wet I couldn't see so I ran downstairs as I was and slipped out the back into the garden and there was the poor fellow at the end of the garden, shivering.

445 —And did you not tell him to go back? asked Gabriel.

446 —I implored of him to go home at once and told him he would get his death in the rain. But he said he did not want to live. I can see his eyes as well as well! He was standing at the end of the wall where there was a tree.

447 —And did he go home? asked Gabriel.

448 —Yes, he went home. And when I was only a week in the convent he died and he was buried in Oughterard where his people came from. O, the day I heard that, that he was dead!

449 She stopped, choking with sobs, and, overcome by emotion, flung herself face downward on the bed, sobbing in the quilt. Gabriel held her hand for a moment longer, irresolutely, and then, shy of intruding on her grief, let it fall gently and walked quietly to the window.

450 She was fast asleep.

451 Gabriel, leaning on his elbow, looked for a few moments unresentfully on her tangled hair and half-open mouth, listening to her deep-drawn breath. So she had had that romance in her life: a man had died for her sake. It hardly pained him now to think how poor a part, he, her husband, had played in her life. He watched her while she slept as though he and she had never lived together as man and wife. His curious eyes rested long upon her face and on her hair: and, as he thought of what she must have been then, in that time of her first girlish beauty, a strange friendly pity for her entered his soul. He did not like to say even to himself that her face was no longer beautiful but he knew that it was no longer the face for which Michael Furey had braved death.

452 Perhaps she had not told him all the story. His eyes moved to the chair over which she had thrown some of her clothes. A petticoat string dangled to the floor. One boot stood upright, its limp upper fallen down: the fellow of it lay upon its side. He wondered at his riot of emotions of an hour before. From what had it proceeded? From his aunt's supper, from his own foolish speech, from the wine and dancing, the merry-making when saying good-night in the hall, the pleasure of the walk along the river in the snow. Poor Aunt Julia! She, too, would soon be a shade with the shade of Patrick Morkan and his horse. He had caught that haggard look upon her face for a moment when she was singing *Arrayed for the Bridal.* Soon, perhaps, he would be sitting in that same drawing-room, dressed in black, his silk hat on his knees. The blinds would be drawn down and Aunt Kate would be sitting beside him, crying and blowing her nose and telling him how Julia had died. He would cast about his mind for some words that might console her, and would find only lame and useless ones. Yes, yes: that would happen very soon.

453 The air of the room chilled his shoulders. He stretched himself cautiously along under the sheets and lay down beside his wife. One by one they were all becoming shades. Better pass boldly into that other world, in the full

glory of some passion, than fade and wither dismally with age. He thought of how she who lay beside him had locked in her heart for so many years that image of her lover's eyes when he had told her that he did not wish to live.

454 Generous tears filled Gabriel's eyes. He had never felt like that himself towards any woman but he knew that such a feeling must be love. The tears gathered more thickly in his eyes and in the partial darkness he imagined he saw the form of a young man standing under a dripping tree. Other forms were near. His soul had approached that region where dwell the vast hosts of the dead. He was conscious of, but could not apprehend, their wayward and flickering existence. His own identity was fading out into a grey impalpable world: the solid world itself which these dead had one time reared and lived in was dissolving and dwindling.

455 A few light taps upon the pane made him turn to the window. It had begun to snow again. He watched sleepily the flakes, silver and dark, falling obliquely against the lamplight. The time had come for him to set out on his journey westward. Yes, the newspapers were right: snow was general all over Ireland. It was falling on every part of the dark central plain, on the treeless hills, falling softly upon the Bog of Allen and, farther westward, softly falling into the dark mutinous Shannon waves. It was falling, too, upon every part of the lonely churchyard on the hill where Michael Furey lay buried. It lay thickly drifted on the crooked crosses and headstones, on the spears of the little gate, on the barren thorns. His soul swooned slowly as he heard the snow falling faintly through the universe and faintly falling, like the descent of their last end, upon all the living and the dead.

—1907

✧ ✧ ✧

D. H. Lawrence

(1885-1930)

The Horse Dealer's Daughter

Lawrence's working-class origins in the English Midlands provided him with autobiographical subject matter for *Sons and Lovers* (1913) and characters and setting for novels like *The Rainbow* (1915) and *Women in Love* (1920). Born in Nottinghamshire to a coal miner and a teacher, Lawrence was encouraged in his reading by his mother. After receiving his teaching certificate from University College in Nottingham, Lawrence taught briefly, then began to publish poetry and fiction. His first novel, *The White Peacock*, appeared in 1911. Lawrence's long marriage to Frieda von Richtofen (a cousin of the German "Red Baron" of World War I fame) suffered many strains but endured until his death. Lawrence's interest in Freudian psychology and the dynamics of human sexuality made him controversial during his career and perhaps still overshadows his skills as a chronicler of English life in agricultural villages changed forever by the Industrial Revolution. Still, *Lady Chatterley's Lover* (1928), with its frank language and depictions of sex, remains a landmark in the battle against literary censorship, even though an unexpurgated edition did not appear in England until thirty years after the author's death. *Lady Chatterley's Lover* has proven popular with film makers, with a third version announced in 1992. *Sons and Lovers, Women in Love,* and *The Rainbow* have also been made into films, as have such short stories as "The Rocking Horse Winner" and "The Horse Dealer's Daughter."

"Well, Mabel, and what are you going to do with yourself?" asked Joe, with foolish flippancy. He felt quite safe himself. Without listening for an answer, he turned aside, worked a grain of tobacco to the tip of his tongue and spat it out. He did not care about anything, since he felt safe himself.

2 The three brothers and the sister sat round the desolate breakfast table, attempting some sort of desultory consultation. The morning's post had given the final tap to the family fortune, and all was over. The dreary dining room itself, with its heavy mahogany furniture, looked as if it were waiting to be done away with.

3 But the consultation amounted to nothing. There was a strange air of ineffectuality about the three men, as they sprawled at table, smoking and reflecting vaguely on their own condition. The girl was alone, a rather short, sullen-looking young woman of twenty-seven. She did not share the same life as her brothers. She would have been good-looking, save for the impassive fixity of her face, "bull-dog," as her brothers called it.

4 There was a confused tramping of horses' feet outside. The three men all sprawled round in their chairs to watch. Beyond the dark holly bushes that separated the strip of lawn from the highroad, they could see a cavalcade of shire horses swinging out of their own yard, being taken for exercise. This was the last time. These were the last horses that would go through their hands. The young men watched with critical, callous looks. They were all frightened at the collapse of their lives, and the sense of disaster in which they were involved left them no inner freedom.

5 Yet they were three fine, well-set fellows enough. Joe, the eldest, was a man of thirty-three, broad and handsome in a hot, flushed way. His face was red, he twisted his black moustache over a thick finger, his eyes were shallow and restless. He had a sensual way of uncovering his teeth when he laughed, and his bearing was stupid. Now he watched the horses with a glazed look of helplessness in his eyes, a certain stupor of downfall.

6 The great draught-horses swung past. They were tied head to tail, four of them, and they heaved along to where a lane branched off from the highroad, planting their great hoofs floutingly in the fine black mud, swinging their great rounded haunches sumptuously, and trotting a few sudden steps as they were led into the lane, round the corner. Every movement showed a massive, slumbrous strength, and a stupidity which held them in subjection. The groom at the head looked back, jerking the leading rope. And the cavalcade moved out of sight up the lane, the tail of the last horse, bobbed up tight and stiff, held out taut from the swinging great haunches as they rocked behind the hedges in a motion-like sleep.

7 Joe watched with glazed hopeless eyes. The horses were almost like his own body to him. He felt he was done for now. Luckily he was engaged to a woman as old as himself, and therefore her father, who was steward of a neighboring estate, would provide him with a job. He would marry and go into harness. His life was over, he would be a subject animal now.

8 He turned uneasily aside, the retreating steps of the horses echoing in his ears. Then, with foolish restlessness, he reached for the scraps of bacon rind from the plates, and making a faint whistling sound, flung them to the terrier that lay against the fender. He watched the dog swallow them, and waited till the creature looked into his eyes. Then a faint grin came on his face, and in a high, foolish voice he said:

9 "You won't get much more bacon, shall you, you little bitch?"

10 The dog faintly and dismally wagged its tail, then lowered its haunches, circled round, and lay down again.

11 There was another helpless silence at the table. Joe sprawled uneasily in his seat, not willing to go till the family conclave was dissolved. Fred Henry, the second brother, was erect, cleanlimbed, alert. He had watched the passing of the horses with more sangfroid. If he was an animal, like Joe, he was an animal which controls, not one which is controlled. He was master of any horse, and he carried himself with a well-tempered air of mastery. But he was not master of the situations of life. He pushed his coarse brown moustache upwards, off his lip, and glanced irritably at his sister, who sat impassive and inscrutable.

12 "You'll go and stop with Lucy for a bit, shan't you?" he asked. The girl did not answer.

13 "I don't see what else you can do," persisted Fred Henry.

14 "Go as a skivvy,"° Joe interpolated laconically.

15 The girl did not move a muscle.

16 "If I was her, I should go in for training for a nurse," said Malcolm, the youngest of them all. He was the baby of the family, a young man of twenty-two, with a fresh, jaunty *museau.*°

17 But Mabel did not take any notice of him. They had talked at her and round her for so many years, that she hardly heard them at all.

18 The marble clock on the mantelpiece softly chimed the half-hour, the dog rose uneasily from the hearthrug and looked at the party at the breakfast table. But still they sat on in effectual conclave.

19 "Oh, all right," said Joe suddenly, apropos of nothing. "I'll get a move on."

20 He pushed back his chair, straddled his knees with a downward jerk, to get them free, in horsey fashion, and went to the fire. Still he did not go out of the room; he was curious to know what the others would do or say. He began to charge his pipe, looking down at the dog and saying, in a high, affected voice:

21 "Going' wi' me? Going wi' me are ter? Tha'rt goin' further tha that counts on just now, dost hear?"

22 The dog faintly wagged its tail, the man stuck out his jaw and covered his pipe with his hands, and puffed intently, losing himself in the tobacco, looking down all the while at the dog with an absent brown eye. The dog looked at him in mournful distrust. Joe stood with his knees stuck out, in real horsey fashion.

23 "Have you had a letter from Lucy?" Fred Henry asked of his sister.

24 "Last week," came the neutral reply.

25 "And what does she say?"

26 There was no answer.

27 "Does she *ask* you to go and stop there?" persisted Fred Henry.

28 "She says I can if I like."

29 "Well, then, you'd better. Tell her you'll come on Monday." This was received in silence.

30 "That's what you'll do then, is it?" said Fred Henry, in some exasperation.

31 But she made no answer. There was a silence of futility and irritation in the room. Malcolm grinned fatuously.

32 "You'll have to make up your mind between now and next Wednesday," said Joe loudly, "or else find yourself lodgings on the curbstone."

33 The face of the young woman darkened, but she sat on immutable.

---

skivvy servant girl
museau jaw (literally, muzzle or snout)

34 "Here's Jack Fergusson!" exclaimed Malcolm, who was looking aimlessly out of the window.

35 "Where?" exclaimed Joe, loudly.

36 "Just gone past."

37 "Coming in?"

38 Malcolm craned his neck to see the gate.

39 "Yes," he said.

40 There was a silence. Mabel sat on like one condemned, at the head of the table. Then a whistle was heard from the kitchen. The dog got up and barked sharply. Joe opened the door and shouted:

41 "Come on."

42 After a moment a young man entered. He was muffled up in overcoat and a purple woolen scarf, and his tweed cap, which he did not remove, was pulled down on his head. He was of medium height, his face was rather long and pale, his eyes looked tired.

43 "Hello, Jack! Well, Jack!" exclaimed Malcolm and Joe. Fred Henry merely said, "Jack."

44 "What's doing?" asked the newcomer, evidently addressing Fred Henry.

45 "Same. We've got to be out by Wednesday. Got a cold?"

46 "I have—got it bad, too."

47 "Why don't you stop in?"

48 "*Me* stop in? When I can't stand on my legs, perhaps I shall have a chance." The young man spoke huskily. He had a slight Scotch accent.

49 "It's a knock-out, isn't it," said Joe, boisterously, "if a doctor goes round croaking with a cold. Looks bad for the patients, doesn't it?"

50 The young doctor looked at him slowly.

51 "Anything the matter with *you*, then?" he asked sarcastically.

52 "Not as I know of. Damn your eyes, I hope not. Why?"

53 "I thought you were very concerned about the patients, wondered if you might be one yourself."

54 "Damn it, no, I've never been patient to no flaming doctor, and hope I never shall be," returned Joe.

55 At this point Mabel rose from the table, and they all seemed to become aware of her existence. She began putting the dishes together. The young doctor looked at her, but did not address her. He had not greeted her. She went out of the room with the tray, her face impassive and unchanged.

56 "When are you off then, all of you?" asked the doctor.

57 "I'm catching the eleven forty," replied Malcolm. "Are you goin' down wi' th' trap, Joe?"

58 "Yes, I've told you I'm going down wi' th' trap, haven't I?"

59 "We'd better be getting her in then. So long, Jack, if I don't see you before I go," said Malcolm, shaking hands.

60 He went out, followed by Joe, who seemed to have his tail between his legs.

61 "Well, this is the devil's own," exclaimed the doctor, when he was left alone with Fred Henry. "Going before Wednesday, are you?"

62 "That's the orders," replied the other.

63 "Where, to Northampton?"

64 "That's it."

65 "The devil!" exclaimed Fergusson, with quiet chagrin.

66 And there was silence between the two.

67 "All settled up, are you?" asked Fergusson.

68 "About."

69 There was another pause.

70 "Well, I shall miss yer, Freddy, boy," said the young doctor.

71 "And I shall miss thee, Jack," returned the other.

72 "Miss you like hell," mused the doctor.

73 Fred Henry turned aside. There was nothing to say. Mabel came in again, to finish clearing the table.

74 "What are *you* going to do, then, Miss Pervin?" asked Fergusson. "Going to your sister's, are you?"

75 Mabel looked at him with her steady, dangerous eyes, that always made him uncomfortable, unsettling his superficial ease.

76 "No," she said.

77 "Well, what in the name of fortune *are* you going to do? Say what you mean to do," cried Fred Henry, with futile intensity.

78 But she only averted her head, and continued her work. She folded the white table-cloth, and put on the chenille cloth.

79 "The sulkiest bitch that ever trod!" muttered her brother.

80 But she finished her task with perfectly impassive face, the young doctor watching her interestedly all the while. Then she went out.

81 Fred Henry stared after her, clenching his lips, his blue eyes fixing in sharp antagonism, as he made a grimace of sour exasperation.

82 "You could bray her into bits, and that's all you'd get out of her," he said in a small, narrowed tone.

83 The doctor smiled faintly.

84 "What's she *going* to do, then?" he asked.

85 "Strike me if *I* know!" returned the other.

86 There was a pause. Then the doctor stirred.

87 "I'll be seeing you to-night, shall I?" he said to his friend.

88 "Ay—where's it to be? Are we going over to Jessdale?"

89 "I don't know. I've got such a cold on me. I'll come round to the Moon and Stars, anyway."

90 "Let Lizzie and May miss their night for once, eh?"

91 "That's it—if I feel as I do now."

92 "All's one—"

93 The two young men went through the passage and down to the back door together. The house was large, but it was servantless now, and desolate. At the back was a small bricked house-yard, and beyond that a big square, graveled fine and red, and having stables on two sides. Sloping, dank, winter-dark fields stretched away on the open sides.

94 But the stables were empty. Joseph Pervin, the father of the family, had been a man of no education, who had become a fairly large horse dealer. The stables had been full of horses, there was a great turmoil and come-and-go of horses and of dealers and grooms. Then the kitchen was full of servants. But of late things had declined. The old man had married a second time, to retrieve his fortunes. Now he was dead and everything was gone to the dogs, there was nothing but debt and threatening.

95 For months, Mabel had been servantless in the big house, keeping the home together in penury for her ineffectual brothers. She had kept house for ten years. But previously it was with unstinted means. Then, however brutal and coarse everything was, the sense of money had kept her proud, confident. The men might be foul-mouthed, the women in the kitchen might have bad reputations, her brothers might have illegitimate children. But so long as there was money, the girl felt herself established, and brutally proud, reserved.

96 No company came to the house, save dealers and coarse men. Mabel had no associates of her own sex, after her sister went away. But she did not mind. She went regularly to church, she attended to her father. And she lived in the memory of her mother, who had died when she was fourteen, and whom she had loved. She had loved her father, too, in a different way, depending upon him, and feeling secure in him, until at the age of fifty-four he married again. And then she had set hard against him. Now he had died and left them all hopelessly in debt.

97 She had suffered badly during the period of poverty. Nothing, however, could shake the curious sullen, animal pride that dominated each member of the family. Now, for Mabel, the end had come. Still she would not cast about her. She would follow her own way just the same. She would always hold the keys of her own situation. Mindless and persistent, she endured from day to day. Why should she think? Why should she answer anybody? It was enough that this was the end, and there was no way out. She need not pass any more darkly along the main street of the small town, avoiding every eye. She need not demean herself any more, going into the shops and buying the cheapest food. This was at an end. She thought of nobody, not even of herself. Mindless and persistent, she seemed in a sort of ecstasy to be coming nearer to her fulfillment, her own glorification, approaching her dead mother, who was glorified.

98 In the afternoon she took a little bag, with shears and sponge and a small scrubbing brush, and went out. It was a gray, wintry day, with saddened, dark green fields and an atmosphere blackened by the smoke of foundries not far off. She went quickly, darkly along the causeway, heeding nobody, through the town to the churchyard.

99 There she always felt secure, as if no one could see her, although as a matter of fact she was exposed to the stare of every one who passed along under the churchyard wall. Nevertheless, once under the shadow of the great looming church, among the graves, she felt immune from the world, reserved within the thick churchyard wall as in another country.

100 Carefully she clipped the grass from the grave, and arranged the pinky white, small chrysanthemums in the tin cross. When this was done, she took an empty jar from a neighboring grave, brought water, and carefully, most scrupulously sponged the marble headstone and the coping-stone. It gave her sincere satisfaction to do this. She felt in immediate contact with the world of her mother. She took minute pains, went through the park in a state bordering on pure happiness, as if in performing this task she came into a subtle, intimate connection with her mother. For the life she followed here in the world was far less real than the world of death she inherited from her mother.

101 The doctor's house was just by the church. Fergusson, being a mere hired assistant, was slave to the countryside. As he hurried now to attend to the outpatients in the surgery, glancing across the graveyard with his quick eyes, he saw the girl at her task at the grave. She seemed so intent and remote, it was like looking into another world. Some mystical element was touched in him. He slowed down as he walked, watching her as if spellbound.

102 She lifted her eyes, feeling him looking. Their eyes met. And each looked away again at once, each feeling, in some way, found out by the other. He lifted his cap and passed on down the road. There remained distinct in his consciousness, like a vision, the memory of her face, lifted from the tombstone in the churchyard, and looking at him with slow, large, portentous eyes. It was portentous, her face. It seemed to mesmerize him. There was a heavy power in her eyes which laid hold of his whole being, as if he had drunk some powerful drug. He had been feeling weak and done before. Now the life came back into him, he felt delivered from his own fretted, daily self.

103 He finished his duties at the surgery as quickly as might be, hastily filling up the bottles of the waiting people with cheap drugs. Then, in perpetual haste, he set off again to visit several cases in another part of his round, before teatime. At all times he preferred to walk if he could, but particularly when he was not well. He fancied the motion restored him.

104 The afternoon was falling. It was gray, deadened, and wintry, with a slow, moist, heavy coldness sinking in and deadening all the faculties. But why should he think or notice? He hastily climbed the hill and turned across the

dark green fields, following the black cindertrack. In the distance, across a shallow dip in the country, the small town was clustered like smouldering ash, a tower, a spire, a heap of low, raw, extinct houses. And on the nearest fringe of the town, sloping into the dip, was Oldmeadow, the Pervins's house. He could see the stables and the outbuildings distinctly, as they lay towards him on the slope. Well, he would not go there many more times! Another resource would be lost to him, another place gone: the only company he cared for in the alien, ugly little town he was losing. Nothing but wok, drudgery, constant hastening from dwelling to dwelling among the colliers and the iron-workers. It wore him out, but at the same time he had a craving for it. It was a stimulant to him to be in the homes of the working people, moving as it were through the innermost body of their life. His nerves were excited and gratified. He could come so near, into the very lives of the rough, inarticulate, powerfully emotional men and women. He grumbled, he said he hated the hellish hole. But as a matter of fact it excited him, the contact with the rough, strongly-feeling people was a stimulant applied direct to his nerves.

105 Below Oldmeadow, in the green, shallow, soddened hollow of fields, lay a square, deep pond. Roving across the landscape, the doctor's quick eye detected a figure in black passing through the gate of the field, down towards the pond. He looked again. It would be Mabel Pervin. His mind suddenly became alive and attentive.

106 Why was she going down there? He pulled up on the path on the slope above, and stood staring. He could just make sure of the small black figure moving in the hollow of the failing day. He seemed to her in the midst of such obscurity, that he was like a clairvoyant, seeing rather with the mind's eye than with ordinary sight. Yet he could see her positively enough, while he kept his eye attentive. He felt, if he looked away from her, in the thick, ugly falling dusk, he would lose her altogether.

107 He followed her minutely as she moved, direct and intent, like something transmitted rather than stirring in voluntary activity, straight down the field towards the pond. There she stood in the bank for a moment. She never raised her head. Then she waded slowly into the water.

108 He stood motionless as the small black figure walked slowly and deliberately towards the center of the pond, very slowly, gradually moving deeper into the motionless water, and still moving forward as the water got up to her breast. Then he could see her no more in the dusk of the dead afternoon.

109 "There!" he exclaimed. "Would you believe it?"

110 And he hastened straight down, running over the wet, soddened fields, pushing through the hedges, down into the depression of callous wintry obscurity. It took him several minutes to come to the pond. He stood on the bank, breathing heavily. He could see nothing. His eyes seemed to penetrate the dead

water. Yes, perhaps that was the dark shadow of her black clothing beneath the surface of the water.

111 He slowly ventured into the pond. The bottom was deep, soft clay, he sank in, and the water clasped dead cold round his legs. As he stirred he could smell the cold, rotten clay that fouled up into the water. It was objectionable in his lungs. Still, repelled and yet not heeding, he moved deeper into the pond. The cold water rose over his thighs, over his loins, upon his abdomen. The lower part of his body was all sunk in the hideous cold element. And the bottom was so deeply soft and uncertain he was afraid of pitching with his mouth underneath. He could not swim, and was afraid.

112 He crouched a little, spreading his hands under the water and moving them round, trying to feel for her. The dead cold pond swayed upon his chest. He moved again, a little deeper, and again, with his hands underneath, he felt all around under the water. And he touched her clothing. But it evaded his fingers. He made a desperate effort to grasp it.

113 And so doing he lost his balance and went under, horribly, suffocating in the foul earthy water, struggling madly for a few moments. At last, after what seemed an eternity, he got his footing, rose again into the air and looked around. He gasped, and knew he was in the world. Then he looked at the water. She had risen near him. He grasped her clothing, and drawing her nearer, turned to take his way to land again.

114 He went very slowly, carefully, absorbed in the slow progress. He rose higher, climbing out of the pond. The water was now only about his legs; he was thankful, full of relief to be out of the clutches of the pond. He lifted her and staggered on to the bank, out of the horror of wet, gray clay.

115 He laid her down on the bank. She was quite unconscious and running with water. He made the water come from her mouth, he worked to restore her. He did not have to work very long before he could feel the breathing begin again in her; she was breathing naturally. He worked a little longer. He could feel her live beneath his hands; she was coming back. He wiped her face, wrapped her in his overcoat, looked round into the dim, dark gray world, then lifted her and staggered down the bank and across the fields.

116 It seemed an unthinkably long way, and his burden so heavy he felt he would never get to the house. But at last he was in the stableyard, and then in the houseyard. He opened the door and went into the house. In the kitchen he laid her down on the hearth-rug, and called. The house was empty. But the fire was burning in the grate.

117 Then again he kneeled to attend to her. She was breathing regularly, her eyes were wide open and as if conscious, but there seemed something missing in her look. She was conscious in herself, but unconscious of her surroundings.

118 He ran upstairs, took blankets from a bed, and put them before the fire to warm. Then he removed her saturated, earthy-smelling clothing, rubbed her dry

with a towel, and wrapped her naked in the blankets. Then he went into the dining-room, to look for spirits. There was a little whisky. He drank a gulp himself, and put some into her mouth.

119 The effect was instantaneous. She looked full into his face, as if she had been seeing him for some time, and yet had only just become conscious of him.

120 "Dr. Fergusson?" she said.

121 "What?" he answered.

122 He was divesting himself of his coat, intending to find some dry clothing upstairs. He could not bear the smell of the dead, clayey water, and he was mortally afraid of his own health.

123 "What did I do?" she asked.

124 "Walked into the pond," he replied. He had begun to shudder like one sick, and could hardly attend to her. Her eyes remained full on him, he seemed to be going dark in his mind, looking back at her helplessly. The shuddering became quieter in him, his life came back in him, dark and unknowing, but strong again.

125 "Was I out of my mind?" she asked, while her eyes were fixed on him all the time.

126 "Maybe, for the moment," he replied. He felt quiet, because his strength came back. The strange fretful strain had left him.

127 "Am I out of my mind now?" she asked.

128 "Are you?" he reflected a moment. "No," he answered truthfully, "I don't see that you are." He turned his face aside. He was afraid now, because he felt dazed, and felt dimly that her power was stronger than his, in this issue. And she continued to looked at him fixedly all the time. "Can you tell me where I shall find some dry things to put on?" he asked.

129 "Did you dive into the pond for me?" she asked.

130 "No," he answered. "I walked in. But I went in overhead as well."

131 There was silence for a moment. He hesitated. He very much wanted to go upstairs to get into dry clothing. But there was another desire in him. And she seemed to hold him. His will seemed to have gone to sleep, and left him, standing there slack before her. But he felt warm inside himself. He did not shudder at all, though his clothes were sodden on him.

132 "Why did you?" she asked.

133 "Because I didn't want you to do such a foolish thing," he said.

134 "It wasn't foolish," she said, still gazing at him as she lay on the floor, with a sofa cushion under her head. "It was the right thing to do. *I* knew best, then."

135 "I'll go and shift these wet things," he said. But still he had not the power to move out of her presence, until she sent him. It was as if she had the life of his body in her hands, and he could not extricate himself. Or perhaps he did not want to.

136 Suddenly she sat up. Then she became aware of her own immediate condition. She felt the blankets about her, she knew her own limbs. For a moment it seemed as if her reason were going. She looked round, with wild eye, as if seeking something. He stood still with fear. She saw her clothing lying scattered.

137 "Who undressed me?" she asked, her eyes resting full and inevitable on his face.

138 "I did," he replied, "to bring you round."

139 For some moments she sat and gazed at him awfully, her lips parted.

140 "Do you love me, then?" she asked.

141 He only stood and stared at her, fascinated. His soul seemed to melt.

142 She shuffled forward on her knees, and put her arms round him, round his legs, as he stood there, pressing her breasts against his knees and thighs, clutching him with strange, convulsive certainty, pressing his thighs against her, drawing him to her face, her throat, as she looked up at him with flaring, humble eyes of transfiguration, triumphant in first possession.

143 "You love me," she murmured, in strange transport, yearning and triumphant and confident. "You love me. I know you love me, I know."

144 And she was passionately kissing his knees, through the wet clothing, passionately and indiscriminately kissing his knees, his legs, as if unaware of everything.

145 He looked down at the tangled wet hair, the wild, bare, animal shoulders. He was amazed, bewildered, and afraid. He had never thought of loving her. He had never wanted to love her. When he rescued her and restored her, he was a doctor, and she was a patient. He had had no single personal thought of her. Nay, this introduction of the personal element was very distasteful to him, a violation of his professional honor. It was horrible to have her there embracing his knees. It was horrible. He revolted from it, violently. And yet—and yet—he had not the power to break away.

146 She looked at him again, with the same supplication of powerful love, and that same transcendent, frightening light of triumph. In view of the delicate flame which seemed to come from her face like a light, he was powerless. And yet he had never intended to love her. He had never intended. And something stubborn in him could not give away.

147 "You love me," she repeated, in a murmur of deep, rhapsodic assurance. "You love me."

148 Her hands were drawing him, drawing him down to her. He was afraid, even a little horrified. For he had, really, no intention of loving her. Yet her hands were drawing him towards her. He put out his hands quickly to steady himself, and grasped her bare shoulder. A flame seemed to burn the hand that grasped her soft shoulder. He had no intention of loving her; his whole will was against his yielding. It was horrible. And yet wonderful was the touch of

her shoulders, beautiful the shining of her face. Was she perhaps mad? He had a horror of yielding to her. Yet something in him ached also.

149 He had been staring away at the door, away from her. But his hand remained on her shoulder. She had gone suddenly very still. He looked down at her. Her eyes were now wide with fear, with doubt, the light was dying from her face, a shadow of terrible grayness was returning. He could not bear the touch of her eyes' question upon him, and the look of death behind the question.

150 With an inward groan he gave way, and let his heart yield towards her. A sudden gentle smile came on his face. And her eyes, which never left his face, slowly, slowly filled with tears. He watched the strange water rise in her eyes, like some slow fountain coming up. And his heart seemed to burn and melt away in his breast.

151 He could not bear to look at her any more. He dropped on his knees and caught her head with his arms and pressed her face against his throat. She was very still. His heart, which seemed to have broken, was burning with a kind of agony in his breast. And he felt her slow, hot tears wetting his throat. But he could not move.

152 He felt the hot tears wet his back and the hollows of his neck, and he remained motionless, suspended through one of man's eternities. Only now it had become indispensable to him to have her face pressed close to him; he could never let her go again. He could never let her head go away from the close clutch of his arm. He wanted to remain like that for ever, with his heart hurting him in a pain that was also life to him. Without knowing, he was looking down on her damp, soft brown hair.

153 Then, as it were suddenly, he smelt the horrid stagnant smell of that water. And at the same moment she drew away from him and looked at him. Her eyes were wistful and unfathomable. He was afraid of them, and he fell to kissing her, not knowing what he was doing. He wanted her eyes not to have that terrible, wistful, unfathomable look.

154 When she turned her face to him again, a faint delicate flush was glowing, and there was again dawning that terrible shining of joy in her eyes, which really terrified him, and yet which he now wanted to see, because he feared the look of doubt still more.

155 "You love me?" she said, rather faltering.

156 "Yes." The word cost him a painful effort. Not because it wasn't true. But because it was too newly true, the *saying* seemed to tear open again his newly torn heart. And he hardly wanted it to be true, even now.

157 She lifted her face to him, and he bent forward and kissed her on the mouth, gently, with the one kiss that is an eternal pledge. And as he kissed her his heart strained again in his breast. He never intended to love her. But now it was over. He had crossed over the gulf to her, and all that he had left behind had shriveled and become void.

158 After the kiss, her eyes again slowly filled with tears. She sat still, away from him, with her face drooped aside, and her hands folded in her lap. The tears fell very slowly. There was complete silence. He too sat there motionless and silent on the hearthrug. The strange pain of his heart that was broken seemed to consume him. That he should love her? That this was love! That he should be ripped open in this way! Him, a doctor! How they would all jeer if they knew! It was agony to him to think they might know.

159 In the curious naked pain of the thought he looked again to her. She was sitting there drooped into a muse. He saw a tear fall, and his heart flared not. He saw for the first time that one of her shoulders was quite uncovered, one arm bare, he could see one of her small breasts; dimly, because it had become almost dark in the room.

160 "Why are you crying?" he asked, in an altered voice.

161 She looked up at him, and behind her tears the consciousness of her situation for the first time brought a dark look of shame to her eyes.

162 "I'm not crying, really," she said, watching him half frightened.

163 He reached his hand, and softly closed it on her bare arm.

164 "I love you! I love you!" he said in a soft, low vibrating voice, unlike himself.

165 She shrank, and dropped her head. The soft, penetrating grip of his hand on her arm distressed her. She looked up at him.

166 "I want to go," she said. "I want to go and get you some dry things."

167 "Why?" he said. "I'm all right."

168 "But I want to go," she said. "And I want you to change your things."

169 He released her arm, and she wrapped herself in the blanket, looking at him rather frightened. And still she did not rise.

170 "Kiss me," she said wistfully.

171 He kissed her, but briefly, half in anger.

172 Then, after a second, she rose nervously, all mixed up in the blanket. He watched her in her confusion, as she tried to extricate herself and wrap herself up so that she could walk. He watched her relentlessly, as she knew. And as she went, the blanket trailing, and as he saw a glimpse of her feet and her white leg, he tried to remember her as she was when he had wrapped her in the blanket. But then he didn't want to remember, because she had been nothing to him then, and his nature revolted from remembering her as she was when she was nothing to him.

173 A tumbling, muffled noise from within the dark house startled him. Then he heard her voice:—"There are clothes." He rose and went to the foot of the stairs, and gathered up the garments she had thrown down. Then he came back to the fire, to rub himself down and dress. He grinned at his own appearance when he had finished.

174 The fire was sinking, so he put on coal. The house was now quite dark, save for the light of a street-lamp that shone in faintly from beyond the holly trees. He lit the gas with matches he found on the mantelpiece. Then he emptied the pockets of his own clothes, and threw all his wet things in a heap into the scullery. After which he gathered up her sodden clothes, gently, and put them in a separate heap on the copper-top in the scullery.

175 It was six o'clock on the clock. His own watch had stopped. He ought to go back to the surgery. He waited, and still she did not come down. So he went to the foot of the stairs and called:

176 "I shall have to go."

177 Almost immediately he heard her coming down. She had on her best dress of black voile, and her hair was tidy, but still damp. She looked at him—and in spite of herself, smiled.

178 "I don't like you in those clothes," she said.

179 "Do I look a sight?" he answered.

180 They were shy of one another.

181 "I'll make you some tea," she said.

182 "No, I must go."

183 "Must you?" And she looked at him again with the wide, strained, doubtful eyes. And again, from the pain of his breast, he knew how he loved her. He went and bent to kiss her, gently, passionately, with his heart's painful kiss.

184 "And my hair smells so horrible," she murmured in distraction. "And I'm so awful, I'm so awful! Oh, no, I'm too awful!" And she broke into bitter, heart-broken sobbing. "You can't want to love me, I'm horrible."

185 "Don't be silly, don't be silly," he said, trying to comfort her, kissing her, holding her in his arms. "I want you, I want to marry you, we're going to be married, quickly, quickly—tomorrow if I can."

186 But she only sobbed terribly, and cried:

187 "I feel awful. I feel awful. I feel I'm horrible to you."

188 "No, I want you, I want you," was all he answered, blindly, with that terrible intonation which frightened her almost more than her horror lest he should not want her.

—1922

✧ ✧ ✧

Katherine Anne Porter

(1890-1980)

The Jilting of Granny Weatherall

Porter's allegorical novel of a voyage to Germany at the beginning of the Nazi era, *Ship of Fools*, was a great popular success in 1962, changing her from a "writer's writer" known mainly for prestigious literary essays, book reviews, and short stories to an international celebrity. Born in Indian Creek, Texas, and educated in Catholic schools in the South, Porter's youth was a study in rebellion, with stints as a reporter and traveling singer and entertainer. The recipient of a Guggenheim Fellowship after the appearance of her first book, Porter subsequently traveled in Mexico and Europe, gathering further material for her stories, which were collected in *Flowering Judas* (1930), *Pale Horse, Pale Rider* (1939), and *The Leaning Tower* (1944). Porter's *Collected Stories* won both a Pulitzer Prize and a National Book Award in 1965, the same year in which Stanley Kramer's popular film version of *Ship of Fools* appeared. Though Porter is not primarily identified as a regional writer, "The Jilting of Granny Weatherall" draws on the rural landscapes of her youth and makes effective use of her upbringing as a southern Roman Catholic. It also makes effective use of stream of consciousness, a technique Porter often employs in her stories. "The Jilting of Granny Weatherall" was made into a film as part of the PBS *American Short Story* series.

She flicked her wrist neatly out of Doctor Harry's pudgy careful fingers and pulled the sheet up to her chin. The brat ought to be in knee breeches. Doctoring around the country with spectacles on his nose! "Get along now, take your schoolbooks and go. There's nothing wrong with me."

2 Doctor Harry spread a warm paw like a cushion on her forehead where the forked green vein danced and made her eyelids twitch. "Now, now, be a good girl, and we'll have you up in no time."

3 "That's no way to speak to a woman nearly eighty years old just because she's down. I'd have you respect your elders, young man."

4 "Well, Missy, excuse me." Doctor Harry patted her cheek. "But I've got to warn you, haven't I? You're a marvel, but you must be careful or you're going to be good and sorry."

5 "Don't tell me what I'm going to be. I'm on my feet now, morally speaking. It's Cornelia. I had to go to bed to get rid of her."

6 Her bones felt loose, and floated around in her skin, and Doctor Harry floated like a balloon around the foot of the bed. He floated and pulled down his waistcoat and swung his glasses on a cord. "Well, stay where you are, it certainly can't hurt you."

7 "Get along and doctor your sick," said Granny Weatherall. "Leave a well woman alone. I'll call for you when I want you . . . Where were you forty years ago when I pulled through milk leg and double pneumonia? You weren't even born. Don't let Cornelia lead you on," she shouted, because Doctor Harry appeared to float up to the ceiling and out. "I pay my own bills, and I don't throw my money away on nonsense!"

8 She meant to wave good-by, but it was too much trouble. Her eyes closed of themselves, it was like a dark curtain drawn around the bed. The pillow rose and floated under her, pleasant as a hammock in a light wind. She listened to the leaves rustling outside the window. No, somebody was swishing newspapers: no, Cornelia and Doctor Harry were whispering together. She leaped broad awake, thinking they whispered in her ear.

9 "She was never like this, *never* like this!" "Well, what can we expect?" "Yes, eighty years old . . . "

10 Well, and what if she was? She still had ears. It was like Cornelia to whisper around doors. She always kept things secret in such a public way. She was always being tactful and kind. Cornelia was dutiful; that was the trouble with her. Dutiful and good: "So good and dutiful," said Granny, "and I'd like to spank her." She saw herself spanking Cornelia and making a fine job of it.

11 "What'd you say, Mother?"

12 Granny felt her face tying up in hard knots.

13 "Can't a body think, I'd like to know?"

14 "I thought you might want something."

15 "I do. I want a lot of things. First off, go away and don't whisper."

16 She lay and drowsed, hoping in her sleep that the children would keep out and let her rest a minute. It had been a long day. Not that she was tired. It was always pleasant to snatch a minute now and then. There was always so much to be done, let me see: tomorrow.

17 Tomorrow was far away and there was nothing to trouble about. Things were finished somehow when the time came; thank God there was always a little margin over for peace: then a person could spread out the plan of life and tuck in the edges orderly. It was good to have everything clean and folded away, with the hair brushes and tonic bottles sitting straight on the white embroi-

dered linen: the day started without fuss and the pantry shelves laid out with rows of jelly glasses and brown jugs and white stone-china jars with blue whirligigs and words painted on them: coffee, tea, sugar, ginger, cinnamon, allspice: and the bronze clock with the lion on top nicely dusted off. The dust that lion could collect in twenty-four hours! The box in the attic with all those letters tied up, she'd have to go through that tomorrow. All those letters—George's letters and John's letters and her letters to them both—lying around for the children to find afterwards made her uneasy. Yes, that would be tomorrow's business. No use to let them know how silly she had been once.

18 While she was rummaging around she found death in her mind and it felt clammy and unfamiliar. She had spent so much time preparing for death there was no need for bringing it up again. Let it take care of itself now. When she was sixty she had felt very old, finished, and went around making farewell trips to see her children and grandchildren, with a secret in her mind: This is the very last of your mother, children! Then she made her will and came down with a long fever. That was all just a notion like a lot of other things, but it was lucky too, for she had once for all got over the idea of dying for a long time. Now she couldn't be worried. She hoped she had better sense now. Her father had lived to be one hundred and two years old and had drunk a noggin of strong hot toddy on his last birthday. He told the reporters it was his daily habit, and he owed his long life to that. He had made quite a scandal and was very pleased about it. She believed she'd just plague Cornelia a little.

19 "Cornelia! Cornelia!" No footsteps, but a sudden hand on her cheek. "Bless you, where have you been?"

20 "Here, Mother."

21 "Well, Cornelia, I want a noggin of hot toddy."

22 "Are you cold, darling?"

23 "I'm chilly, Cornelia. Lying in bed stops the circulation. I must have told you that a thousand times."

24 Well, she could just hear Cornelia telling her husband that Mother was getting a little childish and they'd have to humor her. The thing that most annoyed her was that Cornelia thought she was deaf, dumb, and blind. Little hasty glances and tiny gestures tossed around her and over her head saying, "Don't cross her, let her have her way, she's eighty years old," and she sitting there as if she lived in a thin glass cage. Sometimes Granny almost made up her mind to pack up and move back to her own house where nobody could remind her every minute that she was old.

25 Wait, wait, Cornelia, till your own children whisper behind your back! In her day she had kept a better house and had got more work done. She wasn't too old yet for Lydia to be driving eighty miles for advice when one of the children jumped the track, and Jimmy still dropped in and talked things over: "Now, Mammy, you've a good business head, I want to know what you think of

this? . . . " Old. Cornelia couldn't change the furniture around without asking. Little things, little things! They had been so sweet when they were little. Granny wished the old days were back again with the children young and everything to be done over. It had been a hard pull, but not too much for her. When she thought of all the food she had cooked, and all the clothes she had cut and sewed, and all the gardens she had made—well, the children showed it. There they were, made out of her, and they couldn't get away from that. Sometimes she wanted to see John again and point to them and say, Well, I didn't do so badly, did I? But that would have to wait. That was for tomorrow. She used to think of him as a man, but now all the children were older than their father, and he would be a child beside her if she saw him now. It seemed strange and there was something wrong in the idea. Why, he couldn't possibly recognize her. She had fenced in a hundred acres once, digging the post holes herself and clamping the wires with just a negro boy to help. That changed a woman. John would be looking for a young woman with the peaked Spanish comb in her hair and the painted fan. Digging post holes changed a woman. Riding country roads in the winter when women had their babies was another thing: sitting up nights with sick horses and sick negroes and sick children and hardly every losing one. John, I hardly ever lost one of them! John would see that in a minute, that would be something he could understand, she wouldn't have to explain anything!

26 It made her feel like rolling up her sleeves and putting the whole place to rights again. No matter if Cornelia was determined to be everywhere at once, there were a great many things left undone on this place. She would start tomorrow and do them. It was good to be strong enough for everything, even if all you made melted and changed and slipped under your hands, so that by the time you finished you almost forgot what you were working for. What was it I set out to do? she asked herself intently, but she could not remember. A fog rose over the valley, she saw it marching across the creek swallowing the trees and moving up the hill like an army of ghosts. Soon it would be at the near edge of the orchard, and then it was time to go in and light the lamps. Come in, children, don't stay out in the night air.

27 Lighting the lamps had been beautiful. The children huddled up to her and breathed like little calves waiting at the bars in the twilight. Their eyes followed the match and watched the flame rise and settle in a blue curve, then they moved away from her. The lamp was lit, they didn't have to be scared and hang on to mother any more. Never, never, never more. God, for all my life I thank Thee. Without Thee, my God, I could never have done it. Hail, Mary, full of grace.

28 I want you to pick all the fruit this year and see that nothing is wasted. There's always someone who can use it. Don't let good things rot for want of using. You waste life when you waste good food. Don't let things get lost. It's

bitter to lose things. Now, don't let me get to thinking, not when I am tired and taking a little nap before supper . . .

29 The pillow rose about her shoulders and pressed against her heart and the memory was being squeezed out of it: oh, push down the pillow, somebody: it would smother her if she tried to hold it. Such a fresh breeze blowing and such a green day with no threats in it. But he had not come, just the same. What does a woman do when she has put on the white veil and set out the white cake for a man and he doesn't come? She tried to remember. No, I swear he never harmed me but in that. He never harmed me but in that . . . and what if he did? There was the day, the day, but a whirl of dark smoke rose and covered it, crept up and over into the bright field where everything was planted so carefully in orderly rows. That was hell, she knew hell when she saw it. For sixty years she had prayed against remembering him and against losing her soul in the deep pit of hell, and now the two things were mingled in one and the thought of him was a smoky cloud from hell that moved and crept in her head when she had just got rid of Doctor Harry and was trying to rest a minute. Wounded vanity, Ellen, said a sharp voice in the top of her mind. Don't let your wounded vanity get the upper hand of you. Plenty of girls get jilted. You were jilted, weren't you? Then stand up to it. Her eyelids wavered and let in streamers of blue-gray light like tissue paper over her eyes. She must get up and pull the shades down or she'd never sleep. She was in bed again and the shades were not down. How could that happen? Better turn over, hide from the light, sleeping in the light gave you nightmares. "Mother, how do you feel now?" and a stinging wetness on her forehead. But I don't like having my face washed in cold water!

30 Hapsy? George? Lydia? Jimmy? No, Cornelia, and her features were swollen and full of little puddles. "They're coming, darling, they'll all be here soon." Go wash your face, child, you look funny.

31 Instead of obeying, Cornelia knelt down and put her head on the pillow. She seemed to be talking but there was no sound. "Well, are you tongue-tied? Whose birthday is it? Are you going to give a party?"

32 Cornelia's mouth moved urgently in strange shapes. "Don't do that, you bother me, daughter."

33 "Oh, no, Mother. Oh, no . . . "

34 Nonsense. It was strange about children. They disputed your every word. "No what, Cornelia?"

35 "Here's Doctor Harry."

36 "I won't see that boy again. He just left five minutes ago."

37 "That was this morning, Mother. It's night now. Here's the nurse."

38 "This is Doctor Harry, Mrs. Weatherall. I never saw you look so young and happy!

39 "Ah, I'll never be young again—but I'd be happy if they'd let me lie in peace and get rested."

40 She thought she spoke up loudly, but no one answered. A warm weight on her forehead, a warm bracelet on her wrist, and a breeze went on whispering, trying to tell her something. A shuffle of leaves in the everlasting hand of God. He blew on them and they danced and rattled. "Mother, don't mind, we're going to give you a little hypodermic." "Look here, daughter, how do ants get in this bed? I saw sugar ants yesterday." Did you send for Hapsy too?

41 It was Hapsy she really wanted. She had to go a long way back through a great many rooms to find Hapsy standing with a baby on her arm. She seemed to herself to be Hapsy also, and the baby on Hapsy's arm was Hapsy and himself and herself, all at once, and there was no surprise in the meeting. Then Hapsy melted from within and turned flimsy as gray gauze and the baby was a gauzy shadow, and Hapsy came up close and said, "I thought you'd never come," and looked at her very searchingly and said, "You haven't changed a bit!" They leaned forward to kiss, when Cornelia began whispering from a long way off, "Oh, is there anything you want to tell me? Is there anything I can do for you?"

42 Yes, she had changed her mind after sixty years and she would like to see George. I want you to find George. Find him and be sure to tell him I forgot him. I want him to know I had my husband just the same and my children and my house like any other woman. A good house too and a good husband that I loved and fine children out of him. Better than I hoped for even. Tell him I was given back everything he took away and more. Oh, no, oh, God, no, there was something else besides the house and the man and the children. Oh, surely they were not all? What was it? Something not given back . . . Her breath crowded down under her ribs and grew into a monstrous frightening shape with cutting edges; it bored up into her head, and the agony was unbelievable—Yes, John, get the doctor now, no more talk, my time has come.

43 When this one was born it should be the last. The last. It should have been born first, for it was the one she had truly wanted. Everything came in good time. Nothing left out, left over. She was strong, in three days she would be as well as ever. Better. A woman needed milk in her to have her full health.

44 "Mother, do you hear me?"

45 "I've been telling you—"

46 "Mother, Father Connolly's here."

47 "I went to Holy Communion only last week. Tell him I'm not so sinful as all that."

48 "Father just wants to speak to you."

49 He could speak as much as he pleased. It was like him to drop in and inquire about her soul as if it were a teething baby, and then stay on for a cup of tea and a round of cards and gossip. He always had a funny story of some sort, usually about an Irishman who made his little mistakes and confessed them, and the point lay in some absurd thing he would blurt out in the confessional showing his struggles between native piety and original sin. Granny felt easy about

her soul. Cornelia, where are your manners? Give Father Connolly a chair. She had her secret comfortable understanding with a few favorite saints who cleared a straight road to God for her. All as surely signed and sealed as the papers for the new Forty Acres. Forever . . . heirs and assigns forever. Since the day the wedding cake was not cut, but thrown out and wasted. The whole bottom dropped out of the world, and there she was blind and sweating with nothing under her feet and walls falling away. His hand had caught her under the breast, she had not fallen, there was the freshly polished floor with the green rug on it, just as before. He had cursed like a sailor's parrot and said, "I'll kill him for you." Don't lay a hand on him, for my sake leave something to God. "Now, Ellen, you must believe what I tell you . . . "

50 So there was nothing, nothing to worry about any more, except sometimes in the night one of the children screamed in a nightmare, and they both hustled out shaking and hunting for the matches and calling, "There, wait a minute, here we are!" John, get the doctor now, Hapsy's time has come. But there was Hapsy standing by the bed in a white cap. "Cornelia, tell Hapsy to take off her cap. I can't see her plain."

51 Her eyes opened very wide and the room stood out like a picture she had seen somewhere. Dark colors with the shadows rising towards the ceiling in long angles. The tall black dresser gleamed with nothing on it but John's picture, enlarged from a little one, with John's eyes very black when they should have been blue. You never saw him, so how do you know how he looked? But the man insisted the copy was perfect, it was very rich and handsome. For a picture, yes, but it's not my husband. The table by the bed had a linen cover and a candle and a crucifix. The light was blue from Cornelia's silk lampshades. No sort of light at all, just frippery. You had to live forty years with kerosene lamps to appreciate honest electricity. She felt very strong and she saw Doctor Harry with a rosy nimbus around him.

52 "You look like a saint, Doctor Harry, and I vow that's as near as you'll ever come to it."

53 "She's saying something."

54 "I heard you, Cornelia. What's all this carrying on?"

55 "Father Connolly's saying—"

56 Cornelia's voice staggered and bumped like a cart in a bad road. It rounded corners and turned back again and arrived nowhere. Granny stepped up in the cart very lightly and reached for the reins, but a man sat beside her and she knew him by his hands, driving the cart. She did not look in his face, for she knew without seeing, but looked instead down the road where the trees leaned over and bowed to each other and a thousand birds were singing a Mass. She felt like singing too, but she put her hand in the bosom of her dress and pulled out a rosary, and Father Connolly murmured Latin in a very solemn voice and tickled her feet. My God, will you stop that nonsense? I'm a married woman.

What if he did run away and leave me to face the priest by myself? I found another a whole world better. I wouldn't have exchanged my husband for anybody except St. Michael himself, and you may tell him that for me with a thank you in the bargain.

57 Light flashed on her closed eyelids, and a deep roaring shook her. Cornelia, is that lightning? I hear thunder. There's going to be a storm. Close all the windows. Call the children in . . . "Mother, here we are, all of us." "Is that you, Hapsy?" "Oh, no, I'm Lydia. We drove as fast as we could." Their faces drifted above her, drifted away. The rosary fell out of her hands and Lydia put it back. Jimmy tried to help, their hands fumbled together, and Granny closed two fingers around Jimmy's thumb. Beads wouldn't do, it must be something alive. She was so amazed her thoughts ran round and round. So, my dear Lord, this is my death and I wasn't even thinking about it. My children have come to see me die. But I can't, it's not time. Oh, I always hated surprises. I wanted to give Cornelia the amethyst set—Cornelia, you're to have the amethyst set, but Hapsy's to wear it when she wants, and, Doctor Harry, do shut up. Nobody sent for you. Oh, my dear Lord, do wait a minute. I meant to do something about the Forty Acres, Jimmy doesn't need it and Lydia will later on, with that worthless husband of hers. I meant to finish the altar cloth and send six bottles of wine to Sister Borgia for her dyspepsia. I want to send six bottles of wine to Sister Borgia, Father Connolly, now don't let me forget.

58 Cornelia's voice made short turns and tilted over and crashed, "Oh, Mother, oh, Mother, oh, Mother . . . "

59 "I'm not going, Cornelia. I'm taken by surprise. I can't go."

60 You'll see Hapsy again. What about her? "I thought you'd never come." Granny made a long journey outward, looking for Hapsy. What if I don't find her? What then? Her heart sank down and down, there was no bottom to death, she couldn't come to the end of it. The blue light from Cornelia's lampshade drew into a tiny point in the center of her brain, it flickered and winked like an eye, quietly it fluttered and dwindled. Granny lay curled down within herself, amazed and watchful, staring at the point of light that was herself; her body was now only a deeper mass of shadow in an endless darkness and this darkness would curl around the light and swallow it up. God, give a sign!

61 For the second time there was no sign. Again no bridegroom and the priest in the house. She could not remember any other sorrow because this grief wiped them all away. Oh, no, there's nothing more cruel than this—I'll never forgive it. She stretched her self with a deep breath and blew out the light.

—1929

✧ ✧ ✧

William Faulkner
(1897-1962)

A Rose for Emily

Faulkner (originally spelled "Falkner," but a misprint in an early book led him to change it) spent long periods of his adult life in Hollywood, where he had some success as a screenwriter (a 1991 film, *Barton Fink*, has a character obviously modeled on him), but always returned to Oxford, Mississippi, the site of his fictional Jefferson and Yoknapatawpha County. With Thomas Wolfe and others, he was responsible for the flowering of southern fiction in the early decades of the century, though for Faulkner fame came relatively late in life. Despite the success of *Sanctuary* (1931) and the critical esteem in which other early works like *The Sound and the Fury* (1929) and *As I Lay Dying* (1930) were held, Faulkner proved too difficult for most readers and failed to attract large audiences for what are now considered his best novels. By the late 1940s most of his books were out of print. His reputation was revived when Malcolm Cowley's edition of *The Portable Faulkner* appeared in 1946, but despite the success of *Intruder in the Dust* (1948) he was not as well known as many of his contemporaries when he won the Nobel Prize in 1950. A brilliant innovator of unusual narrative techniques in his novels, Faulkner created of complex genealogies of characters to inhabit the world of his mythical South.

I

When Miss Emily Grierson died, our whole town went to her funeral: The men through a sort of respectful affection for a fallen monument, the women mostly out of curiosity to see the inside of her house, which no one save an old manservant—a combined gardener and cook—had seen in at least ten years.

2 It was a big, squarish frame house that had once been white, decorated with cupolas and spires and scrolled balconies in the heavily lightsome style of the seventies, set on what had once been our most select street. But garages and cotton gins had encroached and obliterated even the august names of that neighborhood; only Miss Emily's house was left, lifting its stubborn and coquettish decay above the cotton wagons and the gasoline pumps—an eyesore among eye-

sores. And now Miss Emily had gone to join the representatives of those august names where they lay in the cedar-bemused cemetery among the ranked and anonymous graves of Union and Confederate soldiers who fell at the battle of Jefferson.

3 Alive, Miss Emily had been a tradition, a duty, and a care; a sort of hereditary obligation upon the town, dating from that day in 1894 when Colonel Sartoris, the mayor—he who fathered the edict that no Negro woman should appear on the streets without an apron—remitted her taxes, the dispensation dating from the death of her father on into perpetuity. Not that Miss Emily would have accepted charity. Colonel Sartoris invented an involved tale to the effect that Miss Emily's father had loaned money to the town, which the town, as a matter of business, preferred this way of repaying. Only a man of Colonel Sartoris' generation and thought could have invented it, and only a woman could have believed it.

4 When the next generation, with its more modern ideas, became mayors and aldermen, this arrangement created some little dissatisfaction. On the first of the year they mailed her a tax notice. February came, and there was no reply. They wrote her a formal letter, asking her to call at the sheriff's office at her convenience. A week later the mayor wrote her himself, offering to call or to send his car for her, and received in reply a note on paper of an archaic shape, in a thin, flowing calligraphy in faded ink, to the effect that she no longer went out at all. The tax notice was also enclosed, without comment.

5 They called a special meeting of the Board of Aldermen. A deputation waited upon her, knocked at the door through which no visitor had passed since she ceased giving china-painting lessons eight or ten years earlier. They were admitted by the old Negro into a dim hall from which a staircase mounted into still more shadow. It smelled of dust and disuse—a close, dank smell. The Negro led them into the parlor. It was furnished in heavy, leather-covered furniture. When the Negro opened the blinds of one window, they could see that the leather was cracked; and when they sat down, a faint dust rose sluggishly about their thighs, spinning with slow motes in the single sunray. On a tarnished gilt easel before the fireplace stood a crayon portrait of Miss Emily's father.

6 They rose when she entered—a small, fat woman in black, with a thin gold chain descending to her waist and vanishing into her belt, leaning on an ebony cane with a tarnished gold head. Her skeleton was small and spare; perhaps that was why what would have been merely plumpness in another was obesity in her. She looked bloated, like a body long submerged in motionless water, and of that pallid hue. Her eyes, lost in the fatty ridges of her face, looked like two small pieces of coal pressed into a lump of dough as they moved from one face to another while the visitors stated their errand.

7 She did not ask them to sit. She just stood in the door and listened quietly until the spokesman came to a stumbling halt. Then they could hear the invisible watch ticking at the end of the gold chain.

8 Her voice was dry and cold. "I have no taxes in Jefferson. Colonel Sartoris explained it to me. Perhaps one of you can gain access to the city records and satisfy yourselves."

9 "But we have. We are the city authorities, Miss Emily. Didn't you get a notice from the sheriff, signed by him?"

10 "I received a paper, yes," Miss Emily said. "Perhaps he considers himself the sheriff . . . I have no taxes in Jefferson."

11 "But there is nothing on the books to show that, you see. We must go by the—"

12 "See Colonel Sartoris. I have no taxes in Jefferson."

13 "But, Miss Emily—"

14 "See Colonel Sartoris." (Colonel Sartoris had been dead almost ten years.) "I have no taxes in Jefferson. Tobe!" The Negro appeared. "Show these gentlemen out."

II

15 So she vanquished them, horse and foot, just as she had vanquished their fathers thirty years before about the smell. That was two years after her father's death and a short time after her sweetheart—the one we believed would marry her—had deserted her. After her father's death she went out very little; after her sweetheart went away people hardly saw her at all. A few of the ladies had the temerity to call, but were not received, and the only sign of life about the place was the Negro man—a young man then—going in and out with a market basket.

16 "Just as if a man—any man—could keep a kitchen properly," the ladies said; so they were not surprised when the smell developed. It was another link between the gross, teeming world and the high and mighty Griersons.

17 A neighbor, a woman, complained to the mayor, Judge Stevens, eighty years old.

18 "But what will you have me do about it, madam?" he said.

19 "Why, send her word to stop it," the woman said. "Isn't there a law?"

20 "I'm sure that won't be necessary," Judge Stevens said. "It's probably just a snake or a rat that nigger of hers killed in the yard. I'll speak to him about it."

21 The next day he received two more complaints, one from a man who came in diffident deprecation. "We really must do something about it, Judge. I'd be the last one in the world to bother Miss Emily, but we've got to do something." That night the Board of Aldermen met—three gray-beards and one younger man, a member of the rising generation.

22 "It's simple enough," he said. "Send her word to have her place cleaned up. Give her a certain time to do it in, and if she don't . . . "

23 "Dammit, sir," Judge Stevens said, "will you accuse a lady to her face of smelling bad?"

24 So the next night, after midnight, four men crossed Miss Emily's lawn and slunk about the house like burglars, sniffing along the base of the brickwork and at the cellar openings while one of them performed a regular sowing motion with his hand out of a sack slung from his shoulder. They broke open the cellar door and sprinkled lime there, and in all the outbuildings. As they recrossed the lawn, a window that had been dark was lighted and Miss Emily sat in it, the light behind her, and her upright torso motionless as that of an idol. They crept quietly across the lawn and into the shadow of the locusts that lined the street. After a week or two the smell went away.

25 That was when people had begun to feel really sorry for her. People in our town, remembering how old lady Wyatt, her great-aunt, had gone completely crazy at last, believed that the Griersons held themselves a little too high for what they really were. None of the young men were quite good enough for Miss Emily and such. We had long thought of them as a tableau, Miss Emily a slender figure in white in the background, her father a spraddled silhouette in the foreground, his back to her and clutching a horsewhip, the two of them framed by the back-flung front door. So when she got to be thirty and was still single, we were not pleased exactly, but vindicated; even with insanity in the family she wouldn't have turned down all of her chances if they had really materialized.

26 When her father died, it got about that the house was all that was left to her; and in a way, people were glad. At last they could pity Miss Emily. Being left alone, and a pauper, she had become humanized. Now she too would know the old thrill and the old despair of a penny more or less.

27 The day after his death all the ladies prepared to call at the house and offer condolence and aid, as is our custom. Miss Emily met them at the door, dressed as usual and with no trace of grief on her face. She told them that her father was not dead. She did that for three days, with the ministers calling on her, and the doctors, trying to persuade her to let them dispose of the body. Just as they were about to resort to law and force, she broke down, and they buried her father quickly.

28 We did not say she was crazy then. We believed she had to do that. We remembered all the young men her father had driven away, and we knew that with nothing left, she would have to cling to that which had robbed her, as people will.

III

29 She was sick for a long time. When we saw her again, her hair was cut short, making her look like a girl, with a vague resemblance to those angels in colored church windows—sort of tragic and serene.

30 The town had just let the contracts for paving the sidewalks, and in the summer after her father's death they began the work. The construction company came with niggers and mules and machinery, and a foreman named Homer Barron, a Yankee—a big, dark, ready man, with a big voice and eyes lighter than his face. The little boys would follow in groups to hear him cuss the niggers, and the niggers singing in time to the rise and fall of picks. Pretty soon he knew everybody in town. Whenever you heard a lot of laughing anywhere about the square, Homer Barron would be in the center of the group. Presently we began to see him and Miss Emily on Sunday afternoons driving in the yellow-wheeled buggy and the matched team of bays from the livery stable.

31 At first we were glad that Miss Emily would have an interest, because the ladies all said, "Of course a Grierson would not think seriously of a Northerner, a day laborer." But there were still others, older people, who said that even grief could not cause a real lady to forget *noblesse oblige*—without calling it *noblesse oblige.* They just said, "Poor Emily. Her kinsfolk should come to her." She had some kin in Alabama; but years ago her father had fallen out with them over the estate of old lady Wyatt, the crazy woman, and there was no communication between the two families. They had not even been represented at the funeral.

32 And as soon as the old people said, "Poor Emily," the whispering began. "Do you suppose it's really so?" they said to one another. "Of course it is. What else could . . . " This behind their hands; rustling of craned silk and satin behind jalousies closed upon the sun of Sunday afternoon as the thin, swift clop-clop-clop of the matched team passed: "Poor Emily."

33 She carried her head high enough—even when we believed that she was fallen. It was as if she demanded more than ever the recognition of her dignity as the last Grierson; as if it had wanted that touch of earthiness to reaffirm her imperviousness. Like when she bought the rat poison, the arsenic. That was over a year after they had begun to say "Poor Emily," and while the two female cousins were visiting her.

34 "I want some poison," she said to the druggist. She was over thirty then, still a slight woman, though thinner than usual, with cold, haughty black eyes in a face the flesh of which was strained across the temples and about the eye-sockets as you imagine a lighthousekeeper's face ought to look. "I want some poison," she said.

35 "Yes, Miss Emily. What kind? For rats and such? I'd recom—"

36 "I want the best you have. I don't care what kind."

37 The druggist named several. "They'll kill anything up to an elephant. But what you want—"

38 "Arsenic," Miss Emily said. "Is that a good one?"

39 "Is . . . arsenic? Yes, ma'am. But what you want—"

40 "I want arsenic."

41 The druggist looked down at her. She looked back at him, erect, her face like a strained flag. "Why, of course," the druggist said. "If that's what you want. But the law requires you to tell what you are going to use it for."

42 Miss Emily just stared at him, her head tilted back in order to look him eye for eye, until he looked away and went and got the arsenic and wrapped it up. The Negro delivery boy brought her the package; the druggist didn't come back. When she opened the package at home there was written on the box, under the skull and bones—"For rats."

IV

43 So the next day we all said, "She will kill herself"; and we said it would be the best thing. When she had first begun to be seen with Homer Barron, we had said, "She will marry him." Then we said, "She will persuade him yet," because Homer himself had remarked—he liked men, and it was known that he drank with the younger men in the Elks' Club—that he was not a marrying man. Later we said, "Poor Emily" behind the jalousies as they passed on Sunday afternoon in the glittering buggy, Miss Emily with her head high and Homer Barron with his hat cocked and a cigar in his teeth, reins and whip in a yellow glove.

44 Then some of the ladies began to say that it was a disgrace to the town and a bad example to the young people. The men did not want to interfere, but at last the ladies forced the Baptist minister—Miss Emily's people were Episcopal—to call upon her. He would never divulge what happened during that interview, but he refused to go back again. The next Sunday they again drove about the streets, and the following day the minister's wife wrote to Miss Emily's relations in Alabama.

45 So she had blood-kin under her roof again and we sat back to watch developments. At first nothing happened. Then we were sure that they were to be married. We learned that Miss Emily had been to the jeweler's and ordered a man's toilet set in silver, with the letters H. B. on each piece. Two days later we learned that she had bought a complete outfit of men's clothing, including a nightshirt, and we said, "They are married." We were really glad. We were glad because the two female cousins were even more Grierson than Miss Emily had ever been.

46 So we were not surprised when Homer Barron—the streets had been finished some time since—was gone. We were a little disappointed that there was not a public blowing-off, but we believed that he had gone on to prepare for Miss Emily's coming, or to give her a chance to get rid of the cousins. (By that time it was a cabal, and we were all Miss Emily's allies to help circumvent the cousins.) Sure enough, after another week they departed. And, as we had expected all along, within three days Homer Barron was back in town. A neighbor saw the Negro man admit him at the kitchen door at dusk one evening.

47 And that was the last we saw of Homer Barron. And of Miss Emily for some time. The Negro man went in and out with the market basket, but the front door remained closed. Now and then we would see her at a window for a moment, as the men did that night when they sprinkled the lime, but for almost six months she did not appear on the streets. Then we knew that this was to be expected too; as if that quality of her father which had thwarted her woman's life so many times had been too virulent and too furious to die.

48 When we next saw Miss Emily, she had grown fat and her hair was turning gray. During the next few years it grew grayer and grayer until it attained an even pepper-and-salt iron-gray, when it ceased turning. Up to the day of her death at seventy-four it was still that vigorous iron-gray, like the hair of an active man.

49 From that time on her front door remained closed, save for a period of six or seven years, when she was about forty, during which she gave lessons in china painting. She fitted up a studio in one of the downstairs rooms, where the daughters and granddaughters of Colonel Sartoris' contemporaries were sent to her with the same regularity and in the same spirit that they were sent to church on Sundays with a twenty-five cent piece for the collection plate. Meanwhile her taxes had been remitted.

50 Then the newer generation became the backbone and the spirit of the town, and the painting pupils grew up and fell away and did not send their children to her with boxes of color and tedious brushes and pictures cut from the ladies' magazines. The front door closed upon the last one and remained closed for good. When the town got free postal delivery, Miss Emily alone refused to let them fasten the metal numbers above her door and attach a mailbox to it. She would not listen to them.

51 Daily, monthly, yearly we watched the Negro grow grayer and more stooped, going in and out with the market basket. Each December we sent her a tax notice, which would be returned by the post office a week later, unclaimed. Now and then we would see her in one of the downstairs windows—she had evidently shut up the top floor of the house—like the carven torso of an idol in a niche, looking or not looking at us, we could never tell which. Thus she passed from generation to generation—dear, inescapable, impervious, tranquil, and perverse.

52 And so she died. Fell ill in the house filled with dust and shadows, with only a doddering Negro man to wait on her. We did not even know she was sick; we had long since given up trying to get any information from the Negro. He talked to no one, probably not even to her, for his voice had grown harsh and rusty, as if from disuse.

53 She died in one of the downstairs rooms, in a heavy walnut bed with a curtain, her gray head propped on a pillow yellow and moldy with age and lack of sunlight.

V

54 The Negro met the first of the ladies at the front door and let them in, with their hushed, sibilant voices and their quick, curious glances, and then he disappeared. He walked right through the house and out the back and was not seen again.

55 The two female cousins came at once. They held the funeral on the second day, with the town coming to look at Miss Emily beneath a mass of bought flowers, with the crayon face of her father musing profoundly above the bier and the ladies sibilant and macabre; and the very old men—some in their brushed Confederate uniforms—on the porch and the lawn, talking of Miss Emily as if she had been a contemporary of theirs, believing that they had danced with her and courted her perhaps, confusing time with its mathematical progression, as the old do, to whom all the past is not a diminishing road but, instead, a huge meadow which no winter ever quite touches, divided from them now by the narrow bottleneck of the most recent decade of years.

56 Already we knew that there was one room in that region above stairs which no one had seen in forty years, and which would have to be forced. They waited until Miss Emily was decently in the ground before they opened it.

57 The violence of breaking down the door seemed to fill this room with pervading dust. A thin, acrid pall as of the tomb seemed to lie everywhere upon this room decked and furnished as for a bridal: upon the valance curtains of faded rose color, upon the rose-shaded lights, upon the dressing table, upon the delicate array of crystal and the man's toilet things backed with tarnished silver, silver so tarnished that the monogram was obscured. Among them lay collar and tie, as if they had just been removed, which, lifted, left upon the surface a pale crescent in the dust. Upon a chair hung the suit, carefully folded; beneath it the two mute shoes and the discarded socks.

58 The man himself lay in the bed.

59 For a long while we just stood there, looking down at the profound and fleshless grin. The body had apparently once lain in the attitude of an embrace, but now the long sleep that outlasts love, that conquers even the grimace of love, had cuckolded him. What was left of him, rotted beneath what was left of the nightshirt, had become inextricable from the bed in which he lay; and upon him and upon the pillow beside him lay that even coating of the patient and biding dust.

60 Then we noticed that in the second pillow was the indentation of a head. One of us lifted something from it, and leaning forward, that faint and invisible dust dry and acrid in the nostrils, we saw a long strand of iron-gray hair.

—1930

✧ ✧ ✧

Ernest Hemingway
(1899-1961)

A Clean, Well-Lighted Place

Hemingway so embodied the image of the successful writer for so long that today, three decades after his suicide, it is difficult to separate the celebrity from the serious artist, the sportsman and carouser from the stylist whose influence on the short story and novel continues to be felt. The complexity of his life and personality still fascinates biographers, even though a half dozen major studies have already appeared. Born to a doctor in Oak Park, Illinois, wounded as a volunteer ambulance driver in Italy during World War I, trained as a reporter on the Kansas City *Star*, Hemingway moved to Paris in the early 1920s, where he was at the center of a brilliant generation of American expatriates that included Gertrude Stein and F. Scott Fitzgerald. His wide-ranging travels are reflected in his work. He spent much time in Spain, which provided material for his first novel, *The Sun Also Rises* (1926), and stories like "A Clean, Well-Lighted Place." In the 1930s he covered the Spanish Civil War, the backdrop for his most popular novel, *For Whom the Bell Tolls* (1940). His African safaris and residence in pre-Castro Cuba were also sources of his fiction. When all else is said, Hemingway's greatest contribution may lie in the terse, stripped-down quality of his early prose, which renders modern alienation with stark concrete details. Hemingway won the Nobel Prize in 1954.

It was late and every one had left the café except an old man who sat in the shadow the leaves of the tree made against the electric light. In the day time the street was dusty, but at night the dew settled the dust and the old man liked to sit late because he was deaf and now at night it was quiet and he felt the difference. The two waiters inside the café knew that the old man was a little drunk, and while he was a good client they knew that if he became too drunk he would leave without paying, so they kept watch on him.

2 "Last week he tried to commit suicide," one waiter said.

3 "Why?"

4 "He was in despair."

5 "What about?"

6 "Nothing."

7 "How do you know it was nothing?"

8 "He has plenty of money."

9 They sat together at a table that was close against the wall near the door of the cafe and looked at the terrace where the tables were all empty except where the old man sat in the shadow of the leaves of the tree that moved slightly in the wind. A girl and a soldier went by in the street. The street light shone on the brass number on his collar. The girl wore no head covering and hurried beside him.

10 "The guard will pick him up," one waiter said.

11 "What does it matter if he gets what he's after?"

12 "He had better get off the street now. The guard will get him. They went by five minutes ago."

13 The old man sitting in the shadow rapped on his saucer with his glass. The younger waiter went over to him.

14 "What do you want?"

15 The old man looked at him. "Another brandy," he said.

16 "You'll be drunk," the waiter said. The old man looked at him. The waiter went away.

17 "He'll stay all night," he said to his colleague. "I'm sleepy now. I never get into bed before three o'clock. He should have killed himself last week."

18 The waiter took the brandy bottle and another saucer from the counter inside the café and marched out to the old man's table. He put down the saucer and poured the glass full of brandy.

19 "You should have killed yourself last week," he said to the deaf man. The old man motioned with his finger. "A little more," he said. The waiter poured on into the glass so that the brandy slopped over and ran down the stem into the top saucer of the pile. "Thank you," the old man said. The waiter took the bottle back inside the café. He sat down at the table with his colleague again.

20 "He's drunk now," he said.

21 "He's drunk every night."

22 "What did he want to kill himself for?"

23 "How should I know?"

24 "How did he do it?"

25 "He hung himself with a rope."

26 "Who cut him down?"

27 "His niece."

28 "Why did they do it?"

29 "Fear for his soul."

30 "How much money has he got?"

31 "He's got plenty."

32 "He must be eighty years old."

33 "Anyway I should say he was eighty."

34 "I wish he would go home. I never get to bed before three o'clock. What kind of hour is that to go to bed?"

35 "He stays up because he likes it."

36 "He's lonely. I'm not lonely. I have a wife waiting in bed for me."

37 "He had a wife once too."

38 "A wife would be no good to him now."

39 "You can't tell. He might be better with a wife."

40 "His niece looks after him."

41 "I know. You said she cut him down."

42 "I wouldn't want to be that old. An old man is a nasty thing."

43 "Not always. This old man is clean. He drinks without spilling. Even now, drunk. Look at him."

44 "I don't want to look at him. I wish he would go home. He has no regard for those who must work."

45 The old man looked from his glass across the square, then over at the waiters.

46 "Another brandy," he said, pointing to his glass. The waiter who was in a hurry came over.

47 "Finished," he said, speaking with that omission of syntax stupid people employ when talking to drunken people or foreigners. "No more tonight. Close now."

48 "Another," said the old man.

49 "No. Finished." The waiter wiped the edge of the table with a towel and shook his head.

50 The old man stood up, slowly counted the saucers, took a leather coin purse from his pocket and paid for the drinks, leaving half a peseta tip.

51 The waiter watched him go down the street, a very old man walking unsteadily but with dignity.

52 "Why didn't you let him stay and drink?" the unhurried waiter asked. They were putting up the shutters. "It is not half-past two."

53 "I want to go home to bed."

54 "What is an hour?"

55 "More to me than to him."

56 "An hour is the same."

57 "You talk like an old man yourself. He can buy a bottle and drink at home."

58 "It's not the same."

59 "No, it is not," agreed the waiter with a wife. He did not wish to be unjust. He was only in a hurry.

60 "And you? You have no fear of going home before the usual hour?"

61 "Are you trying to insult me?"

62 "No, hombre, only to make a joke."

63 "No," the waiter who was in a hurry said, rising from pulling down the metal shutters. "I have confidence. I am all confidence."

64 "You have youth, confidence, and a job," the older waiter said. "You have everything."

65 "And what do you lack?"

66 "Everything but work."

67 "You have everything I have."

68 "No. I have never had confidence and I am not young."

69 "Come on. Stop talking nonsense and lock up."

70 "I am of those who like to stay late at the café," the older waiter said. "With all those who do not want to go to bed. With all those who need a light for the night."

71 "I want to go home and into bed."

72 "We are of two different kinds," the older waiter said. He was not dressed to go home. "It is not only a question of youth and confidence although those things are very beautiful. Each night I am reluctant to close up because there may be some one who needs the café."

73 "Hombre, there are bodegas° open all night long."

74 "You do not understand. This is a clean and pleasant café. It is well lighted. The light is very good and also, now, there are shadows of the leaves."

75 "Good night," said the younger waiter.

76 "Good night," the other said. Turning off the electric light he continued the conversation with himself. It is the light of course but it is necessary that the place be clean and pleasant. You do not want music. Certainly you do not want music. Nor can you stand before a bar with dignity although that is all that is provided for these hours. What did he fear? It was not fear or dread. It was a nothing that he knew too well. It was all a nothing and a man was nothing too. It was only that and light was all it needed and a certain cleanness and order. Some lived in it and never felt it but he knew it all was nada y pues nada y nada y pues nada.° Our nada who are in nada, nada be thy name thy kingdom nada thy will be nada in nada as it is in nada. Give us this nada our daily nada and nada us our nada as we nada our nadas and nada us not into nada but deliver us from nada; pues nada. Hail nothing full of nothing, nothing is with thee. He smiled and stood before a bar with a shining steam pressure coffee machine.

77 "What's yours?" asked the barman.

78 "Nada."

79 "Otro loco más,"° said the barman and turned away.

---

bodegas wine shops
nada y pues . . . nada nothing and then nothing . . .
Otro loco más Another lunatic

80 "A little cup," said the waiter.

81 The barman poured it for him.

82 "The light is very bright and pleasant but the bar is unpolished," the waiter said.

83 The barman looked at him but did not answer. It was too late at night for conversation.

84 "You want another copita?"° the barman asked.

85 "No, thank you," said the waiter and went out. He disliked bars and bodegas. A clean, well-lighted café was a very different thing. Now, without thinking further, he would go home to his room. He would lie in the bed and finally, with daylight, he would go to sleep. After all, he said to himself, it is probably only insomnia. Many must have it.

—1933

✧ ✧ ✧

John Steinbeck
(1902-1968)

The Chrysanthemums

Another American winner of the Nobel Prize, Steinbeck has not attracted as much biographical and critical attention as his contemporaries William Faulkner and Ernest Hemingway, but future generations may view *The Grapes of Wrath* (1939), his epic novel of the Depression and the Oklahoma dust bowl, with the same reverence we reserve for nineteenth-century masterpieces of historical fiction like Thackeray's *Vanity Fair* or Tolstoy's *War and Peace*. If one measure of a great writer is how well he or she manages to capture the temper of the times, then Steinbeck stands as tall as any. Born in Salinas, California, he drew throughout his career on his familiarity with the farming country, ranches, and fishing communities of his native state, especially in novels like *Tortilla Flat* (1935), *Of Mice and Men* (1937), and *Cannery Row* (1945). Steinbeck's short fiction is less well known, though

---

copita little cup

he excelled at the novella form in *The Pearl* (1947). "The Chrysanthemums" comes from *The Long Valley,* a collection of short stories set in the Salinas Valley. Like many of the best American writers of the century, Steinbeck was a humanitarian whose sympathies lay with the common man or woman, though he rarely indulged in the shallow propagandizing that characterized many so-called proletarian novels of the 1930s. Steinbeck was a lifelong student of marine biology, and his sensitivity to the effects of environment on organisms, both animal and human, is reflected in his scrupulous attention to setting.

The high grey-flannel fog of winter closed off the Salinas Valley from the sky and from all the rest of the world. On every side it sat like a lid on the mountains and made of the great valley a closed pot. On the broad, level land floor the gang plows bit deep and left the black earth shining like metal where the shares had cut. On the foothill ranches across the Salinas River, the yellow stubble fields seemed to be bathed in pale cold sunshine, but there was no sunshine in the valley now in December. The thick willow scrub along the river flamed with sharp and positive yellow leaves.

2 It was a time of quiet and of waiting. The air was cold and tender. A light wind blew up from the southwest so that the farmers were mildly hopeful of a good rain before long; but fog and rain do not go together.

3 Across the river, on Henry Allen's foothill ranch there was little work to be done, for the hay was cut and stored and the orchards were plowed up to receive the rain deeply when it should come. The cattle on the higher slopes were becoming shaggy and rough-coated.

4 Elisa Allen, working in her flower garden, looked down across the yard and saw Henry, her husband, talking to two men in business suits. The three of them stood by the tractor shed, each man with one foot on the side of the little Fordson. They smoked cigarettes and studied the machine as they talked.

5 Elisa watched them for a moment and then went back to her work. She was thirty-five. Her face was lean and strong and her eyes were as clear as water. Her figure looked blocked and heavy in her gardening costume, a man's black hat pulled low down over her eyes, clod-hopper shoes, a figured print dress almost completely covered by a big corduroy apron with four big pockets to hold the snips, the trowel and scratcher, the seeds and the knife she worked with. She wore heavy leather gloves to protect her hands while she worked.

6 She was cutting down the old year's chrysanthemum stalks with a pair of short and powerful scissors. She looked down toward the men by the tractor shed now and then. Her face was eager and mature and handsome; even her work with

the scissors was over-eager, over-powerful. The chrysanthemum stems seemed too small and easy for her energy.

7 She brushed a cloud of hair out of her eyes with the back of her glove, and left a smudge of earth on her cheek in doing it. Behind her stood the neat white farm house with red geraniums close-banked around it as high as the windows. It was a hard-swept looking little house with hard-polished windows, and a clean mud-mat on the front steps.

8 Elisa cast another glance toward the tractor shed. The strangers were getting into their Ford coupe. She took off a glove and put her strong fingers down into the forest of new green chrysanthemum sprouts that were growing around the old roots. She spread the leaves and looked down among the close-growing stems. No aphids were there, no sowbugs or snails or cutworms. Her terrier fingers destroyed such pests before they could get started.

9 Elisa started at the sound of her husband's voice. He had come near quietly, and he leaned over the wire fence that protected her flower garden from cattle and dogs and chickens.

10 "At it again," he said. "You've got a strong new crop coming."

11 Elisa straightened her back and pulled on the gardening glove again. "Yes. They'll be strong this coming year." In her tone and on her face there was a little smugness.

12 "You've got a gift with things," Henry observed. "Some of those yellow chrysanthemums you had this year were ten inches across. I wish you'd work out in the orchard and raise some apples that big."

13 Her eyes sharpened. "Maybe I could do it, too. I've a gift with things, all right. My mother had it. She could stick anything in the ground and make it grow. She said it was having planters' hands that knew how to do it."

14 "Well, it sure works with flowers," he said.

15 "Henry, who were those men you were talking to?"

16 "Why, sure, that's what I came to tell you. They were from the Western Meat Company. I sold those thirty head of three-year-old steers. Got nearly my own price, too."

17 "Good," she said. "Good for you."

18 "And I thought," he continued, "I thought how it's Saturday afternoon, and we might go into Salinas for dinner at a restaurant, and then to a picture show—to celebrate, you see."

19 "Good," she repeated. "Oh, yes. That will be good."

20 Henry put on his joking tone. "There's fights tonight. How'd you like to go to the fights?"

21 "Oh, no," she said breathlessly. "No, I wouldn't like fights."

22 "Just fooling, Elisa. We'll go to a movie. Let's see. It's two now. I'm going to take Scotty and bring down those steers from the hill. It'll take us

maybe two hours. We'll go in town about five and have dinner at the Cominos Hotel. Like that?"

23 "Of course I'll like it. It's good to eat away from home."

24 "All right, then. I'll go get up a couple of horses."

25 She said, "I'll have plenty of time to transplant some of these sets, I guess."

26 She heard her husband calling Scotty down by the barn. And a little later she saw the two men ride up the pale yellow hillside in search of the steers.

27 There was a little square sandy bed kept for rooting the chrysanthemums. With her trowel she turned the soil over and over, and smoothed it and patted it firm. Then she dug ten parallel trenches to receive the sets. Back at the chrysanthemum bed she pulled out the little crisp shoots, trimmed off the leaves of each one with her scissors and laid it on a small orderly pile.

28 A squeak of wheels and plod of hoofs came from the road. Elisa looked up. The country road ran along the dense bank of willows and cottonwoods that bordered the river, and up this road came a curious vehicle, curiously drawn. It was an old springwagon, with a round canvas top on it like the cover of a prairie schooner. It was drawn by an old bay horse and a little grey-and-white burro. A big stubble bearded man sat between the cover flaps and drove the crawling team. Underneath the wagon, between the hind wheels, a lean and rangy mongrel dog walked sedately. Words were painted on the canvas, in clumsy, crooked letters. "Pots, pans, knives, sisors, lawn mores, Fixed." Two rows of articles, and the triumphantly definitive "Fixed" below. The black paint had run down in little sharp-points beneath each letter.

29 Elisa, squatting on the ground, watched to see the crazy, loose-jointed wagon pass by. But it didn't pass. It turned into the farm road in front of her house, crooked old wheels skirling and squeaking. The rangy dog darted from between the wheels and ran ahead. Instantly the two ranch shepherds flew out at him. Then all three stopped, and with stiff and quivering tails, with taut straight legs, with ambassadorial dignity, they slowly circled, sniffing daintily. The caravan pulled up to Elisa's wire fence and stopped. Now the newcomer dog, feeling out numbered, lowered his tail and retired under the wagon with raised hackles and bared teeth.

30 The man on the wagon seat called out, "That's a bad dog in a fight when he gets started."

31 Elisa laughed. "I see he is. How soon does he generally get started?"

32 The man caught up her laughter and echoed it heartily. "Sometimes not for weeks and weeks," he said. He climbed stiffly down, over the wheel. The horse and the donkey drooped like unwatered flowers.

33 Elisa saw that he was a very big man. Although his hair and beard were greying, he did not look old. His worn black suit was wrinkled and spotted with grease. The laughter had disappeared from his face and eyes the moment his laughing voice ceased. His eyes were dark, and they were full of the brood-

ing that gets in the eyes of teamsters and of sailors. The calloused hands he rested on the wire fence were cracked, and every crack was a black line. He took off his battered hat.

34 "I'm off my general road, ma'am," he said. "Does this dirt road cut over across the river to the Los Angeles highway?"

35 Elisa stood up and shoved the thick scissors in her apron pocket. "Well, yes, it does, but it winds around and then fords the river. I don't think your team could pull through the sand."

36 He replied with some asperity. "It might surprise you what them beasts can pull through."

37 "When they get started?" she asked.

38 He smiled for a second. "Yes. When they get started."

39 "Well," said Elisa, "I think you'll save time if you go back to the Salinas road and pick up the highway there."

40 He drew a big finger down the chicken wire and made it sing. "I ain't in any hurry, ma'am. I go from Seattle to San Diego and back every year. Takes all my time. About six months each way. I aim to follow nice weather."

41 Elisa took off her gloves and stuffed them in the apron pocket with the scissors. She touched the under edge of her man's hat, searching for fugitive hairs. "That sounds like a nice kind of a way to live," she said.

42 He leaned confidentially over the fence. "Maybe you noticed the writing on my wagon. I mend pots and sharpen knives and scissors. You got any of them things to do?"

43 "Oh, no," she said quickly. "Nothing like that." Her eyes hardened with resistance.

44 "Scissors is the worst thing," he explained. "Most people just ruin scissors trying to sharpen 'em, but I know how. I got a special tool. It's a little bobbit kind of thing, and patented. But it sure does the trick."

45 "No. My scissors are all sharp."

46 "All right, then. Take a pot," he continued earnestly, "a bent pot, or a pot with a hole. I can make it like new so you don't have to buy no new ones. That's a saving for you."

47 "No," she said shortly. "I tell you I have nothing like that for you to do."

48 His face fell to an exaggerated sadness. His voice took on a whining undertone. "I ain't had a thing to do today. Maybe I won't have no supper tonight. You see I'm off my regular road. I know folks on the highway clear from Seattle to San Diego. They save their things for me to sharpen up because they know I do it so good and save them money."

49 "I'm sorry," Elisa said irritably. "I haven't anything for you to do."

50 His eyes left her face and fell to searching the ground. They roamed about until they came to the chrysanthemum bed where she had been working. "What's them plants, ma'am?"

51 The irritation and resistance melted from Elisa's face. "Oh, those are chrysanthemums, giant whites and yellows. I raise them every year, bigger than anybody around here."

52 "Kind of a long-stemmed flower? Looks like a quick puff of colored smoke?" he asked.

53 "That's it. What a nice way to describe them."

54 "They smell kind of nasty till you get used to them," he said.

55 "It's a good bitter smell," she retorted, "not nasty at all."

56 He changed his tone quickly. "I like the smell myself."

57 "I had ten-inch blooms this year," she said.

58 The man leaned farther over the fence. "Look. I know a lady down the road a piece, has got the nicest garden you ever seen. Got nearly every kind of flower but no chrysanthemums. Last time I was mending a copper bottom wash tub for her (that's a hard job but I do it good), she said to me, 'If you ever run acrost some nice chrysanthemums I wish you'd try to get me a few seeds.' That's what she told me."

59 Elisa's eyes grew alert and eager. "She couldn't have known much about chrysanthemums. You *can* raise them from seed, but it's much easier to root the little sprouts you see there."

60 "Oh," he said. "I s'pose I can't take none to her, then."

61 "Why yes you can," Elisa cried. "I can put some in damp sand, and you can carry them right along with you. They'll take root in the pot if you keep them damp. And then she can transplant them."

62 "She'd sure like to have some, ma'am. You say they're nice ones?"

63 "Beautiful," she said. "Oh, beautiful." Her eyes shone. She tore off the battered hat and shook out her dark pretty hair. "I'll put them in a flower pot, and you can take them right with you. Come into the yard."

64 While the man came through the picket gate Elisa ran excitedly along the geranium-bordered path to the back of the house. And she returned carrying a big red flower pot. The gloves were forgotten now. She kneeled on the ground by the starting bed and dug up the sandy soil with her fingers and scooped it into the bright new flower pot. Then she picked up the little pile of shoots she had prepared. With her strong fingers she pressed them into the sand and tamped around them with her knuckles. The man stood over her. "I'll tell you what to do," she said. "You remember so you can tell the lady."

65 "Yes, I'll try to remember."

66 "Well, look. These will take root in about a month. Then she must set them out, about a foot apart in good rich earth like this, see?" She lifted a handful of dark soil for him to look at. "They'll grow fast and tall. Now re-

member this: In July tell her to cut them down, about eight inches from the ground."

67 "Before they bloom?" he asked.

68 "Yes, before they bloom." Her face was tight with eagerness. "They'll grow right up again. About the last of September the buds will start."

69 She stopped and seemed perplexed. "It's the budding that takes the most care," she said hesitantly. "I don't know how to tell you." She looked deep into his eyes, searchingly. Her mouth opened a little, and she seemed to be listening. "I'll try to tell you," she said. "Did you ever hear of planting hands?"

70 "Can't say I have, ma'am."

71 "Well, I can only tell you what it feels like. It's when you're picking off the buds you don't want. Everything goes right down into your fingertips. You watch your fingers work. They do it themselves. You can feel how it is. They pick and pick the buds. They never make a mistake. They're with the plant. Do you see? Your fingers and the plant. You can feel that, right up your arm. They know. They never make a mistake. You can feel it. When you're like that you can't do anything wrong. Do you see that? Can you understand that?"

72 She was kneeling on the ground looking up at him. Her breast swelled passionately.

73 The man's eyes narrowed. He looked away self-consciously. "Maybe I know," he said. "Sometimes in the night in the wagon there—"

74 Elisa's voice grew husky. She broke in on him, "I've never lived as you do, but I know what you mean. When the night is dark—why, the stars are sharp-pointed, and there's quiet. Why, you rise up and up! Every pointed star gets driven into your body. It's like that. Hot and sharp and—lovely."

75 Kneeling there, her hand went out toward his legs in the greasy black trousers. Her hesitant fingers almost touched the cloth. Then her hand dropped to the ground. She crouched low like a fawning dog.

76 He said, "It's nice, just like you say. Only when you don't have no dinner, it ain't."

77 She stood up then, very straight, and her face was ashamed. She held the flower pot out to him and placed it gently in his arms. "Here. Put it in your wagon, on the seat, where you can watch it. Maybe I can find something for you to do."

78 At the back of the house she dug in the can pile and found two old and battered aluminum saucepans. She carried them back and gave them to him. "Here, maybe you can fix these."

79 His manner changed. He became professional. "Good as new I can fix them." At the back of his wagon he set a little anvil, and out of an oily tool box dug a small machine hammer. Elisa came through the gate to watch him while

he pounded out the dents in the kettles. His mouth grew sure and knowing. At a difficult part of the work he sucked his under-lip.

80 "You sleep right in the wagon?" Elisa asked.

81 "Right in the wagon, ma'am. Rain or shine I'm dry as a cow in there."

82 "It must be nice," she said. "It must be very nice. I wish women could do such things."

83 "It ain't the right kind of a life for a woman."

84 Her upper lip raised a little, showing her teeth. "How do you know? How can you tell?" she said.

85 "I don't know, ma'am," he protested. "Of course I don't know. Now here's your kettles, done. You don't have to buy no new ones."

86 "How much?"

87 "Oh, fifty cents'll do. I keep my prices down and my work good. That's why I have all them satisfied customers up and down the highway."

88 Elisa brought him a fifty-cent piece from the house and dropped it in his hand. "You might be surprised to have a rival some time. I can sharpen scissors, too. And I can beat the dents out of little pots. I could show you what a woman might do."

89 He put his hammer back in the oily box and shoved the little anvil out of sight. "It would be a lonely life for a woman, ma'am, and a scarey life, too, with animals creeping under the wagon all night." He climbed over the single-tree, steadying himself with a hand on the burro's white rump. He settled himself in the seat, picked up the lines. "Thank you kindly, ma'am," he said. "I'll do like you told me; I'll go back and catch the Salinas road."

90 "Mind," she called, "if you're long in getting there, keep the sand damp."

91 "Sand, ma'am? . . . Sand? Oh, sure. You mean around the chrysanthemums. Sure I will." He clucked his tongue. The beasts leaned luxuriously into their collars. The mongrel dog took his place between the back wheels. The wagon turned and crawled out the entrance road and back the way it had come, along the river.

92 Elisa stood in front of her wire fence watching the slow progress of the caravan. Her shoulders were straight, her head thrown back, her eyes half-closed, so that the scene came vaguely into them. Her lips moved silently, forming the words "Good-bye—good-bye." Then she whispered, "That's a bright direction. There's a glowing there." The sound of her whisper startled her. She shook herself free and looked about to see whether anyone had been listening. Only the dogs had heard. They lifted their heads toward her from their sleeping in the dust, and then stretched out their chins and settled asleep again. Elisa turned and ran hurriedly into the house.

93 In the kitchen she reached behind the stove and felt the water tank. It was full of hot water from the noonday cooking. In the bathroom she tore off her soiled clothes and flung them into the corner. And then she scrubbed herself

with a little block of pumice, legs and thighs, loins and chest and arms, until her skin was scratched and red. When she had dried herself she stood in front of a mirror in her bedroom and looked at her body. She tightened her stomach and threw out her chest. She turned and looked over her shoulder at her back.

94 After a while she began to dress, slowly. She put on her newest underclothing and her nicest stockings and the dress which was the symbol of her prettiness. She worked carefully on her hair, penciled her eyebrows and rouged her lips.

95 Before she was finished she heard the little thunder of hoofs and the shouts of Henry and his helper as they drove the red steers into the corral. She heard the gate bang shut and set herself for Henry's arrival.

96 His step sounded on the porch. He entered the house calling, "Elisa, where are you?"

97 "In my room, dressing. I'm not ready. There's hot water for your bath. Hurry up. It's getting late."

98 When she heard him splashing in the tub, Elisa laid his dark suit on the bed, and shirt and socks and tie beside it. She stood his polished shoes on the floor beside the bed. Then she went to the porch and sat primly and stiffly down. She looked toward the river road where the willow-line was still yellow with frosted leaves so that under the high grey fog they seemed a thin band of sunshine. This was the only color in the grey afternoon. She sat unmoving for a long time. Her eyes blinked rarely.

99 Henry came banging out of the door shoving his tie inside his vest as he came. Elisa stiffened and her face grew tight. Henry stopped short and looked at her. "Why—why, Elisa. You look so nice!"

100 "Nice? You think I look nice? What do you mean by 'nice'?"

101 Henry blundered on. "I don't know. I mean you look different, strong and happy."

102 "I am strong? Yes, strong. What do you mean 'strong'?"

103 He looked bewildered. "You're playing some kind of a game," he said helplessly. "It's a kind of a play. You look strong enough to break a calf over your knee, happy enough to eat it like a watermelon."

104 For a second she lost her rigidity. "Henry! Don't talk like that. You didn't know what you said." She grew complete again. "I'm strong," she boasted. "I never knew before how strong."

105 Henry looked down toward the tractor shed, and when he brought his eyes back to her, they were his own again. "I'll get out the car. You can put on your coat while I'm starting."

106 Elisa went into the house. She heard him drive to the gate and idle down his motor, and then she took a long time to put on her hat. She pulled it here and

pressed it there. When Henry turned the motor off she slipped into her coat and went out.

107 The little roadster bounced along on the dirt road by the river, raising the birds and driving the rabbits into the brush. Two cranes flapped heavily over the willow-line and dropped into the river-bed.

108 Far ahead on the road Elisa saw a dark speck. She knew.

109 She tried not to look as they passed it, but her eyes would not obey. She whispered to herself sadly, "He might have thrown them off the road. That wouldn't have been much trouble, not very much. But he kept the pot," she explained. "He had to keep the pot. That's why he couldn't get them off the road."

110 The roadster turned a bend and she saw the caravan ahead. She swung full around toward her husband so she could not see the little covered wagon and the mismatched team as the car passed them.

111 In a moment it was over. The thing was done. She did not look back.

112 She said loudly, to be heard above the motor, "It will be good, tonight, a good dinner."

113 "Now you're changed again," Henry complained. He took one hand from the wheel and patted her knee. "I ought to take you in to dinner oftener. It would be good for both of us. We get so heavy out on the ranch."

114 "Henry," she asked, "could we have wine at dinner?"

115 "Sure we could. Say! That will be fine."

116 She was silent for a while; then she said, "Henry, at those prize fights, do the men hurt each other very much?"

117 "Sometimes a little, not often. Why?"

118 "Well, I've read how they break noses, and blood runs down their chests. I've read how the fighting gloves get heavy and soggy with blood."

119 He looked around at her. "What's the matter, Elisa? I didn't know you read things like that." He brought the car to a stop, then turned to the right over the Salinas River bridge.

120 "Do any women ever go to the fights?" she asked.

121 "Oh, sure, some. What's the matter, Elisa? Do you want to go? I don't think you'd like it, but I'll take you if you really want to go."

122 She relaxed limply in the seat. "Oh, no. No. I don't want to go. I'm sure I don't." Her face was turned away from him. "It will be enough if we can have wine. It will be plenty." She turned up her coat collar so he could not see that she was crying weakly—like an old woman.

—1940

✧ ✧ ✧

Richard Wright
(1908-1960)

The Man Who Was Almost a Man

Wright was the son of a Mississippi farm worker and mill hand who abandoned the family when the writer was five and a mother who was forced by poverty to place her son in orphanages during part of his childhood. As he relates in his autobiography, *Black Boy* (1945), he was largely self-educated through extensive reading; while working for the post office in Memphis he discovered the essays of H. L. Mencken, whom he credited as the major influence on his decision to become a writer. In Chicago in the 1930s he became associated with the Federal Writers' Project and, briefly, with the Communist party. He later lived in New York and, for the last fifteen years of his life, Paris, where he was associated with French existentialist writers like Jean-Paul Sartre. Wright's first novel, *Native Son* (1940), based on an actual 1938 murder case, describes the chain of circumstances that lead to a black chauffeur's being tried and executed for the accidental slaying of a wealthy white woman. The success of that book established Wright as the leading black novelist of his generation, and while none of his subsequent works attracted the same level of attention he nevertheless helped define many of the themes that black writers continue to explore today. "The Man Who Was Almost a Man" was filmed as part of the PBS *American Short Story* series.

Dave struck out across the fields, looking homeward through paling light. Whut's the use talkin wid em niggers in the field? Anyhow, his mother was putting supper on the table. Them niggers can't understan nothing. One of these days he was going to get a gun and practice shooting, then they couldn't talk to him as though he were a little boy. He slowed, looking at the ground.

Shucks, Ah ain scareda them even if they are biggern me! Aw, Ah know what Ahma do. Ahm going by ol Joe's sto n git that Sears Roebuck catlog n look at them guns. Mebbe Ma will lemme buy one when she gits mah pay from ol man Hawkins. Ahma beg her t gimme some money. Ahm ol ernough to hava gun. Ahm seventeen. Almost a man. He strode, feeling his long loose-jointed limbs. Shucks, a man oughta hava little gun aftah he done worked hard all day.

2 He came in sight of Joe's store. A yellow lantern glowed on the front porch. He mounted steps and went through the screen door, hearing it bang behind him. There was a strong smell of coal oil and mackerel fish. He felt very confident until he saw fat Joe walk in through the rear door, then his courage began to ooze.

3 "Howdy, Dave! Whutcha want?"

4 "How yuh, Mistah Joe? Aw, Ah don wanna buy nothing. Ah jus wanted t see ef yuhd lemme look at tha catlog erwhile."

5 "Sure! You wanna see it here?"

6 "Nawsuh. Ah wants t take it home wid me. Ah'll bring it back termorrow when Ah come in from the fiels."

7 "You plannin on buying something."

8 "Yessuh."

9 "Your ma lettin you have your own money now?"

10 "Shucks. Mistah Joe, Ahm gittin t be a man like anybody else!"

11 Joe laughed and wiped his greasy white face with a red bandanna.

12 "Whut you plannin on buyin?"

13 Dave looked at the floor, scratched his head, scratched his thigh, and smiled. Then he looked up shyly.

14 "Ah'll tell yuh, Mistah Joe, ef yuh promise yuh won't tell."

15 "I promise."

16 "Waal, Ahma buy a gun."

17 "A gun? What you want with a gun?"

18 "Ah wanna keep it."

19 "You ain't nothing but a boy. You don't need a gun."

20 "Aw, lemme have the catlog, Mistah Joe. Ah'll bring it back."

21 Joe walked through the rear door. Dave was elated. He looked around at barrels of sugar and flour. He heard Joe coming back. He craned his neck to see if he were bringing the book. Yeah, he's got it. Gawddog, he's got it!

22 "Here, but be sure you bring it back. It's the only one I got."

23 "Sho, Mistah Joe."

24 "Say, if you wanna buy a gun, why don't you buy one from me? I gotta gun to sell."

25 "Will it shoot?"

26 "Sure it'll shoot."

27 "Whut kind is it?"

28 "Oh, it's kinda old . . . a left-hand Wheeler. A pistol. A big one."

29 "Is it got bullets in it?"

30 "It's loaded."

31 "Kin Ah see it?"

32 "Where's your money?"

33 "Whut yuh wan fer it?"

34 "I'll let you have it for two dollars."

35 "Just two dollahs? Shucks, Ah could buy that when Ah git mah pay."

36 "I'll have it here when you want it."

37 "Awright, suh. Ah be in fer it."

38 He went through the door, hearing it slam again behind him. Ahma git some money from Ma n buy me a gun! Only two dollahs! He tucked the thick catalogue under his arm and hurried.

39 "Where yuh been, boy?" His mother held a steaming dish of blackeyed peas.

40 "Aw, Ma, Ah jus stopped down the road t talk wid the boys."

41 "Yuh know bettah t keep suppah waitin."

42 He sat down, resting the catalogue on the edge of the table.

43 "Yuh git up from there and git to the well n wash yosef! Ah ain feedin no hogs in mah house!"

44 She grabbed his shoulder and pushed him. He stumbled out of the room, then came back to get the catalogue.

45 "Whut this?"

46 "Aw, Ma, it's jusa catlog."

47 "Who yuh git it from?"

48 "From Joe, down at the sto."

49 "Waal, thas good. We kin use it in the outhouse."

50 "Naw, Ma." He grabbed for it. "Gimme ma catlog, Ma."

51 She held onto it and glared at him.

52 "Quit hollerin at me! Whut's wrong wid yuh? Yuh crazy?"

53 "But Ma, please. It ain mine! It's Joe's! He tol me t bring it back t im termorrow."

54 She gave up the book. He stumbled down the back steps, hugging the thick book under his arm. When he had splashed water on his face and hands, he groped back to the kitchen and fumbled in a corner for the towel. He bumped into a chair; it clattered to the floor. The catalogue sprawled at his feet. When he had dried his eyes he snatched up the book and held it again under his arm. His mother stood watching him.

55 "Now, ef yuh gonna act a fool over that ol book, Ah'll take it n burn it up."

56 "Naw, Ma, please."

57 "Waal, set down n be still!"

58 He sat down and drew the oil lamp close. He thumbed page after page, unaware of the food his mother set on the table. His father came in. Then his small brother.

59 "Whutcha got there, Dave?" his father asked.

60 "Jusa catlog," he answered, not looking up.

61 "Yeah, here they is!" His eyes glowed at blue-and-black revolvers. He glanced up, feeling sudden guilt. His father was watching him. He eased the book under the table and rested it on his knees. After the blessing was asked, he ate. He scooped up peas and swallowed fat meat without chewing. Buttermilk helped to wash it down. He did not want to mention money before his father. He would do much better by cornering his mother when she was alone. He looked at his father uneasily out of the edge of his eye.

62 "Boy, how come yuh don quit foolin wid tha book n eat yo suppah?"

63 "Yessuh."

64 "How you n ol man Hawkins gitten erlong?"

65 "Suh?"

66 "Can't yuh hear? Why don yuh lissen? Ah ast yu how wuz yuh n ol man Hawkins gittin erlong?"

67 "Oh, swell, Pa. Ah plows mo lan than anybody over there."

68 "Waal, yuh oughta keep you mind on what yuh doin."

69 "Yessuh."

70 He poured his plate full of molasses and sopped it up slowly with a chunk of cornbread. When his father and brother had left the kitchen, he still sat and looked again at the guns in the catalogue, longing to muster courage enough to present his case to his mother. Lawd, ef Ah only had tha pretty one! He could almost feel the slickness of the weapon with his fingers. If he had a gun like that he would polish it and keep it shining so it would never rust! N Ah'd keep it loaded, by Gawd!

71 "Ma?" His voice was hesitant.

72 "Hunh?"

73 "Ol man Hawkins give yuh mah money yit?"

74 "Yeah, but ain no usa yuh thinking bout throwin nona it erway. Ahm keeping tha money sos yuh kin have cloes t go to school this winter."

75 He rose and went to her side with the open catalogue in his palms. She was washing dishes, her head bent low over a pan. Shyly he raised the book. When he spoke, his voice was husky, faint.

76 "Ma, Gawd knows Ah wans one of these."

77 "One of whut?" she asked, not raising her eyes.

78 "One of these," he said again, not daring even to point. She glanced up at the page, then at him with wide eyes. "Nigger, is yuh gone plumb crazy?"

79 "Aw, Ma—"

80 "Git outta here! Don yuh talk t me bout no gun! Yuh a fool!"

81 "Ma, Ah kin buy one fer two dollahs."

82 "Not ef Ah knows it, yuh ain!"

83 "But yuh promised me one—"

84 "Ah don care what Ah promised! Yuh ain nothing but a boy yit!"

85 "Ma, ef yuh lemme buy one Ah'll *never* ast yuh fer nothing no mo."

86 "Ah tol yuh t git outta here! Yuh ain gonna toucha penny of tha money fer no gun! Thas how come Ah has Mistah Hawkins t pay yo wages t me, cause Ah knows yuh ain got no sense."

87 "But, Ma, we needa gun. Pa ain got no gun. We needa gun in the house. Yuh kin never tell whut might happen."

88 "Now don yuh try to maka fool outta me, boy! Ef we did hava gun, yuh wouldn't have it!"

89 He laid the catalogue down and slipped his arm around her waist.

90 "Aw, Ma, Ah done worked hard alla summer n ain ast yuh fer nothing, is Ah, now?"

91 "Thas what yuh spose t do!"

92 "But Ma, Ah wans a gun. Yuh kin lemme have two dollahs outta mah money. Please, Ma. I kin give it to Pa . . . Please, Ma! Ah loves yuh, Ma!"

93 When she spoke her voice came soft and low.

94 "What yu wan wida gun, Dave? Yuh don need no gun. Yuh'll git in trouble. N ef yo pa jus thought Ah let yuh have money t buy a gun he'd hava fit."

95 "Ah'll hide it, Ma. It ain but two dollahs."

96 "Lawd, chil, whut's wrong wid yuh?"

97 "Ain nothin wrong, Ma. Ahm almos a man now. Ah wans a gun."

98 "Who gonna sell yuh a gun?"

99 "Ol Joe at the sto."

100 "N it don cos but two dollahs?"

101 "Thas all, Ma. Jus two dollahs. Please, Ma."

102 She was stacking the plates away; her hands moved slowly, reflectively. Dave kept an anxious silence. Finally, she turned to him.

103 "Ah'll let yuh git tha gun if yuh promise me one thing."

104 "What's tha, Ma?"

105 "Yuh bring it straight back t me, yuh hear? It be fer Pa."

106 "Yessum! Lemme go now, Ma."

107 She stooped, turned slightly to one side, raised the hem of her dress, rolled down the top of her stocking, and came up with a slender wad of bills.

108 "Here," she said. "Lawd knows yuh don need no gun. But yer pa does. Yuh bring it right back t me, yuh hear? Ahma put it up. Now ef yuh don, Ahma have yuh pa lick yuh so hard yuh won fergit it."

109 "Yessum."

110 He took the money, ran down the steps, and across the yard.

111 "Dave! Yuuuuuh Daaaaave!"

112 He heard, but he was not going to stop now. "Naw, Lawd!"

113 The first movement he made the following morning was to reach under the pillow for the gun. In the gray light of dawn he held it loosely, feeling a sense of power. Could kill a man with a gun like this. Kill anybody, black or white. And if he were holding his gun in his hand, nobody could run over him; they would have to respect him. It was a big gun, with a long barrel and a heavy handle. He raised and lowered it in his hand, marveling at its weight.

114 He had not come straight home with it as his mother had asked; instead he had stayed out in the fields, holding the weapon in his hand, aiming it now and then at some imaginary foe. But he had not fired it; he had been afraid that his father might hear. Also he was not sure he knew how to fire it.

115 To avoid surrendering the pistol he had not come into the house until he knew that they were all asleep. When his mother had tiptoed to his bedside late that night and demanded the gun, he had first played possum; then he had told her that the gun was hidden outdoors, that he would bring it to her in the morning. Now he lay turning it slowly in his hands. He broke it, took out the cartridges, felt them, and then put them back.

116 He slid out of bed, got a long strip of old flannel from a trunk, wrapped the gun in it, and tied it to his naked thigh while it was still loaded. He did not go in to breakfast. Even though it was not yet daylight he started for Jim Hawkins' plantation. Just as the sun was rising he reached the barns where the mules and plows were kept.

117 "Hey! That you, Dave?"

118 He turned. Jim Hawkins stood eyeing him suspiciously.

119 "What're yuh doing here so early?"

120 "Ah didn't know Ah wuz gittin up so early, Mistah Hawkins. Ah was fixin t hitch up ol Jenny n take her t the fiels."

121 "Good. Since you're so early, how about plowing that stretch down by the woods?"

122 "Suits me, Mistah Hawkins."

123 "O.K. Go to it!"

124 He hitched Jenny to a plow and started across the fields. Hot dog! This was just what he wanted. If he could get down by the woods, he could shoot his gun and nobody would hear. He walked behind the plow, hearing the traces creaking, feeling the gun tied tight to his thigh.

125 When he reached the woods, he plowed two whole rows before he decided to take out the gun. Finally, he stopped, looked in all directions, then untied the gun and held it in his hand. He turned to the mule and smiled.

126 "Know whut this is, Jenny? Naw, yuh wouldn know! Yuhs jusa ol mule! Anyhow, this is a gun, n it kin shoot, by Gawd!"

127 He held the gun at arm's length. Whut t hell, Ahma shoot this thing! He looked at Jenny again.

128 "Lissen here, Jenny! When Ah pull this ol trigger, Ah don wan yuh t run n acka fool now!"

129 Jenny stood with head down, her short ears pricked straight. Dave walked off about twenty feet, held the gun far out from him at arm's length, and turned his head. Hell, he told himself, Ah ain afraid. The gun felt loose in his fingers; he waved it wildly for a moment. Then he shut his eyes and tightened his forefinger. Bloom! A report half deafened him and he thought his right hand was torn from his arm. He heard Jenny whinnying and galloping over the field, and he found himself on his knees, squeezing his fingers hard between his legs. His hand was numb; he jammed it into his mouth, trying to warm it, trying to stop the pain. The gun lay at his feet. He did not quite know what had happened. He stood up and stared at the gun as though it were a living thing. He gritted his teeth and kicked the gun. Yuh almos broke mah arm! He turned to look for Jenny; she was far over the fields, tossing her head and kicking wildly.

130 "Hol on there, ol mule!"

131 When he caught up with her she stood trembling, walling her big white eyes at him. The plow was far away; the traces had broken. Then Dave stopped short, looking, not believing. Jenny was bleeding. Her left side was red and wet with blood. He went closer. Lawd, have mercy! Wondah did Ah shoot this mule? He grabbed for Jenny's mane. She flinched, snorted, whirled, tossing her head.

132 "Hol on now! Hol on."

133 Then he saw the hole in Jenny's side, right between the ribs. It was round, wet, red. A crimson stream streaked down the front leg, flowing fast. Good Gawd! Ah wuzn't shootin at tha mule. He felt panic. He knew he had to stop that blood, or Jenny would bleed to death. He had never seen so much blood in all his life. He chased the mule for half a mile, trying to catch her. Finally she stopped, breathing hard, stumpy tail half arched. He caught her mane and led her back to where the plow and gun lay. Then he stopped and grabbed handfuls of damp black earth and tried to plug the bullet hole. Jenny shuddered, whinnied, and broke from him.

134 "Hol on! Hol on now!"

135 He tried to plug it again, but blood came anyhow. His fingers were hot and sticky. He rubbed dirt into his palms, trying to dry them. Then again he attempted to plug the bullet hole, but Jenny shied away, kicking her heels high. He stood helpless. He had to do something. He ran at Jenny; she dodged him. He watched a red stream of blood flow down Jenny's leg and form a bright pool at her feet.

136 "Jenny . . . Jenny," he called weakly.

137 His lips trembled. She's bleeding t death! He looked in the direction of home, wanting to go back, wanting to get help. But he saw the pistol lying in the damp black clay. He had a queer feeling that if he only did something, this would not be; Jenny would not be there bleeding to death.

138 When he went to her this time, she did not move. She stood with sleepy, dreamy eyes; and when he touched her she gave a low-pitched whinny and knelt to the ground, her front knees slopping in blood.

139 "Jenny . . . Jenny . . . " he whispered.

140 For a long time she held her neck erect; then her head sank, slowly. Her ribs swelled with a mighty heave and she went over.

141 Dave's stomach felt empty, very empty. He picked up the gun and held it gingerly between his thumb and forefinger. He buried it at the foot of a tree. He took a stick and tried to cover the pool of blood with dirt—but what was the use? There was Jenny lying with her mouth open and her eyes walled and glassy. He could not tell Jim Hawkins he had shot his mule. But he had to tell something. Yeah, Ah'll tell em Jenny started gittin wil n fell on the joint of the plow . . . But that would hardly happen to a mule. He walked across the field slowly, head down.

142 It was sunset. Two of Jim Hawkins' men were over near the edge of the woods digging a hole in which to bury Jenny. Dave was surrounded by a knot of people, all of whom were looking down at the dead mule.

143 "I don't see how in the world it happened," said Jim Hawkins for the tenth time.

144 The crowd parted and Dave's mother, father, and small brother pushed into the center.

145 "Where Dave?" his mother called.

146 "There he is," said Jim Hawkins.

147 His mother grabbed him.

148 "Whut happened, Dave? Whut yuh done?"

149 "Nothin."

150 "C mon, boy, talk," his father said.

151 Dave took a deep breath and told the story he knew nobody believed.

152 "Waal," he drawled. "Ah brung ol Jenny down here sos Ah could do mah plowin. Ah plowed bout two rows, just like yuh see." He stopped and pointed at the long rows of upturned earth. "Then somethin musta been wrong wid ol Jenny. She wouldn ack right a-tall. She started snortin n kickin her heels. Ah tried t hol her, but she pulled erway, rearin n goin in. Then when the point of the plow was stickin up in the air, she swung erroun n twisted herself back on it . . . She stuck herself n started t bleed. N fo Ah could do anything, she wuz dead."

153 "Did you ever hear anything like that in all your life?" asked Jim Hawkins.

154 There were white and black standing in the crowd. They murmured. Dave's mother came close to him and looked hard into his face. "Tell the truth, Dave," she said.

155 "Looks like a bullet hole to me," said one man.

156 "Dave, whut yuh do wid the gun?" his mother asked.

157 The crowd surged in, looking at him. He jammed his hands into his pockets, shook his head slowly from left to right, and backed away. His eyes were wide and painful.

158 "Did he hava gun?" asked Jim Hawkins.

159 "By Gawd, Ah tol yuh tha wuz a gun wound," said a man, slapping his thigh.

160 His father caught his shoulders and shook him till his teeth rattled.

161 "Tell whut happened, yuh rascal! Tell whut . . . "

162 Dave looked at Jenny's stiff legs and began to cry.

163 "Whut yuh do wid tha gun?" his mother asked.

164 "What wuz he doin wida gun?" his father asked.

165 "Come on and tell the truth," said Hawkins. "Ain't nobody going to hurt . . . "

166 His mother crowded close to him.

167 "Did yuh shoot tha mule, Dave?"

168 Dave cried, seeing blurred white and black faces.

169 "Ahh ddinn gggo tt sshooot hher . . . Ah ssswear ffo Gawd Ahh ddin . . . Ah wuz a-tryin t sssee ef the old gggun would sshoot—"

170 "Where yuh git the gun from?" his father asked.

171 "Ah got it from Joe, at the sto."

172 "Where yuh git the money?"

173 "Ma give it t me."

174 "He kept worryin me, Bob. Ah had t. Ah tol im t bring the gun right back t me . . . It was fer yuh, the gun."

175 "But how yuh happen to shoot that mule?" asked Jim Hawkins.

176 "Ah wuzn shootin at the mule, Mistah Hawkins. The gun jumped when Ah pulled the trigger . . . N fo Ah knowed anythin Jenny was there a-bleedin."

177 Somebody in the crowd laughed. Jim Hawkins walked close to Dave and looked into his face.

178 "Well, looks like you have bought you a mule, Dave."

179 "Ah swear fo Gawd, Ah didn go t kill the mule, Mistah Hawkins!"

180 "But you killed her!"

181 All the crowd was laughing now. They stood on tiptoe and poked heads over one another's shoulders.

182 "Well, boy, looks like yuh done bought a dead mule! Hahaha!"

183 "Ain tha ershame."

184 "Hohohohoho."

185 Dave stood, head down, twisting his feet in the dirt.

186 "Well, you needn't worry about it, Bob," said Jim Hawkins to Dave's father. "Just let the boy keep on working and pay me two dollars a month."

187 "Whut yuh wan fer yo mule, Mistah Hawkins?"

188 Jim Hawkins screwed up his eyes.

189 "Fifty dollars."

190 "Whut yuh do wid tha gun?" Dave's father demanded.

191 Dave said nothing.

192 "Yuh wan me t take a tree n beat yuh till yuh talk!"

193 "Nawsuh!"

194 "Whut yuh do wid it?"

195 "Ah throwed it erway."

196 "Where?"

197 "Ah . . . Ah throwed it in the creek."

198 "Waal, c mon home. N firs thing in the mawnin git to tha creek n fin tha gun."

199 "Yessuh."

200 "Whut yuh pay fer it?"

201 "Two dollahs."

202 "Take tha gun n git yo money back n carry it to Mistah Hawkins, yuh hear? N don fergit Ahma lam you black bottom good fer this! Now march yosef on home, suh!"

203 Dave turned and walked slowly. He heard people laughing. Dave glared, his eyes welling with tears. Hot anger bubbled in him. Then he swallowed and stumbled on.

204 That night Dave did not sleep. He was glad that he had gotten out of killing the mule so easily, but he was hurt. Something hot seemed to turn over inside him each time he remembered how they had laughed. He tossed on his bed, feeling his hard pillow. N Pa says he's gonna beat me . . . He remembered other beatings, and his back quivered. Naw, naw, Ah sho don wan im t beat me tha way no mo. Dam em all! Nobody ever gave him anything. All he did was work. They treat me like a mule, n then they beat me. He gritted his teeth. N Ma had t tell on me.

205 Well, if he had to, he would take old man Hawkins that two dollars. But that meant selling the gun. And he wanted to keep that gun. Fifty dollars for a dead mule.

206 He turned over, thinking how he had fired the gun. He had an itch to fire it again. Ef other men kin shoota gun, by Gawd, Ah kin! He was still, listening. Mebbe they all sleepin now. The house was still. He heard the soft breathing of

his brother. Yes, now! He would go down and get that gun and see if he could fire it! He eased out of bed and slipped into overalls.

207 The moon was bright. He ran almost all the way to the edge of the woods. He stumbled over the ground, looking for the spot where he had buried the gun. Yeah, here it is. Like a hungry dog scratching for a bone, he pawed it up. He puffed his black cheeks and blew dirt from the trigger and barrel. He broke it and found four cartridges unshot. He looked around; the fields were filled with silence and moonlight. He clutched the gun stiff and hard in his fingers. But, as soon as he wanted to pull the trigger, he shut his eyes and turned his head. Naw, Ah can't shoot wid mah eyes closed n mah head turned. With effort he held his eyes open; then he squeezed. *Blooooom!* He was stiff, not breathing. The gun was still in his hands. Dammit, he'd done it! He fired again. *Blooooom!* He smiled. *Bloooom! Blooooom! Click, click.* There! It was empty. If anybody could shoot a gun, he could. He put the gun into his hip pocket and started across the fields.

208 When he reached the top of a ridge he stood straight and proud in the moonlight, looking at Jim Hawkins' big white house, feeling the gun sagging in his pocket. Lawd, ef Ah had just one mo bullet Ah'd taka shot at tha house. Ah'd like t scare ol man Hawkins jusa little . . . Jusa enough t let im know Dave Saunders is a man.

209 To his left the road curved, running to the tracks of the Illinois Central. He jerked his head, listening. From far off come a faint *hoooof-hoooof; hoooof-hoooof* . . . He stood rigid. Two dollahs a mont. Les see now . . . Tha means it'll take bout two years. Shucks! Ah'll be dam!

210 He started down the road, toward the tracks. Yeah, here she comes! He stood beside the track and held himself stiffly. Here she comes, erroun the ben . . . C mon, yuh slow poke! C mon! He had his hand on his gun; something quivered in his stomach. Then the train thundered past, the gray and brown box cars rumbling and clinking. He gripped the gun tightly; then he jerked his hand out of his pocket. Ah betcha Bill wouldn't do it! Ah betcha . . . The cars slid past, steel grinding upon steel. Ahm ridin yuh ternight, so hep me Gawd! He was hot all over. He hesitated just a moment; then he grabbed, pulled atop of a car, and lay flat. He felt his pocket; the gun was still there. Ahead the long rails were glinting in the moonlight, stretching away, away to somewhere, somewhere where he could be a man . . .

Eudora Welty
(b. 1909)

Livvie

Welty's name invariably surfaces when lists of both outstanding southern and women writers are made. Born in Jackson, Mississippi, she was educated at Mississippi State College for Women and the University of Wisconsin. Except for a brief period in New York City, where she studied advertising, Welty has spent most of her life in her native state, which provides material for her most characteristic work, especially novels like *Delta Wedding* (1946) and *The Ponder Heart* (1956). Like William Faulkner and Flannery O'Connor, Welty is a scrupulous craftsperson. She has managed to exploit fully both the comic and tragic possibilities of a region and at the same time achieve a national reputation that led to her appointment as writer-in-residence at Smith College in Massachusetts. Equally adept as a novelist and writer of short stories, Welty was awarded a Pulitzer Prize in 1973 for *The Optimist's Daughter.* "Livvie" is taken from her 1953 collection *The Wide Net,* which contains stories set in the rural areas along the Natchez Trace. Like her first novel, *The Robber Bridegroom* (1942), "Livvie" combines elements of both American and European folklore with the realistic setting of a farm in the backwoods where a "May-December" marriage comes to an end. *The Collected Stories of Eudora Welty* appeared in 1980.

Solomon carried Livvie twenty-one miles away from her home when he married her. He carried her away up on the Old Natchez Trace into the deep country to live in his house. She was sixteen—an only girl, then. Once people said he thought nobody would ever come along there. He told her himself that it had been a long time, and a day she did not know about, since that road was a traveled road with *people* coming and going. He was good to her, but he kept her in the house. She had not thought that she could not get back. Where she came from, people said an old man did not want anybody in the world to ever find his wife, for fear they would steal her back from him. Solomon asked her before he took her, "Would she be happy?"—very dignified, for he was a colored man that owned his land and had it written down in the courthouse; and she said, "Yes, sir," since he was an old man and she was young and just listened and answered. He asked her, if she was choosing winter, would she pine for spring, and she said, "No indeed." Whatever she said, always, was because he was an old man . . . while nine years went by. All the time, he got old, and he got so old he gave out. At least he slept the whole day in bed, and she was young still.

2 It was a nice house, inside and outside both. In the first place, it had three rooms. The front room was papered in holly paper, with green palmettos from the swamp spaced at careful intervals over the walls. There was fresh newspaper cut with fancy borders on the mantleshelf, on which were propped photographs of old or very young men printed in faint yellow—Solomon's people. Solomon had a houseful of furniture. There was a double settee, a tall scrolled rocker and an organ in the front room, all around a three-legged table with a pink marble top, on which was set a lamp with three gold feet, beside a jelly glass with pretty hen feathers in it. Behind the front room, the other room had the bright iron bed with the polished knobs like a throne, in which Solomon slept all day. There were snow-white curtains of wiry lace at the window, and a lace bedspread belonged on the bed. But what old Solomon slept sound under was a big feather-stitched piece-quilt in the pattern "Trip Around the World," which had twenty-one different colors, four hundred and forty pieces, and a thousand yards of thread, and that was what Solomon's mother made in her life and old age. There was a table holding the Bible, and a trunk with a key. On the wall were two calendars, and a diploma from somewhere in Solomon's family, and under that Livvie's one possession was nailed, a picture of the little white baby of the family she worked for, back in Natchez before she was married. Going through that room and on to the kitchen, there was a big wood stove and a big round table always with a wet top and with the knives and forks in one jelly glass and the spoons in another, and a cut-glass vinegar bottle between, and going out from those, many shallow dishes of pickled peaches, fig preserves, watermelon pickles and blackberry jam always sitting there. The churn sat in the sun, the doors of the safe were always both shut, and there were four baited mouse-traps in the kitchen, one in every corner.

3 The outside of Solomon's house looked nice. It was not painted, but across the porch was an even balance. On each side there was one easy chair with high springs, looking out, and a fern basket hanging over it from the ceiling, and a dishpan of zinnia seedlings growing at its foot on the floor. By the door was a plow-wheel, just a pretty iron circle, nailed up on one wall and a square mirror on the other, a turquoise-blue comb stuck up in the frame, with the wash stand beneath it. On the door was a wooden knob with a pearl in the end, and Solomon's black hat hung on that, if he was in the house.

4 Out front was a clean dirt yard with every vestige of grass patiently uprooted and the ground scarred in deep whorls from the strike of Livvie's broom. Rose bushes with tiny blood-red roses blooming every month grew in threes on either side of the steps. On one side was a peach tree, on the other a pomegranate. Then coming around up the path from the deep cut of the Natchez Trace below was a line of bare crape-myrtle trees with every branch of them ending in a colored bottle, green or blue. There was no word that fell from Solomon's lips to say what they were for, but Livvie knew that there could be a spell put in trees, and she was familiar from the time she was born with the way bottle trees kept evil spirits from coming into the house—by luring them inside the colored bottles, where they cannot get out again. Solomon had made the bottle trees with his own hands over the nine years, in labor amounting to about a tree a year, and without a sign that he had any uneasiness in his heart, for he took as much pride in his precautions against spirits coming in the house as he took in the house, and sometimes in the sun the bottle trees looked prettier than the house did.

5 It was a nice house. It was in a place where the days would go by and surprise anyone that they were over. The lamplight and the firelight would shine out the door after dark, over the still and breathing country, lighting the roses and the bottle trees, and all was quiet there.

6 But there was nobody, nobody at all, not even a white person. And if there had been anybody, Solomon would not have let Livvie look at them, just as he would not let her look at a field hand, or a field hand look at her. There was no house near, except for the cabins of the tenants that were forbidden to her, and there was no house as far as she had been, stealing away down the still, deep Trace. She felt as if she waded a river when she went, for the dead leaves on the ground reached as high as her knees, and when she was all scratched and bleeding she said it was not like a road that went anywhere. One day, climbing up the high bank, she had found a graveyard without a church; with ribbon-grass growing about the foot of an angel (she had climbed up because she thought she saw angel wings), and in the sun, trees shining like burning flames through the great caterpillar nets which enclosed them. Scarey thistles stood looking like the prophets in the Bible in Solomon's house. Indian paint brushes grew over her head, and the mourning dove made the only sound in the world. Oh for a stirring of the leaves, and a breaking of the nets! But not by a ghost, prayed Livvie, jumping down the bank. After Solomon took to his bed, she never went out, except one more time.

7 Livvie knew she made a nice girl to wait on anybody. She fixed things to eat on a tray like a surprise. She could keep from singing when she ironed, and to sit by a bed and fan away the flies, she could be so still she could not hear herself breathe. She could clean up the house and never drop a thing, and wash the dishes without a sound, and she would step outside to churn, for churning

sounded too sad to her, like sobbing, and if it made her home-sick and not Solomon, she did not think of that.

8 But Solomon scarcely opened his eyes to see her, and scarcely tasted his food. He was not sick or paralyzed or in any pain that he mentioned, but he was surely wearing out in the body, and no matter what nice hot thing Livvie would bring him to taste, he would only look at it now, as if he was past seeing how he could add anything more to himself. Before she could beg him, he would go fast asleep. She could not surprise him any more, if he would not taste, and she was afraid that he was never in the world going to taste another thing she brought him—and so how could he last?

9 But one morning it was breakfast time and she cooked his eggs and grits, carried them in on a tray, and called his name. He was sound asleep. He lay in a dignified way with his watch beside him, on his back in the middle of the bed. One hand drew the quilt up high, though it was the first day of spring. Through the white lace curtains a little puffy wind was blowing as if it came from round cheeks. All night the frogs had sung out in the swamp, like a commotion in the room, and he had not stirred, though she lay wide awake and saying, "Shh, frogs!" for fear he would mind them.

10 He looked as if he would like to sleep a little longer, and so she put back the tray and waited a little. When she tiptoed and stayed so quiet, she surrounded her self with a little reverie, and sometimes it seemed to her when she was so stealthy that the quiet she kept was for a sleeping baby, and that she had a baby and was its mother. When she stood at Solomon's bed and looked down at him, she would be thinking, "He sleeps so well," and she would hate to wake him up. And in some other way, too, she was afraid to wake him up because even in his sleep he seemed to be such a strict man.

11 Of course, nailed to the wall over the bed—only she would forget who it was—there was a picture of him when he was young. Then he had a fan of hair over his forehead like a king's crown. Now his hair lay down on his head, the spring had gone out of it. Solomon had a lightish face, with eyebrows scattered but rugged, the way privet grows, strong eyes, with second sight, a strict mouth, and a little gold smile. This was the way he looked in his clothes, but in bed in the daytime he looked like a different and smaller man, even when he was wide awake, and holding the Bible. He looked like somebody kin to himself. And then sometimes when he lay in sleep and she stood fanning the flies away, and the light came in, his face was like new, so smooth and clear that it was like a glass of jelly held to the window, and she could almost look through his forehead and see what he thought.

12 She fanned him and at length he opened his eyes and spoke her name, but he would not taste the nice eggs she had kept warm under a pan.

13 Back in the kitchen she ate heartily, his breakfast and hers, and looked out the open door at what went on. The whole day, and the whole night before, she had felt the stir of spring close to her. It was as present in the house as a young man would be. The moon was in the last quarter and outside they were turning the sod and planting peas and beans. Up and down the red fields, over which smoke from the brush-burning hung showing like a little skirt of sky, a white horse and a white mule pulled the plow. At intervals hoarse shouts came through the air and roused her as if she dozed neglectfully in the shade, and they were telling her, "Jump up!" She could see how over each ribbon of field were moving men and girls, on foot and mounted on mules, with hats set on their heads and bright with tall hoes and forks as if they carried streamers on them and were going to some place on a journey—and how as if at a signal now and then they would all start at once shouting, hollering, cajoling, calling and answering back, running, being leaped on and breaking away, flinging to earth with a shout and lying motionless in the trance of twelve o'clock. The old women came out of the cabins and brought them food they had ready for them, and then all worked together, spread evenly out. The little children came too, like a bouncing stream overflowing the fields, and set upon the men, the women, the dogs, the rushing birds, and the wave-like rows of earth, their little voices almost too high to be heard. In the middle distance like some white-and-gold towers were the haystacks, with black cows coming around to eat their edges. High above everything, the wheel of fields, house, and cabins, and the deep road surrounding like a moat to keep them in, was the turning sky, blue with long, far-flung white mare's tail clouds, serene and still as high flames. And sound asleep while all this went around him that was his, Solomon was like a little still spot in the middle.

14 Even in the house the earth was sweet to breathe. Solomon had never let Livvie go any farther than the chicken house and the well. But what if she would walk now into the heart of the fields and take a hoe and work until she fell stretched out and drenched with her efforts, like other girls, and laid her cheek against the laid-open earth, and shamed the old man with her humbleness and delight? To shame him! A cruel wish would come in uninvited and so fast while she looked out the back door. She washed the dishes and scrubbed the table. She could hear the cries of the little lambs. Her mother, that she had not seen since her wedding day, had said one time, "I rather a man be anything, than a woman be mean."

15 So all morning she kept tasting the chicken broth on the stove, and when it was right she poured off a nice cupful. She carried it in to Solomon, and there he lay having a dream. Now what did he dream about? For she saw him sigh gently as if not to disturb some whole thing he held round in his mind, like a fresh egg. So even an old man dreamed about something pretty. Did he dream of her, while his eyes were shut and sunken, and his small hand with the wedding

ring curled close in sleep around the quilt? He might be dreaming of what time it was, for even through his sleep he kept track of it like a clock, and knew how much of it went by, and waked up knowing where the hands were even before he consulted the silver watch that he never let go. He would sleep with the watch in his palm, and even holding it to his cheek like a child that loves a plaything. Or he might dream of journeys and travels on a steamboat to Natchez. Yet she thought he dreamed of her; but even while she scrutinized him, the rods of the foot of the bed seemed to rise up like a rail fence between them, and she could see that people never could be sure of anything as long as one of them was asleep and the other awake. To look at him dreaming of her when he might be going to die frightened her a little, as if he might carry her with him that way, and she wanted to run out of the room. She took hold of the bed and held on, and Solomon opened his eyes and called her name, but he did not want anything. He would not taste the good broth.

16 Just a little after that, as she was taking up the ashes in the front room for the last time in the year, she heard a sound. It was somebody coming. She pulled the curtains together and looked through the slit.

17 Coming up the path under the bottle trees was a white lady. At first she looked young, but then she looked old. Marvelous to see, a little car stood steaming like a kettle out in the field-track—it had come without a road.

18 Livvie stood listening to the long, repeated knockings at the door, and after a while she opened it just a little. The lady came in through the crack, though she was more than middle-sized and wore a big hat.

19 "My name is Miss Baby Marie," she said.

20 Livvie gazed respectfully at the lady and at the little suitcase she was holding close to her by the handle until the proper moment. The lady's eyes were running over the room, from palmetto to palmetto, but she was saying, "I live at home . . . out from Natchez . . . and get out and show these pretty cosmetic things to the white people and the colored people both . . . all around . . . years and years . . . Both shades of powder and rouge . . . It's the kind of work a girl can do and not go clear 'way from home . . . " And the harder she looked, the more she talked. Suddenly she turned up her nose and said, "It's not Christian or sanitary to put feathers in a vase," and then she took a gold key out of the front of her dress and began unlocking the locks on her suitcase. Her face drew the light, the way it was covered with intense white and red, with a little patty-cake of white between the wrinkles by her upper lip. Little red tassels of hair bobbed under the rusty wires of her picture-hat, as with an air of triumph and secrecy she now drew open her little suitcase and brought out bottle after bottle and jar after jar, which she put down on the table, the mantlepiece, the settee, and the organ.

21 "Did you ever see so many cosmetics in your life?" cried Miss Baby Marie.

22 "No'm," Livvie tried to say, but the cat had her tongue.

23 "Have you ever applied cosmetics?" asked Miss Baby Marie next.

24 "No'm," Livvie tried to say.

25 "Then look!" she said, and pulling out the last thing of all, "Try this!" she said. And in her hand was unclenched a golden lipstick which popped open like magic. A fragrance came out of it like incense, and Livvie cried out suddenly, "Chinaberry flowers!"

26 Her hand took the lipstick, and in an instant she was carried away in the air through the spring, and looking down with a half-drowsy smile from a purple cloud she saw from above a chinaberry tree, dark and smooth and neatly leaved, neat as a guinea hen in the dooryard, and there was her home that she had left. On one side of the tree was her mama holding up her heavy apron, and she could see it was loaded with ripe figs, and on the other side was her papa holding a fish-pole over the pond, and she could see it transparently, the little clear fishes swimming up to the brim.

27 "Oh, no, not chinaberry flowers—secret ingredients," said Miss Baby Marie, "My cosmetics have secret ingredients—not chinaberry flowers."

28 "It's purple," Livvie breathed, and Miss Baby Marie said, "Use it freely. Rub it on."

29 Livvie tiptoed out to the wash stand on the front porch and before the mirror put the paint on her mouth. In the wavery surface her face danced before her like a flame. Miss Baby Marie followed her out, took a look at what she had done, and said, "That's it."

30 Livvie tried to say "Thank you" without moving her parted lips where the paint lay so new.

31 By now Miss Baby Marie stood behind Livvie and looked in the mirror over her shoulder, twisting up the tassels of her hair. "The lipstick I can let you have for only two dollars," she said, close to her neck.

32 "Lady, but I don't have no money, never did have," said Livvie.

33 "Oh, but you don't pay the first time. I make another trip, that's the way I do. I come back again—later."

34 "Oh," said Livvie, pretending she understood everything so as to please the lady.

35 "But if you don't take it now, this may be the last time I'll call at your house," said Miss Baby Marie sharply. "It's far away from anywhere, I'll tell you that. You don't live close to anywhere."

36 "Yes'm. My husband, he keep the *money,*" said Livvie, trembling. "He is strict as he can be. He don't know *you* walk in here—Miss Baby Marie!"

37 "Where is he?"

38 "Right now, he in yonder sound asleep, an old man. I wouldn't ever ask him for anything."

39 Miss Baby Marie took back the lipstick and packed it up. She gathered up the jars for both black and white and got them all inside the suitcase, with the same little fuss of triumph with which she had brought them out. She started away.

40 "Goodbye," she said, making herself look grand from the back, but at the last minute she turned around in the door. Her old hat wobbled as she whispered, "Let me see your husband."

41 Livvie obediently went on tiptoe and opened the door to the other room. Miss Baby Marie came behind her and rose on her toes and looked in.

42 "My, what a little tiny old, old man!" she whispered, clasping her hands and shaking her head over them. "What a beautiful quilt! What a tiny old, old man!"

43 "He can sleep like that all day," whispered Livvie proudly.

44 They looked at him awhile so fast asleep, and then all at once they looked at each other. Somehow that was as if they had a secret, for he had never stirred. Livvie then politely, but all at once, closed the door.

45 "Well! I'd certainly like to leave you with a lipstick!" said Miss Baby Marie vivaciously. She smiled in the door

46 "Lady, but I told you I don't have no money, and never did have."

47 "And never will?" In the air and all around, like a bright halo around the white lady's nodding head, it was a true spring day.

48 "Would you take eggs, lady?" asked Livvie softly.

49 "No, I have plenty of eggs—plenty," said Miss Baby Marie.

50 "I still don't have no money," said Livvie, and Miss Baby Marie took her suitcase and went on somewhere else.

51 Livvie stood watching her go, and all the time she felt her heart beating in her left side. She touched the place with her hand. It seemed as if her heart beat and her whole face flamed from the pulsing color of her lips. She went to sit by Solomon and when he opened his eyes he could not see a change in her. "He's fixin' to die," she said inside. That was the secret. That was when she went out of the house for a little breath of air.

52 She went down the path and down the Natchez Trace a way, and she did not know how far she had gone, but it was not far, when she saw a sight. It was a man, looking like a vision—she standing on one side of the Old Natchez Trace and he standing on the other.

53 As soon as this man caught sight of her, he began to look himself over. Starting at the bottom with his pointed shoes, he began to look up, lifting his peg-top pants the higher to see fully his bright socks. His coat long and wide and leaf green he opened like doors to see his high-up tawny pants and his pants he smoothed downward from the points of his collar, and he wore a luminous baby-pink satin shirt. At the end, he reached gently above his wide platter-shaped

round hat, the color of a plum, and one finger touched at the feather, emerald green, blowing in the spring winds.

54 No matter how she looked, she could never look so fine as he did, and she was not sorry for that, she was pleased.

55 He took three jumps, one down and two up, and was by her side.

56 "My name is Cash," he said.

57 He had a guinea pig in his pocket. They began to walk along. She stared on and on at him, as if he were doing some daring spectacular thing, instead of just walking beside her. It was not simply the city way he was dressed that made her look at him and see hope in its insolence looking back. It was not only the way he moved along kicking the flowers as if he could break through everything in the way and destroy anything in the world, that made her eyes grow bright. It might be, if he had not appeared the way he did appear that day she would never have looked so closely at him, but the time people come makes a difference.

58 They walked through the still leaves of the Natchez Trace, the light and the shade falling through trees about them, the white irises shining like candles on the banks and the new ferns shining like green stars up in the oak branches. They came out at Solomon's house, bottle trees and all. Livvie stopped and hung her head.

59 Cash began whistling a little tune. She did not know what it was, but she had heard it before from a distance, and she had a revelation. Cash was a field hand. He was a transformed field hand. Cash belonged to Solomon. But he had stepped out of his overalls into this. There in front of Solomon's house he laughed. He had a round head, a round face, all of him was young, and he flung his head up, rolled it against the mare's-tail sky in his round hat, and he could laugh just to see Solomon's house sitting there. Livvie looked at it, and there was Solomon's black hat hanging on the peg on the front door, the blackest thing in the world.

60 "I been to Natchez," Cash said, wagging his head around the sky. "*I* taken a trip, *I* ready for Easter!"

61 How was it possible to look so fine before the harvest? Cash must have stolen the money, stolen it from Solomon. He stood in the path and lifted his spread hand high and brought it down again and again in his laughter. He kicked up his heels. A little chill went through her. It was as if Cash was bringing that strong hand down to beat a drum or to rain blows upon a man, such an abandon and menace were in his laugh. Frowning, she went closer to him and his swinging arm drew her in at once and the fright was crushed from her body, as a little match-flame might be smothered out by what it lighted. She gathered the folds of his coat behind him and fastened her red lips to his mouth, and she was dazzled by herself then, the way he had been dazzled with himself to begin with.

62 In that instant she felt something that could not be told—that Solomon's death was at hand, that he was the same to her as if he were dead now. She cried out, and uttering little cries turned and ran for the house.

63 At once Cash was coming, following after, he was running behind her. He came close, and half-way up the path he laughed and passed her. He even picked up a stone and sailed it into the bottle trees. She put her hands over her head, and sounds clattered through the bottle trees like cries of outrage. Cash stamped and plunged zigzag up the front steps and in at the door.

64 When she got there, he had stuck his hands in his pockets and was turning slowly about in the front room. The little guinea pig peeped out. Around Cash, the pinned-up palmettos looked as if a lazy green monkey had walked up and down and around the walls leaving green prints of his hands and feet.

65 She got through the room and his hands were still in his pockets, and she fell upon the closed door to the other room and pushed it open. She ran to Solomon's bed, calling "Solomon! Solomon!" The little shape of the old man never moved at all, wrapped under the quilt as if it were winter still.

66 "Solomon!" She pulled the quilt away, but there was another one under that, and she fell on her knees beside him. He made no sound except a sigh, and then she could hear in the silence the light springy steps of Cash walking and walking in the front room, and the ticking of Solomon's silver watch, which came from the bed. Old Solomon was far away in his sleep, his face looked small, relentless, and devout, as if he were walking somewhere where she could imagine the snow falling.

67 Then there was a noise like a hoof pawing the floor, and the door gave a creak, and Cash appeared beside her. When she looked up, Cash's face was so black it was bright, and so bright and bare of pity that it looked sweet to her. She stood up and held up her head. Cash was so powerful that his presence gave her strength even when she did not need any.

68 Under their eyes Solomon slept. People's faces tell of things and places not known to the one who looks at them while they sleep, and while Solomon slept under the eyes of Livvie and Cash his face told them like a mythical story that all his life he had built, little scrap by little scrap, respect. A beetle could not have been more laborious or more ingenious in the task of its destiny. When Solomon was young, as he was in his picture overhead, it was the infinite thing with him, and he could see no end to the respect he would contrive and keep in a house. He had built a lonely house, the way he would make a cage, but it grew to be the same with him as a great monumental pyramid and sometimes in his absorption of getting it erected he was like the builder slaves of Egypt who forgot or never knew the origin and meaning of the thing to which they gave all their strength of their bodies and used up all their days. Livvie and Cash

could see that as a man might rest from a life-labor he lay in his bed, and they could hear how, wrapped in his quilt, he sighed to himself comfortably in sleep, while in his dreams he might have been an ant, a beetle, a bird, an Egyptian, assembling and carrying on his back and building with his hands, or he might have been an old man of India or a swaddled baby, about to smile and brush all away.

69 Then without warning old Solomon's eyes flew wide open under the hedgelike brows. He was wide awake.

70 And instantly Cash raised his quick arm. A radiant sweat stood on his temples. But he did not bring his arm down—it stayed in the air, as if something might have taken hold.

71 It was not Livvie—she did not move. As if something said "Wait," she stood waiting. Even while her eyes burned under motionless lids, her lips parted in a stiff grimace, and with her arms stiff at her sides she stood above the prone old man and the panting young one, erect and apart.

72 Movement when it came came in Solomon's face. It was an old and strict face, a frail face, but behind it, like a covered light, came an animation that could play hide and seek, that would dart and escape, had always escaped. The mystery flickered in him, and invited from his eyes. It was that very mystery that Cash with his quick arm would have to strike, and that Livvie could not weep for. But Cash only stood holding his arm in the air, when the gentlest flick of his great strength, almost a puff of his breath, would have been enough, if he had known how to give it, to send the old man over the obstruction that kept him away from death.

73 If it could not be that the tiny illumination in the fragile and ancient face caused a crisis, a mystery in the room that would not permit a blow to fall, at least it was certain that Cash, throbbing in his Easter clothes, felt a pang of shame that the vigor of a man would come to such an end that he could not be struck without warning. He took down his hand and stepped back behind Livvie, like a round-eyed schoolboy on whose unsuspecting head the dunce cap has been set.

74 "Young ones can't wait," said Solomon.

75 Livvie shuddered violently, and then in a gush of tears she stooped for a glass of water and handed it to him, but he did not see her.

76 "So here come the young man Livvie wait for. Was no prevention. No prevention. Now I lay eyes on young man and it come to be somebody I know all the time, and been knowing since he were born in a cotton patch, and watched grow up year to year, Cash McCord, growed to size, growed up to come in my house in the end—ragged and barefoot."

77 Solomon gave a cough of distaste. Then he shut his eyes vigorously, and his lips began to move like a chanter's.

78 "When Livvie married, her husband were already somebody. He had paid great cost for his land. He spread sycamore leaves over the ground from wagon to door, day he brought her home, so her foot would not have to touch ground. He carried her through his door. Then he growed old and could not lift her, and she were still young."

79 Livvie's sobs followed his words like a soft melody repeating each thing as he stated it. His lips moved for a little without sound, or she cried too fervently, and unheard he might have been telling his whole life and then he said, "God forgive Solomon for sins great and small. God forgive Solomon for carrying away too young girl for wife and keeping her away from her people and from all the young people would clamor for her back."

80 Then he lifted up his right hand toward Livvie where she stood by the bed and offered her his silver watch. He dangled it before her eyes, and she hushed crying; her tears stopped. For a moment the watch could be heard ticking as it always did, precisely in his proud hand. She lifted it away. Then he took hold of the quilt; then he was dead.

81 Livvie left Solomon dead and went out of the room. Stealthily, nearly without noise, Cash went beside her. He was like a shadow, but his shiny shoes moved over the floor in spangles, and the green downy feather shone like a light in his hat. As they reached the front door, he seized her deftly as a long black cat and dragged her hanging by the waist round and round him, while he turned in a circle, his face bent down to hers. The first moment, she kept one arm and its hand stiff and still, the one that held Solomon's watch. Then the fingers softly let go, all of her was limp, and the watch fell somewhere on the floor. It ticked away in the still room, and all at once there began outside the full song of a bird.

82 They moved around and around the room and into the brightness of the open door, then he stopped and shook her once. She rested in silence in his trembling arms, unprotesting as a bird on a nest. Outside the redbirds were flying and crisscrossing, the sun was in all the bottles on the prisoned trees, and the young peach was shining in the middle of them with the bursting light of spring.

—1943

Ralph Ellison
(b. 1914)

Flying Home

Ellison was born in Oklahoma City, Oklahoma, where his early interests were primarily musical. He played trumpet and knew many prominent jazz musicians of the Depression era. In 1933 he attended Tuskegee Institute, intending to study music, but he was drawn to literature through his study of contemporary writers (especially the poet T. S. Eliot). Ellison left school in 1936 for New York City, where he found work for a time with the Federal Writers Project and began to publish stories and reviews in the late 1930s in progressive magazines like *The New Masses.* Tuskegee and Harlem provided him with material for *Invisible Man* (1952), a brilliant picaresque novel of black life that established him as a major force in American fiction. *Invisible Man* won the National Book Award in 1953 and in 1965 was voted in a *Book Week* poll the most distinguished novel of the postwar period. Ellison has published little subsequently, with two collections of essays, *Shadow and Act* (1964) and *Going to the Territory* (1986), and a handful of short stories having to satisfy readers who have long anticipated a second novel that might somehow help define the changes four decades have wrought in the experience of black America. "Flying Home," a story written during World War II, turns on the historical irony of black Air Corps officers receiving their flight training in the heart of the segregated South.

When Todd came to, he saw two faces suspended above him in a sun so hot and blinding that he could not tell if they were black or white. He stirred, feeling a pain that burned as though his whole body had been laid open to the sun which glared into his eyes. For a moment an old fear of being touched by white hands seized him. Then the very sharpness of the pain began slowly to clear his head. Sounds came to him dimly. He done come to. Who are they? he thought. Naw he ain't, I coulda sworn he was white. Then he heard clearly:

2 "You hurt bad?"

3 Something within him uncoiled. It was a Negro sound.

4 "He's still out," he heard.

5 "Give 'im time . . . Say, son, you hurt bad?"

6 Was he? There was that awful pain. He lay rigid, hearing their breathing and trying to weave a meaning between them and his being stretched painfully upon the ground. He watched them warily, his mind traveling back over a painful distance. Jagged scenes, swiftly unfolding as in a movie trailer, reeled through his mind, and he saw himself piloting a tailspinning plane and landing and falling from the cockpit and trying to stand. Then, as in a great silence, he remembered the sound of crunching bone, and now, looking up into the anxious faces of an old Negro man and a boy from where he lay in the same field, the memory sickened him and he wanted to remember no more.

7 "How you feel, son?"

8 Todd hesitated, as though to answer would be to admit an inacceptable weakness. Then, "It's my ankle," he said.

9 "Which one?"

10 "The left."

11 With a sense of remoteness he watched the old man bend and remove his boot, feeling the pressure ease.

12 "That any better?"

13 "A lot. Thank you."

14 He had the sensation of discussing someone else, that his concern was with some far more important thing, which for some reason escaped him.

15 "You done broke it bad," the old man said. "We have to get you to a doctor."

16 He felt that he had been thrown into a tailspin. He looked at his watch; how long had he been here? He knew there was but one important thing in the world, to get the plane back to the field before his officers were displeased.

17 "Help me up," he said. "Into the ship."

18 "But it's broke too bad . . . "

19 "Give me your arm!"

20 "But, son . . . "

21 Clutching the old man's arm he pulled himself up, keeping his left leg clear, thinking, "I'd never make him understand," as the leather-smooth face came parallel with his own.

22 "Now, let's see."

23 He pushed the old man back, hearing a bird's insistent shrill. He swayed giddily. Blackness washed over him, like infinity.

24 "You best sit down."

25 "No, I'm OK."

26 "But, son. You jus' gonna make it worse . . . "

27 It was a fact that everything in him cried out to deny, even against the flaming pain in his ankle. He would have to try again.

28 "You mess with that ankle they have to cut your foot off," he heard.

29 Holding his breath, he started up again. It pained so badly that he had to bite his lips to keep from crying out and he allowed them to help him down with a pang of despair.

30 "It's best you take it easy. We gon' git you a doctor."

31 Of all the luck, he thought. Of all the rotten luck, now I have done it. The fumes of high-octane gasoline clung in the heat, taunting him.

32 "We kin ride him into town on old Ned," the boy said.

33 Ned? He turned, seeing the boy point toward an ox team browsing where the buried blade of a plow marked the end of a furrow. Thoughts of himself riding an ox through the town, past streets full of white faces, down the concrete runways of the airfield made swift images of humiliation in his mind. With a pang he remembered his girl's last letter. "Todd," she had written, "I don't need the papers to tell me you had the intelligence to fly. And I have always known you to be as brave as anyone else. The papers annoy me. Don't you be contented to prove over and over again that you're brave or skillful just because you're black, Todd. I think they keep beating that dead horse because they don't want to say why you boys are not yet fighting. I'm really disappointed, Todd. Anyone with brains can learn to fly, but then what? What about using it, and who will you use it for? I wish, dear, you'd write about this. I sometimes think they're playing a trick on us. It's very humiliating . . . " He wiped cold sweat from his face, thinking, What does she know of humiliation? She's never been down South. Now the humiliation would come. When you must have them judge you, knowing that they never accept your mistakes as your own but hold it against your whole race—that was humiliation. Yes, and humiliation was when you could never be simply yourself, when you were always a part of this old black ignorant man. Sure, he's all right. Nice and kind and helpful. But he's not you. Well, there's one humiliation I can spare myself.

34 "No," he said. "I have orders not to leave the ship . . . "

35 "Aw," the old man said. Then turning to the boy, "Teddy, then you better hustle down to Mister Graves and get him to come . . . "

36 "No, wait!" he protested before he was fully aware. Graves might be white. "Just have him get word to the field, please. They'll take care of the rest."

37 He saw the boy leave, running.

38 "How far does he have to go?"

39 "Might' nigh a mile."

40 He rested back, looking at the dusty face of his watch. But now they knew something has happened, he thought. In the ship there was a perfectly good radio, but it was useless. The old fellow would never operate it. That buzzard knocked me back a hundred years, he thought. Irony danced with him like the

gnats circling the old man's head. With all I've learned I'm dependent upon this "peasant's" sense of time and space. His leg throbbed. In the plane, instead of time being measured by the rhythms of pain and a kid's legs, the instruments would have told him at a glance. Twisting upon his elbows he saw where dust had powdered the plane's fuselage, feeling the lump form in his throat that was always there when he thought of flight. It's crouched there, he thought, like the abandoned shell of a locust. I'm naked without it. Not a machine, a suit of clothes you wear. And with a sudden embarrassment and wonder he whispered, "It's the only dignity I have . . . "

41 He saw the old man watching, his torn overalls clinging limply to him in the heat. He felt a sharp need to tell the old man what he felt. But that would be meaningless. If I tried to explain why I need to fly back, he'd think I was simply afraid of white officers. But it's more than fear . . . a sense of anguish clung to him like the veil of sweat that hugged his face. He watched the old man, hearing him humming snatches of a tune as he admired the plane. He felt a furtive sense of resentment. Such old men often came to the field to watch the pilots with childish eyes. At first it had made him proud; they had been a meaningful part of a new experience. But soon he realized they did not understand his accomplishments and they came to shame and embarrass him, like the distasteful praise of an idiot. A part of the meaning of flying had gone then, and he had not been able to regain it. If I were a prizefighter I would be more human, he thought. Not a monkey doing tricks, but a man. They were pleased simply that he was a Negro who could fly, and that was not enough. He felt cut off from them by age, by understanding, by sensibility, by technology and by his need to measure himself against the mirror of other men's appreciation. Somehow he felt betrayed, as he had when as a child he grew to discover that his father was dead. Now for him any real appreciation lay with his white officers; and with them he could never be sure. Between ignorant black men and condescending whites, his course of flight seemed mapped by the nature of things away from all needed and natural landmarks. Under some sealed orders, couched in ever more technical and mysterious terms, his path curved swiftly away from both the shame the old man symbolized and the cloudy terrain of white men's regard. Flying blind, he knew but one point of landing and there he would receive his wings. After that the enemy would appreciate his skill and he would assume his deepest meaning, he thought sadly, neither from those who condescended nor from those who praised without understanding, but from the enemy who would recognize his manhood and skill in terms of hate . . .

42 He sighed, seeing the oxen making queer, prehistoric shadows against the dry brown earth.

43 "You just take it easy, son," the old man soothed. "That boy won't take long. Crazy as he is about airplanes."

44 "I can wait," he said.

45 "What kinda airplane you call this here'n?"

46 "An Advanced Trainer," he said, seeing the old man smile. His fingers were like gnarled dark wood against the metal as he touched the low-slung wing.

47 "'Bout how fast can she fly?"

48 "Over two hundred an hour."

49 "Lawd! That's so fast I bet it don't seem like you moving!"

50 Holding himself rigid, Todd opening his flying suit. The shade had gone and he lay in a ball of fire.

51 "You mind if I take a look inside? I was always curious to see . . . "

52 "Help yourself. Just don't touch anything."

53 He heard him climb upon the metal wing, grunting. Now the questions would start. Well, so you don't have to think to answer . . .

54 He saw the old man looking over into the cockpit, his eyes bright as a child's.

55 "You must have to know a lot to work all these here things."

56 He was silent, seeing him step down and kneel beside him.

57 "Son, how come you want to fly way up there in the air?"

58 Because it's the most meaningful act in the world . . . because it makes me less like you, he thought.

59 But he said: "Because I like it, I guess. It's as good a way to fight and die as I know."

60 "Yeah? I guess you right," the old man said. "But how long you think before they gonna let you all fight?"

61 He tensed. This was the question all Negroes asked, put with the same timid hopefulness and longing that always opened a greater void within him than that he had felt beneath the plane the first time he had flown. He felt light-headed. It came to him suddenly that there was something sinister about the conversation, that he was flying unwillingly into unsafe and uncharted regions. If he could only be insulting and tell this old man who was trying to help him to shut up!

62 "I bet you one thing . . . "

63 "Yes?"

64 "That you was plenty scared coming down."

65 He did not answer. Like a dog on a trail the old man seemed to smell out his fears, and he felt anger bubble within him.

66 "You sho' scared me. When I seen you coming down in that thing with it a-rollin' and a-jumpin' like a pitchin' hoss, I thought sho' you was a goner. I almost had me a stroke!"

67 He saw the old man grinning. "Ever'thin's been happening round here this morning, come to think of it."

68 "Like what?" he asked.

69 "Well, first thing I know, here come two white fellers looking for Mister Rudolph, that's Mister Graves's cousin. That got me worked up right away . . ."

70 "Why?"

71 "Why? 'Cause he done broke outta the crazy house, that's why. He liable lo kill somebody," he said. "They oughta have him by now though. Then here you come. First I think it's one of them white boys. Then doggone if you don't fall outta there. Lawd, I'd done heard about you boys but I haven't never seen one o' you-all. Cain't tell you how it felt to see somebody what look like me in a airplane!"

72 The old man talked on, the sound streaming around Todd's thoughts like air flowing over the fuselage of a flying plane. You were a fool, he thought, remembering how before the spin the sun had blazed bright against the billboard signs beyond the town, and how a boy's blue kite had bloomed beneath him, tugging gently in the wind like a strange, odd-shaped flower. He had once flown such kites himself and tried to find the boy at the end of the invisible cord. But he had been flying too high and too fast. He had climbed steeply away in exultation. Too steeply, he thought. And one of the first rules you learn is that if the angle of thrust is too steep the plane goes into a spin. And then, instead of pulling out of it and going into a dive you let a buzzard panic you. A lousy buzzard!

73 "Son, what made all that blood on the glass?"

74 "A buzzard," he said, remembering how the blood and feathers had sprayed back against the hatch. It had been as though he had flown into a storm of blood and blackness.

75 "Well, I declare! They's lots of 'em around here. They after dead things. Don't eat nothing what's alive."

76 "A little bit more and he would have made a meal out of me," Todd said grimly.

77 "They bad luck all right. Teddy's got a name for 'em, calls 'em jimcrows," the old man laughed.

78 "It's a damned good name."

79 "They the damnedest birds. Once I seen a hoss all stretched out like he was sick, you know. So I hollers, 'Gid up from there, suh!' Just to make sho! An' doggone, son, if I don't see two ole jimcrows come flying right up outa that hoss's insides! yessuh! The sun was shinin' on 'em and they couldn't a been no greasier if they'd been eating barbecue."

80 Todd thought he would vomit, his stomach quivered.

81 "You made that up," he said.

82 "Nawsuh! Saw him just like I see you."

83 "Well, I'm glad it was you."

84 "You see lots a funny things down here, son."

85 "No, I'll let you see them," he said.

86 "By the way, the white folks round here don't like to see you boys up there in the sky. They ever bother you?"

87 "No."

88 "Well, they'd like to."

89 "Someone always wants to bother someone else," Todd said. "How do you know?"

90 "I just know."

91 "Well," he said defensively, "no one has bothered us."

92 Blood pounded in his ears as he looked away into space. He tensed, seeing a black spot in the sky, and strained to confirm what he could not clearly see.

93 "What does that look like to you?" he asked excitedly.

94 "Just another bad luck, son."

95 The he saw the movement of wings with disappointment. It was gliding smoothly down, wings outspread, tail feathers gripping the air, down swiftly—gone behind the green screen of trees. It was like a bird he had imagined there, only the sloping branches of the pines remained, sharp against the pale stretch of sky. He lay barely breathing and stared at the point where it had disappeared, caught in a spell of loathing and admiration. Why did they make them so disgusting and yet teach them to fly so well? It's like when I was up in heaven, he heard, starting.

96 The old man was chuckling, rubbing his stubbled chin.

97 "What did you say?"

98 "Sho', I died and went to heaven . . . maybe by time I tell you about it they be done come after you."

99 "I hope so," he said wearily.

100 "You boys ever sit around and swap lies?"

101 "Not often. Is this going to be one?"

102 "Well, I ain't so sho', on account of it took place when I was dead."

103 The old man paused, "That wasn't no lie 'bout the buzzards, though."

104 "All right," he said.

105 "Sho' you want to hear 'bout heaven?"

106 "Please," he answered, resting his head upon his arm.

107 "Well, I went to heaven and right away started to sproutin' me some wings. Six good ones, they was. Just like them the white angels had. I couldn't hardly believe it. I was so glad that I went off on some clouds by myself and tried 'em out. You know, 'cause I didn't want to make a fool outa myself the first thing . . ."

108 It's an old tale, Todd though. Told me years ago. Had forgotten. But at least it will keep him from talking about buzzards.

109 He closed his eyes, listening.

110 " . . . First thing I done was to git up on a low cloud and jump off. And doggone, boy, if them wings didn't work! First I tried the right; then I tried the left; then I tried 'em both together. Then Lawd, I started to move on out among the folks. I let 'em see me . . . "

111 He saw the old man gesturing flight with his arms, his face full of mock pride as he indicated an imaginary crowd, thinking, It'll be in the newspapers, as he heard, " . . . so I went and found me some colored angels—somehow I didn't believe I was an angel till I seen a real black one, ha, yes! Then I was sho'—but they tole me I better come down 'cause us colored folks had to wear a special kin' a harness when we flew. That was how come they wasn't flyin'. Oh, yes, an' you had to be extra strong for a black man even, to fly with one of them harnesses . . . "

112 This is a new turn, Todd thought, what's he driving at?

113 "So I said to myself, I ain't gonna be bothered with no harness! O naw! 'Cause if God let you sprout wings you oughta have sense enough not to let nobody make you wear something what gits in the way of flyin'. So I starts to flyin'. Heck, son," he chuckled, his eyes twinkling, "you know I had to let eve'ybody know that old Jefferson could fly good as anybody else. And I could too, fly smooth as a bird! I could even loop-the-loop—only I had to make sho' to keep my long white robe down roun' my ankles . . . "

114 Todd felt uneasy. He wanted to laugh at the joke, but his body refused, as of an independent will. He felt as he had as a child when after he had chewed a sugar-coated pill which his mother had given him, she had laughed at his efforts to remove the terrible taste.

115 " . . . Well," he heard, I was doin' all right 'til I got to speeding. Found out I could fan up a right strong breeze, I could fly so fast. I could do all kin'sa stunts too. I started flyin' up to the stars and divin' down and zoomin' roun' the moon. Man, I like to scare the devil outa some ole white angels. I was raisin' hell. Not that I meant any harm, son. But I was just feelin' good. It was so good to know I was free at last. I accidentally knocked the tips offa some stars and they tell me I caused a storm and a coupla lynchings down here in Macon County—though I swear I believe them boys what said that was making up lies on me . . . "

116 He's mocking me, Todd thought angrily. He thinks it's a joke. Grinning down at me . . . His throat was dry. He looked at his watch, why the hell didn't they come? Since they had to, why? One day I was flying down one of them heavenly streets. You got yourself into it, Todd thought. Like Jonah in the whale.

117 "Justa throwin' feathers in everybody's face. An' ole Saint Peter called me in. Said, 'Jefferson, tell me two things, what you doin' flyin' without a harness; an' how come you flyin' so fast?' So I tole him I was flyin' without a harness

'cause it got in my way, but I couldn'ta been flyin' so fast, 'cause I wasn't usin' but one wing. Saint Peter said, 'You wasn't flyin' with but one wing?' 'Yessuh,' I says, scared-like. So he says, 'Well, since you got sucha extra fine pair of wings you can leave off yo' harness awhile. But from now on none of that there one-wing flyin', 'cause you gittin' up too damn much speed!"

118 And with one mouth full of bad teeth you're making too damned much talk, thought Todd. Why don't I send him after the boy? His body ached from the hard ground and seeking to shift his position he twisted his ankle and hated himself for crying out.

119 "It gittin' worse."

120 "I . . . I twisted it," he groaned.

121 "Try not to think about it, son. That's what I do."

122 He bit his lip, fighting pain with counter-pain as the voice resumed its rhythmical droning. Jefferson seemed caught in his own creation.

123 " . . . After all that trouble I just floated roun' heaven in slow motion. But I forgot, like colored folks will do, and got to flyin' with one wing again. This time I was restin' my old broken arm and got to flyin' fast enough to shame the devil. I was comin' so fast, Lawd, I got myself called befo' ole Saint Peter again. He said, 'Jeff, didn't I warn you 'bout that speedin'?' 'Yessuh,' I says, 'but it was an accident.' He looked at me sadlike and shook his head and I knowed I was gone. He said, 'Jeff, you and that speedin' is a danger to the heavenly community. If I was to let you keep on flyin', heaven wouldn't be nothin' but uproar. Jeff, you got to go!' Son, I argued and pleaded with that old while man, but it didn't do a bit of good. They rushed me straight to them pearly gates and gimme a parachute and a map of the state of Alabama . . . "

124 Todd heard him laughing so that he could hardly speak, making a screen between them upon which his humiliation glowed like fire.

125 "Maybe you'd better stop awhile," he said, his voice unreal.

126 "Ain't much more," Jefferson laughed. "When they gimme the parachute ole Saint Peter ask me if I wanted to say a few words before I went. I felt so bad I couldn't hardly look at him, specially with all them white angels standin' around. Then somebody laughed and made me mad. So I tole him, 'Well, you done took my wings. And you puttin' me out. You got charge of things so's I can't do nothin' about it. But you got to admit just this: While I was up here I was the flyinest sonofabitch what ever hit heaven!"

127 At the burst of laughter Todd felt such an intense humiliation that only great violence would wash it away. The laughter which shook the old man like a boiling purge set up vibrations of guilt within him which not even the intricate machinery of the plane would have been adequate to transform and he heard himself screaming, "Why do you laugh at me this way?"

128 He hated himself at that moment, but he had lost control. He saw Jefferson's mouth fall open, "What—?"

129 "Answer me!"

130 His blood pounded as though it would surely burst his temples and he tried to reach the old man and fell, screaming, "Can I help it because they won't let us actually fly? Maybe we are a bunch of buzzards feeding on a dead horse, but we can hope to be eagles, can't we? Can't we?"

131 He fell back, exhausted, his ankle pounding. The saliva was like straw in his mouth. If he had the strength he would strangle this old man. This grinning, gray-headed clown who made him feel as he felt when watched by the white officers at the field. And yet this old man had neither power, prestige, rank nor technique. Nothing that could rid him of this terrible feeling. He watched him, seeing his face struggle to express a turmoil of feeling.

132 "What you mean, son? What you talkin' 'bout . . . ?"

133 "Go away. Go tell your tales to the white folks."

134 "But I didn't mean nothin' like that . . . I . . . I wasn't tryin' to hurt your feelings . . . "

135 "Please. Get the hell away from me!"

136 "But I didn't, son. I didn't mean all them things a-tall."

137 Todd shook as with a chill, searching Jefferson's face for a trace of the mockery he had seen there. But now the face was somber and tired and old. He was confused. He could not be sure that there had ever been laughter there, that Jefferson had ever really laughed in his whole life. He saw Jefferson reach out to touch him and shrank away, wondering if anything except the pain, now causing his vision to waver, was real. Perhaps he had imagined it all.

138 "Don't let it get you down, son," the voice said pensively.

139 He heard Jefferson sigh wearily, as though he felt more than he could say. His anger ebbed, leaving only the pain.

140 "I'm sorry," he mumbled.

141 "You just wore out with pain, was all . . . "

142 He saw him through a blur, smiling. And for a second he felt the embarrassed silence of understanding flutter between them.

143 "What you was doin' flyin' over this section, son? Wasn't you scared they might shoot you for a cow?"

144 Todd tensed. Was he being laughed at again? But before he could decide, the pain shook him and a part of him was lying calmly behind the screen of pain that had fallen between them, recalling the first time he had ever seen a plane. It was as though an endless series of hangars had been shaken ajar in the air base of his memory and from each, like a young wasp emerging from its cell, arose the memory of a plane.

145 The first time I ever saw a plane I was very small and planes were new in the world. I was four-and-a-half and the only plane that I had ever seen was a model suspended from the ceiling of the automobile exhibit at the State Fair.

But I did not know that it was only a model. I did not know how large a real plane was, nor how expensive. To me it was a fascinating toy, complete in itself, which my mother said could only be owned by rich little white boys. I stood rigid with admiration, my head straining backwards as I watched the gray little plane describing arcs above the gleaming tops of the automobiles. And I vowed that, rich or poor, someday I would own such a toy. My mother had to drag me out of the exhibit and not even the merry-go-round, the Ferris wheel, or the racing horse could hold my attention for the rest of the Fair. I was too busy imitating the tiny drone of the plane with my lips, and imitating with my hands the motion, swift and circling, that it made in flight.

146 After that I no longer used the pieces of lumber that lay about our back yard to construct wagons and autos . . . now it was used for airplanes. I built biplanes, using pieces of board for wings, a small box for the fuselage, another piece of wood for the rudder. The trip to the Fair had brought something new into my small world. I asked my mother repeatedly when the Fair would come back again. I'd lie in the grass and watch the sky, and each fighting bird became a soaring plane. I would have been good a year just to have seen a plane again. I became a nuisance to everyone with my questions about airplanes. But planes were new to the old folks, too, and there was little that they could tell me. Only my uncle knew some of the answers. And better still, he could carve propellers from pieces of wood that would whirl rapidly in the wind, wobbling noisily upon oiled nails.

147 I wanted a plane more than I'd wanted anything; more than I wanted the red wagon with rubber tires, more than the train that ran on a track with its train of cars. I asked my mother over and over again:

148 "Mamma?"

149 "What do you want, boy?" she'd say.

150 "Mamma, will you get mad if I ask you?" I'd say.

151 "What do you want now? I ain't got time to be answering a lot of fool questions. What you want?"

152 "Mamma, when you gonna get me one . . . ?" I'd ask.

153 "Get you one what?" she'd say.

154 "You know, Mamma; what I been asking you . . . "

155 "Boy," she'd say, "if you don't want a spanking you better come on an' tell me what you talking about so I can get on with my work."

156 "Aw, Mamma, you know . . . "

157 "What I just tell you?" she'd say.

158 "I mean when you gonna buy me a airplane."

159 "AIRPLANE! Boy, is you crazy? How many times I have to tell you to stop that foolishness. I done told you them things cost too much. I bet I'm gon' wham the living daylight out of you if you don't quit worrying me 'bout them things!"

160 But this did not stop me, and a few days later I'd try all over again.

161 Then one day a strange thing happened. It was spring and for some reason I had been hot and irritable all morning. It was a beautiful spring. I could feel it as I played barefoot in the backyard. Blossoms hung from the thorny black locust trees like clusters of fragrant white grapes. Butterflies flickered in the sunlight above the short new dew-wet grass. I had gone in the house for bread and butter and coming out I heard a steady unfamiliar drone. It was unlike anything I had ever heard before. I tried to place the sound. It was no use. It was a sensation like that I had when searching for my father's watch, heard ticking unseen in a room. It made me feel as though I had forgotten to perform some task that my mother had ordered . . . then I located it, overhead. In the sky, flying quite low and about a hundred yards off was a plane! It came so slowly that it seemed barely to move. My mouth hung wide; my bread and butter fell into the dirt. I wanted to jump up and down and cheer. And when the idea struck I trembled with excitement: "Some little white boy's plane's done flew away and all I got to do is stretch out my hands and it'll be mine!" It was a little plane like that at the Fair, flying no higher than the eaves of our roof. Seeing it come steadily forward I felt the world grow warm with promise. I opened the screen and climbed over it and clung there, waiting. I would catch the plane as it came over and swing down fast and run into the house before anyone could see me. Then no one could come to claim the plane. It droned nearer. Then when it hung like a silver cross in the blue directly above me I stretched out my hand and grabbed. It was like sticking my finger through a soap bubble. The plane flew on, as though I had simply blown my breath after it. I grabbed again, frantically, trying to catch the tail. My fingers clutched the air and disappointment surged tight and hard in my throat. Giving one last desperate grasp, I strained forward. My fingers ripped from the screen. I was falling. The ground burst hard against me. I drummed the earth with my heels and when my breath returned, I lay there bawling.

162 My mother rushed through the door.

163 "What's the matter, chile! What on earth is wrong with you?"

164 "It's gone! It's gone!"

165 "What gone?"

166 "The airplane . . . "

167 "Airplane?"

168 "Yessum, jus' like the one at the Fair . . . I . . . I tried to stop it an' it kep' right on going . . . "

169 "When, boy?"

170 "Just now," I cried, through my tears.

171 "Where it go, boy, what way?"

172 "Yonder, there . . . "

173 She scanned the sky, her arms akimbo and her checkered apron flapping in the wind as I pointed to the fading plane. Finally she looked down at me, slowly shaking her head.

174 "It's gone! It's gone!" I cried.

175 "Boy, is you a fool?" she said. "Don't you see that there's a real airplane 'stead of one of them toy ones?"

176 "Real . . . ?" I forgot to cry. "Real?"

177 "Yass, real. Don't you know that thing you reaching for is bigger'n a auto? You here trying to reach for it and I bet it's flying 'bout two hundred miles higher'n this roof." She was disgusted with me. "You come on in this house before somebody else sees what a fool you done turned out to be. You must think these here lil ole arms of you'n is mighty long . . . "

178 I was carried into the house and undressed for bed and the doctor was called. I cried bitterly, as much from the disappointment of finding the plane so far beyond my reach as from the pain.

179 When the doctor came I heard my mother telling him about the plane and asking if anything was wrong with my mind. He explained that I had had a fever for several hours. But I was kept in bed for a week and I constantly saw the plane in my sleep, flying just beyond my fingertips, sailing so slowly that it seemed barely to move. And each time I'd reach out to grab it I'd miss and through each dream I'd hear my grandma warning:

180

Young man, young man,
Yo' arms too short
To box with God . . .

181 "Hey, son!"

182 At first he did not know where he was and looked at the old man pointing, with blurred eves.

183 "Ain't that one of you-all's airplanes comin' after you?"

184 As his vision cleared he saw a small black shape above a distant field, soaring through waves of heat. But he could not be sure and with the pain he feared that somehow a horrible recurring fantasy of being split in twain by the whirling blades of a propeller had come true.

185 "You think he sees us?" he heard.

186 "See? I hope so."

187 "He's comin' like a bat outa hell!"

188 Straining, he heard the faint sound of a motor and hoped it would soon be over.

189 "How you feelin'?"

190 "Like a nightmare," he said.

191 "Hey, he's done curved back the other way!"

192 "Maybe he saw us," he said. "Maybe he's gone to send out the ambulance and ground crew." And, he thought with despair, maybe he didn't even see us.

193 "Where did you send the boy?"

194 "Down to Mister Graves," Jefferson said. "Man what owns this land."

195 "Do you think he phoned?"

196 Jefferson looked at him quickly.

197 "Aw sho'. Dabney Graves is got a bad name on accounta them killings but he'll call though . . ."

198 "What killings?"

199 "Them five fellers . . . ain't you heard?" he asked with surprise.

200 "No."

201 "Everybody knows 'bout Dabney Graves, especially the colored. He done killed enough of us."

202 Todd had the sensation of being caught in a white neighborhood after dark.

203 "What did they do?" he asked.

204 "Thought they was men," Jefferson said, "An' some he owed money, like he do me . . ."

205 "But why do you stay here?"

206 "You black, son."

207 "I know, but . . . "

208 "You have to come by the white folks, too."

209 He turned away from Jefferson's eyes, at once consoled and accused. And I'll have to come by them soon, he thought with despair. Closing his eyes, he heard Jefferson's voice as the sun burned blood-red upon his lips.

210 "I got nowhere to go," Jefferson said, "an' they'd come after me if I did. But Dabney Graves is a funny fellow. He's all the time makin' jokes. He can be means as hell, then he's liable to turn right around and back the colored against the white folks. I seen him do it. But me, I hates him for that more'n anything else. 'Cause just as soon as he gits tired helpin' a man he don't care what happens to him. He just leaves him stone cold. And then the other white folks is double hard on anybody he done helped. For him it's just a joke. He don't give a hilla beans for nobody—but hisself . . . "

211 Todd listened to the thread of detachment in the old man's voice. It was as though he held his words arm's length before him to avoid their destructive meaning.

212 "He'd just as soon do you a favor and then turn right around and have you strung up. Me, I stays outa his way 'cause down here that's what you gotta do."

213 If my ankle would only ease for a while, he thought. The closer I spin toward the earth the blacker I become, flashed through his mind. Sweat ran into his eyes and he was sure that he would never see the plane if his head continued

whirling. He tried to see Jefferson, what it was that Jefferson held in his hand. It was a little black man, another Jefferson! A little black Jefferson that shook with fits of belly-laughter while the other Jefferson looked on with detachment. Then Jefferson looked up from the thing in his hand and turned to speak, but Todd was far away, searching the sky for a plane in a hot dry land on a day and age he had long forgotten. He was going mysteriously with his mother through empty streets where black faces peered from behind drawn shades and someone was rapping at a window and he was looking back to see a hand and a frightened face frantically beckoning from a cracked door and his mother was looking down the empty perspective of the street and shaking her head and hurrying him along and at first it was only a flash he saw and a motor was droning as through the sun-glare he saw it gleaming silver as it circled and he was seeing a burst like a puff of white smoke and hearing his mother yell, Come along, boy, I got no time for them fool airplanes, I got no time, and he saw it a second time, the plane flying high, and the burst appeared suddenly and fell slowly, billowing out and sparkling like fireworks and he was watching and being hurried along as the air filled with a flurry of white pinwheeling cards that caught in the wind and scattered over the rooftops and into the gutters and a woman was running and snatching a card and reading it and screaming and he darted into the shower, grabbing as in winter he grabbed for snowflakes and bounding away at his mother's, Come on here, boy! Come on, I say! and he was watching as she took the card away, seeing her face grow puzzled and turning taut as her voice quavered, "Niggers Stay From the Polls," and died to a moan of terror as he saw the eyeless sockets of a white hood staring at him from the card and above he saw the plane spiraling gracefully, agleam in the sun like a fiery sword. And seeing it soar he was caught, transfixed between a terrible horror and a horrible fascination.

214 The sun was not so high now, and Jefferson was calling and gradually he saw three figures moving across the curving roll of the field.

215 "Look like some doctors, all dressed in white," said Jefferson.

216 They're coming at last, Todd thought. And he felt such a release of tension within him that he thought he would faint. But no sooner did he close his eyes than he was seized and he was struggling with three white men who were forcing his arms into some kind of coat. It was too much for him, his arms were pinned to his sides and as the pain blazed in his eyes, he realized that it was a straitjacket. What filthy joke was this?

217 "That oughta hold him, Mister Graves," he heard.

218 His total energies seemed focused in his eyes as he searched their faces. That was Graves: the other two wore hospital uniforms. He was poised between two poles of fear and hate as he heard the one called Graves saying, "He looks kinda purty in that there suit, boys. I'm glad you dropped by."

219 "This boy ain't crazy, Mister Graves," one of the others said. "He needs a doctor, not us. Don't see how you led us way out here anyway. It might be a joke to you, but your cousin Rudolph liable to kill somebody. White folks or niggers, don't make no difference . . . "

220 Todd saw the man turn red with anger. Graves looked down upon him, chuckling.

221 "This nigguh belongs in a straitjacket, too, boys. I knowed that the minit Jeff's kid said something 'bout a nigguh flyer. You all know you cain't let the nigguh git up that high without his going crazy. The nigguh brain ain't built right for high altitudes."

222 Todd watched the drawling red face, feeling that all the unnamed horror and obscenities that he had ever imagined stood materialized before him

223 "Let's git outa here," one of the attendants said. Todd saw the other reach toward him, realizing for the first time that he lay upon a stretcher as he yelled.

224 "Don't put your hands on me!"

225 They drew back, surprised.

226 "What's that you say, nigguh?" asked Graves.

227 He did not answer and thought that Graves's foot was aimed at his head. It landed on his chest and he could hardly breathe. He coughed helplessly, seeing Graves's lips stretch taut over his yellow teeth, and tried to shift his head. It was as though a half-dead fly was dragging slowly across his face and a bomb seemed to burst within him. Blasts of hot, hysterical laughter tore from his chest, causing his eyes to pop and he felt that the veins in his neck would surely burst. And then a part of him stood behind it all, watching the surprise in Graves's red face and his own hysteria. He thought he would never stop, he would laugh himself to death. It rang in his ears like Jefferson's laughter and he looked for him, centering his eyes desperately upon his face, as though somehow he had become his sole salvation in an insane world of outrage and humiliation. It brought a certain relief. He was suddenly aware that although his body was still contorted it was an echo that no longer rang in his ears. He heard Jefferson's voice with gratitude.

228 "Mister Graves, the Army done tole him not to leave his airplane."

229 "Nigguh, Army or no, you gittin' off my land! That airplane can stay 'cause it was paid for by taxpayers' money. But you gittin' off. An' dead or alive, it don't make no difference to me."

230 Todd was beyond it now, lost in a world of anguish.

231 "Jeff," Graves said, "you and Teddy come and grab holt. I want you to take this here black eagle over to that nigguh airfield and leave him."

232 Jefferson and the boy approached him silently. He looked away, realizing and doubting at once that only they could release him from his overpowering sense of isolation.

233 They bent for the stretcher. One of the attendants moved toward Teddy.

234 "Think you can manage it, boy?"

235 "I think I can, suh," Teddy said.

236 "Well, you better go behind then, and let yo' pa go ahead so's to keep that leg elevated."

237 He saw the white men walking ahead as Jefferson and the boy carried him along in silence. Then they were pausing and he felt a hand wiping his face; then he was moving again. And it was as though he had been lifted out of his isolation, back into the world of men. A new current of communication flowed between the man and boy and himself. They moved him gently. Far away he heard a mockingbird liquidly calling. He raised his eyes, seeing a buzzard poised unmoving in space. For a moment the whole afternoon seemed suspended and he waited for the horror to seize him again. Then like a song within his head he heard the boy's soft humming and saw the dark bird glide into the sun and glow like a bird of flaming gold.

—1944

✧ ✧ ✧

Shirley Jackson
(1919-1965)

The Lottery

Jackson was born in San Francisco and educated at Syracuse University. With her husband, the literary critic Stanley Edgar Hyman, she lived in Bennington, Vermont. There she produced three novels and the popular *Life Among the Savages* (1953), a "disrespectful memoir" of her four children, and a sequel to it, *Raising Demons* (1957). "The Lottery," which created a sensation when it appeared in the *New Yorker* in 1948, remains a fascinating example of an allegory whose ultimate meaning is open to debate. Many readers at the time, for obvious reasons, associated it with the Holocaust, though it should not be approached in such a restrictive manner. "The Lottery" is the only one of Jackson's many short stories that has been widely reprinted (it was also dramatized for television), but she was a versatile writer of humorous articles for popular magazines, psychological novels, and a popular Gothic horror novel, *The Haunting of Hill House* (1959), which was made into a motion picture called *The Haunting* (1963). Jackson published two collections of short stories, *The Lottery* (1949) and *The Magic of Shirley Jackson* (1966).

The morning of June 27th was clear and sunny, with the fresh warmth of a full-summer day; the flowers were blossoming profusely and the grass was richly green. The people of the village began to gather in the square, between the post office and the bank, around ten o'clock; in some towns there were so many people that the lottery took two days and had to be started on June 26th, but in this village, where there were only about three hundred people, the whole lottery took less than two hours, so it could begin at ten o'clock in the morning and still be through in time to allow the villagers to get home for noon dinner.

2 The children assembled first, of course. School was recently over for the summer, and the feeling of liberty sat uneasily on most of them; they tended to gather together quietly for a while before they broke into boisterous play, and their talk was still of the classroom and the teacher, of books and reprimands. Bobby Martin had already stuffed his pockets full of stones, and the other boys soon followed his example, selecting the smoothest and roundest stones; Bobby and Harry Jones and Dickie Delacroix—the villagers pronounced this name "Dellacroy"—eventually made a great pile of stones in one corner of the square and guarded it against the raids of the other boys. The girls stood aside, talking among themselves, looking over their shoulders at the boys, and the very small children rolled in the dust or clung to the hands of their older brothers or sisters.

3 Soon the men began to gather, surveying their own children, speaking of planting and rain, tractors and taxes. They stood together, away from the pile of stones in the corner, and their jokes were quiet and they smiled rather than laughed. The women, wearing faded house dresses and sweaters, came shortly after their menfolk. They greeted one another and exchanged bits of gossip as they went to join their husbands. Soon the women, standing by their husbands, began to call to their children, and the children came reluctantly, having to be called four or five times. Bobby Martin ducked under his mother's grasping hand and ran, laughing, back to the pile of stones. His father spoke up sharply, and Bobby came quickly and took his place between his father and his oldest brother.

4 The lottery was conducted—as were the square dances, the teenage club, the Halloween program—by Mr. Summers, who had time and energy to devote to civic activities. He was a roundfaced, jovial man and he ran the coal business, and people were sorry for him, because he had no children and his wife was a scold. When he arrived in the square, carrying the black wooden box, there was a

murmur of conversation among the villagers and he waved and called, "Little late today, folks." The postmaster, Mr. Graves, followed him, carrying a three-legged stool, and the stool was put in the center of the square and Mr. Summers set the black box down on it. The villagers kept their distance, leaving a space between themselves and the stool, and when Mr. Summers said, "Some of you fellows want to give me a hand?" there was a hesitation before two men, Mr. Martin and his oldest son, Baxter, came forward to hold the box steady on the stool while Mr. Summers stirred up the papers inside it.

5 The original paraphernalia for the lottery had been lost long ago, and the black box now resting on the stool had been put into use even before Old Man Warner, the oldest man in town, was born. Mr. Summers spoke frequently to the villagers about making a new box, but no one liked to upset even as much tradition as was represented by the black box. There was a story that the present box had been made with some pieces of the box that had preceded it, the one that had been constructed when the first people settled down to make a village here. Every year, after the lottery, Mr. Summers began talking again about a new box, but every year the subject was allowed to fade off without anything's being done. The black box grew shabbier each year; by now it was no longer completely black but splintered badly along one side to show the original wood color, and in some places faded or stained.

6 Mr. Martin and his oldest son, Baxter, held the black box securely on the stool until Mr. Summers had stirred the papers thoroughly with his hand. Because so much of the ritual had been forgotten or discarded, Mr. Summers had been successful in having slips of paper substituted for the chips of wood that had been used for generations. Chips of wood, Mr. Summers had argued, had been all very well when the village was tiny, but now that the population was more than three hundred and likely to keep on growing, it was necessary to use something that would fit more easily into the black box. The night before the lottery, Mr. Summers and Mr. Graves made up the slips of paper and put them in the box, and it was then taken to the safe of Mr. Summers's coal company and locked up until Mr. Summers was ready to take it to the square next morning. The rest of the year, the box was put away, sometimes one place, sometimes another; it had spent one year in Mr. Graves's barn and another year underfoot in the post office, and sometimes it was set on a shelf in the Martin grocery and left there.

7 There was a great deal of fussing to be done before Mr. Summers declared the lottery open. There were lists to make up—of heads of families, heads of households in each family, members of each household in each family. There was the proper swearing-in of Mr. Summers by the postmaster, as the official of the lottery; at one time, some people remembered, there had been a recital of some sort, performed by the official of the lottery, a perfunctory, tuneless chant that had been rattled off duly each year; some people believed that the official

of the lottery used to stand just so when he said or sang it, others believed that he was supposed to walk among the people, but years and years ago this part of the ritual had been allowed to lapse. There had been, also, a ritual salute, which the official of the lottery had had to use in addressing each person who came up to draw from the box, but this also had changed with time, until now it was felt necessary only for the official to speak to each person approaching. Mr. Summers was very good at all this; in his clean white shirt and blue jeans, with one hand resting carelessly on the black box, he seemed very proper and important as he talked interminably to Mr. Graves and the Martins.

8 Just as Mr. Summers finally left off talking and turned to the assembled villagers, Mrs. Hutchinson came hurriedly along the path to the square, her sweater thrown over her shoulders, and slid into place in the back of the crowd. "Clean for got what day it was," she said to Mrs. Delacroix, who stood next to her, and they both laughed softly. "Thought my old man was out back stacking wood," Mrs. Hutchinson went on, "and then I looked out the window and the kids were gone, and then I remembered it was the twenty-seventh and came a-running." She dried her hands on her apron, and Mrs. Delacroix said, "You're in time, though. They're still talking away up there."

9 Mrs. Hutchinson craned her neck to see through the crowd and found her husband and children standing near the front. She tapped Mrs. Delacroix on the arm as a farewell and began to make her way through the crowd. The people separated good-humoredly to let her through; two or three people said, in voices just loud enough to be heard across the crowd, "Here comes your Missus, Hutchinson," and "Bill, she made it after all." Mrs. Hutchinson reached her husband, and Mr. Summers, who had been waiting, said cheerfully, "Thought we were going to have to get on without you, Tessie." Mrs. Hutchinson said, grinning, "Wouldn't have me leave m'dishes in the sink, now would you, Joe?," and soft laughter ran through the crowd as the people stirred back into position after Mrs. Hutchinson's arrival.

10 "Well, now," Mr. Summers said soberly, "guess we better get started, get this over with, so's we can go back to work. Anybody ain't here?"

11 "Dunbar," several people said. "Dunbar, Dunbar."

12 Mr. Summers consulted his list. "Clyde Dunbar," he said. "That's right. He's broke his leg, hasn't he? Who's drawing for him?"

13 "Me, I guess," a woman said, and Mr. Summers turned to look at her. "Wife draws for her husband," Mr. Summers said. "Don't you have a grown boy to do it for you, Janey?" Although Mr. Summers and everyone else in the village knew the answer perfectly well, it was the business of the official of the lottery to ask such questions formally. Mr. Summers waited with an expression of polite interest while Mrs. Dunbar answered.

14 "Horace's not but sixteen yet," Mrs. Dunbar said regretfully. "Guess I gotta fill in for the old man this year."

15 "Right," Mr. Summers said. He made a note on the list he was holding. Then he asked, "Watson boy drawing this year?"

16 A tall boy in the crowd raised his hand. "Here," he said. "I'm drawing for m'mother and me." He blinked his eyes nervously and ducked his head as several voices in the crowd said things like "Good fellow, Jack," and "Glad to see your mother's got a man to do it."

17 "Well," Mr. Summers said, "guess that's everyone. Old Man Warner make it?"

18 "Here," a voice said, and Mr. Summers nodded.

19 A sudden hush fell on the crowd as Mr. Summers cleared his throat and looked at the list. "All ready?" he called. "Now, I'll read the names—heads of families first—and the men come up and take a paper out of the box. Keep the paper folded in your hand without looking at it until everyone has had a turn. Everything clear?"

20 The people had done it so many times that they only half listened to the directions; most of them were quiet, wetting their lips, not looking around. Then Mr. Summers raised one hand high and said, "Adams." A man disengaged himself from the crowd and came forward. "Hi, Steve," Mr. Summers said, and Mr. Adams said, "Hi, Joe." They grinned at one another humorlessly and nervously. Then Mr. Adams reached into the black box and took out a folded paper. He held it firmly by one corner as he turned and went hastily back to his place in the crowd, where he stood a little apart from his family, not looking down at his hand.

21 "Allen," Mr. Summers said. "Anderson . . . Bentham."

22 "Seems like there's no time at all between lotteries any more," Mrs. Delacroix said to Mrs. Graves in the back row. "Seems like we got through with the last one only last week."

23 "Time sure goes fast," Mrs. Graves said.

24 "Clark . . . Delacroix."

25 "There goes my old man," Mrs. Delacroix said. She held her breath while her husband went forward.

26 "Dunbar," Mr. Summers said, and Mrs. Dunbar went steadily to the box while one of the women said, "Go on, Janey," and another said, "There she goes."

27 "We're next," Mrs. Graves said. She watched while Mr. Graves came around from the side of the box, greeted Mr. Summers gravely, and selected a slip of paper from the box. By now, all through the crowd there were men holding the small folded papers in their large hands, turning them over and over nervously. Mrs. Dunbar and her two sons stood together, Mrs. Dunbar holding the slip of paper.

28 "Harburt . . . Hutchinson."

29 "Get up there, Bill," Mrs. Hutchinson said, and the people near her laughed.

30 "Jones."

31 "They do say," Mr. Adams said to Old Man Warner, who stood next to him, "that over in the north village they're talking of giving up the lottery."

32 Old Man Warneer snorted. "Pack of crazy fools," he said. "Listening to the young folks, nothing's good enough for *them.* Next thing you know, they'll be wanting to go back to living in caves, nobody work any more, live *that* way for a while. Used to be a saying about 'Lottery in June, corn be heavy soon.' First thing you know, we'd all be eating stewed chickweed and acorns. There's *always* been a lottery," he added petulantly. "Bad enough to see young Joe Summers up there joking with everybody."

33 "Some places have already quit lotteries," Mrs. Adams said.

34 "Nothing but trouble in *that,"* Old Man Warner said stoutly. "Pack of young fools."

35 "Martin." And Bobby Martin watched his father go forward. "Overdyke . . . Percy."

36 "I wish they'd hurry," Mrs. Dunbar said to her older son. "I wish they'd hurry."

37 "They're almost through," her son said.

38 "You get ready to run tell Dad," Mrs. Dunbar said.

39 Mr. Summers called his own name and then stepped forward precisely and selected a slip from the box. Then he called, "Warner."

40 "Seventy-seventh year I been in the lottery," Old Man Warner said as he went through the crowd. "Seventy-seventh time."

41 "Watson." The tall boy came awkwardly through the crowd. Someone said, "Don't be nervous, Jack," and Mr. Summers said, "Take your time, son."

42 "Zanini."

43 After that, there was a long pause, a breathless pause, until Mr. Summers, holding his slip of paper in the air, said, "All right, fellows." For a minute, no one moved, and then all the slips of paper were opened. Suddenly, all women began to speak at once, saying, "Who is it?" "Who's got it?" "Is it the Dunbars?" "Is it the Watsons?" Then the voices began to say, "It's Hutchinson. It's Bill." "Bill Hutchinson's got it."

44 "Go tell your father," Mrs. Dunbar said to her older son.

45 People began to look around to see the Hutchinsons. Bill Hutchinson was standing quiet, staring down at the paper in his hand. Suddenly, Tessie Hutchinson shouted to Mr. Summers, "You didn't give him time enough to take any paper he wanted. I saw you. It wasn't fair!"

46 "Be a good sport, Tessie," Mrs. Delacroix called, and Mrs. Graves said, "All of us took the same chance."

47 "Shut up, Tessie," Bill Hutchinson said.

48 "Well, everyone," Mr. Summers said, "that was done pretty fast, and now we've got to be hurrying a little more to get done in time." He consulted his next list. "Bill," he said, "you draw for the Hutchinson family. You got any other households in the Hutchinsons?"

49 "There's Don and Eva," Mrs. Hutchinson yelled. "Make *them* take their chance!"

50 "Daughters draw with their husbands' families, Tessie," Mr. Summers said gently. "You know that as well as anyone else."

51 "It wasn't fair," Tessie said.

52 "I guess not, Joe," Bill Hutchinson said regretfully. "My daughter draws with her husband's family, that's only fair. And I've got no other family except the kids."

53 "Then, as far as drawing for families is concerned, it's you," Mr. Summers said in explanation, "and as far as drawing for households is concerned, that's you, too. Right?"

54 "Right," Bill Hutchinson said.

55 "How many kids, Bill?" Mr. Summers asked formally.

56 "Three," Bill Hutchinson said. "There's Bill, Jr., and Nancy, and little Dave. And Tessie and me."

57 "All right, then," Mr. Summers said. "Harry, you got their tickets back?"

58 Mr. Graves nodded and held up the slips of paper. "Put them in the box, then," Mr. Summers directed. "Take Bill's and put it in."

59 "I think we ought to start over," Mrs. Hutchinson said, as quietly as she could. "I tell you it wasn't *fair*. You didn't give him time enough to choose. *Every*body saw that."

60 Mr. Graves had selected the five slips and put them in the box, and he dropped all the papers but those onto the ground, where the breeze caught them and lifted them off.

61 "Listen, everybody," Mrs. Hutchinson was saying to the people around her.

62 "Ready, Bill?" Mr. Summers asked, and Bill Hutchinson, with one quick glance around at his wife and children, nodded.

63 "Remember," Mr. Summers said, "take the slips and keep them folded until each person has taken one. Harry, you help little Dave." Mr. Graves took the hand of the little boy, who came willingly with him up to the box. "Take a paper out of the box, Davy," Mr. Summers said. Davy put his hand into the box and laughed. "Take just *one* paper," Mr. Summers said. "Harry, you hold it for him." Mr. Graves took the child's hand and removed the folded paper from the tight fist and held it while little Dave stood next to him and looked up at him wonderingly.

64 "Nancy next," Mr. Summers said. Nancy was twelve, and her school friends breathed heavily as she went forward, switching her skirt, and took a slip daintily from the box. "Bill, Jr.," Mr. Summers said, and Billy, his face red and his feet overlarge, nearly knocked the box over as he got a paper out. "Tessie," Mr. Summers said. She hesitated for a minute, looking around defiantly, and then set her lips and went up to the box. She snatched a paper out and held it behind her.

65 "Bill," Mr. Summers said, and Bill Hutchinson reached into the box and felt around, bringing his hand out at last with the slip of paper in it.

66 The crowd was quiet. A girl whispered, "I hope it's not Nancy," and the sound of the whisper reached the edges of the crowd.

67 "It's not the way it used to be," Old Man Warner said clearly. "People ain't the way they used to be."

68 "All right," Mr. Summers said. "Open the papers. Harry, you open little Dave's."

69 Mr. Graves opened the slip of paper and there was a general sigh through the crowd as he held it up and everyone could see that it was blank. Nancy and Bill, Jr., opened theirs at the same time, and both beamed and laughed, turning around to the crowd and holding their slips of paper above their heads.

70 "Tessie," Mr. Summers said. There was a pause, and then Mr. Summers looked at Bill Hutchinson, and Bill unfolded his paper and showed it. It was blank.

71 "It's Tessie," Mr. Summers said, and his voice was hushed. "Show us her paper, Bill."

72 Bill Hutchinson went over to his wife and forced the slip of paper out of her hand. It had a black spot on it, the black spot Mr. Summers had made the night before with the heavy pencil in the coal-company office. Bill Hutchinson held it up, and there was a stir in the crowd.

73 "All right, folks," Mr. Summers said, "let's finish quickly."

74 Although the villagers had forgotten the ritual and lost the original black box, they still remembered to use stones. The pile of stones the boys had made earlier was ready; there were stones on the ground with the blowing scraps of paper that had come out of the box. Mrs. Delacroix selected a stone so large she had to pick it up with both hands and turned to Mrs. Dunbar. "Come on," she said. "Hurry up."

75 Mrs. Dunbar had small stones in both hands, and she said, gasping for breath, "I can't run at all. You'll have to go ahead and I'll catch up with you."

76 The children had stones already, and someone gave little Davy Hutchinson a few pebbles.

77 Tessie Hutchinson was in the center of a cleared space by now, and she held her hands out desperately as the villagers moved in on her. "It isn't fair," she said. A stone hit her on the side of the head.

78 Old Man Warner was saying, "Come on, come on, everyone." Steve Adams was in the front of the crowd of villagers, with Mrs. Graves beside him.

79 "It isn't fair, it isn't right," Mrs. Hutchinson screamed, and then they were upon her.

—1948

✧ ✧ ✧

Doris Lessing

(b. 1919)

A Woman on a Roof

Lessing was born in Persia, where her father was a bank manager, and grew up in Rhodesia (now Zimbabwe) on an isolated farm, a member of the controlling white minority of the British colony. After quitting school, she eventually settled in London. There, after two failed marriages and the births of three children, she turned to writing, publishing her first novel, *The Grass Is Singing*, in 1950. A member of the Communist party in her youth but disillusioned with it later, Lessing continued to express her political views through writing, becoming an important figure to feminists in the 1960s through the publication of her experimental novel *The Golden Notebook* (1962), an account of a woman writer's failed attempt to attain her own artistic goals. Still, she has managed to remain independent of most labels, and has expanded her interests in many directions, including religious mysticism. Among her many books are novels; collections of short stories; plays; political non-fiction; a five-volume series of novels, *The Children of Violence* (1950-69); and a tetralogy of science fiction novels, *Canopus in Argos: Archives* (1981). "A Woman on a Roof" appeared in her 1963 collection *A Man and Two Women* and thus anticipates by almost a decade many of the themes of later feminist fiction.

It was during the week of hot sun, that June.

2 Three men were at work on the roof, where the leads got so hot they had the idea of throwing water on to cool them. But the water steamed, then sizzled; and they made jokes about getting an egg from some woman in the flats under them, to poach it for their dinner. By two it was not possible to touch the guttering they were replacing, and they speculated about what workmen did in regularly hot countries. Perhaps they should borrow kitchen gloves with the egg? They were all a bit dizzy, not used to the heat; and they shed their coats and stood side by side squeezing themselves into a foot-wide patch of shade against a chimney, careful to keep their feet in the thick socks and boots out of the sun. There was a fine view across several acres of roofs. Not far off a man sat in a deck chair reading the newspapers. Then they saw her, between chimneys, about fifty yards away. She lay face down on a brown blanket. They could see the top part of her: black hair, a flushed solid back, arms spread out.

3 "She's stark naked," said Stanley, sounding annoyed.

4 Harry, the oldest, a man of about forty-five, said: "Looks like it."

5 Young Tom, seventeen, said nothing, but he was excited and grinning.

6 Stanley said: "Someone'll report her if she doesn't watch out."

7 "She thinks no one can see," said Tom, craning his head all ways to see more.

8 At this point the woman, still lying prone, brought her two hands up behind her shoulders with the ends of a scarf in them, tied it behind her back, and sat up. She wore a red scarf tied around her breasts and brief red bikini pants. This being the first day of the sun she was white, flushing red. She sat smoking, and did not look up when Stanley let out a wolf whistle. Harry said: "Small things amuse small minds," leading the way back to their part of the roof, but it was scorching. Harry said: "Wait, I'm going to rig up some shade," and disappeared down the skylight into the building. Now that he'd gone, Stanley and Tom went to the farthest point they could to peer at the woman. She had moved, and all they could see were two pink legs stretched on the blanket. They whistled and shouted but the legs did not move. Harry came back with a blanket and shouted: "Come on, then." He sounded irritated with them. They clambered back to him and he said to Stanley: "What about your missus?" Stanley was newly married, about three months. Stanley said, jeering: "What about my missus?"—preserving his independence. Tom said nothing, but his mind was full of the nearly naked woman. Harry slung the blanket, which he had borrowed from a friendly woman downstairs, from the stem of a television aerial to a row of chimney-pots. This shade fell across the piece of gutter they had to replace. But the shade kept moving, they had to adjust the blanket, and not much progress was made. At last some of the heat left the roof, and they worked fast, making up for lost time. First Stanley, then Tom, made a trip to the end of the roof to see the woman. "She's on her back," Stanley said, adding a jest which made Tom snicker, and the older man smile tolerantly. Tom's report was that

she hadn't moved, but it was a lie. He wanted to keep what he had seen to himself: he had caught her in the act of rolling down the little red pants over her hips, till they were no more than a small triangle. She was on her back, fully visible, glistening with oil.

9 Next morning, as soon as they came up, they went to look. She was already there, face down, arms spread out, naked except for the little red pants. She had turned brown in the night. Yesterday she was a scarlet-and-white woman, today she was a brown woman. Stanley let out a whistle. She lifted her head, startled, as if she'd been asleep, and looked straight over at him. The sun was in her eyes, she blinked and stared, then she dropped her head again. At this gesture of indifference, they all three, Stanley, Tom and old Harry, let out whistles and yells. Harry was doing it in parody of the younger men, making fun of them, but he was also angry. They were all angry because of her utter indifference to the three men watching her.

10 "Bitch," said Stanley.

11 "She should ask us over," said Tom, snickering.

12 Harry recovered himself and reminded Stanley: "If she's married, her old man wouldn't like that."

13 "Christ," said Stanley virtuously, "if my wife lay about like that, for everyone to see, I'd soon stop her."

14 Harry said, smiling: "How do you know, perhaps she's sunning herself at this very moment?"

15 "Not a chance, not on our roof." The safety of his wife put Stanley into a good humor, and they went to work. But today it was hotter than yesterday; and several times one or the other suggested they should tell Matthew, the foreman, and ask to leave the roof until the heat wave was over. But they didn't. There was work to be done in the basement of the big block of flats, but up here they felt free, on a different level from ordinary humanity shut in the streets or the buildings. A lot more people came out on to the roofs that day, for an hour at midday. Some married couples sat side by side in deck chairs, the women's legs stockingless and scarlet, the men in vests with reddening shoulders.

16 The woman stayed on her blanket, turning herself over and over. She ignored them, no matter what they did. When Harry went off to fetch more screws, Stanley said: "Come on." Her roof belonged to a different system of roofs, separated from theirs at one point by about twenty feet. It meant a scrambling climb from one level to another, edging along parapets, clinging to chimneys, while their big boots slipped and slithered, but at last they stood on a small square projecting roof looking straight down at her, close. She sat smoking, reading a book. Tom thought she looked like a poster, or a magazine cover, with the blue sky behind her and her legs stretched out. Behind her a great crane at work on a new building in Oxford Street swung its black arm across roofs in a great arc. Tom imagined himself at work on the crane, adjusting the arm to

swing over and pick her up and swing her back across the sky to drop her near him.

17 They whistled. She looked up at them, cool and remote, then went on reading. Again, they were furious. Or, rather, Stanley was. His sun-heated face was screwed into a rage as he whistled again and again, trying to make her look up. Young Tom stopped whistling. He stood beside Stanley, excited, grinning; but he felt as if he were saying to the woman: Don't associate me with *him,* for his grin was apologetic. Last night he had thought of the unknown woman before he slept, and she had been tender with him. This tenderness he was remembering as he shifted his feet by the jeering, whistling Stanley, and watched the indifferent, healthy brown woman a few feet off, with the gap that plunged to the street between them. Tom thought it was romantic, it was like being high on two hilltops. But there was a shout from Harry, and they clambered back. Stanley's face was hard, really angry. The boy kept looking at him and wondered why he hated the woman so much, for by now he loved her.

18 They played their little games with the blanket, trying to trap shade to work under; but again it was not until nearly four that they could work seriously, and they were exhausted, all three of them. They were grumbling about the weather by now. Stanley was in a thoroughly bad humor. When they made their routine trip to see the woman before they packed up for the day, she was apparently asleep, face down, her back all naked save for the scarlet triangle on her buttocks. "I've got a good mind to report her to the police," said Stanley, and Harry said: "What's eating you? What harm's she doing?"

19 "I tell you, if she was my wife!"

20 "But she isn't, is she?" Tom knew that Harry, like himself, was uneasy at Stanley's reaction. He was normally a sharp young man, quick at his work, making a lot of jokes, good company.

21 "Perhaps it will be cooler tomorrow," said Harry.

22 But it wasn't; it was hotter, if anything, and the weather forecast said the good weather would last. As soon as they were on the roof, Harry went over to see if the woman was there, and Tom knew it was to prevent Stanley going, to put off his bad humor. Harry had grownup children, a boy the same age as Tom, and the youth trusted and looked up to him.

23 Harry came back and said: "She's not there."

24 "I bet her old man has put his foot down," said Stanley, and Harry and Tom caught each other's eyes and smiled behind the young married man's back.

25 Harry suggested they should get permission to work in the basement, and they did, that day. But before packing up Stanley said: "Let's have a breath of fresh air." Again Harry and Tom smiled at each other as they followed Stanley up to the roof, Tom in the devout conviction that he was there to protect the woman from Stanley. It was about five-thirty, and a calm, full sunlight lay over the roofs. The great crane still swung its black arm from Oxford Street to

above their heads. She was not there. Then there was a flutter of white from behind a parapet, and she stood up, in a belted, white dressing gown. She had been there all day, probably, but on a different patch of roof, to hide from them. Stanley did not whistle; he said nothing, but watched the woman bend to collect papers, books, cigarettes, then fold the blanket over her arm. Tom was thinking: If they weren't here, I'd go over and say . . . what? But he knew from his nightly dreams of her that she was kind and friendly. Perhaps she would ask him down to her flat? Perhaps . . . He stood watching her disappear down the skylight. As she went, Stanley let out a shrill derisive yell; she started, and it seemed as if she nearly fell. She clutched to save herself, they could hear things falling. She looked straight at them, angry. Harry said, facetiously: "Better be careful on those slippery ladders, love." Tom knew he said it to save her from Stanley, but she could not know it. She vanished, frowning. Tom was full of a secret delight, because he knew her anger was for the others, not for him.

26 "Roll on some rain," said Stanley, bitter, looking at the blue evening sky.

27 Next day was cloudless, and they decided to finish the work in the basement. They felt excluded, shut in the grey cement basement fitting pipes, from the holiday atmosphere in London in a heat wave. At lunchtime they came up for some air, but while the married couples, and the men in shirt-sleeves or vests, were there, she was not there, either on her usual patch of roof or where she had been yesterday. They all, even Harry, clambered about, between chimney-pots, over parapets, the hot leads stinging their fingers. There was not a sign of her. They took off their shirts and vests and exposed their chests, feeling their feet sweaty and hot. They did not mention the woman. But Tom felt alone again. Last night she had him into her flat: it was big and had fitted white carpets and a bed with a padded white leather headboard. She wore a black filmy negligée and her kindness to Tom thickened his throat as he remembered it. He felt she had betrayed him by not being there.

28 And again after work they climbed up, but still there was nothing to be seen of her. Stanley kept repeating that if it was as hot as this tomorrow he wasn't going to work and that's all there was to it. But they were all there next day. By ten the temperature was in the middle seventies, and it was eighty long before noon. Harry went to the foreman to say it was impossible to work on the leads in that heat; but the foreman said there was nothing else he could put them on, and they'd have to. At midday they stood, silent, watching the skylight on her roof open, and then she slowly emerged in her white gown, holding a bundle of blanket. She looked at them, gravely, then went to the part of the roof where she was hidden from them. Tom was pleased. He felt she was more his when the other men couldn't see her. They had taken off their shirts and vests, but now they put them back again, for they felt the sun bruising their flesh. "She must have the hide of a rhino," said Stanley, tugging at guttering and swearing. They stopped work, and sat in the shade, moving around behind chimney stacks. A

woman came to water a yellow window box opposite them. She was middleaged, wearing a flowered summer dress. Stanley said to her: "We need a drink more than them." She smiled and said: "Better drop down to the pub quick, it'll be closing in a minute." They exchanged pleasantries, and she left them with a smile and a wave.

29 "Not like Lady Godiva," said Stanley. "She can give us a bit of a chat and a smile."

30 "You didn't whistle at *her,"* said Tom, reproving.

31 "Listen to him," said Stanley, "you didn't whistle, then?"

32 But the boy felt as if he hadn't whistled, as if only Harry and Stanley had. He was making plans, when it was time to knock off work, to get left behind and somehow make his way over to the woman. The weather report said the hot spell was due to break, so he had to move quickly. But there was no chance of being left.

33 The other two decided to knock off work at four, because they were exhausted. As they went down, Tom quickly climbed a parapet and hoisted himself higher by pulling his weight up a chimney. He caught a glimpse of her lying on her back, her knees up, eyes closed, a brown woman lolling in the sun. He slipped and clattered down, as Stanley looked for information: "She's gone down," he said. He felt as if he had protected her from Stanley, and that she must be grateful to him. He could feel the bond between the woman and himself.

34 Next day, they stood around on the landing below the roof, reluctant to climb up into the heat. The woman who had lent Harry the blanket came out and offered them a cup of tea. They accepted gratefully, and sat around Mrs. Pritchett's kitchen an hour or so, chatting. She was married to an airline pilot. A smart blonde, of about thirty, she had an eye for the handsome sharp-eyed Stanley; and the two teased each other while Harry sat in a comer, watching, indulgent, though his expression reminded Stanley that he was married. And young Tom felt envious of Stanley's ease in badinage; felt, too, that Stanley's getting off with Mrs. Pritchett left his romance with the woman on the roof safe and intact.

35 "I thought they said the heat wave'd break," said Stanley, sullen, as the time approached when they really would have to climb up into the sunlight.

36 "You don't like it, then?" asked Mrs. Pritchett.

37 "All right for some," said Stanley. "Nothing to do but lie about as if it was a beach up there. Do you ever go up?"

38 "Went up once," said Mrs. Pritchett. "But it's a dirty place up there, and it's too hot."

39 "Quite right too," said Stanley.

40 Then they went up, leaving the cool neat little flat and the friendly Mrs. Pritchett.

41 As soon as they were up they saw her. The three men looked at her, resentful at her ease in this punishing sun. Then Harry said, because of the expression on Stanley's face: "Come on, we've got to pretend to work, at least."

42 They had to wrench another length of guttering that ran beside a parapet out of its bed, so that they could replace it. Stanley took it in his two hands, tugged, swore, stood up. "Fuck it," he said, and sat down under a chimney. He lit a cigarette. "Fuck them," he said. "What do they think we are, lizards? I've got blisters all over my hands." Then he jumped up and climbed over the roofs and stood with his back to them. He put his fingers either side of his mouth and let out a shrill whistle. Tom and Harry squatted, not looking at each other, watching him. They could just see the woman's head, the beginnings of her brown shoulders. Stanley whistled again. Then he began stamping with his feet, and whistled and yelled and screamed at the woman, his face getting scarlet. He seemed quite mad, as he stamped and whistled, while the woman did not move, she did not move a muscle.

43 "Barmy," said Tom.

44 "Yes," said Harry, disapproving.

45 Suddenly the older man came to a decision. It was, Tom knew, to save some sort of scandal or real trouble over the woman. Harry stood up and began packing tools into a length of oily cloth. "Stanley," he said, commanding. At first Stanley took no notice, but Harry said: "Stanley, we're packing it in, I'll tell Matthew."

46 Stanley came back, cheeks mottled, eyes glaring.

47 "Can't go on like this," said Harry. "It'll break in a day or so. I'm going to tell Matthew we've got sunstroke, and if he doesn't like it, it's too bad." Even Harry sounded aggrieved, Tom noted. The small, competent man, the family man with his grey hair, who was never at a loss, sounded really off balance. "Come on," he said, angry. He fitted himself into the open square in the roof, and went down, watching his feet on the ladder. Then Stanley went, with not a glance at the woman. Then Tom, who, his throat beating with excitement, silently promised her on a backward glance: Wait for me, wait, I'm coming.

48 On the pavement Stanley said: "I'm going home." He looked white now, so perhaps he really did have sunstroke. Harry went off to find the foreman, who was at work on the plumbing of some flats down the street. Tom slipped back, not into the building they had been working on, but the building on whose roof the woman lay. He went straight up, no one stopping him. The skylight stood open, with an iron ladder leading up. He emerged on to the roof a couple of yards from her. She sat up, pushing back her black hair with both hands. The scarf across her breasts bound them tight, and brown flesh bulged around it. Her legs were brown and smooth. She stared at him in silence. The boy stood grinning, foolish, claiming the tenderness he expected from her.

49 "What do you want?" she asked.

50 "I . . . I came to . . . make your acquaintance," he stammered, grinning, pleading with her.

51 They looked at each other, the slight, scarlet-faced excited boy, and the serious, nearly naked woman. Then, without a word, she lay down on her brown blanket, ignoring him.

52 "You like the sun, do you?" he enquired of her glistening back.

53 Not a word. He felt panic, thinking of how she had held him in her arms, stroked his hair, brought him where he sat, lordly, in her bed, a glass of some exhilarating liquor he had never tasted in life. He felt that if he knelt down, stroked her shoulders, her hair, she would turn and clasp him in her arms.

54 He said: "The sun's all right for you, isn't it?"

55 She raised her head, set her chin on two small fists: "Go away," she said. He did not move. "Listen," she said, in a slow reasonable voice, where anger was kept in check, though with difficulty; looking at him, her face weary with anger, "if you get a kick out of seeing women in bikinis, why don't you take a sixpenny bus ride to the Lido? You'd see dozens of them, without all this mountaineering."

56 She hadn't understood him. He felt her unfairness pale him. He stammered: "But I like you, I've been watching you and . . . "

57 "Thanks," she said, and dropped her face again, turned away from him.

58 She lay there. He stood there. She said nothing. She had simply shut him out. He stood, saying nothing at all, for some minutes. He thought: She'll have to say something if I stay. But the minutes went past, with no sign of them in her, except in the tension of her back, her thighs, her arms—the tension of waiting for him to go.

59 He looked up at the sky, where the sun seemed to spin in heat; and over the roofs where he and his mates had been earlier. He could see the heat quivering where they had worked. And they expect us to work in these conditions! he thought, filled with righteous indignation. The woman hadn't moved. A bit of hot wind blew her black hair softly; it shone, and was iridescent. He remembered how he had stroked it last night.

60 Resentment of her at last moved him off and away down the ladder, through the building, into the street. He got drunk then, in hatred of her.

61 Next day when he woke the sky was grey. He looked at the wet grey and thought, vicious: Well, that's fixed you, hasn't it now? That's fixed you good and proper.

62 The three men were at work early on the cool leads, surrounded by damp drizzling roofs where no one came to sun themselves, black roofs, slimy with rain. Because it was cool now, they would finish the job that day, if they hurried.

—1963

Flannery O'Connor
(1925-1964)

Everything That Rises Must Converge

O'Connor was one of the first of many important writers to emerge from the Writers' Workshop of the University of Iowa, where she received an M.F.A. in creative writing. Born in Savannah, Georgia, she earlier attended Georgia State College for Women, graduating in 1945. Plagued by disseminated lupus, the same incurable illness that killed her father in 1941, O'Connor spent most of the last decade of her life living with her mother on a dairy farm near Milledgeville, Georgia, where she wrote and raised peacocks. Unusual among modern American writers in the seriousness of her Christianity (she was a devout Roman Catholic in the largely Protestant South), O'Connor focuses an uncompromising moral eye on the violence and spiritual disorder of the modern world. She is sometimes called a "southern gothic" writer because of her fascination with the grotesque, though today she seems far ahead of her time in depicting a region in which the social and religious certainties of the past are becoming extinct almost overnight. O'Connor's published work includes two short novels, *Wise Blood* (1952) and *The Violent Bear It Away* (1960), and two collections of short stories, *A Good Man Is Hard To Find* (1955) and *Everything That Rises Must Converge*, published posthumously in 1965. A collection of essays and miscellaneous prose, *Mystery and Manners* (1961), and her selected letters, *The Habit of Being* (1979), reveal an engaging social side of her personality that is not always apparent in her fiction.

Her doctor had told Julian's mother that she must lose twenty pounds on account of her blood pressure, so on Wednesday nights Julian had to take her downtown on the bus for a reducing class at the Y. The reducing class was designed for working girls over fifty, who weighed from 165 to 200 pounds. His mother was one of the slimmer ones, but she said ladies did not tell their age or weight. She would not ride the buses by herself at night since they had been integrated, and because the reducing class was one of her few pleasures, necessary for her health, and *free,* she said Julian could at least put himself out to take her, considering all she did for him. Julian did not like to consider all she did for him, but every Wednesday night he braced himself and took her.

2 She was almost ready to go, standing before the hall mirror, putting on her hat, while he, his hands behind him, appeared pinned to the door frame, waiting like Saint Sebastian for the arrows to begin piercing him. The hat was new and had cost her seven dollars and a half. She kept saying, "Maybe I shouldn't have paid that for it. No, I shouldn't have. I'll take it off and return it tomorrow. I shouldn't have bought it."

3 Julian raised his eyes to heaven. "Yes, you should have bought it," he said. "Put it on and let's go." It was a hideous hat. A purple velvet flap came down on one side of it and stood up on the other; the rest of it was green and looked like a cushion with the stuffing out. He decided it was less comical than jaunty and pathetic. Everything that gave her pleasure was small and depressed him.

4 She lifted the hat one more time and set it down slowly on top of her head. Two wings of gray hair protruded on either side of her florid face, but her eyes, sky-blue, were as innocent and untouched by experience as they must have been when she was ten. Were it not that she was a widow who had struggled fiercely to feed and clothe and put him through school and who was supporting him still, "until he got on his feet," she might have been a little girl that he had to take to town.

5 "It's all right, it's all right," he said. "Let's go." He opened the door himself and started down the walk to get her going. The sky was a dying violet and the houses stood out darkly against it, bulbous liver-colored monstrosities of a uniform ugliness though no two were alike. Since this had been a fashionable neighborhood forty years ago, his mother persisted in thinking they did well to have an apartment in it. Each house had a narrow collar of dirt around it in which sat, usually, a grubby child. Julian walked with his hands in his pockets, his head down and thrust forward and his eyes glazed with the determination to make himself completely numb during the time he would be sacrificed to her pleasure.

6 The door closed and he turned to find the dumpy figure, surmounted by the atrocious hat, coming toward him. "Well," she said, "you only live once and paying a little more for it, I at least won't meet myself coming and going."

7 "Some day I'll start making money," Julian said gloomily—he knew he never would—"and you can have one of those jokes whenever you take the fit." But first they would move. He visualized a place where the nearest neighbors would be three miles away on either side.

8 "I think you're doing fine," she said, drawing on her gloves. "You've only been out of school a year. Rome wasn't built in a day."

9 She was one of the few members of the Y reducing class who arrived in hat and gloves and who had a son who had been to college. "It takes time," she said,

"and the world is in such a mess. This hat looked better on me than any of the others, though when she brought it out I said, 'Take that thing back. I wouldn't have it on my head,' and she said, 'Now wait till you see it on,' and when she put it on me, I said, 'We-ull,' and she said, 'If you ask me, that hat does something for you and you do something for the hat, and besides,' she said, 'with that hat, you won't meet yourself coming and going.'"

10 Julian thought he could have stood his lot better if she had been selfish, if she had been an old hag who drank and screamed at him. He walked along, saturated in depression, as if in the midst of his martyrdom he had lost his faith. Catching sight of his long, hopeless, irritated face, she stopped suddenly with a grief-stricken look, and pulled back on his arm. "Wait on me," she said. "I'm going back to the house and take this thing off and tomorrow I'm going to return it. I was out of of my head. I can pay the gas bill with that seven-fifty."

11 He caught her arm in a vicious grip. "You are not going to take it back," he said. "I like it."

12 "Well," she said, "I don't think I ought . . . "

13 "Shut up and enjoy it," he muttered, more depressed than ever.

14 "With the world in the mess it's in," she said, "it's a wonder we can enjoy anything. I tell you, the bottom rail is on the top."

15 Julian sighed.

16 "Of course," she said, "if you know who you are, you can go anywhere." She said this every time he took her to the reducing class. "Most of them in it are not our kind of people," she said, "but I can be gracious to anybody. I know who I am."

17 "They don't give a damn for your graciousness," Julian said savagely. "Knowing who you are is good for one generation only. You haven't the foggiest idea where you stand now or who you are."

18 She stopped and allowed her eyes to flash at him. "I most certainly do know who I am," she said, "and if you don't know who you are, I'm ashamed of you."

19 "Oh hell," Julian said.

20 "Your great-grandfather was a former governor of this state," she said. "Your grandfather was a prosperous landowner. Your grandmother was a Godhigh."

21 "Will you look around you," he said tensely, "and see where you are now?" and he swept his arm jerkily out to indicate the neighborhood, which the growing darkness at least made less dingy.

22 "You remain what you are," she said. "Your great-grandfather had a plantation and two hundred slaves."

23 "There are no more slaves," he said irritably.

24 "They were better off when they were," she said. He groaned to see that she was off on that topic. She rolled onto it every few days like a train on an open

track. He knew every stop, every junction, every swamp along the way, and knew the exact point at which her conclusion would roll majestically into the station: "It's ridiculous. It's simply not realistic. They should rise, yes, but on their own side of the fence."

25 "Let's skip it," Julian said.

26 "The ones I feel sorry for," she said, "are the ones that are half white. They're tragic."

27 "Will you skip it?"

28 "Suppose we were half white. We would certainly have mixed feelings."

29 "I have mixed feelings now," he groaned.

30 "Well let's talk about something pleasant," she said. "I remember going to Grandpa's when I was a little girl. Then the house had double stairways that went up to what was really the second floor—all the cooking was done on the first. I used to like to stay down in the kitchen on account of the way the walls smelled. I would sit with my nose pressed against the plaster and take deep breaths. Actually the place belonged to the Godhighs but your grandfather Chestny paid the mortgage and saved it for them. They were in reduced circumstances," she said, "but reduced or not, they never forgot who they were."

31 "Doubtless that decayed mansion reminded them," Julian muttered. He never spoke of it without contempt or thought of it without longing. He had seen it once when he was a child before it had been sold. The double stairways had rotted and been torn down. Negroes were living in it. But it remained in his mind as his mother had known it. It appeared in his dreams regularly. He would stand on the wide porch, listening to the rustle of oak leaves, then wander through the high-ceilinged hall into the parlor that opened onto it and gaze at the worn rugs and faded draperies. It occurred to him that it was he, not she, who could have appreciated it. He preferred its threadbare elegance to anything he could name and it was because of it that all the neighborhoods they had lived in had been a torment to him—whereas she had hardly known the difference. She called her insensitivity "being adjustable."

32 "And I remember the old darky who was my nurse, Caroline. There was no better person in the world. I've always had a great respect for my colored friends," she said. "I'd do anything in the world for them and they'd . . . "

33 "Will you for God's sake get off that subject?" Julian said. When he got on a bus by himself, he made it a point to sit down beside a Negro, in reparation as it were for his mother's sins.

34 "You're mighty touchy tonight," she said. "Do you feel all right?"

35 "Yes I feel all right," he said. "Now lay off."

36 She pursed her lips. "Well, you certainly are in a vile humor," she observed, "I just won't speak to you at all."

37 They had reached the bus stop. There was no bus in sight and Julian, his hands still jammed in his pockets and his head thrust forward, scowled down

the empty street. The frustration of having to wait on the bus as well as ride on it began to creep up his neck like a hot hand. The presence of his mother was borne in upon him as she gave a pained sigh. He looked at her bleakly. She was holding herself very erect under the preposterous hat, wearing it like a banner of her imaginary dignity. There was in him an evil urge to break her spirit. He suddenly unloosened his tie and pulled it off and put it in his pocket.

38 She stiffened. "Why must you look like *that* when you take me to town?" she said. "Why must you deliberately embarrass me?"

39 "If you'll never learn where you are," he said, "you can at least learn where I am."

40 "You look like a—thug," she said.

41 "Then I must be one," he murmured.

42 "I'll just go home," she said. "I will not bother you. If you can't do a little thing like that for me . . . "

43 Rolling his eyes upward, he put his tie back on. "Restored to my class," he muttered. He thrust his face toward her and hissed. "True culture is in the mind, the *mind,*" he said, and tapped his head, "the mind."

44 "It's in the heart," she said, "and in how you do things is because of who you *are.*"

45 "Nobody in the damn bus cares who you are."

46 "I care who I am," she said icily.

47 The lighted bus appeared on top of the next hill and as it approached, they moved out into the street to meet it. He put his hand under her elbow and hoisted her up on the creaking step. She entered with a little smile, as if she were going into a drawing room where everyone had been waiting for her. While he put in the tokens, she sat down on one of the broad front seats for three which faced the aisle. A thin woman with protruding teeth and long yellow hair was sitting on the end of it. His mother moved up beside her and left room for Julian beside herself. He sat down and looked at the floor across the aisle where a pair of thin feet in red and white canvas sandals were planted.

48 His mother immediately began a general conversation meant to attract anyone who felt like talking. "Can it get any hotter?" she said and removed from her purse a folding fan, black with a Japanese scene on it, which she began to flutter before her.

49 "I reckon it might could," the woman with the protruding teeth said, "but I know for a fact my apartment couldn't get no hotter."

50 "It must get the afternoon sun," his mother said. She sat forward and looked up and down the bus. It was half filled. Everybody was white. "I see we have the bus to ourselves," she said. Julian cringed.

51 "For a change," said the woman across the aisle, the owner of the red and white canvas sandals. "I come on one the other day and they were thick as fleas—up front and all through."

52 "The world is in a mess everywhere," his mother said. "I don't know how we've let it get in this fix."

53 "What gets my goat is all those boys from good families stealing automobile tires," the woman with the protruding teeth said. "I told my boy, I said you may not be rich but you been raised right and if I ever catch you in any such mess, they can send you on to the reformatory. Be exactly where you belong."

54 "Training tells," his mother said. "Is your boy in high school?"

55 "Ninth grade," the woman said.

56 "My son just finished college last year. He wants to write but he's selling typewriters until he gets started," his mother said.

57 The woman leaned forward and peered at Julian. He threw her such a malevolent look that she subsided against the seat. On the floor across the aisle there was an abandoned newspaper. He got up and got it and opened it out in front of him. His mother discreetly continued the conversation in a lower tone but the woman across the aisle said in a loud voice, "Well that's nice. Selling typewriters is close to writing. He can go right from one to the other."

58 "I tell him," his mother said, "that Rome wasn't built in a day."

59 Behind the newspaper Julian was withdrawing into the inner compartment of his mind where he spent most of his time. This was a kind of mental bubble in which he established himself when he could not bear to be a part of what was going on around him. From it he could see out and judge but in it he was safe from any kind of penetration from without. It was the only place where he felt free of the general idiocy of his fellows. His mother had never entered it but from it he could see her with absolute clarity.

60 The old lady was clever enough and he thought that if she had started from any of the right premises, more might have been expected of her. She lived according to the laws of her own fantasy world, outside of which he had never seen her set foot. The law of it was to sacrifice herself for him after she had first created the necessity to do so by making a mess of things. If he had permitted her sacrifices, it was only because her lack of foresight had made them necessary. All of her life had been a struggle to act like a Chestny without the Chestny goods, and to give him everything she thought a Chestny ought to have; but since, said she, it was fun to struggle, why complain? And when you had won, as she had won, what fun to look back on the hard times! He could not forgive her that she had enjoyed the struggle and that she thought *she* had won.

61 What she meant when she said she had won was that she had brought him up successfully and had sent him to college and that he had turned out so well—good looking (her teeth had gone unfilled so that his could be straightened), intelligent (he realized he was too intelligent to be a success), and with a future ahead of him (there was of course no future ahead of him). She excused his gloominess on the grounds that he was still growing up and his radical ideas on his lack of practical experience. She said he didn't yet know a thing about

"life," that he hadn't even entered the real world—when already he was as disenchanted with it as a man of fifty.

62 The further irony of all this was that in spite of her, he had turned out so well. In spite of going to only a third-rate college, he had, on his own initiative, come out with a first-rate education; in spite of growing up dominated by a small mind, he had ended up with a large one; in spite of all her foolish views, he was free of prejudice and unafraid to face facts. Most miraculous of all, instead of being blinded by love for her as she was for him, he had cut himself emotionally free of her and could see her with complete objectivity. He was not dominated by his mother.

63 The bus stopped with a sudden jerk and shook him from his meditation. A woman from the back lurched forward with little steps and barely escaped falling in his newspaper as she righted herself. She got off and a large Negro got on. Julian kept his paper lowered to watch. It gave him a certain satisfaction to see injustice in daily operation. It confirmed his view that with a few exceptions there was no one worth knowing within a radius of three hundred miles. The Negro was well dressed and carried a briefcase. He looked around and then sat down on the other end of the seat where the woman with the red and white canvas sandals was sitting. He immediately unfolded a newspaper and obscured himself behind it. Julian's mother's elbow at once prodded insistently into his ribs. "Now you see why I won't ride on these buses by myself," she whispered.

64 The woman with the red and white canvas sandals had risen at the same time the Negro sat down and had gone further back in the bus and taken the seat of the woman who had got off. His mother leaned forward and cast her an approving look.

65 Julian rose, crossed the aisle, and sat down in the place of the woman with the canvas sandals. From this position, he looked serenely across at his mother. Her face had turned an angry red. He stared at her, making his eyes the eyes of a stranger. He felt his tension suddenly lift as if he had openly declared war on her.

66 He would have liked to get in conversation with the Negro and to talk with him about art or politics or any subject that would be above the comprehension of those around them, but the man remained entrenched behind his paper. He was either ignoring the change of seating or had never noticed it. There was no way for Julian to convey his sympathy.

67 His mother kept her eyes fixed reproachfully on his face. The woman with the protruding teeth was looking at him avidly as if he were a type of monster new to her.

68 "Do you have a light?" he asked the Negro.

69 Without looking away from his paper, the man reached in his pocket and handed him a packet of matches.

70 "Thanks," Julian said. For a moment he held the matches foolishly. A NO SMOKING sign looked down upon him from over the door. This alone would not have deterred him; he had no cigarettes. He had quit smoking some months before because he could not afford it. "Sorry," he muttered and handed back the matches. The Negro lowered the paper and gave him an annoyed look. He took the matches and raised the paper again.

71 His mother continued to gaze at him but she did not take advantage of his momentary discomfort. Her eyes retained their battered look. Her face seemed to be unnaturally red, as if her blood pressure had risen. Julian allowed no glimmer of sympathy to show on his face. Having got the advantage, he wanted desperately to keep it and carry it through. He would have liked to teach her a lesson that would last her a while, but there seemed no way to continue the point. The Negro refused to come out from behind his paper.

72 Julian folded his arms and looked stolidly before him, facing her but as if he did not see her, as if he had ceased to recognize her existence. He visualized a scene in which, the bus having reached their stop, he would remain in his seat and when she said, "Aren't you going to get off?" he would look at her as at a stranger who had rashly addressed him. The corner they got off on was usually deserted, but it was well lighted and it would not hurt her to walk by herself the four blocks to the Y. He decided to wait until the time came and then decide whether or not he would let her get off by herself. He would have to be at the Y at ten to bring her back, but he could leave her wondering if he was going to show up. There was no reason for her to think she could always depend on him.

73 He retired again into the high-ceilinged room sparsely settled with large pieces of antique furniture. His soul expanded momentarily but then he became aware of his mother across from him and the vision shriveled. He studied her coldly. Her feet in little pumps dangled like a child's and did not quite reach the floor. She was training on him an exaggerated look of reproach. He felt completely detached from her. At that moment he could with pleasure have slapped her as he would have slapped a particularly obnoxious child in his charge.

74 He began to imagine various unlikely ways by which he could teach her a lesson. He might make friends with some distinguished Negro professor or lawyer and bring him home to spend the evening. He would be entirely justified but her blood pressure would rise to 300. He could not push her to the extent of making her have a stroke, and moreover, he had never been successful at making any Negro friends. He had tried to strike up an acquaintance on the bus with some of the better types, with ones that looked like professors or ministers or lawyers. One morning he had sat down next to a distinguished-looking dark brown man who had answered his questions with a sonorous solemnity but who had turned out to be an undertaker. Another day he had sat down beside a cigar-smoking Negro with a diamond ring on his finger, but after a few stilted

pleasantries, the Negro had rung the buzzer and risen, slipping two lottery tickets into Julian's hand as he climbed over him to leave.

75 He imagined his mother lying desperately ill and his being able to secure only a Negro doctor for her. He toyed with that idea for a few minutes and then dropped it for a momentary vision of himself participating as a sympathizer in a sit-in demonstration. This was possible but he did not linger with it. Instead, he approached the ultimate horror. He brought home a beautiful suspiciously Negroid woman. Prepare yourself, he said. There is nothing you can do about it. This is the woman I've chosen. She's intelligent, dignified, even good, and she's suffered and she hasn't thought it *fun*. Now persecute us, go ahead and persecute us. Drive her out of here, but remember, you're driving me too. His eyes were narrowed and through the indignation he had generated, he saw his mother across the aisle, purple-faced, shrunken to the dwarf-like proportions of her moral nature, sitting like a mummy beneath the ridiculous banner of her hat.

76 He was tilted out of his fantasy again as the bus stopped. The door opened with a sucking hiss and out of the dark a large, gaily dressed, sullen-looking colored woman got on with a little boy. The child, who might have been four, had on a short plaid suit and a Tyrolean hat with a blue feather in it. Julian hoped that he would sit down beside him and that the woman would push in beside his mother. He could think of no better arrangement.

77 As she waited for her tokens, the woman was surveying the seating possibilities—he hoped with the idea of sitting where she was least wanted. There was something familiar-looking about her but Julian could not place what it was. She was a giant of a woman. Her face was set not only to meet opposition but to seek it out. The downward tilt of her large lower lip was like a warning sign: DON'T TAMPER WITH ME. Her bulging figure was encased in a green crepe dress and her feet overflowed in red shoes. She had on a hideous hat. A purple velvet flap came down on one side of it and stood up on the other; the rest of it was green and looked like a cushion with the stuffing out. She carried a mammoth red pocketbook that bulged throughout as if it were stuffed with rocks.

78 To Julian's disappointment, the little boy climbed up on the empty seat beside his mother. His mother lumped all children, black and white, into the common category, "cute," and she thought little Negroes were on the whole cuter than little white children. She smiled at the little boy as he climbed on the seat.

79 Meanwhile the woman was bearing down upon the empty seat beside Julian. To his annoyance, she squeezed herself into it. He saw his mother's face change as the woman settled herself next to him and he realized with satisfaction that this was more objectionable to her than it was to him. Her face seemed almost gray and there was a look of dull recognition in her eyes, as if suddenly she had sickened at some awful confrontation. Julian saw that it was because she

and the woman had, in a sense, swapped sons. Though his mother would not realize the symbolic significance of this, she would feel it. His amusement showed plainly on his face.

80 The woman next to him muttered something unintelligible to herself. He was conscious of a kind of bristling next to him, a muted growling like that of an angry cat. He could not see anything but the red pocketbook upright on the bulging green thighs. He visualized the woman as she had stood waiting for her tokens—the ponderous figure, rising from the red shoes upward over the solid hips, the mammoth bosom, the haughty face, to the green and purple hat.

81 His eyes widened.

82 The vision of the two hats, identical, broke upon him with the radiance of a brilliant sunrise. His face was suddenly lit with joy. He could not believe that Fate had thrust upon his mother such a lesson. He gave a loud chuckle so that she would look at him and see that he saw. She turned her eyes on him slowly. The blue in them seemed to have turned a bruised purple. For a moment he had an uncomfortable sense of her innocence, but it lasted only a second before principle rescued him. Justice entitled him to laugh. His grin hardened until it said to her as plainly as if he were saying aloud: Your punishment exactly fits your pettiness. This should teach you a permanent lesson.

83 Her eyes shifted to the woman. She seemed unable to bear looking at him and to find the woman preferable. He became conscious again of the bristling presence at his side. The woman was rumbling like a volcano about to become active. His mother's mouth began to twitch slightly at one corner. With a sinking heart, he saw incipient signs of recovery on her face and realized that this was going to strike her suddenly as funny and was going to be no lesson at all. She kept her eyes on the woman and an amused smile came over her face as if the woman were a monkey that had stolen her hat. The little Negro was looking up at her with large fascinated eyes. He had been trying to attract her attention for some time.

84 "Carver!" the woman said suddenly. "Come heah!"

85 When he saw that the spotlight was on him at last, Carver drew his feet up and turned himself toward Julian's mother and giggled.

86 "Carver!" the woman said. "You heah me? Come heah!"

87 Carver slid down from the seat but remained squatting with his back against the base of it, his head turned slyly around toward Julian's mother, who was smiling at him. The woman reached a hand across the aisle and snatched him to her. He righted himself and hung backwards on her knees, grinning at Julian's mother. "Isn't he cute?" Julian's mother said to the woman with the protruding teeth.

88 "I reckon he is," the woman said without conviction.

89 The Negress yanked him upright but he eased out of her grip and shot across the aisle and scrambled, giggling wildly, onto the seat beside his love.

90 "I think he likes me," Julian's mother said, and smiled at the woman. It was the smile she used when she was being particularly gracious to an inferior. Julian saw everything lost. The lesson had rolled off her like rain on a roof.

91 The woman stood up and yanked the little boy off the seat as if she were snatching him from contagion. Julian could feel the rage in her at having no weapon like his mother's smile. She gave the child a sharp slap across his leg. He howled once and then thrust his head into her stomach and kicked his feet against her shins. "Be-have," she said vehemently.

92 The bus stopped and the Negro who had been reading the newspaper got off. The woman moved over and set the little boy down with a thump between herself and Julian. She held him firmly by the knee. In a moment he put his hands in front of his face and peeped at Julian's mother through his fingers.

93 "I see yoooooooo!" she said and put her hand in front of her face and peeped at him.

94 The woman slapped his hand down. "Quit yo' foolishness," she said, "before I knock the living Jesus out of you!"

95 Julian was thankful that the next stop was theirs. He reached up and pulled the cord. The woman reached up and pulled it at the same time. Oh my God, he thought. He had the terrible intuition that when they got off the bus together, his mother would open her purse and give the little boy a nickel. The gesture would be as natural to her as breathing. The bus stopped and the woman got up and lunged to the front, dragging the child, who wished to stay on, after her. Julian and his mother got up and followed. As they neared the door, Julian tried to relieve her of her pocketbook.

96 "No," she murmured, "I want to give the little boy a nickel."

97 "No!" Julian hissed. "No!"

98 She smiled down at the child and opened her bag. The bus door opened and the woman picked him up by the arm and descended with him, hanging at her hip. Once in the street she set him down and shook him.

99 Julian's mother had to close her purse while she got down the bus step but as soon as her feet were on the ground, she opened it again and began to rummage inside. "I can't find but a penny," she whispered, "but it looks like a new one."

100 "Don't do it!" Julian said fiercely between his teeth. There was a streetlight on the corner and she hurried to get under it so that she could better see into her pocketbook. The woman was heading off rapidly down the street with the child still hanging backward on her hand.

101 "Oh little boy!" Julian's mother called and took a few quick steps and caught up with them just beyond the lamp-post. "Here's a bright new penny for you," and she held out the coin, which shone bronze in the dim light.

102 The huge woman turned and for a moment stood, her shoulders lifted and her face frozen with frustrated rage, and stared at Julian's mother. Then all at once she seemed to explode like a piece of machinery that had been given one ounce of pressure too much. Julian saw the black fist swing out with the red pocketbook. He shut his eyes and cringed as he heard the woman shout, "He don't take nobody's pennies!" When he opened his eyes, the woman was disappearing down the street with the little boy staring wide-eyed over her shoulder. Julian's mother was sitting on the sidewalk.

103 "I told you not to do that," Julian said angrily. "I told you not to do that!"

104 He stood over her for a minute, gritting his teeth. Her legs were stretched out in front of her and her hat was on her lap. He squatted down and looked her in the face. It was totally expressionless. "You got exactly what you deserved," he said. "Now get up."

105 He picked up her pocketbook and put what had fallen out back in it. He picked the hat up off her lap. The penny caught his eye on the sidewalk and he picked that up and let it drop before her eyes into the purse. Then he stood up and leaned over and held his hands out to pull her up. She remained immobile. He sighed. Rising above them on either side were black apartment buildings, marked with irregular rectangles of light. At the end of the block a man came out of a door and walked off in the opposite direction. "All right," he said, "suppose somebody happens by and wants to know why you're sitting on the sidewalk?"

106 She took the hand and, breathing hard, pulled heavily up on it and then stood for a moment, swaying slightly as if the spots of light in the darkness were circling around her. Her eyes, shadowed and confused, finally settled on his face. He did not try to conceal his irritation. "I hope this teaches you a lesson," he said. She leaned forward and her eyes raked his face. She seemed trying to determine his identity. Then, as if she found nothing familiar about him, she started off with a headlong movement in the wrong direction.

107 "Aren't you going on to the Y?" he asked.

108 "Home," she muttered.

109 "Well, are we walking?"

110 For answer she kept going. Julian followed along, his hands behind him. He saw no reason to let the lesson she had had go without backing it up with an explanation of its meaning. She might as well be made to understand what had happened to her. "Don't think that was just an uppity Negro woman," he said. "That was the whole colored race which will no longer take your condescending pennies. That was your black double. She can wear the same hat as you, and to be sure," he added gratuitously (because he thought it was funny), "it looked better on her than it did on you. What all this means," he said, "is that the old world is gone. The old manners are obsolete and your graciousness is not worth

a damn." He thought bitterly of the house that had been lost for him. "You aren't who you think you are," he said.

111 She continued to plow ahead, paying no attention to him. Her hair had come undone on one side. She dropped her pocketbook and took no notice. He stooped and picked it up and handed it to her but she did not take it.

112 "You needn't act as if the world had come to an end," he said, "because it hasn't. From now on you've got to live in a new world and face a few realities for a change. Buck up," he said, "it won't kill you."

113 She was breathing fast.

114 "Let's wait on the bus," he said.

115 "Home," she said thickly.

116 "I hate to see you behave like this," he said. "Just like a child. I should be able to expect more of you." He decided to stop where he was and make her stop and wait for a bus. "I'm not going any farther," he said, stopping. "We're going on the bus."

117 She continued to go on as if she had not heard him. He took a few steps and caught her arm and stopped her. He looked into her face and caught his breath. He was looking into a face he had never seen before. "Tell Grandpa to come get me," she said.

118 He stared, stricken.

119 "Tell Caroline to come get me," she said.

120 Stunned, he let her go and she lurched forward again, walking as if one leg were shorter than the other. A tide of darkness seemed to be sweeping her from him. "Mother!" he cried. "Darling, sweetheart, wait!" Crumpling, she fell to the pavement. He dashed forward and fell at her side, crying, "Mamma, Mamma!" He turned her over. Her face was fiercely distorted. One eye, large and staring, moved slightly to the left as if it had become unmoored. The other remained fixed on him, raked his face again, found nothing and closed.

121 "Wait here, wait here!" he cried and jumped up and began to run for help toward a cluster of lights he saw in the distance ahead of him. "Help, help!" he shouted, but his voice was thin, scarcely a thread of sound. The lights drifted farther away the faster he ran and his feet moved numbly as if they carried him nowhere. The tide of darkness seemed to sweep him back to her, postponing from moment to moment his entry into the world of guilt and sorrow.

—1961

✧ ✧ ✧

Gabriel García Márquez
(b. 1928)

The Handsomest Drowned Man in the World

A Tale for Children

Márquez's brilliant seriocomic historical novel, *One Hundred Years of Solitude* (1967), is one of the landmarks of contemporary fiction, rapidly becoming an international best seller. The term "magical realism" is often used to describe his unique blend of folklore, historical fact, naturalism, and fantasy, much of it centering in the fictional village of Macondo. A native of Colombia, Márquez, the eldest of twelve children, was born in Aracataca, a small town that is the model for the isolated, decaying settlements found in his fiction. Márquez was trained as a journalist, first coming to public attention in 1955 with his investigative reporting (collected in *Relato de un naufrage*) about the governmental cover-up that followed the sinking of a Colombian navy vessel. After residence in Paris in the late 1950s, he worked for a time as a correspondent for Fidel Castro's official news agency. He has also lived in Mexico and Spain. Other works by Márquez include the short story collections *No One Writes to the Colonel* (1968), *Leaf Storm and Other Stories* (1972), and *Innocent Erendira and Other Stories* (1978). His novel *Love in the Time of Cholera* was a major success in 1988. He was awarded the Nobel Prize in 1982.

The first children who saw the dark and slinky bulge approaching through the sea let themselves think it was an empty ship. Then they saw it had no flags or masts and they thought it was a whale. But when it washed up on the beach, they removed the clumps of seaweed, the jellyfish tentacles, and the

---

Translated by Gregory Rabassa

remains of fish and flotsam, and only then did they see that it was a drowned man.

2 They had been playing with him all afternoon, burying him in the sand and digging him up again, when someone chanced to see them and spread the alarm in the village. The men who carried him to the nearest house noticed that he weighed more than any dead man they had ever known, almost as much as a horse, and they said to each other that maybe he'd been floating too long and the water had got into his bones. When they laid him on the floor they said he'd been taller than all other men because there was barely enough room for him in the house, but they thought that maybe the ability to keep on growing after death was part of the nature of certain drowned men. He had the smell of the sea about him and only his shape gave one to suppose that it was the corpse of a human being, because the skin was covered with a crust of mud and scales.

3 They did not even have to clean off his face to know that the dead man was a stranger. The village was made up of only twenty-odd wooden houses that had stone courtyards with no flowers and which were spread about on the end of a desertlike cape. There was so little land that mothers always went about with the fear that the wind would carry off their children and the few dead that the years had caused among them had to be thrown off the cliffs. But the sea was calm and bountiful and all the men fit into seven boats. So when they found the drowned man they simply had to look at one another to see that they were all there. That night they did not go out to work at sea. While the men went to find out if anyone was missing in neighboring villages, the women stayed behind to care for the drowned man. They took the mud off with grass swabs, they removed the underwater stones entangled in his hair, and they scraped the crust off with tools used for scaling fish. As they were doing that they noticed that the vegetation on him came from faraway oceans and deep water and that his clothes were in tatters, as if he had sailed through labyrinths of coral. They noticed too that he bore his death with pride, for he did not have the lonely look of other drowned men who came out of the sea or that haggard, needy look of men who drowned in rivers. But only when they finished cleaning him off did they become aware of the kind of man he was and it left them breathless. Not only was he the tallest, strongest, most virile, and best built man they had ever seen, but even though they were looking at him there was no room for him in their imagination.

4 They could not find a bed in the village large enough to lay him on nor was there a table solid enough to use for his wake. The tallest men's holiday pants would not fit him, nor the fattest ones' Sunday shirts, nor the shoes of the one with the biggest feet. Fascinated by his huge size and his beauty, the women then decided to make him some pants from a large piece of sail and a shirt from some bridal brabant linen so that he could continue through his death with dignity. As they sewed, sitting in a circle and gazing at the corpse between

stitches, it seemed to them that the wind had never been so steady nor the sea so restless as on that night and they supposed that the change had something to do with the dead man. They thought that if that magnificent man had lived in the village, his house would have had the widest doors, the highest ceiling, and the strongest floor, his bedstead would have been made from a midship frame held together by iron bolts, and his wife would have been the happiest woman. They thought that he would have had so much authority that he could have drawn fish out of the sea simply by calling their names and that he would have put so much work into his land that springs would have burst forth from among the rocks so that he would have been able to plant flowers on the cliffs. They secretly compared him to their own men, thinking that for all their lives theirs were incapable of doing what he could do in one night, and they ended up dismissing them deep in their hearts as the weakest, meanest, and most useless creatures on earth. They were wandering through that maze of fantasy when the oldest woman, who as the oldest had looked upon the drowned man with more compassion than passion, sighed:

5 "He has the face of someone called Esteban."

6 It was true. Most of them had only to take another look at him to see that he could not have any other name. The more stubborn among them, who were the youngest, still lived for a few hours with the illusion that when they put his clothes on and he lay among the flowers in patent leather shoes his name might be Lautaro. But it was a vain illusion. There had not been enough canvas, the poorly cut and worse sewn pants were too tight, and the hidden strength of his heart popped the buttons on his shirt. After midnight the whistling of the wind died down and the sea fell into its Wednesday drowsiness. The silence put an end to any last doubts: he was Esteban. The women who had dressed him, who had combed his hair, had cut his nails and shaved him were unable to hold back a shudder of pity when they had to resign themselves to his being dragged along the ground. It was then that they understood how unhappy he must have been with that huge body since it bothered him even after death. They could see him in life, condemned to going through doors sideways, cracking his head on crossbeams, remaining on his feet during visits, not knowing what to do with his soft, pink, sea lion hands while the lady of the house looked for her most resistant chair and begged him, frightened to death, sit here, Esteban, please, and he, leaning against the wall, smiling, don't bother, ma'am, I'm fine where I am, his heels raw and his back roasted from having done the same thing so many times whenever he paid a visit, don't bother, ma'am, I'm fine where I am, just to avoid the embarrassment of breaking up the chair, and never knowing perhaps that the ones who said don't go, Esteban, at least wait till the coffee's ready, were the ones who later on would whisper the big boob finally left, how nice, the handsome fool has gone. That was what the women were thinking beside the body a little before dawn. Later, when they covered his face with a handkerchief

so that the light would not bother him, he looked so forever dead, so defenseless, so much like their men that the first furrows of tears opened in their hearts. It was one of the younger ones who began the weeping. The others, coming to, went from sighs to wails, and the more they sobbed the more they felt like weeping, because the drowned man was becoming all the more Esteban for them, and so they wept so much, for he was the most destitute, most peaceful, and most obliging man on earth, poor Esteban. So when the men returned with the news that the drowned man was not from the neighboring villages either, the women felt an opening of jubilation in the midst of their tears.

7 "Praise the Lord," they sighed, "he's ours!"

8 The men thought the fuss was only womanish frivolity. Fatigued because of the difficult nighttime inquiries, all they wanted was to get rid of the bother of the newcomer once and for all before the sun grew strong on that arid, windless day. They improvised a litter with the remains of foremasts and gaffs, tying it together with rigging so that it would bear the weight of the body until they reached the cliffs. They wanted to tie the anchor from a cargo ship to him so that he would sink easily into the deepest waves, where fish are blind and divers die of nostalgia, and bad currents would not bring him back to shore, as had happened with other bodies. But the more they hurried, the more the women thought of ways to waste time. They walked about like startled hens, pecking with the sea charms on their breasts, some interfering on one side to put a scapular of the good wind on the drowned man, some on the other side to put a wrist compass on him, and after a great deal of *get away from there, woman, stay out of the way, look, you almost made me fall on top of the dead man,* the men began to feel mistrust in their livers and started grumbling about why so many main-altar decorations for a stranger, because no matter how many nails and holy-water jars he had on him, the sharks would chew him all the same, but the women kept piling on their junk relics, running back and forth, stumbling, while they released in sighs what they did not in tears, so that the men finally exploded with *since when has there ever been such a fuss over a drifting corpse, a drowned nobody, a piece of cold Wednesday meat.* One of the women, mortified by so much lack of care, then removed the handkerchief from the dead man's face and the men were left breathless too.

9 He was Esteban. It was not necessary to repeat it for them to recognize him. If they had been told Sir Walter Raleigh, even they might have been impressed with his gringo accent, the macaw on his shoulder, his cannibal-killing blunderbuss, but there could be only one Esteban in the world and there he was, stretched out like a sperm whale, shoeless, wearing the pants of an undersized child, and with those stony nails that had to be cut with a knife. They only had to take the handkerchief off his face to see that he was ashamed, that it was not his fault that he was so big or so heavy or so handsome, and if he had known that this was going to happen, he would have looked for a more discreet place to

drown in, seriously, I even would have tied the anchor off a galleon around my neck and staggered off a cliff like someone who doesn't like things in order not to be upsetting people now with this Wednesday dead body, as you people say, in order not to he bothering anyone with this filthy piece of cold meat that doesn't have anything to do with me. There was so much truth in his manner that even the most mistrustful men, the ones who felt the bitterness of cloudless nights at sea fearing that their women would tire of dreaming about them and begin to dream of drowned men, even they and others who were harder still shuddered in the marrow of their bones at Esteban's sincerity.

10 That was how they came to hold the most splendid funeral they could conceive of for an abandoned drowned man. Some women who had gone to get flowers in the neighboring villages returned with other women who could not believe what they had been told, and those women went back for more flowers when they saw the dead man, and they brought more and more until there were so many flowers and so many people that it was hard to walk about. At the final moment it pained them to return him to the waters as an orphan and they chose a father and mother from among the best people, and aunts and uncles and cousins, so that through him all the inhabitants of the village became kinsmen. Some sailors who heard weeping from a distance went off course and people heard of one who had himself tied to the mainmast, remembering ancient fables about sirens. While they fought for the privilege of carrying him on their shoulders along the steep escarpment by the cliffs, men and women became aware for the first time of the desolation of their streets, the dryness of their courtyards, the narrowness of their dreams as they faced the splendor and beauty of their drowned man. They let him go without an anchor so that he could come back if he wished and whenever he wished, and they all held their breath for the fraction of centuries the body took to fall into the abyss. They did not need to look at one another to realize that they were no longer all present, that they would never be. But they also knew that everything would be different from then on, that their houses would have wider doors, higher ceilings, and stronger floors so that Esteban's memory could go everywhere without bumping into beams and so that no one in the future would dare whisper the big boob finally died, too bad, the handsome fool has finally died, because they were going to paint their house fronts gay colors to make Esteban's memory eternal and they were going to break their backs digging for springs among the stones and planting flowers on the cliffs so that in future years at dawn the passengers on great liners would awaken, suffocated by the smell of gardens on the high seas, and the captain would have to come down from the bridge in his dress uniform, with his astrolabe, his pole star, and his row of war medals and, pointing to the promontory of roses on the horizon, he would say in fourteen languages, look there, where the wind is so peaceful now that it's gone to sleep beneath the beds, over there,

where the sun's so bright that the sunflowers don't know which way to turn, yes, that's Esteban's village.

—1968

✧ ✧ ✧

Chinua Achebe

(b. 1930)

Civil Peace

Achebe was born in Ogidi, Nigeria, and after graduation from University College in Ibadan and study at London University was employed by the Nigerian Broadcasting Service, where he served for years as a producer. After the appearance of his first novel, *Things Fall Apart*, in 1958 (the title is taken from William Butler Yeats's apocalyptic poem "The Second Coming") he became one of the most widely acclaimed writers to emerge from the former British colonies of Africa. The author of several novels as well as a collection of short stories, Achebe has taught in the United States at U.C.L.A., Stanford, and the University of Massachusetts at Amherst. One of his chief services to contemporary literature was his editorship of the African Writers Series, which sponsored the first publications of many of his fellow Nigerian writers. Achebe draws heavily on the oral traditions of his native country, but he has been successful in adapting European fiction-writing techniques to deal with subjects that are truly African. One of his main themes grows out of the ugly contrast between the degradation imposed by colonialism and the relative failure of most post-colonial governments to materially improve on the past for the betterment of the lives of their citizens.

Jonathan Iwegbu counted himself extraordinarily lucky. "Happy survival!" meant so much more to him than just a current fashion of greeting old friends in the first hazy days of peace. It went deep to his heart. He had come out of the war with five inestimable blessings—his head, his wife Maria's head, and the heads of three out of their four children. As a bonus he also had his old bicycle—a miracle too but naturally not to be compared to the safety of five human heads.

2 The bicycle had a little history of its own. One day at the height of the war it was commandeered "for urgent military action." Hard as its loss would have been to him he would still have let it go without a thought had he not had some doubts about the genuineness of the officer. It wasn't his disreputable rags, nor the toes peeping out of one blue and one brown canvas shoe, nor yet the two stars of his rank done obviously in a hurry in biro° that troubled Jonathan; many good and heroic soldiers looked the same or worse. It was rather a certain lack of grip and firmness in his manner. So Jonathan, suspecting he might be amenable to influence, rummaged in his raffia bag and produced the two pounds with which he had been going to buy firewood which his wife, Maria, retailed to camp officials for extra stockfish and cornmeal, and got his bicycle back. That night he buried it in the little clearing in the bush where the dead of the camp, including his own youngest son, were buried. When he dug it up again a year later after the surrender all it needed was a little palm oil greasing. "Nothing puzzles God," he said in wonder.

3 He put it to immediate use as a taxi and accumulated a small pile of Biafran money ferrying camp officials and their families across the four-mile stretch to the nearest tarred road. His standard charge per trip was six pounds and those who had the money were only glad to be rid of some of it in this way. At the end of a fortnight he had made a small fortune of one hundred and fifteen pounds.

4 Then he made the journey to Enugu and found another miracle waiting for him. It was unbelievable. He rubbed his eyes and looked again and it was still standing there before him. But, needless to say, even that monumental blessing must be accounted also totally inferior to the five heads in the family. This newest miracle was his little house in Ogui Overside. Indeed nothing puzzles God! Only two houses away a huge concrete edifice some wealthy contractor had put up just before the war was a mountain of rubble. And here was Jonathan's little zinc house of no regrets built with mud blocks quite intact! Of course the doors and windows were missing and five sheets off the roof. But what was that? And anyhow he had returned to Enugu early enough to pick up bits of old zinc and wood and soggy sheets of cardboard lying around the neighborhood before thousands more came out of their forest holes looking for the same things. He got a destitute carpenter with one old hammer, a blunt plane, and a few bent and rusty nails in his tool bag to turn this assortment of wood, paper, and metal into door and window shutters for five Nigerian shillings or fifty Biafran pounds. He paid the pounds, and moved in with his overjoyed family carrying five heads on their shoulders.

---

biro ball-point pen

5 His children picked mangoes near the military cemetery and sold them to soldiers' wives for a few pennies—real pennies this time—and his wife started making breakfast akara balls for neighbors in a hurry to start life again. With his family earnings he took his bicycle to the villages around and bought fresh palm wine which he mixed generously in his rooms with the water which had recently started running again in the public tap down the road, and opened up a bar for soldiers and other lucky people with good money.

6 At first he went daily, then every other day, and finally once a week, to the offices of the Coal Corporation where he used to be a miner, to find out what was what. The only thing he did find out in the end was that that little house of his was even a greater blessing than he had thought. Some of his fellow ex-miners who had nowhere to return at the end of the day's waiting just slept outside the doors of the offices and cooked what meal they could scrounge together in Bournvita tins. As the weeks lengthened and still nobody could say what was what Jonathan discontinued his weekly visits altogether and faced his palm-wine bar.

7 But nothing puzzles God. Came the day of the windfall when after five days of endless scuffles in queues and counterqueues in the sun outside the Treasury he had twenty pounds counted into his palms as ex gratia award for the rebel money he had turned in. It was like Christmas for him and for many others like him when the payments began. They called it (since few could manage its proper official name) *egg-rasher.*

8 As soon as the pound notes were placed in his palm Jonathan simply closed it tight over them and buried fist and money inside his trouser pocket. He had to be extra careful because he had seen a man a couple of days earlier collapse into near-madness in an instant before that oceanic crowd because no sooner had he got his twenty pounds than some heartless ruffian picked it off him. Though it was not right that a man in such an extremity of agony should be blamed yet many in the queues that day were able to remark quietly at the victim's carelessness, especially after he pulled out the innards of his pocket and revealed a hole in it big enough to pass a thief's head. But of course he had insisted that the money had been in the other pocket, pulling it out too to show its comparative wholeness. So one had to be careful.

9 Jonathan soon transferred the money to his left hand and pocket so as to leave his right free for shaking hands should the need arise, though by fixing his gaze at such an elevation as to miss all approaching human faces he made sure that the need did not arise, until he got home.

10 He was normally a heavy sleeper but that night he heard all the neighborhood noises die down one after another. Even the night watchman who knocked the hour on some metal somewhere in the distance had fallen silent after knocking one o'clock. That must have been the last thought in Jonathan's mind

before he was finally carried away himself. He couldn't have been gone for long, though, when he was violently awakened again.

11 "Who is knocking?" whispered his wife lying beside him on the floor.

12 "I don't know," he whispered back breathlessly.

13 The second time the knocking came it was so loud and imperious that the rickety old door could have fallen down.

14 "Who is knocking?" he asked them, his voice parched and trembling.

15 "Na tief-man and him people," came the cool reply. "Make you hopen de door." This was followed by the heaviest knocking of all.

16 Maria was the first to raise the alarm, then he followed and all their children.

17 *"Police-o! Thieves-o! Neighbors-o! Police o! We are lost! We are dead! Neighbors, are you asleep? Wake up! Police-o!"*

18 "You done finish?" asked the voice outside. "Make we help you small. Oya, everybody!"

19 *"Police-o! Tief-man-so! Neighbors-o! we done loss-o! Police-o!. . . "*

20 There were at least five other voices besides the leader's.

21 Jonathan and his family were now completely paralyzed by terror. Maria and the children sobbed inaudibly like lost souls. Jonathan groaned continuously.

22 The silence that followed the thieves' alarm vibrated horribly. Jonathan all but begged their leader to speak again and be done with it.

23 "My frien," said he at long last, "we don try our best for call dem but I tink say dem all done sleep-o . . . So wetin we go do now? Sometaim you wan call soja? Or you wan make we call dem for you? Soja better pass police. No be so?"

24 "Na so!" replied his men. Jonathan thought he heard even more voices now than before and groaned heavily. His legs were sagging under him and his throat felt like sandpaper.

25 "My frien, why you no de talk again. I de ask you say you wan make we call soja?"

26 "No."

27 "Awrighto. Now make we talk business. We no be bad tief. We no like for make trouble. Trouble done finish. War done finish and all the katakata° wey de for inside. No Civil War again. This time na Civil Peace. No be so?"

28 "Na so!" answered the horrible chorus.

29 "What do you want from me? I am a poor man. Everything I had went with this war. Why do you come to me? You know people who have money. We . . . "

---

katakata shit

30 "Awright! We know say you no get plenty money. But we sef no get even anini.° So derefore make you open dis window and give us one hundred pound and we go commot. Otherwise we de come for inside now to show you guitar-boy like dis . . . "

31 A volley of automatic fire rang through the sky. Maria and the children began to weep aloud again.

32 "Ah, missisi de cry again. No need for dat. We done talk say we na good tief. We just take our small money and go nwayorly. No molest. Abi we de molest?"

33 "At all!" sand the chorus.

34 "My friends," began Jonathan hoarsely. "I hear what you say and I thank you. If I had one hundred pounds . . . "

35 "Lookia my frien, no be play we come play for your house. If we make mistake and step for inside you no go like am-o. So derefore . . . "

36 "To God who made me; if you come inside and find one hundred pounds, take and shoot me and shoot my wife and children. I swear to God. The only money I have in this life is this twenty pounds *egg-rasher* they gave me today . . . "

37 "OK. Time de go. Make you open dis window and bring the twenty pound. We go manage am like dat."

38 There were now loud murmurs of dissent among the chorus: "Na lie de man de lie; e get plenty money . . . Make we go inside and search properly well . . . Wetin be twenty pound? . . . "

39 "Shurrup!" rang the leader's voice like a lone shot in the sky and silenced the murmuring at once. "Are you dere? Bring the money quick!"

40 "I am coming," said Jonathan fumbling in the darkness with the key of the small wooden box he kept by his side on the mat.

41 At the first sign of light as neighbors and others assembled to commiserate with him he was already strapping his five-gallon demijohn to his bicycle carrier and his wife, sweating in the open fire, was turning over akara balls in a wide clay bowl of boiling oil. In the corner his eldest son was rinsing out dregs of yesterday's palm wine from old beer bottles.

42 "I count it as nothing," he told his sympathizers, his eyes on the rope he was tying. "What is *egg-rasher?* Did I depend on it last week? Or is it greater than other things that went with the war? I say, let *egg-rasher* perish in the flames! Let it go where everything else has gone. Nothing puzzles God."

—1971

---

anini penny

✧ ✧ ✧

Alice Munro
(b. 1931)

Wild Swans

Munro was born on a farm in Wingham, Ontario, and educated at the University of Ontario, where she received her degree in 1952. Her first book appeared in 1968, and she has continued to publish collections of short stories regularly. Asked about her devotion to short fiction, Munro told *Contemporary Authors*: "I never intended to be a short story writer—I started writing them because I didn't have time to write anything else—I had three children. And then I got used to writing short stories, so I see my materials that way, and now I don't think I'll ever write a novel." Parent-child relations and the discovery of personal freedom are constant themes in Munro's work, especially in *The Beggar Maid: Stories of Rose and Flo* (1982), a series of stories about a woman and her stepdaughter that is the source of "Wild Swans." Munro has won both the Governor General's Literary Award and the Canadian Booksellers' award, befitting her status as one of her country's most distinguished writers.

Flo said to watch for White Slavers. She said this was how they operated: an old woman, a motherly or grandmotherly sort, made friends while riding beside you on a bus or train. She offered you candy, which was drugged. Pretty soon you began to droop and mumble, were in no condition to speak for yourself. Oh, help, the woman said, my daughter (granddaughter) is sick, please somebody help me get her off so that she can recover in the fresh air. Up stepped a polite gentleman, pretending to be a stranger, offering assistance. Together, at the next stop, they hustled you off the train or bus, and that was the last the ordinary world ever saw of you. They kept you a prisoner in the White Slave place (to which you had been transported drugged and bound so you wouldn't even know where you were), until such time as you were thoroughly degraded and in despair, your insides torn up by drunken men and invested with vile disease, your mind destroyed by drugs, your hair and teeth fallen out. It took about three years, for you to get to this state. You wouldn't want to go home, then, maybe couldn't remember home, or find your way if you did. So they let you out on the streets.

2 Flo took ten dollars and put it in a little cloth bag which she sewed to the strap of Rose's slip. Another thing likely to happen was that Rose would get her purse stolen.

3 Watch out, Flo said as well, for people dressed up as ministers. They were the worst. That disguise was commonly adopted by White Slavers, as well as those after your money.

4 Rose said she didn't see how she could tell which ones were disguised.

5 Flo had worked in Toronto once. She had worked as a waitress in a coffee shop in Union Station. That was how she knew all she knew. She never saw sunlight, in those days, except on her days off. But she saw plenty else. She saw a man cut another man's stomach with a knife, just pull out his shirt and do a tidy cut, as if it was a watermelon not a stomach. The stomach's owner just sat looking down surprised, with no time to protest. Flo implied that that was nothing, in Toronto. She saw two bad women (that was what Flo called whores, running the two words together, like badminton) get into a fight, and a man laughed at them, other men stopped and laughed and egged them on, and they had their fists full of each other's hair. At last the police came and took them away, still howling and yelping.

6 She saw a child die of a fit, too. Its face was black as ink.

7 "Well I'm not scared," said Rose provokingly. "There's the police, anyway."

8 "Oh, them! They'd be the first ones to diddle you!"

9 She did not believe anything Flo said on the subject of sex. Consider the undertaker.

10 A little bald man, very neatly dressed, would come into the store sometimes and speak to Flo with a placating expression.

11 "I only wanted a bag of candy. And maybe a few packages of gum. And one or two chocolate bars. Could you go to the trouble of wrapping them?"

12 Flo in her mock-deferential tone would assure him that she could. She wrapped them in heavy-duty white paper, so they were something like presents. He took his time with the selection, humming and chatting, then dawdled for a while. He might ask how Flo was feeling. And how Rose was, if she was there.

13 "You look pale. Young girls need fresh air." To Flo he would say, "You work too hard. You've worked hard all your life."

14 "No rest for the wicked," Flo would say agreeably.

15 When he went out she hurried to the window. There it was—the old black hearse with its purple curtains.

16 "He'll be after them today!" Flo would say as the hearse rolled away at a gentle pace, almost a funeral pace. The little man had been an undertaker, but he was retired now. The hearse was retired too. His sons had taken over the

undertaking and bought a new one. He drove the old hearse all over the country, looking for women. So Flo said. Rose could not believe it. Flo said he gave them the gum and the candy. Rose said he probably ate them himself. Flo said he had been seen, he had been heard. In mild weather he drove with the windows down, singing, to himself or to somebody out of sight in the back.

17 Her brow is like the snowdrift
Her throat is like the swan

Flo imitated him singing. Gently overtaking some woman walking on a back road, or resting at a country crossroads. All compliments and courtesy and chocolate bars, offering a ride. Of course every woman who reported being asked said she had turned him down. He never pestered anybody, drove politely on. He called in at houses, and if the husband was home he seemed to like just as well as anything to sit and chat. Wives said that was all he ever did anyway but Flo did not believe it.

18 "Some women are taken in," she said. "A number." She liked to speculate on what the hearse was like inside. Plush. Plush on the walls and the roof and the floor. Soft purple, the color of the curtains, the color of dark lilacs.

19 All nonsense, Rose thought. Who could believe it, of a man that age?

20 Rose was going to Toronto on the train for the first time by herself. She had been once before, but that was with Flo, long before her father died. They took along their own sandwiches and bought milk from the vendor on the train. It was sour. Sour chocolate milk. Rose kept taking tiny sips, unwilling to admit that something so much desired could fail her. Flo sniffed it, then hunted up and down the train until she found the old man in his red jacket, with no teeth and the tray hanging around his neck. She invited him to sample the chocolate milk. She invited people nearby to smell it. He let her have some ginger ale for nothing. It was slightly warm.

21 "I let him know," Flo said looking around after he had left. "You have to let them know."

22 A woman agreed with her but most people looked out the window. Rose drank the warm ginger ale. Either that, or the scene with the vendor, or the conversation Flo and the agreeing woman now got into about where they came from, why they were going to Toronto, and Rose's morning constipation which was why she was lacking color, or the small amount of chocolate milk she had got inside her, caused her to throw up in the train toilet. All day long she was afraid people in Toronto could smell vomit on her coat.

23 This time Flo started the trip off by saying, "Keep an eye on her, she's never been away from home before!" to the conductor, then looking around and laughing, to show that was jokingly meant. Then she had to get off. It seemed

the conductor had no more need for jokes than Rose had, and no intention of keeping an eye on anybody. He never spoke to Rose except to ask for her ticket. She had a window seat, and was soon extraordinarily happy. She felt Flo receding, West Hanratty flying away from her, her own wearying self discarded as easily as everything else. She loved the towns less and less known. A woman was standing at her back door in her nightgown, not caring if everybody on the train saw her. They were traveling south, out of the snow belt, into an earlier spring, a tenderer sort of landscape. People could grow peach trees in their backyards.

24 Rose collected in her mind the things she had to look for in Toronto. First, things for Flo. Special stockings for her varicose veins. A special kind of cement for sticking handles on pots. And a full set of dominoes.

25 For herself Rose wanted to buy hair-remover to put on her arms and legs, and if possible an arrangement of inflatable cushions, supposed to reduce your hips and thighs. She thought they probably had hair-remover in the drugstore in Hanratty, but the woman in there was a friend of Flo's and told everything. She told Flo who bought hair dye and slimming medicine and French safes. As for the cushion business, you could send away for it but there was sure to be a comment at the Post Office, and Flo knew people there as well. She also planned to buy some bangles, and an angora sweater. She had great hopes of silver bangles and powder-blue angora. She thought they could transform her, make her calm and slender and take the frizz out of her hair, dry her underarms and turn her complexion to pearl.

26 The money for these things, as well as the money for the trip, came from a prize Rose had won, for writing an essay called "Art and Science in the World of Tomorrow." To her surprise, Flo asked if she could read it, and while she was reading it, she remarked that they must have thought they had to give Rose the prize for swallowing the dictionary. Then she said shyly, "It's very interesting."

27 She would have to spend the night at Cela McKinney's. Cela McKinney was her father's cousin. She had married a hotel manager and thought she had gone up in the world. But the hotel manager came home one day and sat down on the dining room floor between two chairs and said, "I am never going to leave this house again." Nothing unusual had happened, he had just decided not to go out of the house again, and he didn't, until he died. That had made Cela McKinney odd and nervous. She locked her doors at eight o'clock. She was also very stingy. Supper was usually oatmeal porridge, with raisins. Her house was dark and narrow and smelled like a bank.

28 The train was filling up. At Brantford a man asked if she would mind if he sat down beside her.

29 "It's cooler out than you'd think," he said. He offered her part of his newspaper. She said no thanks.

30 Then lest he think her rude she said it really was cooler. She went on looking out the window at the spring morning. There was no snow left, down here. The trees and bushes seemed to have a paler bark than they did at home. Even the sunlight looked different. It was as different from home, here, as the coast of the Mediterranean would be, or the valleys of California.

31 "Filthy windows, you'd think they'd take more care," the man said. "Do you travel much by train?"

32 She said no.

33 Water was lying in the fields. He nodded at it and said there was a lot this year.

34 "Heavy snows."

35 She noticed his saying *snows,* a poetic-sounding word. Anyone at home would have said *snow.*

36 "I had an unusual experience the other day. I was driving out in the country. In fact I was on my way to see one of my parishioners, a lady with a heart condition—"

37 She looked quickly at his collar. He was wearing an ordinary shirt and tie and a dark blue suit.

38 "Oh, yes," he said. "I'm a United Church minister. But I don't always wear my uniform. I wear it for preaching in. I'm off duty today.

39 "Well as I said I was driving through the country and I saw some Canada geese down on a pond, and I took another look, and there were some swans down with them. A whole great flock of swans. What a lovely sight they were. They would be on their spring migration, I expect, heading up north. What a spectacle. I never saw anything like it."

40 Rose was unable to think appreciatively of the wild swans because she was afraid he was going to lead the conversation from them to Nature in general and then to God, the way a minister would feel obliged to do. But he did not, he stopped with the swans.

41 "A very fine sight. You would have enjoyed them."

42 He was between fifty and sixty years old, Rose thought. He was short, and energetic-looking, with a square ruddy face and bright waves of gray hair combed straight up from his forehead. When she realized he was not going to mention God she felt she ought to show her gratitude.

43 She said they must have been lovely.

44 "It wasn't even a regular pond, it was only some water lying in a field. It was just luck the water was lying there and they came down and I came driving by at the right time. Just luck. They come in at the east end of Lake Erie, I think. But I never was lucky enough to see them before."

45 She turned by degrees to the window, and he returned to his paper. She remained slightly smiling, so as not to seem rude, not to seem to be rejecting conversation altogether. The morning really was cool, and she had taken down

her coat off the hook where she put it when she first got on the train, she had spread it over herself, like a lap robe. She had set her purse on the floor when the minister sat down, to give him room. He took the sections of the paper apart, shaking and rustling them in a leisurely, rather showy, way. He seemed to her the sort of person who does everything in a showy way. A ministerial way. He brushed aside the sections he didn't want at the moment. A corner of newspaper touched her leg, just at the edge of her coat.

46 She thought for some time that it was the paper. Then she said to herself, what if it is a hand? That was the kind of thing she could imagine. She would sometimes look at men's hands, at the fuzz on their forearms, their concentrating profiles. She would think about everything they could do. Even the stupid ones. For instance the driver-salesman who brought the bread to Flo's store. The ripeness and confidence of manner, the settled mixture of ease and alertness with which he handled the bread truck. A fold of mature belly over the belt did not displease her. Another time she had her eye on the French teacher at school. Not a Frenchman at all, really, his name was McLaren, but Rose thought teaching French had rubbed off on him, made him look like one. Quick and sallow; sharp shoulders; hooked nose and sad eyes. She saw him lapping and coiling his way through slow pleasures, a perfect autocrat of indulgences. She had a considerable longing to be somebody's object. Pounded, pleasured, reduced, exhausted.

47 But what if it was a hand? What if it really was a hand? She shifted slightly, moved as much as she could toward the window. Her imagination seemed to have created this reality, a reality she was not prepared for at all. She found it alarming. She was concentrating on that leg, that bit of skin with the stocking over it. She could not bring herself to look. Was there a pressure, or was there not? She shifted again. Her legs had been, and remained, tightly closed. It was. It was a hand. It was a hand's pressure.

48 *Please don't.* That was what she tried to say. She shaped the words in her mind, tried them out, then couldn't get them past her lips. Why was that? The embarrassment, was it, the fear that people might hear? People were all around them, the seats were full.

49 It was not only that.

50 She did manage to look at him, not raising her head but turning it cautiously. He had tilted his seat back and closed his eyes. There was his dark blue suit sleeve, disappearing under the newspaper. He had arranged the paper so that it overlapped Rose's coat. His hand was underneath, simply resting, as if flung out in sleep.

51 Now, Rose could have shifted the newspaper and removed her coat. If he was not asleep, he would have been obliged to draw back his hand. If he was asleep, if he did not draw it back, she could have whispered, *Excuse me,* and set his hand firmly on his own knee. This solution, so obvious and foolproof, did not occur to her. And she would have to wonder, why not? The minister's hand

was not, or not yet, at all welcome to her. It made her feel uncomfortable, resentful, slightly disgusted, trapped and wary. But she could not take charge of it, to reject it. She could not insist that it was there, when he seemed to be insisting that it was not. How could she declare him responsible, when he lay there so harmless and trusting, resting himself before his busy day, with such a pleased and healthy face? A man older than her father would be, if he were living, a man used to deference, an appreciator of Nature, delighter in wild swans. If she did say *Please don't* she was sure he would ignore her, as if overlooking some silliness or impoliteness on her part. She knew that as soon as she said it she would hope he had not heard.

52 But there was more to it than that. Curiosity. More constant, more imperious, than any lust. A lust in itself, that will make you draw back and wait, wait too long, risk almost anything, just to see what will happen. *To see what will happen.*

53 The hand began, over the next several miles, the most delicate, the most timid, pressures and investigations. Not asleep. Or if he was, his hand wasn't. She did feel disgust. She felt a faint, wandering nausea. She thought of flesh: lumps of flesh, pink snouts, fat tongues, blunt fingers, all on their way trotting and creeping and lolling and rubbing, looking for their comfort. She thought of cats in heat rubbing themselves along the top of board fences, yowling with their miserable complaint. It was pitiful, infantile, this itching and shoving and squeezing. Spongy tissues, inflamed membranes, tormented nerve-ends, shameful smells; humiliation.

54 All that was starting. His hand, that she wouldn't ever have wanted to hold, that she wouldn't have squeezed back, his stubborn patient hand was able, after all, to get the ferns to rustle and the streams to flow, to waken a sly luxuriance.

55 Nevertheless, she would rather not. She would still rather not. Please remove this, she said out the window. Stop it, please, she said to the stumps and barns. The hand moved up her leg past the top of her stocking to her bare skin, had moved higher, under her suspender, reached her underpants and the lower part of her belly. Her legs were still crossed, pinched together. While her legs stayed crossed she could lay claim to innocence, she had not admitted anything. She could still believe that she would stop this in a minute. Nothing was going to happen, nothing more. Her legs were never going to open.

56 But they were. They were. As the train crossed the Niagara Escarpment above Dundas, as they looked down at the preglacial valley, the silver-wooded rubble of little hills, as they came sliding down to the shores of Lake Ontario, she would make this slow, and silent, and definite, declaration, perhaps disappointing as much as satisfying the hand's owner. He would not lift his eyelids, his face would not alter, his fingers would not hesitate, but would go powerfully and discreetly to work. Invasion, and welcome, and sunlight flashing far and wide on the lake water; miles of bare orchards stirring round Burlington.

57 This was disgrace, this was beggary. But what harm in that, we say to ourselves at such moments, what harm in anything, the worse the better, as we ride the cold wave of greed, of greedy assent. A stranger's hand, or root vegetables or humble kitchen tools that people tell jokes about; the world is tumbling with innocent-seeming objects ready to declare themselves, slippery and obliging. She was careful of her breathing. She could not believe this. Victim and accomplice she was borne past Glassco's Jams and Marmalades, past the big pulsating pipes of oil refineries. They glided into suburbs where bedsheets, and towels used to wipe up intimate stains, flapped leeringly on the clotheslines, where even the children seemed to be frolicking lewdly in the school-yards, and the very truckdrivers stopped at the railway crossings must be thrusting their thumbs gleefully into curled hands. Such cunning antics now, such popular visions. The gates and towers of the Exhibition Grounds came into view, the painted domes and pillars floated marvelously against her eyelids' rosy sky. Then flew apart in celebration. You could have had such a flock of birds, wild swans, even, wakened under one big dome together, exploding from it, taking to the sky.

58 She bit the edge of her tongue. Very soon the conductor passed through the train, to stir the travelers, warn them back to life.

59 In the darkness under the station the United Church minister, refreshed, opened his eyes and got his paper folded together, then asked if she would like some help with her coat. His gallantry was self-satisfied, dismissive. No, said Rose, with a sore tongue. He hurried out of the train ahead of her. She did not see him in the station. She never saw him again in her life. But he remained on call, so to speak, for years and years, ready to slip into place at a critical moment, without even any regard, later on, for husband or lovers. What recommended him? She could never understand it. His simplicity, his arrogance, his perversely appealing lack of handsomeness, even of ordinary grown-up masculinity? When he stood up she saw that he was shorter even than she had thought, that his face was pink and shiny, that there was something crude and pushy and childish about him.

60 Was he a minister, really, or was that only what he said? Flo had mentioned people who were not ministers, dressed up as if they were. Not real ministers dressed as if they were not. Or, stranger still, men who were not real ministers pretending to be real but dressed as if they were not. But that she had come as close as she had, to what could happen, was an unwelcome thing. Rose walked through Union Station feeling the little bag with the ten dollars rubbing at her, knew she would feel it all day long, rubbing its reminder against her skin.

61 She couldn't stop getting Flo's messages, even with that. She remembered, because she was in Union Station, that there was a girl named Mavis working here, in the Gift Shop, when Flo was working in the coffee shop. Mavis had

warts on her eyelids that looked like they were going to turn into sties but they didn't, they went away. Maybe she had them removed, Flo didn't ask. She was very good-looking, without them. There was a movie star in those days she looked a lot like. The movie star's name was Frances Farmer.

62 Frances Farmer. Rose had never heard of her.

63 That was the name. And Mavis went and bought herself a big hat that dipped over one eye and a dress entirely made of lace. She went off for the weekend to Georgian Bay, to a resort up there. She booked herself in under the name of Florence Farmer. To give everybody the idea she was really the other one, Frances Farmer, but calling herself Florence because she was on holiday and didn't want to be recognized. She had a little cigarette holder that was black and mother-of-pearl. She could have been arrested, Flo said. For the *nerve.*

64 Rose almost went over to the Gift Shop, to see if Mavis was still there and if she could recognize her. She thought it would be an especially fine thing, to manage a transformation like that. To dare it; to get away with it, to enter on preposterous adventures in your own, but newly named, skin.

—1978

✧ ✧ ✧

John Updike
(b. 1932)

A & P

Updike's novels so consistently appear on the best-seller lists that his brilliant forays into light verse, serious poetry, the literary essay and book review, and the short story are often overshadowed by his achievement in longer forms. Born in Shillingford, in rural Pennsylvania, he attended Harvard, where he contributed humor and cartoons to the *Harvard Lampoon*, and later studied art in England. After his return to the United States, he worked for three years for the *New Yorker*, to which he remains a regular contributor of book reviews on a wide range of subjects. Updike is a prolific writer who has won many awards, including the National Book Award in 1963 and both the Pulitzer prize and an American Book Award in 1982, yet he remains difficult to classify. Still, his series of novels about the life of a contemporary American "everyman," Harry "Rabbit" Angstrom—*Rabbit Run* (1960); *Rabbit Redux* (1971); and *Rabbit Is Rich*

(1981)—has solidified his reputation as one of the most astute observers of the American middle class. His best seller *The Witches of Eastwick* (1984) was made into a popular motion picture. "A & P" comes from his 1962 collection of short stories *Pigeon Feathers.*

In walks three girls in nothing but bathing suits. I'm in the third checkout slot, with my back to the door, so I don't see them until they're over by the bread. The one that caught my eye first was the one in the plaid green two-piece. She was a chunky kid, with a good tan and a sweet broad soft-looking can with those two crescents of white just under it, where the sun never seems to hit, at the top of the backs of her legs. I stood there with my hand on a box of HiHo crackers trying to remember if I rang it up or not. I ring it up again and the customer starts giving me hell. She's one of these cash-register-watchers, a witch about fifty with rouge on her cheekbones and no eyebrows, and I know it made her day to trip me up. She'd been watching cash registers for fifty years and probably never seen a mistake before.

2 By the time I got her feathers smoothed and her goodies into a bag—she gives me a little snort in passing, if she'd been born at the right time they would have burned her over in Salem—by the time I get her on her way the girls had circled around the bread and were coming back, without a pushcart, back my way along the counters, in the aisle between the check-outs and the Special bins. They didn't even have shoes on. There was this chunky one, with the two-piece—it was bright green and the seams on the bra were still sharp and her belly was still pretty pale so I guessed she just got it (the suit)—there was this one, with one of those chubby berry-faces, the lips all bunched together under her nose, this one, and a tall one, with black hair that hadn't quite frizzed right, and one of these sunburns right across under the eyes, and a chin that was too long—you know, the kind of girl other girls think is very "striking" and "attractive" but never quite makes it, as they very well know, which is why they like her so much—and then the third one, that wasn't quite so tall. She was the queen. She kind of led them, the other two peeking around and making their shoulders round. She didn't look around, not this queen, she just walked straight on slowly, on these long white prima-donna legs. She came down a little hard on her heels, as if she didn't walk in her bare feet that much, putting down her heels and then letting the weight move along to her toes as if she was testing the floor with every step, putting a little deliberate extra action into it. You never know for sure how girls' minds work (do you really think it's a mind in there or just a little buzz like a bee in a glass jar?) but you got the idea she had talked the other two into coming in here with her, and now she was showing them how to do it, walk slow and hold yourself straight.

3 She had on a kind of dirty-pink—beige maybe, I don't know—bathing suit with a little nubble all over it and, what got me, the straps were down. They were off her shoulders looped loose around the cool tops of her arms, and I guess as a result the suit had slipped a little on her, so all around the top of the cloth there was this shining rim. If it hadn't been there you wouldn't have known there could have been anything whiter than those shoulders. With the straps pushed off, there was nothing between the top of the suit and the top of her head except just *her*, this clean bare plane of the top of her chest down from the shoulder bones like a dented sheet of metal tilted in the light. I mean, it was more than pretty.

4 She had sort of oaky hair that the sun and salt had bleached, done up in a bun that was unravelling, and a kind of prim face. Walking into the A & P with your straps down, I suppose it's the only kind of face you *can* have. She held her head so high her neck, coming up out of those white shoulders, looked kind of stretched, but I didn't mind. The longer her neck was, the more of her there was.

5 She must have felt in the corner of her eye me and over my shoulder Stokesie in the second slot watching, but she didn't tip. Not this queen. She kept her eyes moving across the racks, and stopped, and turned so slow it made my stomach rub the inside of my apron, and buzzed to the other two, who kind of huddled against her for relief, and then they all three of them went up the cat and dog food-breakfastcereal-macaroni-rice-raisins-seasonings-spreads-spaghetti-soft drinks-crackers-and-cookies aisle. From the third slot I look straight up this aisle to the meat counter, and I watched them all the way. The fat one with the tan sort of fumbled with the cookies, but on second thought she put the packages back. The sheep pushing their carts down the aisle—the girls were walking against the usual traffic (not that we have one-way signs or anything)—were pretty hilarious. You could see them, when Queenie's white shoulders dawned on them, kind of jerk, or hop, or hiccup, but their eyes snapped back to their own baskets and on they pushed. I bet you could set off dynamite in an A & P and the people would by and large keep reaching and checking oatmeal off their lists and muttering "Let me see, there was a third thing, began with A, asparagus, no, ah, yes, applesauce!" or whatever it is they do mutter. But there was no doubt, this jiggled them. A few house slaves in pin curlers even look around after pushing their carts past to make sure what they had seen was correct.

6 You know, it's one thing to have a girl in a bathing suit down on the beach, where what with the glare nobody can look at each other much anyway, and another thing in the cool of the A & P, under the fluorescent lights, against all those stacked packages, with her feet padding along naked over our checkerboard green-and-cream rubber-tile floor.

7 "Oh, Daddy," Stokesie said beside me. "I feel so faint."

8 "Darling," I said. "Hold me tight." Stokesie's married, with two babies chalked up on his fuselage already, but as far as I can tell that's the only difference. He's twenty-two, and I was nineteen this April.

9 "Is it done?" he asks, the responsible married man finding his voice. I forgot to say he thinks he's going to be manager some sunny day, maybe in 1990 when it's called the Great Alexandrov and Petrooshki Tea Company or something.

10 What he meant was, our town is five miles from a beach, with a big summer colony out on the Point, but we're right in the middle of town, and the women generally put on a shirt or shorts or something before they get out of the car into the street. And anyway these are usually women with six children and varicose veins mapping their legs and nobody, including them, could care less. As I say, we're right in the middle of town, and if you stand at our front doors you can see two banks and the Congregational church and the newspaper store and three real estate offices and about twenty-seven old freeloaders tearing up Central Street because the sewer broke again. It's not as if we're on the Cape; we're north of Boston and there's people in this town haven't seen the ocean for twenty years.

11 The girls had reached the meat counter and were asking McMahon something. He pointed, they pointed, and they shuffled out of sight behind a pyramid of Diet Delight peaches. All that was left for us to see was old McMahon patting his mouth and looking after them sizing up their joints. Poor kids, I began to feel sorry for them, they couldn't help it.

12 Now here comes the sad part of the story, at least my family says it's sad, but I don't think it's so sad myself. The store's pretty empty, it being Thursday afternoon, so there was nothing much to do except lean on the register and wait for the girls to show up again. The whole store was like a pinball machine and I didn't know which tunnel they'd come out of. After a while they come around out of the far aisle, around the light bulbs, records at discount of the Caribbean Six or Tony Martin Sings or some such gunk you wonder they waste the wax on, sixpacks of candy bars, and plastic toys done up in cellophane that fall apart when a kid looks at them anyway. Around they come, Queenie still leading the way, and holding a little gray jar in her hand. Slots Three through Seven are unmanned and I could see her wondering between Stokes and me, but Stokesie with his usual luck draws an old party in baggy gray pants who stumbles up with four giant cans of pineapple juice (what do these bums *do* with all that pineapple juice? I've often asked myself) so the girls come to me. Queenie puts down the jar and I take it into my fingers icy cold. Kingfish Fancy Herring Snacks in Pure Sour Cream: 49¢. Now her hands are empty, not a ring or a bracelet, bare as God made them, and I wonder where the money's coming from. Still with that prim look she lifts a folded dollar bill out of the hollow at the

center of her nubbled pink top. The jar went heavy in my hand. Really, I thought that was so cute.

13 Then everybody's luck begins to run out. Lengel comes in from haggling with a truck full of cabbages on the lot and is about to scuttle into that door marked MANAGER behind which he hides all day when the girls touch his eye. Lengel's pretty dreary, teaches Sunday school and the rest, but he doesn't miss that much. He comes over and says, "Girls, this isn't the beach."

14 Queenie blushes, though maybe it's just a brush of sunburn I was noticing for the first time, now that she was so close. "My mother asked me to pick up a jar of herring snacks." Her voice kind of startled me, the way voices do when you see the people first, coming out so flat and dumb yet kind of tony, too, the way it ticked over "pick up" and "snacks." All of a sudden I slid right down her voice into her living room. Her father and the other men were standing around in ice-cream coats and bow ties and the women were in sandals picking up herring snacks on toothpicks off a big glass plate and they were all holding drinks the color of water with olives and sprigs of mint in them. When my parents have somebody over they get lemonade and if it's a real racy affair Schlitz in tall glasses with "They'll Do It Every Time" cartoons stencilled on.

15 "That's all right," Lengel said. "But this isn't the beach." His repeating this struck me as funny, as if it had just occurred to him, and he had been thinking all these years the A & P was a great big dune and he was the head lifeguard. He didn't like my smiling—as I say he doesn't miss much—but he concentrates on giving the girls that sad Sunday-school-superintendent stare.

16 Queenie's blush is no sunburn now, and the plump one in plaid, that I liked better from the back—a really sweet can—pipes up, "We weren't doing any shopping. We just came in for the one thing."

17 "That makes no difference," Lengel tells her, and I could see from the way his eyes went that he hadn't noticed she was wearing a two-piece before. "We want you decently dressed when you come in here."

18 "We *are* decent," Queenie says suddenly, her lower lip pushing, getting sore now that she remembers her place, a place from which the crowd that runs the A & P must look pretty crummy. Fancy Herring Snacks flashed in her very blue eyes.

19 "Girls, I don't want to argue with you. After this come in here with your shoulders covered. It's our policy." He turns his back. That's policy for you. Policy is what the kingpins want. What the others want is juvenile delinquency.

20 All this while, the customers had been showing up with their carts but, you know, sheep, seeing a scene, they had all bunched up on Stokesie, who shook open a paper bag as gently as peeling a peach, not wanting to miss a word. I could feel in the silence everybody getting nervous, most of all Lengel, who asks me, "Sammy, have you rung up this purchase?"

21 I thought and said "No" but it wasn't about that I was thinking. I go through the punches, 4, 9, GROC, TOT—it's more complicated than you think, and after you do it often enough, it begins to make a little song, that you hear words to, in my case "Hello *(bing)* there, you *(gung)* hap-py *pee*pul *(splat)!"*—the *splat* being the drawer flying out. I uncrease the bill, tenderly as you may imagine, it just having come from between the two smoothest scoops of vanilla I had ever known were there, and pass a half and a penny into her narrow pink palm, and nestle the herrings in a bag and twist its neck and hand it over, all the time thinking.

22 The girls, and who'd blame them, are in a hurry to get out, so I say "I quit" to Lengel quick enough for them to hear, hoping they'll stop and watch me, their unsuspected hero. They keep right on going, into the electric eye; the door flies open and they flicker across the lot to their car, Queenie and Plaid and Big Tall Goony-Goony (not that as raw material she was so bad), leaving me with Lengel and a kink in his eyebrow.

23 "Did you say something, Sammy?"

24 "I said I quit."

25 "I thought you did."

26 "You didn't have to embarrass them."

27 "It was they who were embarrassing us."

28 I started to say something that came out "Fiddle-de-doo." It's a saying of my grandmother's, and I know she would have been pleased.

29 "I don't think you know what you're saying," Lengel said.

30 "I know you don't," I said. "But I do." I pull the bow at the back of my apron and start shrugging it off my shoulders. A couple customers that had been heading for my slot begin to knock against each other, like scared pigs in a chute.

31 Lengel sighs and begins to look very patient and old and gray. He's been a friend of my parents for years. "Sammy, you don't want to do this to your Mom and Dad," he tells me. It's true, I don't. But it seems to me that once you begin a gesture it's fatal not to go through with it. I fold the apron, "Sammy" stitched in red on the pocket, and put it on the counter, and drop the bow tie on top of it. The bow tie is theirs, if you've ever wondered. "You'll feel this for the rest of your life," Lengel says, and I know that's true, too, but remembering how he made that pretty girl blush makes me so scrunchy inside I punch the No Sale tab and the machine whirs "pee-pul" and the drawer splats out. One advantage to this scene taking place in summer, I can follow this up with a clean exit, there's no fumbling around getting your coat and galoshes, I just saunter into the electric eye in my white shirt that my mother ironed the night before, and the door heaves itself open, and outside the sunshine is skating around on the asphalt.

32 I look around for my girls, but they're gone, of course. There wasn't anybody but some young married screaming with her children about some candy

they didn't get by the door of a powder-blue Falcon station wagon. Looking back in the big windows, over the bags of peat moss and aluminum lawn furniture stacked on the pavement, I could see Lengel in my place in the slot, checking the sheep through. His face was dark gray and his back stiff, as if he'd just had an injection of iron, and my stomach kind of fell as I felt how hard the world was going to be to me hereafter.

—1962

✧ ✧ ✧

Raymond Carver
(1938-1988)

Cathedral

Carver's reputation as a master of the contemporary short story was still growing at the end of his life, which ended prematurely after a bout with lung cancer. A native of Clatskanie, Oregon, Carver worked at a number of unskilled jobs in his early years. Married and the father of two before he was twenty, he knew the working class more intimately than have many American writers. Carver worked his way through Humboldt State College (now the University of California at Humboldt) and, like many major figures in contemporary American writing, was a graduate of the Writers' Workshop of the University of Iowa. It is interesting to note that Carver's publishing career is bracketed by collections of poetry; *A New Path to the Waterfall* appeared posthumously in 1989. The compression of language he learned as a poet may in part account for the lean quality of his prose, what has been called, perhaps inaccurately, "minimalist." Carver's last years were spent with his second wife, poet Tess Gallagher, and he taught at a number of universities. His personal victory over alcoholism paralleled the remarkable literary triumphs of these final years, which included receipt of a prestigious MacArthur Fellowship. *Where I'm Calling From: New and Selected Stories* appeared in 1988.

This blind man, an old friend of my wife's, he was on his way to spend the night. His wife had died. So he was visiting the dead wife's relatives in

Connecticut. He called my wife from his in-laws'. Arrangements were made. He would come by train, a five-hour trip, and my wife would meet him at the station. She hadn't seen him since she worked for him one summer in Seattle ten years ago. But she and the blind man had kept in touch. They made tapes and mailed them back and forth. I wasn't enthusiastic about his visit. He was no one I knew. And his being blind bothered me. My idea of blindness came from the movies. In the movies, the blind moved slowly and never laughed. Sometimes they were led by seeing-eye dogs. A blind man in my house was not something I looked forward to.

2 That summer in Seattle she had needed a job. She didn't have any money. The man she was going to marry at the end of the summer was in officers' training school. He didn't have any money, either. But she was in love with the guy, and he was in love with her, etc. She'd seen something in the paper: HELP WANTED—*Reading to Blind Man,* and a telephone number. She phoned and went over, was hired on the spot. She'd worked with this blind man all summer. She read stuff to him, case studies, reports, that sort of thing. She helped him organize his little office in the county social-service department. They'd become good friends, my wife and the blind man. How do I know these things? She told me. And she told me something else. On her last day in the office, the blind man asked if he could touch her face. She agreed to this. She told me he touched his fingers to every part of her face, her nose—even her neck! She never forgot it. She even tried to write a poem about it. She was always trying to write a poem. She wrote a poem or two every year, usually after something really important had happened to her.

3 When we first started going out together, she showed me the poem. In the poem, she recalled his fingers and the way they had moved around over her face. In the poem, she talked about what she had felt at the time, about what went through her mind when the blind man touched her nose and lips. I can remember I didn't think much of the poem. Of course, I didn't tell her that. Maybe I just don't understand poetry. I admit it's not the first thing I reach for when I pick up something to read.

4 Anyway, this man who'd first enjoyed her favors, the officer-to-be, he'd been her childhood sweetheart. So okay. I'm saying that at the end of the summer she let the blind man run his hands over her face, said good-bye to him, married her childhood etc., who was now a commissioned officer, and she moved away from Seattle. But they'd kept in touch, she and the blind man. She made the first contact after a year or so. She called him up one night from an Air Force base in Alabama. She wanted to talk. They talked. He asked her to send a tape and tell him about her life. She did this. She sent the tape. On the tape, she told the blind man about her husband and about their life together in the military. She told the blind man she loved her husband but she didn't like it where they lived and she didn't like it that he was part of the military industrial thing. She told the

blind man she'd written a poem and he was in it. She told him that she was writing a poem about what it was like to be an Air Force officer's wife. The poem wasn't finished yet. She was still writing it. The blind man made a tape. He sent her the tape. She made a tape. This went on for years. My wife's officer was posted to one base and then another. She sent tapes from Moody AFB, McGuire, McConnell, and finally Travis, near Sacramento, where one night she got to feeling lonely and cut off from people she kept losing in that moving around life. She got to feeling she couldn't go it another step. She went in and swallowed all the pills and capsules in the medicine chest and washed them down with a bottle of gin. Then she got into a hot bath and passed out.

5 But instead of dying, she got sick. She threw up. Her officer—why should he have a name? he was the childhood sweetheart, and what more does he want?—came home from somewhere, found her, and called the ambulance. In time, she put it all on a tape and sent the tape to the blind man. Over the years, she put all kinds of stuff on tapes and sent the tapes off lickety-split. Next to writing a poem every year, I think it was her chief means of recreation. On one tape, she told the blind man she'd decided to live away from her officer for a time. On another tape, she told him about her divorce. She and I began going out, and of course she told her blind man about it. She told him everything, or so it seemed to me. Once she asked me if I'd like to hear the latest tape from the blind man. This was a year ago. I was on the tape, she said. So I said okay, I'd listen to it. I got us drinks and we settled down in the living room. We made ready to listen. First she inserted the tape into the player and adjusted a couple of dials. Then she pushed a lever. The tape squeaked and someone began to talk in this loud voice. She lowered the volume. After a few minutes of harmless chitchat, I heard my own name in the mouth of this stranger, this blind man I didn't even know! And then this: "From all you've said about him, I can only conclude—" But we were interrupted, a knock at the door, something, and we didn't ever get back to the tape. Maybe it was just as well. I'd heard all I wanted to.

6 Now this same blind man was coming to sleep in my house.

7 "Maybe I could take him bowling," I said to my wife. She was at the draining board doing scalloped potatoes. She put down the knife she was using and turned around.

8 "If you love me," she said, "you can do this for me. If you don't love me, okay. But if you had a friend, any friend, and the friend came to visit, I'd make him feel comfortable." She wiped her hands with the dish towel.

9 "I don't have any blind friends," I said.

10 "You don't have *any* friends," she said. "Period. Besides," she said, "goddamn it, his wife's just died! Don't you understand that? The man's lost his wife!"

11 I didn't answer. She'd told me a little about the blind man's wife. Her name was Beulah. Beulah! That's a name for a colored woman.

12 "Was his wife a Negro?" I asked.

13 "Are you crazy?" my wife said. "Have you just flipped or something?" She picked up a potato. I saw it hit the floor, then roll under the stove. "What's wrong with you?" she said. "Are you drunk?"

14 "I'm just asking," I said.

15 Right then my wife filled me in with more detail than I cared to know. I made a drink and sat at the kitchen table to listen. Pieces of the story began to fall into place.

16 Beulah had gone to work for the blind man the summer after my wife had stopped working for him. Pretty soon Beulah and the blind man had themselves a church wedding. It was a little wedding—who'd want to go to such a wedding in the first place?—just the two of them, plus the minister and the minister's wife. But it was a church wedding just the same. It was what Beulah had wanted, he'd said. But even then Beulah must have been carrying the cancer in her glands. After they had been inseparable for eight years—my wife's word, *inseparable*—Beulah's health went into a rapid decline. She died in a Seattle hospital room, the blind man sitting beside the bed and holding on to her hand. They'd married, lived and worked together, slept together—had sex, sure—and then the blind man had to bury her. All this without his having ever seen what the goddamned woman looked like. It was beyond my understanding. Hearing this, I felt sorry for the blind man for a little bit. And then I found myself thinking what a pitiful life this woman must have led. Imagine a woman who could never see herself as she was seen in the eyes of her loved one. A woman who could go on day after day and never receive the smallest compliment from her beloved. A woman whose husband could never read the expression on her face, be it misery or something better. Someone who could wear makeup or not—what difference to him? She could, if she wanted, wear green eye-shadow around one eye, a straight pin in her nostril, yellow slacks, and purple shoes, no matter. And then to slip off into death, the blind man's hand on her hand, his blind eyes streaming tears—I'm imagining now—her last thought maybe this: that he never even knew what she looked like, and she on an express to the grave. Robert was left with a small insurance policy and a half of a twenty-peso Mexican coin. The other half of the coin went into the box with her. Pathetic.

17 So when the time rolled around, my wife went to the depot to pick him up. With nothing to do but wait—sure, I blamed him for that—I was having a drink and watching the TV when I heard the car pull into the drive. I got up from the sofa with my drink and went to the window to have a look.

18 I saw my wife laughing as she parked the car. I saw her get out of the car and shut the door. She was still wearing a smile. Just amazing. She went around to the other side of the car to where the blind man was already starting to get

out. This blind man, feature this, he was wearing a full beard! A beard on a blind man! Too much, I say. The blind man reached into the backseat and dragged out a suitcase. My wife took his arm, shut the car door, and, talking all the way, moved him down the drive and then up the steps to the front porch. I turned off the TV. I finished my drink, rinsed the glass, dried my hands. Then I went to the door.

19 My wife said, "I want you to meet Robert. Robert, this is my husband. I've told you all about him." She was beaming. She had this blind man by his coat sleeve.

20 The blind man let go of his suitcase and up came his hand.

21 I took it. He squeezed hard, held my hand, and then he let it go.

22 "I feel like we've already met," he boomed.

23 "Likewise," I said. I didn't know what else to say. Then I said, "Welcome. I've heard a lot about you." We began to move then, a little group, from the porch into the living room, my wife guiding him by the arm. The blind man was carrying his suitcase in his other hand. My wife said things like, "To your left here, Robert. That's right. Now watch it, there's a chair. That's it. Sit down right here. This is the sofa. We just bought this sofa two weeks ago."

24 I started to say something about the old sofa. I'd liked that old sofa. But I didn't say anything. Then I wanted to say something else, small talk, about the scenic ride along the Hudson. How going *to* New York, you should sit on the right-hand side of the train, and coming *from* New York, the left hand side.

25 "Did you have a good train ride?" I said. "Which side of the train did you sit on, by the way?"

26 "What a question, which side!" my wife said. "What's it matter which side?" she said.

27 "I just asked," I said.

28 "Right side," the blind man said. "I hadn't been on a train in nearly forty years. Not since I was a kid. With my folks. That's been a long time. I'd nearly forgotten the sensation. I have winter in my beard now," he said. "So I've been told, anyway. Do I look distinguished, my dear?" the blind man said to my wife.

29 "You look distinguished, Robert," she said. "Robert," she said. "Robert, it's just so good to see you."

30 My wife finally took her eyes off the blind man and looked at me. I had the feeling she didn't like what she saw. I shrugged.

31 I've never met, or personally known, anyone who was blind. This blind man was late forties, a heavy-set, balding man with stooped shoulders, as if he carried a great weight there. He wore brown slacks, brown shoes, a light-brown shirt, a tie, a sports coat. Spiffy. He also had this full beard. But he didn't use a cane and he didn't wear dark glasses. I'd always thought dark glasses were a must for the blind. Fact was, I wished he had a pair. At first glance, his eyes looked

like anyone else's eyes. But if you looked close, there was something different about them. Too much white in the iris, for one thing, and the pupils seemed to move around in the sockets without his knowing it or being able to stop it. Creepy. As I stared at his face, I saw the left pupil turn in toward his nose while the other made an effort to keep in one place. But it was only an effort, for that eye was on the roam without his knowing it or wanting it to be.

32 I said, "Let me get you a drink. What's your pleasure? We have a little of everything. It's one of our pastimes."

33 "Bub, I'm a Scotch man myself," he said fast enough in this big voice.

34 "Right," I said. Bub! "Sure you are. I knew it."

35 He let his fingers touch his suitcase, which was sitting alongside the sofa. He was taking his bearings. I didn't blame him for that.

36 "I'll move that up to your room," my wife said.

37 "No, that's fine," the blind man said loudly. "It can go up when I go up."

38 "A little water with the Scotch?" I said.

39 "Very little," he said.

40 "I knew it," I said.

41 He said, "Just a tad. The Irish actor, Barry Fitzgerald? I'm like that fellow. When I drink water, Fitzgerald said, I drink water. When I drink whiskey, I drink whiskey." My wife laughed. The blind man brought his hand up under his beard. He lifted his beard slowly and let it drop.

42 I did the drinks, three big glasses of Scotch with a splash of water in each. Then we made ourselves comfortable and talked about Robert's travels. First the long flight from the West Coast to Connecticut, we covered that. Then from Connecticut up here by train. We had another drink concerning that leg of the trip.

43 I remembered having read somewhere that the blind didn't smoke because, as speculation had it, they couldn't see the smoke they exhaled. I thought I knew that much and that much only about blind people. But this blind man smoked his cigarette down to the nubbin and then lit another one. This blind man filled his ashtray and my wife emptied it.

44 When we sat down at the table for dinner, we had another drink. My wife heaped Robert's plate with cube steak, scalloped potatoes, green beans. I buttered him up two slices of bread. I said, "Here's bread and butter for you." I swallowed some of my drink. "Now let us pray," I said, and the blind man lowered his head. My wife looked at me, her mouth agape. "Pray the phone won't ring and the food doesn't get cold," I said.

45 We dug in. We ate everything there was to eat on the table. We ate like there was no tomorrow. We didn't talk. We ate. We scarfed. We grazed that table. We were into serious eating. The blind man had right away located his foods, he knew just where everything was on his plate. I watched with admiration as he used his knife and fork on the meat. He'd cut two pieces of meat, fork

the meat into his mouth, and then go all out for the scalloped potatoes, the beans next, and then he'd tear off a hunk of buttered bread and eat that. He'd follow this up with a big drink of milk. It didn't seem to bother him to use his fingers once in a while, either.

46 We finished everything, including half a strawberry pie. For a few moments, we sat as if stunned. Sweat beaded on our faces. Finally, we got up from the table and left the dirty plates. We didn't look back. We took ourselves into the living room and sank into our places again. Robert and my wife sat on the sofa. I took the big chair. We had us two or three more drinks while they talked about the major things that had come to pass for them in the past ten years. For the most part, I just listened. Now and then I joined in. I didn't want him to think I'd left the room, and I didn't want her to think I was feeling left out. They talked of things that had happened to them—to them!—these past ten years. I waited in vain to hear my name on my wife's sweet lips: "And then my dear husband came into my life"—something like that. But I heard nothing of the sort. More talk of Robert. Robert had done a little of everything, it seemed, a regular blind jack-of-all-trades. But most recently he and his wife had had an Amway distributorship, from which, I gathered, they'd earned their living, such as it was. The blind man was also a ham radio operator. He talked in his loud voice about conversations he'd had with fellow operators in Guam, in the Philippines, in Alaska, and even in Tahiti. He said he'd have a lot of friends there if he ever wanted to go visit those places. From time to time, he'd turn his blind face toward me, put his hand under his beard, ask me something. How long had I been in my present position? (Three years.) Did I like my work? (I didn't.) Was I going to stay with it? (What were the options?) Finally, when I thought he was beginning to run down, I got up and turned on the TV.

47 My wife looked at me with irritation. She was heading toward a boil. Then she looked at the blind man and said, "Robert, do you have a TV?"

48 The blind man said, "My dear, I have two TVs. I have a color set and a black-and-white thing, an old relic. It's funny, but if I turn the TV on, and I'm always turning it on, I turn on the color set. It's funny, don't you think?"

49 I didn't know what to say to that. I had absolutely nothing to say to that. No opinion. So I watched the news program and tried to listen to what the announcer was saying.

50 "This is a color TV," the blind man said. "Don't ask me how, but I can tell."

51 "We traded up a while ago," I said.

52 The blind man had another taste of his drink. He lifted his beard, sniffed it, and let it fall. He leaned forward on the sofa. He positioned his ashtray on the coffee table, then put the lighter to his cigarette. He leaned back on the sofa and crossed his legs at the ankles.

53 My wife covered her mouth, and then she yawned. She stretched. She said, "I think I'll go upstairs and put on my robe. I think I'll change into something else. Robert, you make yourself comfortable," she said.

54 "I'm comfortable," the blind man said.

55 "I want you to feel comfortable in this house," she said.

56 "I am comfortable," the blind man said.

57 After she'd left the room, he and I listened to the weather report and then to the sports roundup. By that time, she'd been gone so long I didn't know if she was going to come back. I thought she might have gone to bed. I wished she'd come back downstairs. I didn't want to be left alone with a blind man. I asked him if he wanted another drink, and he said sure. Then I asked if he wanted to smoke some dope with me. I said I'd just rolled a number. I hadn't, but I planned to do so in about two shakes.

58 "I'll try some with you," he said.

59 "Damn right," I said. "That's the stuff."

60 I got our drinks and sat down on the sofa with him. Then I rolled us two fat numbers. I lit one and passed it. I brought it to his fingers. He took it and inhaled.

61 "Hold it as long as you can," I said. I could tell he didn't know the first thing.

62 My wife came back downstairs wearing her pink robe and her pink slippers.

63 "What do I smell?" she said.

64 "We thought we'd have us some cannabis," I said.

65 My wife gave me a savage look. Then she looked at the blind man and said, "Robert, I didn't know you smoked."

66 He said, "I do now, my dear. There's a first time for everything. But I don't feel anything yet."

67 "This stuff is pretty mellow," I said. "This stuff is mild. It's dope you can reason with," I said. "It doesn't mess you up."

68 "Not much it doesn't, bub," he said, and laughed.

69 My wife sat on the sofa between the blind man and me. I passed her the number. She took it and toked and then passed it back to me. "Which way is this going?" she said. Then she said, "I shouldn't be smoking this. I can hardly keep my eyes open as it is. That dinner did me in. I shouldn't have eaten so much."

70 "It was the strawberry pie," the blind man said. "That's what did it," he said, and he laughed his big laugh. Then he shook his head.

71 "There's more strawberry pie," I said.

72 "Do you want some more, Robert?" my wife said.

73 "Maybe in a little while," he said.

74 We gave our attention to the TV. My wife yawned again. She said, "Your bed is made up when you feel like going to bed, Robert. I know you must have had a long day. When you're ready to go to bed, say so." She pulled his arm. "Robert?"

75 He came to and said, "I've had a real nice time. This beats tapes, doesn't it?"

76 I said, "Coming at you," and I put the number between his fingers. He inhaled, held the smoke, and then let it go. It was like he'd been doing it since he was nine years old.

77 "Thanks, bub," he said. "But I think this is all for me. I think I'm beginning to feel it," he said. He held the burning roach out for my wife.

78 "Same here," she said. "Ditto. Me, too." She took the roach and passed it to me. "I may just sit here for a while between you two guys with my eyes closed. But don't let me bother you, okay? Either one of you. If it bothers you, say so. Otherwise, I may just sit here with my eyes closed until you're ready to go to bed," she said. "Your bed's made up, Robert, when you're ready. It's right next to our room at the top of the stairs. We'll show you up when you're ready. You wake me up now, you guys, if I fall asleep." She said that and then she closed her eyes and went to sleep.

79 The news program ended. I got up and changed the channel. I sat back down on the sofa. I wished my wife hadn't pooped out. Her head lay across the back of the sofa, her mouth open. She'd turned so that her robe slipped away from her legs, exposing a juicy thigh. I reached to draw her robe back over her, and it was then that I glanced at the blind man. What the hell! I flipped the robe open again.

80 "You say when you want some strawberry pie," I said.

81 "I will," he said.

82 I said, "Are you tired? Do you want me to take you up to your bed? Are you ready to hit the hay?"

83 "Not yet," he said. "No, I'll stay up with you, bub. If that's all right. I'll stay up until you're ready to turn in. We haven't had a chance to talk. Know what I mean? I feel like me and her monopolized the evening." He lifted his beard and he let it fall. He picked up his cigarettes and his lighter.

84 "That's all right," I said. Then I said, "I'm glad for the company."

85 And I guess I was. Every night I smoked dope and stayed up as long as I could before I fell asleep. My wife and I hardly ever went to bed at the same time. When I did go to sleep, I had these dreams. Sometimes I'd wake up from one of them, my heart going crazy.

86 Something about the church and the Middle Ages was on the TV. Not your run-of-the-mill TV fare. I wanted to watch something else. I turned to the other channels. But there was nothing on them, either. So I turned back to the first channel and apologized.

87 "Bub, it's all right," the blind man said. "It's fine with me. Whatever you want to watch is okay. I'm always learning something. Learning never ends. It won't hurt me to learn something tonight. I got ears," he said.

88 We didn't say anything for a time. He was leaning forward with his head turned at me, his right ear aimed in the direction of the set. Very disconcerting. Now and then his eyelids drooped and then they snapped open again. Now and then he put his fingers into his beard and tugged, like he was thinking about something he was hearing on the television.

89 On the screen, a group of men wearing cowls was being set upon and tormented by men dressed in skeleton costumes and men dressed as devils. The men dressed as devils wore devil masks, horns, and long tails. This pageant was part of a procession. The Englishman who was narrating the thing said it took place in Spain once a year. I tried to explain to the blind man what was happening.

90 "Skeletons," he said. "I know about skeletons," he said, and he nodded.

91 The TV showed this one cathedral. Then there was a long, slow look at another one. Finally, the picture switched to the famous one in Paris, with its flying buttresses and its spires reaching up to the clouds. The camera pulled away to show the whole of the cathedral rising above the skyline.

92 There were times when the Englishman who was telling the thing would shut up, would simply let the camera move around the cathedrals. Or else the camera would tour the countryside, men in fields walking behind oxen. I waited as long as I could. Then I felt I had to say something. I said, "They're showing the outside of this cathedral now. Gargoyles. Little statues carved to look like monsters. Now I guess they're in Italy. Yeah, they're in Italy. There's paintings on the walls of this one church."

93 "Are those fresco paintings, bub?" he asked, and he sipped from his drink.

94 I reached for my glass. But it was empty. I tried to remember what I could remember. "You're asking me are those frescoes?" I said. "That's a good question. I don't know."

95 The camera moved to a cathedral outside Lisbon. The differences in the Portuguese cathedral compared with the French and Italian were not that great. But they were there. Mostly the interior stuff. Then something occurred to me, and I said, "Something has occurred to me. Do you have any idea what a cathedral is? What they look like, that is? Do you follow me? If somebody says cathedral to you, do you have any notion what they're talking about? Do you know the difference between that and a Baptist church, say?"

96 He let the smoke dribble from his mouth. "I know they took hundreds of workers fifty or a hundred years to build," he said. "I just heard the man say that, of course. I know generations of the same families worked on a cathedral. I heard him say that, too. The men who began their life's work on them, they never lived to see the completion of their work. In that wise, bub, they're no

different from the rest of us, right?" He laughed. Then his eyelids drooped again. His head nodded. He seemed to be snoozing. Maybe he was imagining himself in Portugal. The TV was showing another cathedral now. This one was in Germany. The Englishman's voice droned on. "Cathedrals," the blind man said. He sat up and rolled his head back and forth. "If you want the truth, bub, that's about all I know. What I just said. What I heard him say. But maybe you could describe one to me? I wish you'd do it. I'd like that. If you want to know, I really don't have a good idea."

97 I stared hard at the shot of the cathedral on the TV. How could I even begin to describe it? But say my life depended on it. Say my life was being threatened by an insane guy who said I had to do it or else.

98 I stared some more at the cathedral before the picture flipped off into the countryside. There was no use. I turned to the blind man and said, "To begin with, they're very tall." I was looking around the room for clues. "They reach way up. Up and up. Toward the sky. They're so big, some of them, they have to have these supports. To help hold them up, so to speak. These supports are called buttresses. They remind me of viaducts, for some reasons. But maybe you don't know viaducts, either? Sometimes the cathedrals have devils and such carved into the front. Sometimes lords and ladies. Don't ask me why this is," I said.

99 He was nodding. The whole upper part of his body seemed to be moving back and forth.

100 "I'm not doing so good, am I?" I said.

101 He stopped nodding and leaned forward on the edge of the sofa. As he listened to me, he was running his fingers through his beard. I wasn't getting through to him, I could see that. But he waited for me to go on just the same. He nodded, like he was trying to encourage me. I tried to think what else to say. "They're really big," I said. "They're massive. They're built of stone. Marble, too, sometimes. In those olden days, when they built cathedrals, men wanted to be close to God. In those olden days, God was an important part of everyone's life. You could tell this from their cathedral-building. I'm sorry," I said, "but it looks like that's the best I can do for you. I'm just no good at it."

102 "That's all right, bub," the blind man said. "Hey, listen. I hope you don't mind my asking you. Can I ask you something? Let me ask you a simple question, yes or no. I'm just curious and there's no offense. You're my host. But let me ask if you are in any way religious? You don't mind my asking?"

103 I shook my head. He couldn't see that, though. A wink is the same as a nod to a blind man. "I guess I don't believe in it. In anything. Sometimes it's hard. You know what I'm saying?"

104 "Sure, I do," he said.

105 "Right," I said.

106 The Englishman was still holding forth. My wife sighed in her sleep. She drew a long breath and went on with her sleeping.

107 "You'll have to forgive me," I said. "But I can't tell you what a cathedral looks like. It just isn't in me to do it. I can't do any more than I've done."

108 The blind man sat very still, his head down, as he listened to me.

109 I said, "The truth is, cathedrals don't mean anything special to me. Nothing. Cathedrals. They're something to look at on late-night TV. That's all they are."

110 It was then that the blind man cleared his throat. He brought something up. He took a handkerchief from his back pocket. Then he said, "I get it, bub. It's okay. It happens. Don't worry about it," he said. "Hey, listen to me. Will you do me a favor? I got an idea. Why don't you find us some heavy paper? And a pen. We'll do something. We'll draw one together. Get us a pen and some heavy paper. Go on, bub, get the stuff," he said.

111 So I went upstairs. My legs felt like they didn't have any strength in them. They felt like they did after I'd done some running. In my wife's room, I looked around. I found some ballpoints in a little basket on her table. And then I tried to think where to look for the kind of paper he was talking about.

112 Downstairs, in the kitchen, I found a shopping bag with onion skins in the bottom of the bag. I emptied the bag and shook it. I brought it into the living room and sat down with it near his legs. I moved some things, smoothed the wrinkles from the bag, spread it out on the coffee table.

113 The blind man got down from the sofa and sat next to me on the carpet.

114 He ran his fingers over the paper. He went up and down the sides of the paper. The edges, even the edges. He fingered the corners.

115 "All right," he said. "All right, let's do her."

116 He found my hand, the hand with the pen. He closed his hand over my hand. "Go ahead, bub, draw," he said. "Draw. You'll see. I'll follow along with you. It'll be okay. Just begin now like I'm telling you. You'll see. Draw," the blind man said.

117 So I began. First I drew a box that looked like a house. It could have been the house I lived in. Then I put a roof on it. At either end of the roof, I drew spires. Crazy.

118 "Swell," he said. "Terrific. You're doing fine," he said. "Never thought anything like this could happen in your lifetime, did you, bub? Well, it's a strange life, we all know that. Go on now. Keep it up."

119 I put in windows with arches. I drew flying buttresses. I hung great doors. I couldn't stop. The TV station went off the air. I put down the pen and closed and opened my fingers. The blind man felt around over the paper. He moved the tips of his fingers over the paper, all over what I had drawn, and he nodded.

120 "Doing fine," the blind man said.

121 I took up the pen again, and he found my hand. I kept at it. I'm no artist. But I kept drawing just the same.

122 My wife opened up her eyes and gazed as us. She sat up on the sofa, her robe hanging open. She said, "What are you doing? Tell me, I want to know."

123 I didn't answer her. The blind man said, "We're drawing a cathedral. Me and him are working on it. Press hard," he said to me. "That's right. That's good," he said. "Sure. You got it, bub, I can tell. You didn't think you could. But you can, can't you? You're cooking with gas now. You know what I'm saying? We're going to really have us something here in a minute. How's the old arm?" he said. "Put some people in there now. What's a cathedral without people?"

124 My wife said, "What's going on? Robert, what are you doing? What's going on?"

125 "It's all right," he said to her. "Close your eyes now," the blind man said to me.

126 I did it. I closed them just like he said.

127 "Are they closed?" he said. "Don't fudge."

128 "They're closed," I said.

129 "Keep them that way," he said. He said, "Don't stop now. Draw."

130 So we kept on with it. His fingers rode my fingers as my hand went over the paper. It was like nothing else in my life up to now.

131 Then he said, "I think that's it. I think you got it," he said. "Take a look. What do you think?"

132 But I had my eyes closed. I thought I'd keep them that way for a little longer. I thought it was something I ought to do.

133 "Well?" he said. "Are you looking?"

134 My eyes were still closed. I was in my house. I knew that. But I didn't feel like I was inside anything.

135 "It's really something," I said.

—1981

Joyce Carol Oates
(b. 1938)

Where Are You Going, Where Have You Been?

Oates is a prolific writer who has published over sixty books since her first one appeared in 1963, and she shows few signs of slowing her output. Her books—whether novels, collections of stories, or non fiction memoirs on subjects like boxing—always draw serious critical attention and more often than not land on the best-seller lists. She has also written under the pseudonym "Rosamond Smith." Born in Lockport, New York, she holds degrees from Syracuse University and the University of Wisconsin, and she is writer-in-residence at Princeton University, where she also co-directs, with her husband, Ontario Review Press. Oates's work is often violent, a fact for which she has been criticized repeatedly. In response, she has remarked that these comments are "always ignorant, always sexist," implying that different standards are often applied to the work of women authors whose realism may be too strong for some tastes. Few readers would argue that her stories and novels exceed the violence of the society they depict. Her novel *them*, about black people in Detroit, won a National Book Award in 1970, and Oates has since garnered many other honors. "Where Are You Going, Where Have You Been?" is based on a *Life* magazine story about a serial rapist and killer known as "the Pied Piper of Tucson." In 1985 the story was filmed by Joyce Chopra as *Smooth Talk*.

To Bob Dylan

Her name was Connie. She was fifteen and she had a quick nervous giggling habit of craning her neck to glance into mirrors or checking other people's faces to make sure her own was all right. Her mother, who noticed everything and knew everything and who hadn't much reason any longer to look at her own face, always scolded Connie about it. "Stop gawking at yourself, who are you? You think you're so pretty?" she would say. Connie would raise her eyebrows at these familiar complaints and look right through her mother, into a shadowy vision of herself as she was right at that moment: she knew she was pretty and that was everything. Her mother had been pretty once too, if you could believe those old snapshots in the album, but now her looks were gone and that was why she was always after Connie.

2 "Why don't you keep your room clean like your sister? How've you got your hair fixed—what the hell stinks? Hair spray? You don't see your sister using that junk."

3 Her sister June was twenty-four and still lived at home. She was a secretary in the high school Connie attended, and if that wasn't bad enough—with her in the same building—she was so plain and chunky and steady that Connie had to hear her praised all the time by her mother and her mother's sisters. June did this, June did that, she saved money and helped clean the house and cooked and Connie couldn't do a thing, her mind was all filled with trashy daydreams. Their father was away at work most of the time and when he came home he wanted supper and he read the newspaper at supper and after supper he went to bed. He didn't bother talking much to them, but around his bent head Connie's mother kept picking at her until Connie wished her mother was dead and she herself was dead and it was all over. "She makes me want to throw up sometimes," she complained to her friends. She had a high, breathless, amused voice which made everything she said sound a little forced, whether it was sincere or not.

4 There was one good thing: June went places with girlfriends of hers, girls who were just as plain and steady as she, and so when Connie wanted to do that her mother had no objections. The father of Connie's best girlfriend drove the girls the three miles to town and left them off at a shopping plaza, so that they could walk through the stores or go to a movie, and when he came to pick them up again at eleven he never bothered to ask what they had done.

5 They must have been familiar sights, walking around that shopping plaza in their shorts and flat ballerina slippers that always scuffed the sidewalk, with charm bracelets jingling on their thin wrists; they would lean together to whisper and laugh secretly if someone passed by who amused or interested them. Connie had long dark blond hair that drew anyone's eye to it, and she wore part of it pulled up on her head and puffed out and the rest of it she let fall down her back. She wore a pull over jersey blouse that looked one way when she was at home and another way when she was away from home. Everything about her had two sides to it, one for home and one for anywhere that was not home: her walk that could be childlike and bobbing, or languid enough to make anyone think she was hearing music in her head, her mouth which was pale and smirking most of the time, but bright and pink on these evenings out, her laugh which

was cynical and drawling at home—"Ha, ha, very funny"—but high-pitched and nervous anywhere else, like the jingling of the charms on her bracelet.

6 Sometimes they did go shopping or to a movie, but sometimes they went across the highway, ducking fast across the busy road, to a drive-in restaurant where older kids hung out. The restaurant was shaped like a big bottle, though squatter than a real bottle, and on its cap was a revolving figure of a grinning boy who held a hamburger aloft. One night in midsummer they ran across, breathless with daring, and right away someone leaned out a car window and invited them over, but it was just a boy from high school they didn't like. It made them feel good to be able to ignore him. They went up through the maze of parked and cruising cars to the bright-lit, fly-infested restaurant, their faces pleased and expectant as if they were entering a sacred building that loomed out of the night to give them what haven and what blessing they yearned for. They sat at the counter and crossed their legs at the ankles, their thin shoulders rigid with excitement, and listened to the music that made everything so good: the music was always in the background like music at a church service, it was something to depend upon.

7 A boy named Eddie came in to talk with them. He sat backward on his stool, turning himself jerkily around in semicircles and then stopping and turning again, and after a while he asked Connie if she would like something to eat. She said she did and so she tapped her friend's arm on her way out—her friend pulled her face up into a brave droll look—and Connie said she would meet her at eleven, across the way. "I just hate to leave her like that," Connie said earnestly, but the boy said that she wouldn't be alone for long. So they went out to his car and on the way Connie couldn't help but let her eyes wander over the windshields and faces all around her, her face gleaming with a joy that had nothing to do with Eddie or even this place; it might have been the music. She drew her shoulders up and sucked in her breath with the pure pleasure of being alive, and just at that moment she happened to glance at a face just a few feet from hers. It was a boy with shaggy black hair, in a convertible jalopy painted gold. He stared at her and then his lips widened into a grin. Connie slit her eyes at him and turned away, but she couldn't help glancing back and there he was still watching her. He wagged a finger and laughed and said, "Gonna get you, baby," and Connie turned away again without Eddie noticing anything.

8 She spent three hours with him, at the restaurant where they ate hamburgers and drank Cokes in wax cups that were always sweating, and then down an alley a mile or so away, and when he left her off at five to eleven only the movie house was still open at the plaza. Her girlfriend was there, talking with a boy. When Connie came up the two girls smiled at each other and Connie said, "How was the movie?" and the girl said, "You should know." They rode off with the girl's father, sleepy and pleased, and Connie couldn't help but look at the darkened shopping plaza with its big empty parking lot and its signs that

were faded and ghostly now, and over at the drive-in restaurant where cars were still circling tirelessly. She couldn't hear the music at this distance.

9 Next morning June asked her how the movie was and Connie said, "So-so."

10 She and that girl and occasionally another girl went out several times a week that way, and the rest of the time Connie spent around the house—it was summer vacation—getting in her mother's way and thinking, dreaming, about the boys she met. But all the boys fell back and dissolved into a single face that was not even a face, but an idea, a feeling, mixed up with the urgent insistent pounding of the music and the humid night air of July. Connie's mother kept dragging her back to the daylight by finding things for her to do or saying, suddenly, "What's this about the Pettinger girl?"

11 And Connie would say nervously, "Oh, her. That dope." She always drew thick clear lines between herself and such girls, and her mother was simple and kindly enough to believe her. Her mother was so simple, Connie thought, that it was maybe cruel to fool her so much. Her mother went scuffling around the house in old bedroom slippers and complained over the telephone to one sister about the other, then the other called up and the two of them complained about the third one. If June's name was mentioned her mother's tone was approving, and if Connie's name was mentioned it was disapproving. This did not really mean she disliked Connie and actually Connie thought that her mother preferred her to June because she was prettier, but the two of them kept up a pretense of exasperation, a sense that they were tugging and struggling over something of little value to either of them. Sometimes, over coffee, they were almost friends, but something would come up—some vexation that was like a fly buzzing suddenly around their heads—and their faces went hard with contempt.

12 One Sunday Connie got up at eleven—none of them bothered with church—and washed her hair so that it could dry all day long, in the sun. Her parents and sister were going to a barbecue at an aunt's house and Connie said no, she wasn't interested, rolling her eyes to let her mother know just what she thought of it. "Stay home alone then," her mother said sharply. Connie sat out back in a lawn chair and watched them drive away, her father quiet and bald, hunched around so that he could back the car out, her mother with a look that was still angry and not at all softened through the windshield, and in the back seat poor old June all dressed up as if she didn't know what a barbecue was, with all the running yelling kids and the flies. Connie sat with her eyes closed in the sun, dreaming and dazed with the warmth about her as if this were a kind of love, the caresses of love, and her mind slipped over onto thoughts of the boy she had been with the night before and how nice he had been, how sweet it always was, not the way someone like June would suppose but sweet, gentle, the way it was in movies and promised in songs; and when she opened her eyes she hardly

knew where she was, the back yard ran off into weeds and a fence line of trees and behind it the sky was perfectly blue and still. The asbestos "ranch house" that was now three years old startled her—it looked small. She shook her head as if to get awake.

13 It was too hot. She went inside the house and turned on the radio to drown out the quiet. She sat on the edge of her bed, barefoot, and listened for an hour and a half to a program called XYZ Sunday Jamboree, record after record of hard, fast, shrieking songs she sang along with, interspersed by exclamations from "Bobby King": "An' look here you girls at Napoleon's—Son and Charley want you to pay real close attention to this song coming up!"

14 And Connie paid close attention herself, bathed in a glow of slow-pulsed joy that seemed to rise mysteriously out of the music itself and lay languidly about the airless little room, breathed in and breathed out with each gentle rise and fall of her chest.

15 After a while she heard a car coming up the drive. She sat up at once, startled, because it couldn't be her father so soon. The gravel kept crunching all the way in from the road—the driveway was long—and Connie ran to the window. It was a car she didn't know. It was an open jalopy, painted a bright gold that caught the sunlight opaquely. Her heart began to pound and her fingers snatched at her hair, checking it, and she whispered "Christ, Christ," wondering how bad she looked. The car came to a stop at the side door and the horn sounded four short taps as if this were a signal Connie knew.

16 She went into the kitchen and approached the door slowly, then hung out the screen door, her bare toes curling down off the step. There were two boys in the car and now she recognized the driver: he had shaggy, shabby black hair that looked crazy as a wig and he was grinning at her.

17 "I ain't late, am I?" he said.

18 "Who the hell do you think you are?" Connie said.

19 "Toldja I'd be out, didn't I?"

20 "I don't even know who you are."

21 She spoke sullenly, careful to show no interest or pleasure, and he spoke in a fast bright monotone. Connie looked past him to the other boy, taking her time. He had fair brown hair, with a lock that fell onto his forehead. His sideburns gave him a fierce, embarrassed look, but so far he hadn't even bothered to glance at her. Both boys wore sunglasses. The driver's glasses were metallic and mirrored everything in miniature.

22 "You wanta come for a ride?" he said.

23 Connie smirked and let her hair fall loose over one shoulder.

24 "Don'tcha like my car? New paint job," he said. "Hey."

25 "What?"

26 "You're cute."

27 She pretended to fidget, chasing flies away from the door.

28 "Don'tcha believe me, or what?" he said.

29 "Look, I don't even know who you are," Connie said in disgust.

30 "Hey, Ellie's got a radio, see. Mine's broke down." He lifted his friend's arm and showed her the little transistor the boy was holding, and now Connie began to hear the music. It was the same program that was playing inside the house.

31 "Bobby King?" she said.

32 "I listen to him all the time. I think he's great."

33 "He's kind of great," Connie said reluctantly.

34 "Listen, that guy's *great.* He knows where the action is."

35 Connie blushed a little, because the glasses made it impossible for her to see just what this boy was looking at. She couldn't decide if she liked him or if he was just a jerk, and so she dawdled in the doorway and wouldn't come down or go back inside. She said, "What's all that stuff painted on your car?"

36 "Can'tcha read it?" He opened the door very carefully, as if he was afraid it might fall off. He slid out just as carefully, planting his feet firmly on the ground, the tiny metallic world in his glasses slowing down like gelatine hardening and in the midst of it Connie's bright green blouse. "This here is my name, to begin with," he said. ARNOLD FRIEND was written in tarlike black letters on the side, with a drawing of a round grinning face that reminded Connie of a pumpkin, except it wore sunglasses. "I wanta introduce myself, I'm Arnold Friend and that's my real name and I'm gonna be your friend, honey, and inside the car's Ellie Oscar, he's kinda shy." Ellie brought his transistor radio up to his shoulder and balanced it there. "Now these numbers are a secret code, honey," Arnold Friend explained. He read off the numbers 33, 19, 17 and raised his eyebrows at her to see what she thought of that, but she didn't think much of it. The left rear fender had been smashed and around it was written, on the gleaming gold background—DONE BY CRAZY WOMAN DRIVER. Connie had to laugh at that. Arnold Friend was pleased at her laughter and looked up at her. "Around the other side's a lot more—you wanta come and see them?"

37 "No."

38 "Why not?"

39 "Why should I?"

40 "Don'tcha wanta see what's on the car? Don'tcha wanta go for a ride?"

41 "I don't know."

42 "Why not?"

43 "I got things to do."

44 "Like what?"

45 "Things."

46 He laughed as if she had said something funny. He slapped his thighs. He was standing in a strange way, leaning back against the car as if he were balanc-

ing himself. He wasn't tall, only an inch or so taller than she would be if she came down to him. Connie liked the way he was dressed, which was the way all of them dressed: tight faded jeans stuffed into black, scuffed boots, a belt that pulled his waist in and showed how lean he was, and a white pullover shirt that was a little soiled and showed the hard small muscles of his arms and shoulders. He looked as if he probably did hard work, lifting and carrying things. Even his neck looked muscular. And his face was a familiar face, somehow—the jaw and chin and cheeks slightly darkened, because he hadn't shaved for a day or two, and the nose long and hawklike, sniffing as if she were a treat he was going to gobble up and it was all a joke.

47 "Connie, you ain't telling the truth. This is your day set aside for a ride with me and you know it," he said, still laughing. The way he straightened and recovered from his fit of laughing showed that it had been all fake.

48 "How do you know what my name is?" she said suspiciously.

49 "It's Connie."

50 "Maybe and maybe not."

51 "I know my Connie," he said, wagging his finger. Now she remembered him even better, back at the restaurant, and her cheeks warmed at the thought of how she sucked in her breath just at the moment she passed him—how she must have looked to him. And he had remembered her. "Ellie and I come out here especially for you," he said. "Ellie can sit in back. How about it?"

52 "Where?"

53 "Where what?"

54 "Where're we going?"

55 He looked at her. He took off the sunglasses and she saw how pale the skin around his eyes was, like holes that were not in shadow but instead in light. His eyes were like chips of broken glass that catch the light in an amiable way. He smiled. It was as if the idea of going for a ride somewhere, to some place, was a new idea to him.

56 "Just for a ride, Connie sweetheart."

57 "I never said my name was Connie," she said.

58 "But I know what it is. I know your name and all about you, lots of things," Arnold Friend said. He had not moved yet but stood still leaning back against the side of his jalopy. "I took a special interest in you, such a pretty girl, and found out all about you like I know your parents and sister are gone somewheres and I know where and how long they're going to be gone, and I know who you were with last night, and your best girlfriend's name is Betty. Right?"

59 He spoke in a simple lilting voice, exactly as if he were reciting the words to a song. His smile assured her that everything was fine. In the car Ellie turned up the volume on his radio and did not bother to look around at them.

60 "Ellie can sit in the back seat," Arnold Friend said. He indicated his friend with a casual jerk of his chin, as if Ellie did not count and she should not bother with him.

61 "How'd you find out all that stuff?" Connie said.

62 "Listen: Betty Schultz and Tony Fitch and Jimmy Pettinger and Nancy Pettinger," he said, in a chant. "Raymond Stanley and Bob Hutter—"

63 "Do you know all those kids?"

64 "I know everybody."

65 "Look, you're kidding. You're not from around here."

66 "Sure ."

67 "But—how come we never saw you before?"

68 "Sure you saw me before," he said. He looked down at his boots, as if he were a little offended. "You just don't remember."

69 "I guess I'd remember you," Connie said.

70 "Yeah?" He looked up at this, beaming. He was pleased. He began to mark time with the music from Ellie's radio, tapping his fists lightly together. Connie looked away from his smile to the car, which was painted so bright it almost hurt her eyes to look at it. She looked at that name, ARNOLD FRIEND. And up at the front fender was an expression that was familiar—MAN THE FLYING SAUCERS. It was an expression kids had used the year before, but didn't use this year. She looked at if for a while as if the words meant something to her that she did not yet know.

71 "What're you thinking about? Huh?" Arnold Friend demanded. "Not worried about your hair blowing around in the car, are you?"

72 "No."

73 "Think I maybe can't drive good?"

74 "How do I know?"

75 "You're a hard girl to handle. How come?" he said. "Don't you know I'm your friend? Didn't you see me put my sign in the air when you walked by?"

76 "What sign?"

77 "My sign." And he drew an X in the air, leaning out toward her. They were maybe ten feet apart. After his hand fell back to his side the X was still in the air, almost visible. Connie let the screen door close and stood perfectly still inside it, listening to the music from her radio and the boy's blend together. She stared at Arnold Friend. He stood there so stiffly relaxed, pretending to be relaxed, with one hand idly on the door handle as if he were keeping himself up that way and had no intention of ever moving again. She recognized most things about him, the tight jeans that showed his thighs and buttocks and the greasy leather boots and the tight shirt, and even that slippery friendly smile of his, that sleepy dreamy smile that all the boys used to get across ideas they didn't want to put into words. She recognized all this and also the singsong way he talked, slightly mocking, kidding, but serious and a little melancholy, and she

recognized the way he tapped one fist against the other in homage to the perpetual music behind him. But all these things did not come together.

78 She said suddenly, "Hey, how old are you?"

79 His smile faded. She could see then that he wasn't a kid, he was much older—thirty, maybe more. At this knowledge her heart began to pound faster.

80 "That's a crazy thing to ask. Can'tcha see I'm your own age?"

81 "Like hell you are."

82 "Or maybe a coupla years older, I'm eighteen."

83 "Eighteen?" she said doubtfully.

84 He grinned to reassure her and lines appeared at the corners of his mouth. His teeth were big and white. He grinned so broadly his eyes became slits and she saw how thick the lashes were, thick and black as if painted with a black tar-like material. Then he seemed to become embarrassed, abruptly, and looked over his shoulder at Ellie. *"Him,* he's crazy," he said. "Ain't he a riot, he's a nut, a real character." Ellie was still listening to the music. His sunglasses told nothing about what he was thinking. He wore a bright orange shirt unbuttoned halfway to show his chest, which was a pale, bluish chest and not muscular like Arnold Friend's. His shirt collar was turned up all around and the very tips of the collar pointed out past his chin as if they were protecting him. He was pressing the transistor radio up against his ear and sat there in a kind of daze, right in the sun.

85 "He's kinda strange," Connie said.

86 "Hey, she says you're kinda strange! Kinda strange!" Arnold Friend cried. He pounded on the car to get Ellie's attention. Ellie turned for the first time and Connie saw with shock that he wasn't a kid either—he had a fair, hairless face, cheeks reddened slightly as if the veins grew too close to the surface of his skin, the face of a forty-year-old baby. Connie felt a wave of dizziness rise in her at this sight and she stared at him as if waiting for something to change the shock of the moment, make it all right again. Ellie's lips kept shaping words, mumbling along, with the words blasting in his ear.

87 "Maybe you two better go away," Connie said faintly.

88 "What? How come?" Arnold Friend cried. "We come out here to take you for a ride. It's Sunday." He had the voice of the man on the radio now. It was the same voice, Connie thought. "Don'tcha know it's Sunday all day and honey, no matter who you were with last night today you're with Arnold Friend and don't you forget it!—Maybe you better step out here," he said, and this last was in a different voice. It was a little flatter, as if the heat was finally getting to him.

89 "No. I got things to do."

90 "Hey."

91 "You two better leave."

92 "We ain't leaving until you come with us."

93 "Like hell I am—"

94 "Connie, don't fool around with me. I mean, I mean, don't fool *around,*" he said, shaking his head. He laughed incredulously. He placed his sunglasses on top of his head, carefully, as if he were indeed wearing a wig, and brought the stems down behind his ears. Connie stared at him, another wave of dizziness and fear rising in her so that for a moment he wasn't even in focus but was just a blur, standing there against his gold car, and she had the idea that he had driven up the driveway all right but had come from nowhere before that and belonged nowhere and that everything about him and even about the music that was so familiar to her was only half real.

95 "If my father comes and sees you—"

96 "He ain't coming. He's at barbecue."

97 "How do you know that?"

98 "Aunt Tillie's. Right now they're—uh—they're drinking. Sitting around," he said vaguely, squinting as if he were staring all the way to town and over to Aunt Tillie's back yard. Then the vision seemed to get clear and he nodded energetically. "Yeah. Sitting around. There's your sister in a blue dress, huh? And high heels, the poor sad bitch—nothing like you, sweetheart! And your mother's helping some fat woman with the corn, they're cleaning the corn—husking the corn—"

99 "What fat woman?" Connie cried.

100 "How do I know what fat woman. I don't know every goddam fat woman in the world!" Arnold Friend laughed.

101 "Oh, that's Mrs. Hornby . . . Who invited her?" Connie said. She felt a little light-headed. Her breath was coming quickly.

102 "She's too fat. I don't like them fat. I like them the way you are, honey," he said, smiling sleepily at her. They stared at each other for a while, through the screen door. He said softly, "Now what you're going to do is this: you're going to come out that door. You're going to sit up front with me and Ellie's going to sit in the back, the hell with Ellie, right? This isn't Ellie's date. You're my date. I'm your lover, honey."

103 "What? You're crazy—"

104 "Yes, I'm your lover. You don't know what that is but you will," he said. "I know that too. I know all about you. But look: it's real nice and you couldn't ask for nobody better than me, or more polite. I always keep my word. I'll tell you how it is, I'm always nice at first, the first time. I'll hold you so tight you won't think you have to try to get away or pretend anything because you'll know you can't. And I'll come inside you where it's all secret and you'll give in to me and you'll love me—"

105 "Shut up! You're crazy!" Connie said. She backed away from the door. She put her hands against her ears as if she'd heard something terrible, something not meant for her. "People don't talk like that, you're crazy," she muttered. Her heart was almost too big now for her chest and its pumping made sweat break

out all over her. She looked out to see Arnold Friend pause and then take a step toward the porch lurching. He almost fell. But, like a clever drunken man, he managed to catch his balance. He wobbled in his high boots and grabbed hold of one of the porch posts.

106 "Honey?" he said. "You still listening?"

107 "Get the hell out of here!"

108 "Be nice, honey. Listen."

109 "I'm going to call the police—"

110 He wobbled again and out of the side of his mouth came a fast spat curse, an aside not meant for her to hear. But even this "Christ!" sounded forced. Then he began to smile again. She watched this smile come, awkward as if he were smiling from inside a mask. His whole face was a mask, she thought wildly, tanned down onto his throat but then running out as if he had plastered makeup on his face but had forgotten about his throat.

111 "Honey—? Listen, here's how it is. I always tell the truth and I promise you this: I ain't coming in that house after you."

112 "You better not! I'm going to call the police if you—if you don't—"

113 "Honey," he said, talking right through her voice, "honey, I'm not coming in there but you are coming out here. You know why?"

114 She was panting. The kitchen looked like a place she had never seen before, some room she had run inside but which wasn't good enough, wasn't going to help her. The kitchen window had never had a curtain, after three years, and there were dishes in the sink for her to do—probably—and if you ran your hand across the table you'd probably feel something sticky there.

115 "You listening, honey? Hey?"

116 "—going to call the police—"

117 "Soon as you touch the phone I don't need to keep my promise and can come inside. You won't want that."

118 She rushed forward and tried to lock the door. Her fingers were shaking. "But why lock it," Arnold Friend said gently, talking right into her face. "It's just a screen door. It's just nothing." One of his boots was at a strange angle, as if his foot wasn't in it. It pointed out to the left, bent at the ankle. "I mean, anybody can break through a screen door and glass and wood and iron or anything else if he needs to, anybody at all and specially Arnold Friend. If the place got lit up with a fire honey you'd come runnin' out into my arms, right into my arms an' safe at home—like you knew I was your lover and'd stopped fooling around. I don't mind a nice shy girl but I don't like no fooling around." Part of those words were spoken with a slight rhythmic lilt, and Connie somehow recognized them—the echo of a song from last year, about a girl rushing into her boyfriend's arms and coming home again—

119 Connie stood barefoot on the linoleum floor, staring at him. "What do you want?" she whispered.

120 "I want you," he said.

121 "What?"

122 "Seen you that night and thought, that's the one, yes sir. I never needed to look any more."

123 "But my father's coming back. He's coming to get me. I had to wash my hair first—" She spoke in a dry, rapid voice, hardly raising it for him to hear.

124 "No, your Daddy is not coming and yes, you had to wash your hair and you washed it for me. It's nice and shining and all for me, I thank you, sweetheart," he said, with a mock bow, but again he almost lost his balance. He had to bend and adjust his boots. Evidently his feet did not go all the way down; the boots must have been stuffed with something so that he would seem taller. Connie stared out at him and behind him Ellie in the car, who seemed to be looking off toward Connie's right into nothing. This Ellie said, pulling the words out of the air one after another as if he were just discovering them, "You want me to pull out the phone?"

125 "Shut your mouth and keep it shut," Arnold Friend said, his face red from bending over or maybe from embarrassment because Connie had seen his boots. "This ain't none of your business."

126 "What—what are you doing? What do you want?" Connie said. "If I call the police they'll get you, they'll arrest you—"

127 "Promise was not to come in unless you touch that phone, and I'll keep that promise," he said. He resumed his erect position and tried to force his shoulders back. He sounded like a hero in a movie, declaring something important. He spoke too loudly and it was as if he were speaking to someone behind Connie. "I ain't made plans for coming in that house where I don't belong but just for you to come out to me, the way you should. Don't you know who I am?"

128 "You're crazy," she whispered. She backed away from the door but did not want to go into another part of the house, as if this would give him permission to come through the door. "What do you . . . You're crazy, you . . . "

129 "Huh? What're you saying, honey?"

130 Her eyes darted everywhere in the kitchen. She could not remember what it was, this room.

131 "This is how it is, honey: you come out and we'll drive away, have a nice ride. But if you don't come out we're gonna wait till your people come home and then they're all going to get it."

132 "You want that telephone pulled out?" Ellie said. He held the radio away from his ear and grimaced, as if without the radio the air was too much for him.

133 "I toldja shut up, Ellie," Arnold Friend said, "you're deaf, get a hearing aid, right? Fix yourself up. This little girl's no trouble and's gonna be nice to me, so Ellie keep to yourself, this ain't your date—right? Don't hem in on me.

Don't hog. Don't crush. Don't bird dog. Don't trail me," he said in a rapid meaningless voice, as if he were running through all the expressions he'd learned but was no longer sure which one of them was in style, then rushing on to new ones, making them up with his eyes closed, "Don't crawl under my fence, don't squeeze in my chipmunk hole, don't sniff my glue, suck my popsicle, keep your own greasy fingers on yourself!" He shaded his eyes and peered in at Connie, who was backed against the kitchen table. "Don't mind him honey he's just a creep. He's a dope. Right? I'm the boy for you and like I said you come out here nice like a lady and give me your hand, and nobody else gets hurt, I mean, your nice old bald-headed daddy and your mummy and your sister in her high heels. Because listen: why bring them in this?"

134 "Leave me alone," Connie whispered.

135 "Hey, you know that old woman down the road, the one with the chickens and stuff—you know her?"

136 "She's dead!"

137 "Dead? What? You know her?" Arnold Friend said.

138 "She's dead—"

139 "Don't you like her?"

140 "She's dead—she's—she isn't here any more—"

141 "But don't you like her, I mean, you got something against her? Some grudge or something?" Then his voice dipped as if he were conscious of a rudeness. He touched the sunglasses perched on top of his head as if to make sure they were still there. "Now you be a good girl."

142 "What are you going to do?"

143 "Just two things, or maybe three," Arnold Friend said. "But I promise it won't last long and you'll like me the way you get to like people you're close to. You will. It's all over for you here, so come on out. You don't want your people in any trouble, do you?"

144 She turned and bumped against a chair or something, hurting her leg, but she ran into the back room and picked up the telephone. Something roared in her ear, a tiny roaring, and she was so sick with fear that she could do nothing but listen to it—the telephone was clammy and very heavy and her fingers groped down to the dial but were too weak to touch it. She began to scream into the phone, into the roaring. She cried out, she cried for her mother, she felt her breath start jerking back and forth in her lungs as if it were something Arnold Friend were stabbing her with again and again with no tenderness. A noisy sorrowful wailing rose all about her and she was locked inside it the way she was locked inside the house.

145 After a while she could hear again. She was sitting on the floor with her wet back against the wall.

146 Arnold Friend was saying from the door, "That's a good girl. Put the phone back."

147 She kicked the phone away from her.

148 "No, honey. Pick it up. Put it back right."

149 She picked it up and put it back. The dial tone stopped.

150 "That's a good girl. Now come outside."

151 She was hollow with what had been fear, but what was now just an emptiness. All that screaming had blasted it out of her. She sat, one leg cramped under her, and deep inside her brain was something like a pinpoint of light that kept going and would not let her relax. She thought, I'm not going to see my mother again. She thought, I'm not going to sleep in my bed again. Her bright green blouse was all wet.

152 Arnold Friend said, in a gentle-loud voice that was like a stage voice, "The place where you came from ain't there any more, and where you had in mind to go is canceled out. This place you are now—inside your daddy's house—is nothing but a cardboard box I can knock down any time. You know that and always did know it. You hear me?"

153 She thought, I have got to think. I have to know what to do.

154 "We'll go out to a nice field, out in the country here where it smells so nice and it's sunny," Arnold Friend said. "I'll have my arms tight around you so you won't need to try to get away and I'll show you what love is like, what it does. The hell with this house! It looks solid all right," he said. He ran a fingernail down the screen and the noise did not make Connie shiver, as it would have the day before. "Now put your hand on your heart, honey. Feel that? That feels solid too but we know better, be nice to me, be sweet like you can because what else is there for a girl like you but to be sweet and pretty and give in?—and get away before her people come back?"

155 She felt her pounding heart. Her hand seemed to enclose it. She thought for the first time in her life that it was nothing that was hers, that belonged to her, but just a pounding, living thing inside this body that wasn't really hers either.

156 "You don't want them to get hurt," Arnold Friend went on. "Now get up, honey. Get up all by yourself."

157 She stood up.

158 "Now turn this way. That's right. Come over here to me—Ellie, put that away, didn't I tell you? You dope. You miserable creepy dope," Arnold Friend said. His words were not angry but only part of an incantation. The incantation was kindly. "Now come out through the kitchen to me honey, and let's see a smile, try it, you're a brave sweet little girl and now they're eating corn and hot dogs cooked to bursting over an outdoor fire, and they don't know one thing about you and never did and honey you're better than them because not a one of them would have done this for you."

159 Connie felt the linoleum under her feet; it was cool. She brushed her hair back out of her eyes. Arnold Friend let go of the post tentatively and opened his

arms for her, his elbows pointing in toward each other and his wrists limp, to show that this was an embarrassed embrace and a little mocking, he didn't want to make her self-conscious.

160 She put out her hand against the screen. She watched herself push the door slowly open as if she were safe back somewhere in the other doorway, watching this body and this head of long hair moving out into the sunlight where Arnold Friend waited.

161 "My sweet little blue-eyed girl," he said, in a half-sung sigh that had nothing to do with her brown eyes but was taken up just the same by the vast sunlit reaches of the land behind him and on all sides of him, so much land that Connie had never seen before and did not recognize except to know that she was going to it.

—1966

Margaret Atwood
(b. 1939)

Rape Fantasies

Atwood is a leading figure among Canadian writers; she is as skilled a poet as she is a fiction writer. She is also an internationally known feminist spokesperson, widely in demand for appearances on symposia on women's issues. Atwood was named by *Ms.* magazine as Woman of the Year for 1986. Born in Ottawa, Ontario, she graduated from the University of Toronto in 1962, the same year that her first book appeared, and later did graduate work at Radcliffe and Harvard. She has published two volumes of selected poems, over a dozen novels and collections of short stories, and a book of literary criticism. In addition she served as editor of two anthologies of Canadian literature and has served as writer-in-residence at universities in Canada, the United States, and abroad. *The Handmaid's Tale* (1985), a work that presents a future dystopia controlled by a fundamentalist patriarchy, was a best seller and was filmed in 1990. "Rape Fantasies," with its underlying theme of the trivialization of sexual violence in a mass-media culture, embodies many of the issues touched on in contemporary women's studies.

The way they're going on about it in the magazines you'd think it was just invented, and not only that but it's something terrific, like a vaccine for cancer. They put it in capital letters on the front cover, and inside they have these questionnaires like the ones they used to have about whether you were a good enough wife or an endomorph or an ectomorph, remember that? with the scoring upside down on page 73, and then these numbered do-it-yourself dealies, you know? RAPE, TEN THINGS TO DO ABOUT IT, like it was ten new hairdos or something. I mean, what's so new about it?

2 So at work they all have to talk about it because no matter what magazine you open, there it is, staring you right between the eyes, and they're beginning to have it on the television, too. Personally I'd prefer a June Allyson movie anytime but they don't make them anymore and they don't even have them that much on the Late Show. For instance, day before yesterday, that would be Wednesday, thank god it's Friday as they say, we were sitting around in the women's lunch room—the *lunch* room, I mean you'd think you could get some peace and quiet in there—and Chrissy closes up the magazine she's been reading and says, "How about it, girls, do you have rape fantasies?"

3 The four of us were having our game of bridge the way we always do, and I had a bare twelve points counting the singleton with not that much of a bid in anything. So I said one club, hoping Sondra would remember about the one club convention, because the time before when I used that she thought I really meant clubs and she bid us up to three, and all I had was four little ones with nothing higher than a six, and we went down two and on top of that we were vulnerable. She is not the world's best bridge player. I mean, neither am I but there's a limit.

4 Darlene passed but the damage was done, Sondra's head went round like it was on ball bearings and she said, "*What* fantasies?"

5 "Rape fantasies," Chrissy said. She's a receptionist and she looks like one; she's pretty but cool as a cucumber, like she's been painted all over with nail polish, if you know what I mean. Varnished. "It says here all women have rape fantasies."

6 "For Chrissake, I'm eating an egg sandwich," I said, "and I bid one club and Darlene passed."

7 "You mean, like some guy jumping you in an alley or something," Sondra said. She was eating her lunch, we all eat our lunches during the game, and she bit into a piece of that celery she always brings and started to chew away on it with this thoughtful expression in her eyes and I knew we might as well pack it in as far as the game was concerned.

8 "Yeah, sort of like that," Chrissy said. She was blushing a little, you could see it even under her makeup.

9 "I don't think you should go out alone at night," Darlene said, "you put yourself in a position," and I may have been mistaken but she was looking at me.

She's the oldest, she's forty-one though you wouldn't know it and neither does she, but I looked it up in the employees' file. I like to guess a person's age and then look it up to see if I'm right. I let myself have an extra pack of cigarettes if I am, though I'm trying to cut down. I figure it's harmless as long as you don't tell. I mean, not everyone has access to that file, it's more or less confidential. But it's all right if I tell you, I don't expect you'll ever meet her, though you never know, it's a small world. Anyway.

10 "For *heaven's* sake, it's only *Toronto,*" Greta said. She worked in Detroit for three years and she never lets you forget it, it's like she thinks she's a war hero or something, we should all admire her just for the fact that she's still walking this earth, though she was really living in Windsor the whole time, she just worked in Detroit. Which for me doesn't really count. It's where you sleep, right?

11 "Well, do you?" Chrissy said. She was obviously trying to tell us about hers but she wasn't about to go first, she's cautious, that one.

12 "I certainly don't," Darlene said, and she wrinkled up her nose, like this, and I had to laugh. "I think it's disgusting." She's divorced, I read that in the file too, she never talks about it. It must've been years ago anyway. She got up and went over to the coffee machine and turned her back on us as though she wasn't going to have anything more to do with it.

13 "Well," Greta said. I could see it was going to be between her and Chrissy. They're both blondes, I don't mean that in a bitchy way but they do try to outdress each other. Greta would like to get out of Filing, she'd like to be a receptionist too so she could meet more people. You don't meet much of anyone in Filing except other people in Filing. Me, I don't mind it so much, I have outside interests.

14 "Well," Greta said, "I sometimes think about, you know my apartment? It's got this little balcony, I like to sit out there in the summer and I have a few plants out there. I never bother that much about locking the door to the balcony, it's one of those sliding glass ones, I'm on the eighteenth floor for heaven's sake, I've got a good view of the lake and the CN Tower and all. But I'm sitting around one night in my housecoat, watching TV with my shoes off, you know how you do, and I see this guy's feet,, coming down past the window, and the next thing you know he's standing on the balcony, he's let himself down by a rope with a hook on the end of it from the floor above, that's the nineteenth, and before I can even get up off the chesterfield he's inside the apartment. He's all dressed in black with black gloves on"—I knew right away what show she got the black gloves off because I saw the same one—"and then he, well, you know."

15 "You know what?" Chrissy said, but Greta said, "And afterwards he tells me that he goes all over the outside of the apartment building like that, from one floor to another, with his rope and his hook . . . and then he goes out to the balcony and tosses his rope, and he climbs up it and disappears."

16 "Just like Tarzan," I said, but nobody laughed.

17 "Is that all?" Chrissy said. "Don't you ever think about, well, I think about being in the bathtub, with no clothes on . . . "

18 "So, who takes a bath in their clothes?" I said, you have to admit it's stupid when you come to think of it, but she just went on, " . . . with lots of bubbles, what I use is Vitabath, it's more expensive but it's so relaxing, and my hair pinned up, and the door opens and this fellow's standing there . . . "

19 "How'd he get in?" Greta said.

20 "Oh, I don't know, through a window or something. Well, I can't very well get out of the bathtub, the bathroom's too small and besides he's blocking the doorway, so I just lie there, and he starts to very slowly take his own clothes off, and then he gets into the bathtub with me."

21 "Don't you scream or anything?" said Darlene. She'd come back with her cup of coffee, she was getting really interested. "I'd scream like bloody murder."

22 "Who'd hear me?" Chrissy said. "Besides, all the articles say it's better not to resist, that way you don't get hurt."

23 "Anyway you might get bubbles up your nose," I said, "from the deep breathing," and I swear all four of them looked at me like I was in bad taste, like I'd insulted the Virgin Mary or something. I mean, I don't see what's wrong with a little joke now and then. Life's too short, right?"

24 "Listen," I said, "those aren't *rape* fantasies. I mean, you aren't getting *raped*, it's just some guy you haven't met formally who happens to be more attractive than Derek Cummins"—he's the Assistant Manager, he wears elevator shoes or at any rate they have these thick soles and he has this funny way of talking, we call him Derek Duck—"and you have a good time. Rape is when they've got a knife or something and you don't want to."

25 "So what about you, Estelle," Chrissy said, she was miffed because I laughed at her fantasy, she thought I was putting her down. Sondra was miffed too, by this time she'd finished her celery and she wanted to tell about hers, but she hadn't got in fast enough.

26 "All right, let me tell you one," I said. "I'm walking down this dark street at night and this fellow comes up and grabs my arm. Now it so happens that I have a plastic lemon in my purse, you know how it always says you should carry a plastic lemon in your purse? I don't really do it, I tried it once but the darn thing leaked all over my checkbook, but in this fantasy I have one, and I say to him, 'You're intending to rape me, right?' and he nods, so I open my purse to get the plastic lemon, and I can't find it! My purse is full of all this junk, Kleenex and cigarettes and my change purse and my lipstick and my driver's license, you know the kind of stuff; so I ask him to hold out his hands, like this, and I pile all this junk into them and down at the bottom there's the plastic lemon, and I

can't get the top off. So I hand it to him and he's very obliging, he twists the top off and hands it back to me, and I squirt him in the eye."

27 I hope you don't think that's too vicious. Come to think of it, it is a bit mean, especially when he was so polite and all.

28 *"That's* your rape fantasy?" Chrissy says. "I don't believe it."

29 "She's a card," Darlene says, she and I are the ones that've been here the longest and she never will forget the time I got drunk at the office party and insisted I was going to dance under the table instead of on top of it, I did a sort of Cossack number but then I hit my head on the bottom of the table—actually it was a desk—when I went to get up, and I knocked myself out cold. She's decided that's the mark of an original mind and she tells everyone new about it and I'm not sure that's fair. Though I did do it.

30 "I'm being totally honest," I say. I always am and they know it. There's no point in being anything else, is the way I look at it, and sooner or later the truth will come out so you might as well not waste the time, right? "You should hear the one about the Easy-Off Oven Cleaner."

31 But that was the end of the lunch hour, with one bridge game shot to hell, and the next day we spent most of the time arguing over whether to start a new game or play out the hands we had left over from the day before, so Sondra never did get a chance to tell about her rape fantasy.

32 It started me thinking though, about my own rape fantasies. Maybe I'm abnormal or something, I mean I have fantasies about handsome strangers coming in through the window too, like Mr. Clean, I wish one would, please god somebody without flat feet and big sweat marks on his shirt, and over five feet five, believe me being tall is a handicap though it's getting better, tall guys are starting to like someone whose nose reaches higher than their belly button. But if you're being totally honest you can't count those as rape fantasies. In a real rape fantasy, what you should feel is this anxiety, like when you think about your apartment building catching on fire and whether you should use the elevator or the stairs or maybe just stick your head under a wet towel, and you try to remember everything you've read about what to do but you can't decide.

33 For instance, I'm walking along this dark street at night and this short, ugly fellow comes up and grabs my arm, and not only is he ugly, you know, with a sort of puffy nothing face, like those fellows you have to talk to in the bank when your account's overdrawn—of course I don't mean they're all like that—but he's absolutely covered in pimples. So he gets me pinned against the wall, he's short but he's heavy, and he starts to undo himself and the zipper gets stuck. I mean, one of the most significant moments in a girl's life, it's almost like getting married or having a baby or something, and he sticks the zipper.

34 So I say, kind of disgusted, "Oh for Chrissake," and he starts to cry. He tells me he's never been able to get anything right in his entire life, and this is the last straw, he's going to jump off a bridge.

35 "Look," I say, I feel so sorry for him, in my rape fantasies I always end up feeling sorry for the guy, I mean there has to be something *wrong* with them, if it was Clint Eastwood it'd be different but worse luck it never is. I was the kind of little girl who buried dead robins, know what I mean? It used to drive my mother nuts, she didn't like me touching them, because of the germs I guess. So I say, "Listen, I know how you feel. You really should do something about those pimples, if you got rid of them you'd be quite good looking, honest; then you wouldn't have to go around doing stuff like this. I had them myself once," I say, to comfort him, but in fact I did, and it ends up I give him the name of my old dermatologist, the one I had in high school, that was back in Leamington, except I used to go to St. Catharine's for the dermatologist. I'm telling you, I was really lonely when I first came here; I thought it was going to be such a big adventure and all, but it's a lot harder to meet people in a city. But I guess it's different for a guy.

36 Or I'm lying in bed with this terrible cold, my face is all swollen up, my eyes are red and my nose is dripping like a leaky tap, and this fellow comes in through the window and *he* has a terrible cold too, it's a new kind of flu that's been going around. So he says, "I'b goig do rabe you"—I hope you don't mind me holding my nose like this but that's the way I imagine it—and he lets out this terrific sneeze, which slows him down a bit, also I'm no object of beauty myself, you'd have to be some kind of pervert to want to rape someone with a cold like mine, it'd be like raping a bottle of LePages mucilage the way my nose is running. He's looking wildly around the room, and I realize it's because he doesn't have a piece of Kleenex! "Id's ride here," I say, and I pass him the Kleenex, god knows why he even bothered to get out of bed, you'd think if you were going to go around climbing in windows you'd wait till you were healthier, right? I mean, that takes a certain amount of energy. So I ask him why doesn't he let me fix him a Neo-Citran and scotch, that's what I always take, you still have the cold but you don't feel it, so I do and we end up watching the Late Show together. I mean, they aren't all sex maniacs, the rest of the time they must lead a normal life. I figure they enjoy watching the Late Show just like anybody else.

37 I do have a scarier one though . . . where the fellow says he's hearing angel voices that're telling him he's got to kill me, you know, you read about things like that all the time in the papers. In this one I'm not in the apartment where I live now, I'm back in my mother's house in Leamington and the fellow's been hiding in the cellar, he grabs my arm when I go downstairs to get a jar of jam and he's got hold of the axe too, out of the garage, that one is really scary. I mean, what do you say to a nut like that?

38 So I start to shake but after a minute I get control of myself and I say, is he sure the angel voices have got the right person, because I hear the same angel voices and they've been telling me for some time that I'm going to give birth to

the reincarnation of St. Anne who in turn has the Virgin Mary and right after that comes Jesus Christ and the end of the world, and he wouldn't want to interfere with that, would he? So he gets confused and listens some more, and then he asks for a sign and I show him my vaccination mark, you can see it's sort of an odd-shaped one, it got infected because I scratched the top off and that does it, he apologizes and climbs out the coal chute again, which is how he got in in the first place, and I say to myself there's some advantage in having been brought up a Catholic even though I haven't been to church since they changed the service into English, it just isn't the same, you might as well be a Protestant. I must write to Mother and tell her to nail up that coal chute, it always has bothered me. Funny, I couldn't tell you at all what this man looks like but I know exactly what kind of shoes he's wearing, because that's the last I see of him, his shoes going up the coal chute, and they're the old-fashioned kind that lace up the ankles, even though he's a young fellow. That's strange, isn't it?

39 Let me tell you though I really sweat until I see him safely out of there and I go upstairs right away and make myself a cup of tea. I don't think about that one much. My mother always said you shouldn't dwell on unpleasant things and I generally agree with that, I mean, dwelling on them doesn't make them go away. Though not dwelling on them doesn't make them go away either, when you come to think of it.

40 Sometimes I have these short ones where the fellow grabs my arm but I'm really a Kung-Fu expert, can you believe it, in real life I'm sure it would just be a conk on the head and that's that, like getting your tonsils out, you'd wake up and it would be all over except for the sore places, and you'd be lucky if your neck wasn't broken or something, I could never even hit the volleyball in gym and a volleyball is fairly large, you know?—and I just go *zap* with my fingers into his eyes and that's it, he falls over, or I flip him against a wall or something. But I could never really stick my fingers in anyone's eyes, could you? It would feel like hot jello and I don't even like cold jello, just thinking about it gives me the creeps. I feel a bit guilty about that one, I mean how would you like walking around knowing someone's been blinded for life because of you?

41 But maybe it's different for a guy.

42 The most touching one I have is when the fellow grabs my arm and I say, sad and kind of dignified, "You'd be raping a corpse." That pulls him up short and I explain that I've just found out I have leukemia and the doctors have only given me a few months to live. That's why I'm out pacing the streets alone at night, I need to think, you know, come to terms with myself. I don't really have leukemia but in the fantasy I do, I guess I chose that particular disease because a girl in my grade four class died of it, the whole class sent her flowers when she was in the hospital. I didn't understand then that she was going to die and I wanted to have leukemia too so I could get flowers. Kids are funny, aren't they? Well, it turns out that he has leukemia himself, and *he* only has a few months to

live, that's why he's going around raping people, he's very bitter because he's so young and his life is being taken from him before he's really lived it. So we walk along gently under the street lights, it's spring and sort of misty, and we end up going for coffee, we're happy we've found the only other person in the world who can understand what we're going through, it's almost like fate, and after a while we just sort of look at each other and our hands touch, and he comes back with me and moves into my apartment and we spend our last months together before we die, we just sort of don't wake up in the morning, though I've never decided which one of us gets to die first. If it's him I have to go on and fantasize about the funeral, if it's me I don't have to worry about that, so it just about depends on how tired I am at the time. You may not believe this but sometimes I even start crying. I cry at the ends of movies, even the ones that aren't all that sad, so I guess it's the same thing. My mother's like that too.

43 The funny thing about these fantasies is that the man is always someone I don't know, and the statistics in the magazines, well, most of them anyway, they say it's often someone you do know, at least a little bit, like your boss or something—I mean, it wouldn't be *my* boss, he's over sixty and I'm sure he couldn't rape his way out of a paper bag, poor old thing, but it might be someone like Derek Duck, in his elevator shoes, perish the thought—or someone you just met, who invites you up for a drink, it's getting so you can hardly be sociable anymore, and how are you supposed to meet people if you can't trust them even that basic amount? You can't spend your whole life in the Filing Department or cooped up in your own apartment with all the doors and windows locked and the shades down. I'm not what you would call a drinker but I like to go out now and then for a drink or two in a nice place, even if I am by myself, I'm with Women's Lib on that even though I can't agree with a lot of other things they say. Like here for instance, the waiters all know me and if anyone, you know, bothers me . . . I don't know why I'm telling you all this, except I think it helps you get to know a person, especially at first, hearing some of the things they think about. At work they call me the office worry wart, but it isn't so much like worrying, it's more like figuring out what you should do in an emergency, like I said before.

44 Anyway, another thing about it is that there's a lot of conversation, in fact I spend most of my time, in the fantasy that is, wondering what I'm going to say and what he's going to say, I think it would be better if you could get a conversation going. Like, how could a fellow do that to a person he's just had a long conversation with, once you let them know you're human, you have a life too, I don't see how they could go ahead with it, right? I mean, I know it happens but I just don't understand it, that's the part I really don't understand.

—1975

Bobbie Ann Mason

(b. 1940)

Shiloh

Mason was born in Mayfield, Kentucky, and grew up on a dairy farm run by her parents. The rural background of her youth figures in many of her best stories, though one of Mason's favorite subjects is the assimilation of the countryside and the South into a larger American culture. Mason's characters may dream of living in log cabins, but they also take adult education courses, watch *Donahue*, and shop in supermarkets and malls. After taking degrees from the University of Kentucky and the University of Connecticut, she published her first two books, both works of literary criticism, in the mid 1970s. One of them, *The Girl Sleuth*, was a feminist guide to the exploits of the fictional detectives like Nancy Drew that Mason read as a child. After years of attempts, Mason's stories began to appear in prestigious magazines, most prominently the *New Yorker*, and the publication of *Shiloh and Other Stories* (1982) established her as an important new voice in American fiction. She has since published a second collection of short stories and two novels, one of which, *In Country* (1985), was filmed in 1989. "Shiloh," like several of the stories in the collection from which it is taken, gains considerable immediacy from Mason's use of present tense and her sure sense of regional speech patterns.

Leroy Moffitt's wife, Norma Jean, is working on her pectorals. She lifts three-pound dumbbells to warm up, then progresses to a twenty-pound barbell. Standing with her legs apart, she reminds Leroy of Wonder Woman.

2 "I'd give anything if I could just get these muscles to where they're real hard," says Norma Jean. "Feel this arm. It's not as hard as the other one."

3 "That's 'cause you're right-handed," says Leroy, dodging as she swings the barbell in an arc.

4 "Do you think so?"

5 "Sure."

6 Leroy is a truckdriver. He injured his leg in a highway accident four months ago, and his physical therapy which involves weights and a pulley, prompted Norma Jean to try building herself up. Now she is attending a body-building class. Leroy has been collecting temporary disability since his tractor-trailer jackknifed in Missouri, badly twisting his left leg in its socket. He has a steel pin in his hip. He will probably not be able to drive his rig again. It sits in the backyard, like a gigantic bird that has flown home to roost. Leroy has been home in Kentucky for three months, and his leg is almost healed, but the accident frightened him and he does not want to drive any more long hauls. He is not sure what to do next. In the meantime, he makes things from craft kits. He started by building a miniature log cabin from notched Popsicle sticks. He varnished it and place it on the TV set, where it remains. It reminds him of a rustic Nativity scene. Then he tried string art (sailing ships on black velvet), a macrame owl kit, a snap-together B-17 Flying Fortress, and a lamp made out of a model truck, with a light fixture screwed in the top of the cab. At first the kits were diversions, something to kill time, but now he is thinking about building a full-scale log house from a kit. It would be considerably cheaper than building a regular house, and besides, Leroy has grown to appreciate how things are put together. He has begun to realize that in all the years he was on the road he never took time to examine anything. He was always flying past scenery.

7 "They won't let you build a log cabin in any of the new subdivisions," Norma Jean tells him.

8 "They will if I tell them it's for you," he says, teasing her. Ever since they were married, he has promised Norma Jean he would build her a new home one day. They have always rented, and the house they live in is small and nondescript. It does not even feel like a home, Leroy realizes now.

9 Norma Jean works at the Rexall drugstore, and she has acquired an amazing amount of information about cosmetics. When she explains to Leroy the three stages of complexion care, involving creams, toners, and moisturizers, he thinks happily of other petroleum products—axle grease, diesel fuel. This is a connection between him and Norma Jean. Since he has been home, he has felt unusually tender about his wife and guilty over his long absences. But he can't tell what she feels about him. Norma Jean has never complained about his traveling; she has never made hurt remarks, like calling his truck a "widow-maker." He is reasonably certain she has been faithful to him, but he wishes she would celebrate his permanent home-coming more happily. Norma Jean is often startled to find Leroy at home, and he thinks she seems a little disappointed about it. Perhaps he reminds her too much of the early days of their marriage, before he went on the road. They had a child who died as an infant, years ago. They never speak about their memories of Randy, which have almost faded, but now that Leroy is home all the time, they sometimes feel awkward around each other, and Leroy wonders if one of them should mention the child. He has the

feeling that they are waking up out of a dream together—that they must create a new marriage, start afresh. They are lucky they are still married. Leroy has read that for most people losing a child destroys the marriage—or else he heard this on *Donahue*. He can't always remember where he learns things anymore.

10 At Christmas, Leroy bought an electric organ for Norma Jean. She used to play the piano when she was in high school. "It don't leave you," she told him once. "It's like riding a bicycle."

11 The new instrument had so many keys and buttons that she was bewildered by it at first. She touched the keys tentatively, pushed some buttons, then pecked out "Chopsticks." It came out in an amplified fox-trot rhythm, with marimba sounds.

12 "It's an orchestra!" she cried.

13 The organ had a pecan-look finish and eighteen preset chords, with optional flute, violin, trumpet, clarinet, and banjo accompaniments. Norma Jean mastered the organ almost immediately. At first she played Christmas songs. Then she bought *The Sixties Songbook* and learned every tune in it, adding variations to each with the rows of brightly colored buttons.

14 "I didn't like these old songs back then," she said. "But I have this crazy feeling I missed something."

15 "You didn't miss a thing," said Leroy.

16 Leroy likes to lie on the couch and smoke a joint and listen to Norma Jean play "Can't Take My Eyes Off You" and "I'll Be Back." He is back again. After fifteen years on the road, he is finally settling down with the woman he loves. She is still pretty. Her skin is flawless. Her frosted curls resemble pencil trimmings.

17 Now that Leroy has come home to stay, he notices how much the town has changed. Subdivisions are spreading across western Kentucky like an oil slick. The sign at the edge of town says "Pop: 11,500"—only seven hundred more than it said twenty years before. Leroy can't figure out who is living in all the new houses. The farmers who used to gather around the courthouse square on Saturday afternoons to play checkers and spit tobacco juice have gone. It has been years since Leroy has thought about the farmers, and they have disappeared without his noticing.

18 Leroy meets a kid named Stevie Hamilton in the parking lot at the new shopping center. While they pretend to be strangers meeting over a stalled car, Stevie tosses an ounce of marijuana under the front seat of Leroy's car. Stevie is wearing orange jogging shoes and a T-shirt that says CHATTAHOOCHEE SUPER RAT. His father is a prominent doctor who lives in one of the expensive subdivisions in a new white-columned brick house that looks like a funeral parlor. In the phone book under his name there is a separate number, with the listing "Teenagers."

19 "Where do you get this stuff?" asks Leroy. "From your pappy?"

20 "That's for me to know and you to find out," Stevie says. He is slit-eyed and skinny.

21 "What else you got?"

22 "What you interested in?"

23 "Nothing special. Just wondered."

24 Leroy used to take speed on the road. Now he has to go slowly. He needs to be mellow. He leans back against the car and says, "I'm aiming to build me a log house, soon as I get time. My wife, though, I don't think she likes the idea."

25 "Well, let me know when you want me again," Stevie says. He has a cigarette in his cupped palm, as though sheltering it from the wind. He takes a long drag, then stomps it on the asphalt and slouches away.

26 Stevie's father was two years ahead of Leroy in high school. Leroy is thirty-four. He married Norma Jean when they were both eighteen, and their child Randy was born a few months later, but he died at the age of four months and three days. He would be about Stevie's age now. Norma Jean and Leroy were at the drive-in, watching a double feature (*Dr. Strangelove* and *Lover Come Back*), and the baby was sleeping in the back seat. When the first movie ended, the baby was dead. It was the sudden infant death syndrome. Leroy remembers handing Randy to a nurse at the emergency room, as though he were offering her a large doll as a present. A dead baby feels like a sack of flour. "It just happens sometimes," said the doctor, in what Leroy always recalls as a nonchalant tone. Leroy can hardly remember the child anymore, but he still sees vividly a scene from *Dr. Strangelove* in which the President of the United States was talking in a folksy voice on the hot line to the Soviet premier about the bomber accidentally headed toward Russia. He was in the War Room, and the world map was lit up. Leroy remembers Norma Jean standing catatonically beside him in the hospital and himself thinking: Who is this strange girl? He had forgotten who she was. Now scientists are saying that crib death is caused by a virus. Nobody knows anything, Leroy thinks. The answers are always changing.

27 When Leroy gets home from the shopping center, Norma Jean's mother, Mabel Beasley, is there. Until this year, Leroy has not realized how much time she spends with Norma Jean. When she visits, she inspects the closets and then the plants, informing Norma Jean when a plant is droopy or yellow. Mabel calls the plants "flowers," although there are never any blooms. She also notices if Norma Jean's laundry is piling up. Mabel is a short, overweight woman whose tight, brown-dyed curls look more like a wig than the actual wig she sometimes wears. Today she has brought Norma Jean an off-white dust ruffle she made for the bed; Mabel works in a custom upholstery shop.

28 "This is the tenth one I made this year," Mabel says. "I got started and couldn't stop."

29 "It's real pretty," says Norma Jean.

30 "Now we can hide things under the bed," says Leroy, who gets along with his mother-in-law primarily by joking with her. Mabel has never really forgiven him for disgracing her by getting Norma Jean pregnant. When the baby died, she said that fate was mocking her.

31 "What's that thing?" Mabel says to Leroy in a loud voice, pointing to a tangle of yarn on a piece of canvas.

32 Leroy holds it up for Mabel to see. "It's my needlepoint," he explains. "This is a *Star Trek* pillow cover."

33 "That's what a woman would do," says Mabel. "Great day in the morning!"

34 "All the big football players on TV do it," he says.

35 "Why, Leroy, you're always trying to fool me. I don't believe you for one minute. You don't know what to do with yourself—that's the whole trouble. Sewing!"

36 "I'm aiming to build us a log house," says Leroy. "Soon as my plans come."

37 "Like *heck* you are," says Norma Jean. She takes Leroy's needlepoint and shoves it into a drawer. "You have to find a job first. Nobody can afford to build now anyway."

38 Mabel straightens her girdle and says, "I still think before you get tied down y'all ought to take a little run to Shiloh."

39 "One of these days, Mama," Norma Jean says impatiently.

40 Mabel is talking about Shiloh, Tennessee. For the past few years, she has been urging Leroy and Norma Jean to visit the Civil War battleground there. Mabel went there on her honeymoon—the only real trip she ever took. Her husband died of a perforated ulcer when Norma Jean was ten, but Mabel, who was accepted into the United Daughters of the Confederacy in 1975, is still preoccupied with going back to Shiloh.

41 "I've been to kingdom come and back in that truck out yonder," Leroy says to Mabel, "but we never yet set foot in that battleground. Ain't that something? How did I miss it?"

42 "It's not even that far," Mabel says.

43 After Mabel leaves, Norma Jean reads to Leroy from a list she has made. "Things you could do," she announces. "You could get a job as a guard at Union Carbide, where they'd let you set on a stool. You could get on at the lumberyard. You could do a little carpenter work, if you want to build so bad. You could—"

44 "I can't do something where I'd have to stand up all day."

45 "You ought to try standing up all day behind a cosmetics counter. It's amazing that I have strong feet, coming from two parents that never had strong feet at all." At the moment Norma Jean is holding on to the kitchen counter, raising her knees one at a time as she talks. She is wearing two-pound ankle weights.

46 "Don't worry," says Leroy. "I'll do something."

47 "You could truck calves to slaughter for somebody. You wouldn't have to drive any big old truck for that."

48 "I'm going to build you this house," says Leroy. "I want to make you a real home."

49 "I don't want to live in any log cabin."

50 "It's not a cabin. It's a house."

51 "I don't care. It looks like a cabin."

52 "You and me together could lift those logs. It's just like lifting weights."

53 Norma Jean doesn't answer. Under her breath, she is counting. Now she is marching through the kitchen. She is doing goose steps.

54 Before his accident, when Leroy came home he used to stay in the house with Norma Jean, watching TV in bed and playing cards. She would cook fried chicken, picnic ham, chocolate pie—all his favorites. Now he is home alone much of the time. In the mornings, Norma Jean disappears, leaving a cooling place in the bed. She eats a cereal called Body Buddies, and she leaves the bowl on the table, with the soggy tan balls floating in a milk puddle. He sees things about Norma Jean that he never realized before. When she chops onions, she stares off into a corner, as if she can't bear to look. She puts on her house slippers almost precisely at nine o'clock every evening and nudges her jogging shoes under the couch. She saves bread heels for the birds. Leroy watches the birds at the feeder. He notices the peculiar way goldfinches fly past the window. They close their wings, then fall, then spread their wings to catch and lift themselves. He wonders if they close their eyes when they fall. Norma Jean closes her eyes when they are in bed. She wants the lights turned out. Even then, he is sure she closes her eyes.

55 He goes for long drives around town. He tends to drive a car rather carelessly. Power steering and an automatic shift make a car feel so small and inconsequential that his body is hardly involved in the driving process. His injured leg stretches out comfortably. Once or twice he has almost hit something, but even the prospect of an accident seems minor in a car. He cruises the new subdivisions, feeling like a criminal rehearsing for a robbery. Norma Jean is probably right about a log house being inappropriate here in the new subdivision. All the houses look grand and complicated. They depress him.

56 One day when Leroy comes home from a drive he finds Norma Jean in tears. She is in the kitchen making a potato and mushroom-soup casserole, with grated cheese topping. She is crying because her mother caught her smoking.

57 "I didn't hear her coming. I was standing here puffing away pretty as you please," Norma Jean says, wiping her eyes.

58 "I knew it would happen sooner or later," says Leroy, putting his arm around her.

59 "She don't know the meaning of the word 'knock,'" says Norma Jean. "It's a wonder she hadn't caught me years ago."

60 "Think of it this way," Leroy says. "What if she caught me with a joint?"

61 "You better not let her!" Norma Jean shrieks. "I'm warning you, Leroy Moffitt!"

62 "I'm just kidding. Here, play me a tune. That'll help you relax."

63 Norma Jean puts the casserole in the oven and sets the timer. Then she plays a ragtime tune, with horns and banjo, as Leroy lights up a joint and lies on the couch, laughing to himself about Mabel's catching him at it. He thinks of Stevie Hamilton—a doctor's son pushing grass. Everything is funny. The whole town seems crazy and small. He is reminded of Virgil Mathis, a boastful policeman Leroy used to shoot pool with. Virgil recently led a drug bust in a back room at a bowling alley, where he seized ten thousand dollars' worth of marijuana. The newspaper had a picture of him holding up the bags of grass and grinning widely. Right now, Leroy can imagine Virgil breaking down the door and arresting him with a lungful of smoke. Virgil would probably have been alerted to the scene because of all the racket Norma Jean is making. Now she sounds like a hard-rock band. Norma Jean is terrific. When she switches to a Latin-rhythm version of "Sunshine Superman," Leroy hums along. Norma Jean's foot goes up and down, up and down.

64 "Well, what do you think?" Leroy says, when Norma Jean pauses to search through her music.

65 "What do I think about what?"

66 His mind has gone blank. Then he says, "I'll sell my rig and build us a house." That wasn't what he wanted to say. He wanted to know what she thought—what she *really* thought—about them.

67 "Don't start in on that again," says Norma Jean. She begins playing "Who'll Be the Next in Line?"

68 Leroy used to tell hitchhikers his whole life story—about his travels, his hometown, the baby. He would end with a question: "Well, what do you think?" It was just a rhetorical question. In time, he had the feeling that he'd been telling the same story over and over to the same hitchhikers. He quit talking to hitchhikers when he realized how his voice sounded—whining and self-pitying, like some teenage-tragedy song. Now Leroy has the sudden impulse to tell Norma Jean about himself, as if he had just met her. They have known each other so long they have forgotten a lot about each other. They could become reacquainted. But when the oven timer goes off and she runs to the kitchen, he forgets why he wants to do this.

69 The next day, Mabel drops by. It is Saturday and Norma Jean is cleaning. Leroy is studying the plans of his log house, which have finally come in the mail. He has them spread out on the table—big sheets of stiff blue paper, with

diagrams and numbers printed in white. While Norma Jean runs the vacuum, Mabel drinks coffee. She sets her coffee cup on a blueprint.

70 "I'm just waiting for time to pass," she says to Leroy, drumming her fingers on the table.

71 As soon as Norma Jean switches off the vacuum, Mabel says in a loud voice, "Did you hear about the datsun dog that killed the baby?"

72 Norma Jean says, "The word is 'dachshund.'"

73 "They put the dog on trial. It chewed the baby's legs off. The mother was in the next room all the time." She raises her voice. "They thought it was neglect."

74 Norma Jean is holding her ears. Leroy manages to open the refrigerator and get some Diet Pepsi to offer Mabel. Mabel still has some coffee and she waves away the Pepsi.

75 "Datsuns are like that," Mabel says. "They're jealous dogs. They'll tear a place to pieces if you don't keep an eye on them."

76 "You better watch out what you're saying, Mabel," says Leroy.

77 "Well, facts is facts."

78 Leroy looks out the window at his rig. It is like a huge piece of furniture gathering dust in the backyard. Pretty soon it will be an antique. He hears the vacuum cleaner. Norma Jean seems to be cleaning the living room rug again.

79 Later, she says to Leroy, "She just said that about the baby because she caught me smoking. She's trying to pay me back."

80 "What are you talking about?" Leroy says, nervously shuffling blueprints.

81 "You know good and well," Norma Jean says. She is sitting in a kitchen chair with her feet up and her arms wrapped around her knees. She looks small and helpless. She says, "The very idea, her bringing up a subject like that! Saying it was neglect."

82 "She didn't mean that," Leroy says.

83 "She might not have *thought* she meant it. She always says things like that. You don't know how she goes on."

84 "But she didn't really mean it. She was just talking."

85 Leroy opens a king-sized bottle of beer and pours it into two glasses, dividing it carefully. He hands a glass to Norma Jean and she takes it from him mechanically. For a long time, they sit by the kitchen window watching the birds at the feeder.

86 Something is happening. Norma Jean is going to night school. She has graduated from her six-week body-building course and now she is taking an adult-education course in composition at Paducah Community College. She spends her evenings outlining paragraphs.

87 "First, you have a topic sentence," she explains to Leroy. "Then you divide it up. Your secondary topic has to be connected to your primary topic."

88 To Leroy, this sounds intimidating. "I never was any good in English," he says.

89 "It makes a lot of sense."

90 "What are you doing this for, anyhow?"

91 She shrugs. "It's something to do." She stands up and lifts her dumbbells a few times.

92 "Driving a rig, nobody cared about my English."

93 "I'm not criticizing your English."

94 Norma Jean used to say, "If I lose ten minutes' sleep, I just drag all day." Now she stays up late, writing compositions. She got a B on her first paper—a how-to theme on soup-based casseroles. Recently Norma Jean has been cooking unusual foods—tacos, lasagna, Bombay chicken. She doesn't play the organ anymore, though her second paper was called "Why Music Is Important to Me." She sits at the kitchen table, concentrating on her outlines, while Leroy plays with his log house plans, practicing with a set of Lincoln Logs. The thought of getting a truckload of notched, numbered logs scares him, and he wants to be prepared. As he and Norma Jean work together at the kitchen table, Leroy has the hopeful thought that they are sharing something, but he knows he is a fool to think this. Norma Jean is miles away. He knows he is going to lose her. Like Mabel, he is just waiting for time to pass.

95 One day, Mabel is there before Norma Jean gets home from work, and Leroy finds himself confiding in her. Mabel, he realizes, must know Norma Jean better than he does.

96 "I don't know what's got into that girl," Mabel says. "She used to go to bed with the chickens. Now you say she's up all hours. Plus her a-smoking. I like to died."

97 "I want to make her this beautiful home," Leroy says, indicating the Lincoln Logs. "I don't think she even wants it. Maybe she was happier with me gone."

98 "She don't know what to make of you, coming home like this."

99 "Is that it?"

100 Mabel takes the roof off his Lincoln Log cabin. "You couldn't get me in a log cabin," she says. "I was raised in one. It's no picnic, let me tell you."

101 "They're different now," says Leroy.

102 "I tell you what," Mabel says, smiling oddly at Leroy.

103 "What?"

104 "Take her on down to Shiloh. Y'all need to get out together, stir a little. Her brain's all balled up over them books."

105 Leroy can see traces of Norma Jean's features in her mother's face. Mabel's worn face has the texture of crinkled cotton, but suddenly she looks pretty. It occurs to Leroy that Mabel has been hinting all along that she wants them to take her with them to Shiloh.

106 "Let's all go to Shiloh," he says. "You and me and her. Come Sunday."

107 Mabel throws up her hand in protest. "Oh, no, not me. Young folks want to be by theirselves."

108 When Norma Jean comes in with groceries, Leroy says excitedly, "Your mama here's been dying to go to Shiloh for thirty-five years. It's about time we went, don't you think?"

109 "I'm not going to butt in on anybody's second honeymoon," Mabel says.

110 "Who's going on a honeymoon, for Christ's sake?" Norma Jean says loudly.

111 "I never raised no daughter of mine to talk that-a-way," Mabel says.

112 "You ain't seen nothing yet," says Norma Jean. She starts putting away boxes and cans, slamming cabinet doors.

113 "There's a log cabin at Shiloh," Mabel says. "It was there during the battle. There's bullet holes in it."

114 "When are you going to *shut up* about Shiloh, Mama?" asks Norma Jean.

115 "I always thought Shiloh was the prettiest place, so full of history," Mabel goes on. "I just hoped y'all could see it once before I die, so you could tell me about it." Later, she whispers to Leroy, "You do what I said. A little change is what she needs."

116 "Your name means 'the king,'" Norma Jean says to Leroy that evening. He is trying to get her to go to Shiloh, and she is reading a book about another century.

117 "Well, I reckon I ought to be right proud."

118 "I guess so."

119 "Am I still king around here?"

120 Norma Jean flexes her biceps and feels them for hardness. "I'm not fooling around with anybody, if that's what you mean," she says.

121 "Would you tell me if you were?"

122 "I don't know."

123 "What does *your* name mean?"

124 "It was Marilyn Monroe's real name."

125 "No kidding!"

126 "Norma comes from the Normans. They were invaders," she says. She closes her book and looks hard at Leroy. "I'll go to Shiloh with you if you'll stop staring at me."

127 On Sunday, Norma Jean packs a picnic and they go to Shiloh. To Leroy's relief Mabel says she does not want to come with them. Norma Jean drives, and Leroy, sitting beside her, feels like some boring hitchhiker she has picked up. He tries some conversation, but she answers him in monosyllables. At Shiloh, she drives aimlessly through the park, past bluffs and trails and steep ravines.

Shiloh is an immense place, and Leroy cannot see it as a battleground. It is not what he expected. He thought it would look like a golf course. Monuments are everywhere, showing through the thick clusters of trees. Norma Jean passes the log cabin Mabel mentioned. It is surrounded by tourists looking for bullet holes.

128 "That's not the kind of log house I've got in mind," says Leroy apologetically.

129 "I know *that.*"

130 "This is a pretty place. Your mama was right."

131 "It's O.K.," says Norma Jean. "Well, we've seen it. I hope she's satisfied."

132 They burst out laughing together.

133 At the park museum, a movie on Shiloh is shown every half hour, but they decide that they don't want to see it. They buy a souvenir Confederate flag for Mabel, and then they find a picnic spot near the cemetery. Norma Jean has brought a picnic cooler, with pimiento sandwiches, soft drinks, and Yodels. Leroy eats a sandwich and then smokes a joint, hiding it behind the picnic cooler. Norma Jean has quit smoking altogether. She is picking cake crumbs from the cellophane wrapper, like a fussy bird.

134 Leroy says, "So the boys in gray ended up in Corinth. The Union soldiers zapped 'em finally. April 7, 1862."

135 They both know that he doesn't know any history. He is just talking about some of the historical plaques they have read. He feels awkward, like a boy on a date with an older girl. They are still just making conversation.

136 "Corinth is where Mama eloped to," says Norma Jean.

137 They sit in silence and stare at the cemetery for the Union dead and, beyond, at a tall cluster of trees. Campers are parked nearby, bumper to bumper, and small children in bright clothing are cavorting and squealing. Norma Jean wads up the cake wrapper and squeezes it tightly in her hand. Without looking at Leroy, she says, "I want to leave you."

138 Leroy takes a bottle of Coke out of the cooler and flips off the cap. He holds the bottle poised near his mouth but cannot remember to take a drink. Finally he says, "No, you don't."

139 "Yes, I do."

140 "I won't let you."

141 "You can't stop me."

142 "Don't do me that way."

143 Leroy knows Norma Jean will have her own way. "Didn't I promise to be home from now on?" he says.

144 "In some ways, a woman prefers a man who wanders," says Norma Jean. "That sounds crazy, I know."

145 "You're not crazy." Leroy remembers to drink from his Coke. Then he says, "Yes, you *are* crazy. You and me could start all over again. Right back at the beginning."

146 "We *have* started all over again," says Norma Jean. "And this is how it turned out."

147 "What did I do wrong?"

148 "Nothing."

149 "Is this one of those women's lib things?" Leroy asks.

150 "Don't be funny."

151 The cemetery, a green slope dotted with white markers, looks like a subdivision site. Leroy is trying to comprehend that his marriage is breaking up, but for some reason he is wondering about white slabs in a graveyard.

152 "Everything was fine till Mama caught me smoking," says Norma Jean, standing up. "That set something off."

153 "What are you talking about?"

154 "She won't leave me alone—*you* won't leave me alone." Norma Jean seems to be crying, but she is looking away from him. "I feel eighteen again. I can't face that all over again." She starts walking away. "No, it *wasn't* fine. I don't know what I'm saying. Forget it."

155 Leroy takes a lungful of smoke and closes his eyes as Norma Jean's words sink in. He tries to focus on the fact that thirty-five hundred soldiers died on the grounds around him. He can only think of that war as a board game with plastic soldiers. Leroy almost smiles, as he compares the Confederates' daring attack on the Union camps and Virgil Mathis's raid on the bowling alley. General Grant, drunk and furious, shoved the Southerners back to Corinth, where Mabel and Jet Beasley were married years later, when Mabel was still thin and good-looking. The next day, Mabel and Jet visited the battleground, and then Norma Jean was born, and then she married Leroy and they had a baby, which they lost, and now Leroy and Norma Jean are here at the same battleground. Leroy knows he is leaving out a lot. He is leaving out the insides of history. History was always just names and dates to him. It occurs to him that building a house of logs is similarly empty—too simple. And the real inner workings of a marriage, like most of history, have escaped him. Now he sees that building a log house is the dumbest idea he could have had. It was clumsy of him to think Norma Jean would want a log house. It was a crazy idea. He'll have to think of something else, quickly. He will wad the blueprints into tight balls and fling them into the lake. Then he'll get moving again. He opens his eyes. Norma Jean has moved away and is walking through the cemetery, following a serpentine brick path.

156 Leroy gets up to follow his wife, but his good leg is asleep and his bad leg still hurts him. Norma Jean is far away, walking rapidly toward the bluff by the river, and he tries to hobble toward her. Some children run past him,

screaming noisily. Norma Jean has reached the bluff, and she is looking out over the Tennessee River. Now she turns toward Leroy and waves her arms. Is she beckoning to him? She seems to be doing an exercise for her chest muscles. The sky is unusually pale—the color of the dust ruffle Mabel made for their bed.

—1982

✧ ✧ ✧

Alice Walker
(b. 1944)

Everyday Use

Walker's Pulitzer Prize-winning epistolary novel *The Color Purple* (1982) and its 1985 film version have made her the most famous black woman writer in contemporary America, perhaps the most widely read of any American woman of color. A native of Eatonton, Georgia, Walker was the eighth child of an impoverished farm couple. She attended Spelman College in Atlanta and Sarah Lawrence College in New York on scholarships, graduating in 1965. Walker began her literary career as a poet, eventually publishing six volumes of poetry. Her short story collections and novels, including *The Temple of My Familiar* (1989) and *Possessing the Secret of Joy* (1992), which takes as its subject the controversial practice of female circumcision among African tribes, continue to reach large audiences and have solidified her reputation as one of the major figures in contemporary literature. Walker has coined the term "womanist" to stand for the black feminist concerns of much of her fiction. "Everyday Use," a story from the early 1970s, is simultaneously a satisfying piece of realistic social commentary and a subtly satirical variation on the ancient fable of the city mouse and the country mouse.

For your grandmama

I will wait for her in the yard that Maggie and I made so clean and wavy yesterday afternoon. A yard like this is more comfortable than most people know. It is not just a yard. It is like an extended living room. When the hard clay is swept clean as a floor and the fine sand around the edges lined with tiny, irregular grooves anyone can come and sit and look up into the elm tree and wait for the breezes that never come inside the house.

2 Maggie will be nervous until after her sister goes: she will stand hopelessly in corners homely and ashamed of the burn scars down her arms and legs, eyeing her sister with a mixture of envy and awe. She thinks her sister has held life always in the palm of one hand, that "no" is a word the world never learned to say to her.

3 You've no doubt seen those TV shows where the child who has "made it" is confronted, as a surprise, by her own mother and father, tottering in weakly from backstage. (A pleasant surprise, of course: What would they do if parent and child came on the show only to curse out and insult each other?) On TV mother and child embrace and smile into each other's faces. Sometimes the mother and father weep, the child wraps them in her arms and leans across the table to tell how she would not have made it without their help. I have seen these programs.

4 Sometimes I dream a dream in which Dee and I are suddenly brought together on a TV program of this sort. Out of a dark and soft-seated limousine I am ushered into a bright room filled with many people. There I meet a smiling, gray, sporty man like Johnny Carson who shakes my hand and tells me what a fine girl I have. Then we are on the stage and Dee is embracing me with tears in her eyes. She pins on my dress a large orchid, even though she has told me once that she thinks orchids are tacky flowers.

5 In real life I am a large, big-boned woman with rough, man-working hands. In the winter I wear flannel nightgowns to bed and overalls during the day. I can kill and clean a hog as mercilessly as a man. My fat keeps me hot in zero weather. I can work outside all day, breaking ice to get water for washing. I can eat pork liver cooked over the open fire minutes after it comes steaming from the hog. One winter I knocked a bull calf straight in the brain between the eyes with a sledge hammer and had the meat hung up to chill before nightfall. But of course all this does not show on television. I am the way my daughter would want me to be: a hundred pounds lighter, my skin like an uncooked barley pancake. My hair glistens in the hot bright lights. Johnny Carson has much to do to keep up with my quick and witty tongue.

6 But that is a mistake. I know even before I wake up. Who ever knew a Johnson with a quick tongue? Who can even imagine me looking a strange white man in the eye? It seems to me I have talked to them always with one foot raised in flight, with my head turned in whichever way is farthest from them. Dee, though. She would always look anyone in the eye. Hesitation was no part of her nature.

7 "How do I look, Mama?" Maggie says, showing just enough of her thin body enveloped in pink skirt and red blouse for me to know she's there, almost hidden by the door.

8 "Come out into the yard," I say.

9 Have you ever seen a lame animal, perhaps a dog run over by some careless person rich enough to own a car, sidle up to someone who is ignorant enough to be kind to him? That is the way my Maggie walks. She has been like this, chin on chest, eyes on ground, feet in shuffle, ever since the fire that burned the other house to the ground.

10 Dee is lighter than Maggie, with nicer hair and a fuller figure. She's a woman now, though sometimes I forget. How long ago was it that the other house burned? Ten, twelve years? Sometimes I can still hear the flames and feel Maggie's arms sticking to me, her hair smoking and her dress falling off her in little black papery flakes. Her eyes seemed stretched open, blazed open by the flames reflected in them. And Dee. I see her standing off under the sweet gum tree she used to dig gum out of; a look of concentration on her face as she watched the last dingy gray board of the house fall in toward the red-hot brick chimney. Why don't you do a dance around the ashes? I'd wanted to ask her. She had hated the house that much.

11 I used to think she hated Maggie, too. But that was before we raised the money, the church and me, to send her to Augusta to school. She used to read to us without pity; forcing words, lies, other folks' habits, whole lives upon us two, sitting trapped and ignorant underneath her voice. She washed us in a river of make-believe, burned us with a lot of knowledge we didn't necessarily need to know. Pressed us to her with the serious way she read, to shove us away at just the moment, like dimwits, we seemed about to understand.

12 Dee wanted nice things. A yellow organdy dress to wear to her graduation from high school; black pumps to match a green suit she'd made from an old suit somebody gave me. She was determined to stare down any disaster in her efforts. Her eyelids would not flicker for minutes at a time. Often I fought off the temptation to shake her. At sixteen she had a style of her own: and knew what style was.

13 I never had an education myself. After second grade the school was closed down. Don't ask me why: in 1927 colored asked fewer questions than they do now. Sometimes Maggie reads to me. She stumbles along good-naturedly but can't see well. She knows she is not bright. Like good looks and money, quickness passed her by. She will marry John Thomas (who has mossy teeth in an earnest face) and then I'll be free to sit here and I guess just sing church songs to myself. Although I never was a good singer. Never could carry a tune. I was always better at a man's job. I used to love to milk till I was hoofed in the side

in '49. Cows are soothing and slow and don't bother you, unless you try to milk them the wrong way.

14 I have deliberately turned my back on the house. It is three rooms, just like the one that burned, except the roof is tin; they don't make shingle roofs any more. There are no real windows, just some holes cut in the sides, like the port-holes in a ship, but not round and not square, with rawhide holding the shutters up on the outside. This house is in a pasture, too, like the other one. No doubt when Dee sees it she will want to tear it down. She wrote me once that no matter where we "choose" to live, she will manage to come see us. But she will never bring her friends. Maggie and I thought about this and Maggie asked me, "Mama, when did Dee ever *have* any friends?"

15 She had a few. Furtive boys in pink shirts hanging about on washday after school. Nervous girls who never laughed. Impressed with her they worshiped the well-turned phrase, the cute shape, the scalding humor that erupted like bubbles in lye. She read to them.

16 When she was courting Jimmy T she didn't have much time to pay to us, but turned all her faultfinding power on him. He *flew* to marry a cheap gal from a family of ignorant flashy people. She hardly had time to recompose herself.

17 When she comes I will meet—but there they are!

18 Maggie attempts to make a dash for the house, in her shuffling way, but I stay her with my hand. "Come back here," I say. And she stops and tries to dig a well in the sand with her toe.

19 It is hard to see them clearly through the strong sun. But even the first glimpse of leg out of the car tells me it is Dee. Her feet were always neat-looking, as if God himself had shaped them with a certain style. From the other side of the car comes a short, stocky man. Hair is all over his head a foot long and hanging from his chin like a kinky mule tail. I hear Maggie suck in her breath. "Uhnnnh," is what it sounds like. Like when you see the wriggling end of a snake just in front of your foot on the road. "Uhnnnh."

20 Dee next. A dress down to the ground, in this hot weather. A dress so loud it hurts my eyes. There are yellows and oranges enough to throw back the light of the sun. I feel my whole face warming from the heat waves it throws out. Earrings, too, gold and hanging down to her shoulders. Bracelets dangling and making noises when she moves her arm up to shake the folds of the dress out of her armpits. The dress is loose and flows, and as she walks closer, I like it. I hear Maggie go "Uhnnnh" again. It is her sister's hair. It stands straight up like the wool on a sheep. It is black as night and around the edges are two long pig-tails that rope about like small lizards disappearing behind her ears.

21 "Wa-su-zo-Tean-o!" she says, coming on in that gliding way the dress makes her move. The short stocky fellow with the hair to his navel is all

grinning and he follows up with "Asalamalakim, my mother and sister!" He moves to hug Maggie but she falls back, right up against the back of my chair. I feel her trembling there and when I look up I see the perspiration falling off her chin.

22 "Don't get up," says Dee. Since I am stout it takes something of a push. You can see me trying to move a second or two before I make it. She turns, showing white heels through her sandals, and goes back to the car. Out she peeks next with a Polaroid. She stoops down quickly and lines up picture after picture of me sitting there in front of the house with Maggie cowering behind me. She never takes a shot without making sure the house is included. When a cow comes nibbling around the edge of the yard she snaps it and me and Maggie and the house. Then she puts the Polaroid in the back seat of the car, and comes up and kisses me on the forehead.

23 Meanwhile Asalamalakim is going through the motions with Maggie's hand. Maggie's hand is as limp as a fish, and probably as cold, despite the sweat, and she keeps trying to pull it back. It looks like Asalamalakim wants to shake hands but wants to do it fancy. Or maybe he don't know how people shake hands. Anyhow, he soon gives up on Maggie.

24 "Well," I say. "Dee."

25 "No, Mama," she says. "Not 'Dee,' Wangero Leewanika Kemanjo!"

26 "What happened to 'Dee'?" I wanted to know.

27 "She's dead," Wangero said. "I couldn't bear it any longer being named after the people who oppress me."

28 "You know as well as me you was named after your aunt Dicie," I said. Dicie is my sister. She named Dee. We called her "Big Dee" after Dee was born.

29 "But who was *she* named after?" asked Wangero.

30 "I guess after Grandma Dee," I said.

31 "And who was she named after?" asked Wangero.

32 "Her mother," I said, and saw Wangero was getting tired. "That's about as far back as I can trace it," I said. Though, in fact, I probably could have carried it back beyond the Civil War through the branches.

33 "Well," said Asalamalakim, "there you are."

34 "Uhnnnh," I heard Maggie say.

35 "There I was not," I said, "before 'Dicie' cropped up in our family, so why should I try to trace it that far back?"

36 He just stood there grinning, looking down on me like somebody inspecting a Model A car. Every once in a while he and Wangero sent eye signals over my head.

37 "How do you pronounce this name?" I asked.

38 "You don't have to call me by it if you don't want to," said Wangero.

39 "Why shouldn't I?" I asked. "If that's what you want us to call you, we'll call you."

40 "I know it might sound awkward at first," said Wangero.

41 "I'll get used to it," I said. "Ream it out again."

42 Well, soon we got the name out of the way. Asalamalakim had a name twice as long and three times as hard. After I tripped over it two or three times he told me to just to call him Hakim-a-barber. I wanted to ask him was he a barber, but I didn't really think he was, so I didn't ask.

43 "You must belong to those beef-cattle peoples down the road," I said. They said "Asalamalakim" when they met you, too, but they didn't shake hands. Always too busy: feeding the cattle, fixing the fences, putting up salt-lick shelters, throwing down hay. When the white folks poisoned some of the herd the men stayed up all night with rifles in their hands. I walked a mile and a half just to see the sight.

44 Hakim-a-barber said, "I accept some of their doctrines, but farming and raising cattle is not my style." (They didn't tell me, and I didn't ask, whether Wangero [Dee] had really gone and married him.)

45 We sat down to eat and right away he said he didn't eat collards and pork was unclean. Wangero, though, went on through the chitlins and corn bread, the greens and everything else. She talked a blue streak over the sweet potatoes. Everything delighted her. Even the fact that we still used the benches her daddy made for the table when we couldn't afford to buy chairs.

46 "Oh, Mama!" she cried. Then turned to Hakim-a-barber. "I never knew how lovely these benches are. You can feel the rump prints," she said, running her hands underneath her and along the bench. Then she gave a sigh and her hand closed over Grandma Dee's butter dish. "That's it!" she said. "I knew there was something I wanted to ask you if I could have." She jumped up from the table and went over in the corner where the churn stood, the milk in it clabber by now. She looked at the churn and looked at it.

47 "This churn top is what I need," she said. "Didn't Uncle Buddy whittle it out of a tree you all used to have?"

48 "Yes," I said.

49 "Uh huh," she said happily. "And I want the dasher, too."

50 "Uncle Buddy whittle that, too?" asked the barber.

51 Dee (Wangero) looked up at me.

52 "Aunt Dee's first husband whittled the dash," said Maggie so low you almost couldn't hear her. "His name was Henry, but they called him Stash."

53 "Maggie's brain is like an elephant's," Wangero said, laughing. "I can use the churn top as a centerpiece for the alcove table," she said, sliding a plate over the churn, "and I'll think of something artistic to do with the dasher."

54 When she finished wrapping the dasher the handle stuck out. I took it for a moment in my hands. You didn't even have to look close to see where hands pushing the dasher up and down to make butter had left a kind of sink in the wood. In fact, there were a lot of small sinks; you could see where thumbs and

fingers had sunk into the wood. It was beautiful light yellow wood, from a tree that grew in the yard where Big Dee and Stash had lived.

55 After dinner Dee (Wangero) went to the trunk at the foot of my bed and started rifling through it. Maggie hung back in the kitchen over the dishpan. Out came Wangero with two quilts. They had been pieced by Grandma Dee and then Big Dee and me had hung them on the quilt frames on the front porch and quilted them. One was in the Lone Star pattern. The other was Walk Around the Mountain. In both of them were scraps of dresses Grandma Dee had worn fifty and more years ago. Bits and pieces of Grandpa Jarrell's paisley shirts. And one teeny faded blue piece, about the piece of a penny matchbox, that was from Great Grandpa Ezra's uniform that he wore in the Civil War.

56 "Mama," Wangero said sweet as a bird. "Can I have these old quilts?"

57 I heard something fall in the kitchen, and a minute later the kitchen door slammed.

58 "Why don't you take one or two of the others?" I asked. "These old things was just done by me and Big Dee from some tops your grandma pieced before she died."

59 "No," said Wangero. "I don't want those. They are stitched around the borders by machine."

60 "That's make them last better," I said.

61 "That's not the point," said Wangero. "These are all pieces of dresses Grandma used to wear. She did all this stitching by hand. Imagine!" She held the quilts securely in her arms, stroking them.

62 "Some of the pieces, like those lavender ones, come from old clothes her mother handed down to her," I said, moving up to touch the quilts. Dee (Wangero) moved back just enough so that I couldn't reach the quilts. They already belonged to her.

63 "Imagine!" she breathed again, clutching them closely to her bosom.

64 "The truth is," I said, "I promised to give them quilts to Maggie, for when she marries John Thomas."

65 She gasped like a bee had stung her.

66 "Maggie can't appreciate these quilts!" she said. "She'd probably be backward enough to put them to everyday use."

67 "I reckon she would," I said. "God knows I been saving 'em for long enough with nobody using 'em. I hope she will!" I didn't want to bring up how I had offered Dee (Wangero) a quilt when she went away to college. Then she had told me they were old-fashioned, out of style.

68 "But they're *priceless!"* she was saying now, furiously; for she has a temper. "Maggie would put them on the bed and in five years they'd be in rags. Less than that!"

69 "She can always make some more," I said. "Maggie knows how to quilt."

70 Dee (Wangero) looked at me with hatred. "You just will not understand. The point is these quilts, *these* quilts!"

71 "Well," I said, stumped. "What would *you* do with them?"

72 "Hang them," she said. As if that was the only thing you *could* do with quilts.

73 Maggie by now was standing in the door. I could almost hear the sound her feet made as they scraped over each other.

74 "She can have them, Mama," she said, like somebody used to never winning anything, or having anything reserved for her. "I can 'member Grandma Dee without the quilts."

75 I looked at her hard. She had filled her bottom lip with checkerberry snuff and it gave her face a kind of dopey, hangdog look. It was Grandma Dee and Big Dee who taught her how to quilt herself. She stood there with her scarred hands hidden in the folds of her skirt. She looked at her sister with something like fear but she wasn't mad at her. This was Maggie's portion. This was the way she knew God to work.

76 When I looked at her like that something hit me in the top of my head and ran down to the soles of my feet. Just like when I'm in church and the spirit of God touches me and I get happy and shout. I did something I never had done before: hugged Maggie to me, then dragged her on into the room, snatched the quilts out of Miss Wangero's hands and dumped them into Maggie's lap. Maggie just sat there on my bed with her mouth open.

77 "Take one or two of the others," I said to Dee.

78 But she turned without a word and went out to Hakim-a-barber.

79 "You just don't understand," she said, as Maggie and I came out to the car.

80 "What don't I understand?" I wanted to know.

81 "Your heritage," she said. And then she turned to Maggie, kissed her, and said, "You ought to try to make something of yourself, too, Maggie. It's really a new day for us. But from the way you and Mama still live you'd never know it."

82 She put on some sunglasses that hid everything above the tip of her nose and her chin.

83 Maggie smiled; maybe at the sunglasses. But a real smile, not scared. After we watched the car dust settle I asked Maggie to bring me a dip of snuff. And then the two of us sat there just enjoying, until it was time to go in the house and go to bed.

—1973

Denise Chávez
(b. 1948)

The Last of the Menu Girls

A native of Las Cruces, New Mexico, Chávez is the child of an attorney and a schoolteacher and holds degrees from New Mexico State University, Trinity University, and the University of New Mexico. Chávez has edited a collection of poetry by female prison inmates, and she is an accomplished playwright who has seen over twenty of her one-act plays produced. *The Last of the Menu Girls* was published in 1986 by Arte Público, an important publisher of contemporary writing by Hispanic Americans. It is a collection of seven related stories about the coming of age of Rocío Esquibel, a character whose biography often parallels the author's own. The title story was winner of the 1985 fiction award given by *Puerto del Sol,* an important literary magazine of the Southwest. Chávez characterizes herself as a "performance writer," and she is a spirited reader of her own stories. During the year in which she taught at the University of Houston, Chávez oversaw the production of a dramatic version of "The Last of the Menu Girls."

NAME: Rocío Esquibel
2 AGE: Seventeen
3 PREVIOUS EXPERIENCE WITH THE SICK AND DYING: My Great Aunt Eutilia
4 PRESENT EMPLOYMENT: Work-study aide at Altavista Memorial

5 I never wanted to be a nurse. My mother's aunt died in our house, seventy-seven years old and crying in her metal crib: "Put a pillow on the floor. I can jump," she cried. "Go on, let me jump. I want to get away from here, far away."

6 Eutilia's mattress was covered with chipped clothlike sheaves of yellowed plastic. She wet herself, was a small child, undependable, helpless. She was an old lady with a broken hip, dying without having gotten down from that rented

bed. Her blankets were sewn by my mother: corduroy patches, bright yellows, blues and greens, and still she wanted to jump!

7 "Turn her over, turn her over, turn her, wait a minute, wait—turn . . . "

8 Eutilia faced the wall. It was plastered white. The foamed, concrete turnings of some workman's trowel revealed daydreams: people's faces, white clouds, phantom pianos slowly playing half lost melodies, "Las Mañanitas," "Cielito Lindo,"° songs formulated in expectation, dissolved into confusion. Eutilia's blurred faces, far off tunes faded into the white walls, into jagged, broken waves.

9 I never wanted to be a nurse, ever. All that gore and blood and grief. I was not as squeamish as my sister Mercy, who could not stand to put her hands into a sinkful of dirty dishes filled with floating food—wet bread, stringy vegetables and bits of softened meat. Still, I didn't like the touch, the smells. How could I? When I touched my mother's feet, I looked away, held my nose with one hand, the other with fingers laced along her toes, pulling and popping them into place. "It really helps my arthritis, baby—you don't know. Pull my toes, I'll give you a dollar, find my girdle, and I'll give you two. Ouch. Ouch. Not so hard. There, that's good. Look at my feet. You see the veins? Look at them. Aren't they ugly? And up here, look where I had the operations . . . ugly, they stripped them and still they hurt me."

10 She rubbed her battered flesh wistfully, placed a delicate and lovely hand on her right thigh. Mother said proudly, truthfully, "I still have lovely thighs."

11 PREVIOUS EXPERIENCE WITH THE SICK AND DYING: Let me think . . .

12 Great Aunt Eutilia came to live with us one summer and seven months later she died in my father's old study, the walls lined with books, whatever answers were there—unread.

13 Great Aunt Eutilia smelled like the mercilessly sick. At first, a vague, softened aroma of tiredness and spilled food. And later, the full-blown emptyings of the dying: gas, putrefaction and fetid lucidity. Her body poured out long held-back odors. She wet her diapers and sheets and knocked over medicines and glasses of tepid water, leaving in the air an unpleasant smell.

14 I danced around her bed in my dreams, naked, smiling, jubilant. It was an exultant adolescent dance for my dying aunt. It was necessary, compulsive. It was a primitive dance, a full moon offering that led me slithering into her room with breasts naked and oily at thirteen . . .

15 No one home but me.

Las Mañanitas Little Morning **Cielito Lindo** Beautiful Little Sky

16 Led me to her room, my father's refuge, those halcyon days now that he was gone—and all that remained were dusty books, cast iron bookends, reminders of the spaces he filled. Down the steps I leaped into Eutilia's faded and foggy consciousness where I whirled and danced and sang: I am your flesh and my mother's flesh and you are . . . are . . . Eutilia stared at me. I turned away.

17 I danced around Eutilia's bed. I hugged the screen door, my breasts indented in the meshed wire. In the darkness Eutilia moaned, my body wet, her body dry. Steamy we were, and full of prayers.

18 Could I have absolved your dying by my life? Could I have lessened your agony with my spirit-filled dance in the deep darkness? The blue fan stirred, then whipped nonstop the solid air; little razors sliced through consciousness and prodded the sick and dying woman, whose whitened eves screeched: Ay! Ay! Let me jump, put a pillow, I want to go away . . . let me . . . let me . . .

19 One day while playing "Cielito Lindo" on the piano in the living room, Eutilia got up and fell to the side of the piano stool. Her foot caught on the rug, "¡Ay! ¡Ay! ¡Ay! ¡Ay! Canta y no llores . . . "°

20 All requests were silenced. Eutilia rested in her tattered hospital gown, having shredded it to pieces. She was surrounded by little white strips of raveled cloth. Uncle Toño, her babysitter, after watching the evening news, found her naked and in a bed of cloth. She stared at the ceiling, having played the piano far into the night. She listened to sounds coming from around the back of her head. Just listened. Just looked. Just shredded. Shredded the rented gown, shredded it. When the lady of the house returned and asked how was she, meaning, does she breathe, Toño answered, "Fine."

21 Christ on his crucifix! He'd never gone into the room to check on her. Later, when they found her, Toño cried, his cousin laughed. They hugged each other, then cried, then laughed, then cried. Eutilia's fingers never rested. They played beautiful tunes. She was a little girl in tatters in her metal bed with sideboards that went up and down, up and down . . .

22 The young girls danced they played they danced they filled out forms.

23 PREVIOUS EMPLOYMENT: None.

24 There was always a first job, as there was the first summer of the very first boyfriend. That was the summer of our first swamp cooler. The heat bore down and congealed sweat. It made rivulets trace the body's meridian and, before it stopped, was wiped away, never quite dismissed.

Canta y no llores Sing and don't cry

25 On the tops of the neighbors' houses old swamp coolers, with their jerky grating and droning moans, strained to ease the southern implacabilities. Whrr whrr cough whrr.

26 Regino Suárez climbed up and down the roof, first forgetting his hammer and then the cooler filter. His boy, Eliterio, stood at the bottom of the steps that led to the sun deck and squinted dumbly at the blazing sun. For several days Regino tramped over my dark purple bedroom. I had shut the curtains to both father and son and rested in violet contemplation of my first boyfriend.

27 Regino stomped his way to the other side of the house where Eutilia lay in her metal crib, trying to sleep, her weary eyes uncomprehending. The noise was upsetting, she could not play. The small blue fan wheezed freshness. Regino hammered and paced then climbed down. When lunchtime came, a carload of fat daughters drove Regino and the handsome son away.

28 If Eutilia could have read a book, it would have been the *Bible* or maybe her novena to the Santo Niño de Atocha, he was her boy . . .

29 PREVIOUS EXPERIENCE WITH THE SICK AND DYING:

30 This question reminds me of a story my mother told me about a very old woman, Doña Mercedes, who was dying of cancer. Doña Mercedes lived with her daughter, Corina, who was my mother's friend. The old woman lay in bed, day after day, moaning and crying softly, not actually crying out, but whimpering in a sad, hopeless way. "Don't move me," she begged when her daughter tried to change the sheets or bathe her. Every day this ordeal of maintenance became worse. It was a painful thing and full of dread for the old woman, the once fastidious and upright Doña Mercedes. She had been a lady, straight and imposing, and with a headful of rich dark hair. Her ancestors were from Spain. "You mustn't move me, Corina," Doña Mercedes pleaded, "never please. Leave me alone. mi'jita,"° and so the daughter acquiesced. Cleaning around her tortured flesh and delicately wiping where they could, the two women attended to Doña Mercedes. She died in the daytime, as she had wanted.

31 When the young women went to lift the old lady from her death bed, they struggled to pull her from the sheets; and, when finally they turned her on her side, they saw huge gaping holes in her back where the cancer had eaten through the flesh. The sheets were stained, the bedsores lost in a red wash of bloody pus. Doña Mercedes' cancer had eaten its way through her back and onto those sheets. "Don't move me, please don't move me," she had cried.

32 The two young women stuffed piles of shredded disinfected rags soaked in Lysol into Doña Mercedes' chest cavity, filling it, and horrified, with

---

mi'jita my little daughter

cloths over their mouths, said the prayers for the dead. Everyone remembered her as tall and straight and very Spanish

33 PRESENT EMPLOYMENT: Work-study aide at Altavista Memorial Hospital.

34 I never wanted to be a nurse. Never. The smells. The pain. What was I to do then, working in a hospital, in that place of white women, whiter men with square faces? I had no skills. Once in the seventh grade I'd gotten a penmanship award. Swirling R's in boredom, the ABC's ad infinitum. Instead of dipping chocolate cones at the Dairy Queen next door to the hospital, I found myself a frightened girl in a black skirt and white blouse standing near the stairwell to the cafeteria.

35 I stared up at a painting of a dark-haired woman in a stiff nurse's cap and grey tunic, tending to men in old fashioned service uniforms. There was a beauty in that woman's face whoever she was. I saw myself in her, helping all of mankind, forgetting and absolving all my own sick, my own dying, especially relatives, all of them so far away, removed. I never wanted to be like Great Aunt Eutilia, or Doña Mercedes with the holes in her back, or my mother, her scarred legs, her whitened thighs.

36 MR. SMITH

37 Mr. Smith sat at his desk surrounded by requisition forms. He looked up to me with glassy eyes like filmy paperweights.

38 MOTHER OF GOD, MR. SMITH WAS A WALLEYED HUNCHBACK!

39 "Mr. Smith, I'm Rocío Esquibel, the work-study student from the university and I was sent down here to talk to you about my job."

40 "Down here, down here," he laughed, as if it were a private joke. "Oh, yes, you must be the new girl. Menus," he mumbled. "Now just have a seat and we'll see what we can do. Would you like some iced tea?"

41 It was nine o'clock in the morning, too early for tea. "No, well, yes, that would be nice."

42 "It's good tea, everyone likes it. Here, I'll get you some." Mr. Smith got up, more hunchbacked than I'd imagined. He tiptoed out of the room whispering, "Tea, got to get this girl some tea."

43 There was a bit of the gruesome Golom in him, a bit of the twisted spider in the dark. Was I to work for this gnome? I wanted to rescue souls, not play attendant to this crippled, dried up specimen, this cartilaginous insect with his misshapen head and eyes that peered out to me like the marbled eyes of statues

one sees in museums. History preserves its freaks. God, was my job to do the same? No, never!

44 I faced Dietary Awards, Degrees in Food Management, menus for Low Salt and Fluids; the word Jello leaped out at every turn. I touched the walls. They were moist, never having seen the light.

45 In my dreams, Mr. Smith was encased in green Jello; his formaldehyde breath reminded me of other smells—decaying, saddened dead things; my great aunt, biology class in high school, my friend Dolores Casaus. Each of us held a tray with a dead frog pinned in place, served to us by a tall stoop-shouldered Viking turned farmer, our biology teacher Mr. Franke, pink-eyed, half blind. Dolores and I cut into the chest cavity and explored that small universe of dead cold fibers. Dolores stopped at the frog's stomach, then squeezed out its last meal, a green mash, spinach-colored, a viscous fluid—that was all that remained in that miniaturized, unresponding organ, all that was left of potential life.

46 Before Eutilia died she ate a little, mostly drank juice through bent and dripping hospital straws. The straws littered the floor where she'd knocked them over in her wild frenzy to escape. "Diooooooos," she cried in that shrill voice. "Dios mio, Diosito, por favor. Ay, I won't tell your mama, just help me get away . . . Diosito de mi vida . . . Diosito de mi corázon . . . agua, agua . . . por favor, por favor . . . "°

47 Mr. Smith returned with my iced tea.

48 "Sugar?"

49 Sugar, yes, sugar. Lots of it. Was I to spend all summer in this smelly cage? What was I to do? What? And for whom? I had no business here. It was summertime and my life stretched out magically in front of me: there was my boyfriend, my freedom. Senior year had been the happiest of my life; was it to change?

50 "Anytime you want to come down and get a glass of tea, you go right ahead. We always have it on hand. Everyone likes my tea," he said with pride.

51 "About the job?" I asked.

52 Mr. Smith handed me a pile of green forms. They were menus.

53 In the center of the menu was listed the day of the week, and to the left and coming down in a neat order were the three meals, breakfast, lunch and dinner. Each menu had various choices for each meal.

Diooooooos . . . por favor Ooooh, God; My God, dear God, please; God of my life . . . God of my heart . . . water, water . . . please, please

54 LUNCH:

☐ Salisbury Steak	☐ Mashed potatoes and gravy
☐ Fish sticks	☐ Macaroni and cheese
☐ Enchiladas	☐ Broccoli and onions
☐ Rice almondine	
Drinks	*Dessert*
☐ Coffee	☐ Jello
☐ Tea	☐ Carrot cake
☐ 7-Up	☐ Ice Cream, vanilla
☐ Other	

55 "Here you see a menu for Friday, listing the three meals. Let's take lunch. You have a choice of Salisbury steak, enchiladas, they're really good, Trini makes them, she's been working for me for twenty years. Her son George Jr. works for me, too, probably his kids one day." At this possibility, Mr. Smith laughed at himself. "Oh, and fish sticks. You a . . . ?"

56 "Our Lady of the Holy Scapular."

57 "Sometimes I'll get a menu back with a thank you written on the side. 'Thanks for the liver, it was real good', or 'I haven't had rice pudding since I was a boy.' Makes me feel good to know we've made our patients happy."

58 Mr. Smith paused, reflecting on the positive aspects of his job.

59 "Mind you, these menus are only for people on regular diets, not everybody, but a lot of people. I take care of the other special diets, that doesn't concern you. I have a girl working for me now, Arlene Rutschman. You know . . . "

60 My mind raced forward, backward. Arlene Rutschman, the Arlene from Holy Scapular, Arlene of the soft voice, the limp mannerisms, the plain, too goodly face, Arlene, president of Our Lady's Sodality, in her white and navy blue beanie, her bobby socks and horn-rimmed glasses, the Arlene of the school dances with her perpetual escort, Bennie Lara, the toothy better-than-no-date date, the Arlene of the high grades, the muscular, yet turned-in legs, the curly unattractive hair, *that* Arlene, the dud?

61 "Yes, I know her."

62 "Good!"

63 "We went to school together."

64 "Wonderful!"

65 "She works here?"

66 "Oh, she's a nice girl. She'll help you, show you what to do, how to distribute the menus."

67 "Distribute the menus?"

68 "Now you just sit there, drink your tea and tell me about yourself."

69 This was the first of many conversations with Mr. Smith, the hunchbacked dietician, a man who was never anything but kind to me.

70 "Hey," he said proudly, "these are my kids. Norma and Bardwell. Norma's in Junior High, majoring in boys, and Bardwell is graduating from the Military Institute."

71 "Bardwell. That's an unusual name," I said as I stared at a series of 5 x 7's on Mr. Smith's desk.

72 "Bardwell, well, that was my father's name. Bardwell B. Smith. The Bard, they called him!" At this he chuckled to himself, myopically recalling his father, tracing with his strange eyes patterns of living flesh and bone.

73 "He used to recite."

74 The children looked fairly normal. Norma was slight, with a broad toothy smile. Bardwell, or Bobby, as he was called, was not unhandsome in his uniform, if it weren't for one ragged splayed ear that slightly cupped forward, as if listening to something.

75 Mr. Smith's image was nowhere in sight. "Camera shy," he said. To the right of Mr. Smith's desk hung a plastic gold framed prayer beginning with the words: "Oh Lord of Pots and Pans." To the left, near a dried out watercooler was a sign, "Bless This Mess."

76 Over the weeks I began to know something of Mr. Smith's convoluted life, its anchorings. His wife and children came to life, and Mr. Smith acquired a name: Marion, and a vague disconcerting sexuality. It was upsetting for me to imagine him fathering Norma and Bardwell. I stared into the framed glossies full of disbelief. Who was Mrs. Smith? What was she like?

77 Eutilia never had any children. She'd been married to José Esparza, a good man, a handsome man. They ran a store in Agua Tibia. They prospered, until one day, early in the morning, about three a.m., several men from El Otro Lado° called out to them in the house. "Don José, wake up! We need to buy supplies." Eutilia was afraid, said, "No, José, don't let them in." He told her, "Woman, what are we here for?" And she said, "But at this hour, José? At this hour?" Don José let them into the store. The two men came in carrying two sacks, one that was empty, and another that they said was full of money. They went through the store, picking out hats, clothing, tins of corned beef, and stuffing them into the empty sack. "So many things, José," Eutilia whispered, "*too* many things!" "Oh no," one man replied, "we have the money, don't you trust us, José?" "Cómo no, compadre,"° he replied easily. "We need the goods, don't be afraid, compadre." "Too many things, too many things," Eutilia sighed, huddled in the darkness in her robe. She was a small woman, with the body of a little girl. Eutilia looked

---

El Otro Lado The other side (of the tracks, e.g.) **Cómo no, compadre** Of course, pal

at José, and it was then that they both knew. When the two men had loaded up, they turned to Don José, took out a gun, which was hidden in a sack, and said, "So sorry, compadre, but you know . . . stay there, don't follow us." Eutilia hugged the darkness, saying nothing for the longest time. José was a handsome man, but dumb.

78 The village children made fun of José Esparza, laughed at him and pinned notes and pieces of paper to his pants. "Tonto, tonto"° and "I am a fool." He never saw these notes, wondered why they laughed.

79 "I've brought you a gift, a bag of rocks"; all fathers have said that to their children. Except Don José Esparza. He had no children, despite his looks. "At times a monkey can do better than a prince," la comadre° Lucaya used to say to anyone who would listen.

80 The bodies of patients twisted and moaned and cried out, and cursed, but for the two of us in that basement world, all was quiet save for the occasional clinking of an iced tea glass and the sporadic sound of Mr. Smith clearing his throat.

81 "There's no hurry," Mr. Smith always said. "Now you just take your time. Always in a hurry. A young person like you."

82 ARLENE RUTSCHMAN

83 "You're so lucky that you can speak Spanish," Arlene intoned. She stood tiptoes, held her breath, then knocked gently on the patient's door. No sound. A swifter knock. "I could never remember what a turnip was," she said.

84 "Whatjawant?" a voice bellowed.

85 "I'm the menu girl; can I take your order?"

86 Arlene's high tremulous little girl's voice trailed off, "Good morning, Mr. Samaniego! What'll it be? No, it's not today you leave, tomorrow, after lunch. Your wife is coming to get you. So, what'll it be for your third-to-the-last meal? Now we got poached or fried eggs. Poached. P-o-a-c-h-e-d. That's like a little hard in the middle, but a little soft on the outside. Firm. No, not like scrambled. Different. Okay, you want scrambled. Juice? We got grape or orange. You like grape? Two grape. And some coffee, black."

87 A tall Anglo man, gaunt and yellowed like an old newspaper, his eyes rubbed black like an old raccoon's, ranged the hallway. The man talked quietly to himself and smoked numbers of cigarettes as he weaved between attendants with half-filled urinals and lugubrious I.V.'s. He reminded me of my father's friends, angular Anglos in their late fifties, men with names like Bud or Earl,

---

Tonto stupid **la comadre** the godmother of one's daughter

men who owned garages or steak houses, men with firm hairy arms, clear blue eyes and tattoos from the war.

88 "That's Mr. Ellis, 206," Arlene whispered, "jaundice."

89 "Oh," I said, curiously contemptuous and nervous at the same time, unhappy and reeling from the phrase, "I'm the menu girl!" How'd I ever manage to get such a dumb job? At least the Candy Stripers wore a cute uniform, and they got to do fun things like deliver flowers and candy.

90 "Here comes Mrs. Samaniego. The wife."

91 "Mr. Ellis's wife?" I said, with concern.

92 "No, Mr. Samaniego's wife, Donelda." Arlene pointed to a wizened and giggly old woman who was sneaking by the information desk, past the silver-haired volunteer, several squirmy grandchildren in tow. Visiting hours began at two p.m., but Donelda Samaniego had come early to beat the rush. From the hallway, Arlene and I heard loud smacks, much kidding and general merriment. The room smelled of tamales.

93 "Old Mr. Phillips in 304, that's the Medical Floor, he gets his cath at eleven, so don't go ask him about his menu then. It upsets his stomach."

94 Mrs. Daniels in 210 told Arlene weakly, "Honey, yes, you, honey, who's the other girl? Who is she? You'll just have to come back later. I don't feel good. I'm a dying woman, can't you see that?" When we came back an hour later, Mrs. Daniels was asleep, snoring loudly.

95 Mrs. Gustafson, a sad wet-eyed, well-dressed woman in her late sixties, dismissed us from the shade of drawn curtains as her husband, G.P. "Gus" Gustafson, the judge, took long and fitful naps only to wake up again, then go back to sleep, beginning once more his inexorable round of disappearances.

96 "Yesterday I weighed myself in the hall and I'm getting fat. Oh, and you're so thin."

97 "The hips," I said, "the hips."

98 "You know, you remind me of that painting," Arlene said, thoughtfully.

99 "Which?"

100 "Not which, who. The one in the stairwell. Florence Nightingale, she looks like you."

101 "That's who that is!"

102 "The eyes."

103 "She does?"

104 "The eyes."

105 "The eyes?"

106 "And the hair."

107 "The eyes and the hair? Maybe the hair, but not the eyes."

108 "Yes."

109 "I don't think so."

110 "Oh yes! Every time I look at it."

111 "Me?"

112 Arlene and I sat talking at our table in the cafeteria. that later was to become *my* table. It faced the dining room. From that vantage point I could see everything and not be seen.

113 We talked, two friends almost, if only she weren't so, so, little girlish with ribbons. Arlene was still dating Bennie and was majoring in either home ec or biology. They seemed the same in my mind: babies, menus and frogs. Loathsome, unpleasant things.

114 It was there, in the coolness of the cafeteria, in that respite from the green forms, at our special table, drinking tea, laughing with Arlene, that I, still shy, still judgmental, still wondering and still afraid, under the influence of caffeine, decided to stick it out. I would not quit the job.

115 "How's Mr. Prieto in 200?"

116 "He left yesterday, but he'll be coming back. He's dying."

117 "Did you see old Mr. Carter? They strapped him to the wheelchair finally."

118 "It was about time. He kept falling over."

119 "Mrs. Domínguez went to bland."

120 "She was doing so well."

121 "You think so? She couldn't hardly chew. She kept choking."

122 "And that grouch, what's her name, the head nurse, Stevens in 214 . . . "

123 "She's the head nurse? I didn't know that—god, I filled out her menu for her . . . she was sleeping and I . . . no wonder she was mad . . . how did I know she was the head nurse?"

124 "It's okay. She's going home or coming back, I can't remember which. Esperanza González is gonna be in charge."

125 "She was real mad."

126 "Forget it, it's okay."

127 "The woman will never forgive me, I'll lose my job," I sighed.

128 I walked home past the Diary Queen. It took five minutes at the most. I stopped midway at the ditch's edge, where the earth rose and where there was concrete embankment on which to sit. To some this was the quiet place, where neighborhood lovers met on summer nights to kiss, and where older couples paused between their evening walks to rest. It was also the talking place, where all the neighbor kids discussed life while eating hot fudge sundaes with nuts. The bench was large: four could sit on it comfortably. It faced an open field in the middle of which stood a huge apricot tree. Lastly, the bench was a stopping place, the "throne," we called it. We took off hot shoes and dipped our cramped feet into the cool ditch water, as we sat facing the southern sun at the quiet talking place, at our thrones, not thinking anything, eyes closed, but sun. The great red velvet sun.

129 One night I dreamed of food, wading through hallways of food, inside some dark evil stomach. My boyfriend waved to me from the ditch's bank. I sat

on the throne, ran alongside his car, a blue Ford, in which he sat, on clear plastic seat covers, with that hungry Church-of-Christ smile of his. He drove away, and when he returned, the car was small and I was too big to get inside.

130 Eutilia stirred. She was tired. She did not recognize anyone. I danced around the bed, crossed myself, en el nombre del padre, del hijo y del espíritu santo,° crossed forehead, chin and breast, begged for forgiveness even as I danced.

131 And on waking, I remembered. *Nabos. Turnips.* But of course.

132 It seemed right to me to be working in a hospital, to be helping people, and yet: why was I only a menu girl? Once a menu was completed, another would take its place and the next day another. It was a never ending round of food and more food. I thought of Judge Gustafson.

133 When Arlene took a short vacation to the Luray Caverns, I became the official menu girl. That week was the happiest of my entire summer.

134 That week I fell in love.

135 ELIZABETH RAINEY

136 Elizabeth Rainey, Room 240, was in for a D and C. I didn't know what a D and C was, but I knew it was mysterious and to me, of course, this meant it had to do with sex. Elizabeth Rainey was propped up in bed with many pillows, a soft blue, homemade quilt at the foot of her bed. Her cheeks were flushed, her red lips quivering. She looked fragile, and yet her face betrayed a harsh indelicate bitterness. She wore a creme-colored gown on which her loose hair fell about her like a cape. She was a beautiful woman, full-bodied, with the translucent beauty certain women have in the midst of sorrow—clear and unadorned, her eyes bright with inexplicable and self-contained suffering.

137 She cried out to me rudely, as if I personally had offended her. "What do you want? Can't you see I want to be alone. Now close the door and go away! Go away!"

138 "I'm here to get your menu." I could not bring myself to say, I'm the menu girl.

139 "Go away, go away, I don't want anything. I don't want to eat. Close the door!"

140 Elizabeth Rainey pulled her face away from me and turned to the wall, and, with deep and self punishing exasperation, grit her teeth, and from the depths of her self-loathing a small inarticulate cry escaped—"Oooooh."

---

en el nombre . . . santo in the name of the father, the son, and the holy ghost

141 I ran out, frightened by her pain, yet excited somehow. She was so beautiful and so alone. I wanted in my little girl's way to hold her, hold her tight and in my woman's way never to feel her pain, ever, whatever it was.

142 "Go away, go away," she said, her trembling mouth rimmed with pain. "go away!"

143 She didn't want to eat, told me to go away. How many people yelled to me to go away that summer, have yelled since then, countless people, of all ages, sick people, really sick people, dying people, people who were well and still rudely tied into their needs for privacy and space, affronted by these constant impositions from, of all people, the menu girl!

144 "Move over and move out, would you? Go away! Leave me alone!"

145 And yet, of everyone who told me to go away, it was this woman in her solitary anguish who touched me the most deeply. How could I, age seventeen, not knowing love, how could I presume to reach out to this young woman in her sorrow, touch her and say, "I know, I understand."

146 Instead, I shrank back into myself and trembled behind the door. I never went back into her room. How could I? It was too terrible a vision, for in her I saw myself, all life, all suffering. What I saw both chilled and burned me. I stood long in that darkened doorway, confused in the presence of human pain. I wanted to reach out . . . I wanted to . . . I wanted to . . . But *how?*

147 As long as I live I will carry Elizabeth Rainey's image with me: in a creme-colored gown she is propped up, her hair fanning pillows in a room full of deep sweet acrid and overspent flowers. Oh, I may have been that summer girl, but yes, I knew, I understood. I would have danced for her, Eutilia, had I but dared.

148 DOLORES CASAUS

149 Dolores of the frog entrails episode, who'd played my sister Ismene in the world literature class play, was now a nurse's aide on the surgical floor, changing sheets, giving enemas and taking rectal temperatures.

150 It was she who taught me how to take blood pressure, wrapping the cuff around the arm, counting the seconds and then multiplying beats. As a friend, she was rude, impudent, delightful; as an aide, most dedicated. One day for an experiment, with me as a guinea pig, she took the blood pressure of my right leg. That day I hobbled around the hospital, the leg cramped and weak. In high school Dolores had been my double, my confidante and the best ouija board partner I ever had. When we set our fingers to the board, the dial raced and spun, flinging out letters—notes from the long dead, the crying out. Together we

contacted la Llorona° and would have unraveled *that* mystery if Sister Esperidiana hadn't caught us in the religion room during lunchtime communing with that distressed spirit who had so much to tell!

151 Dolores was engaged. She had a hope chest. She wasn't going to college because she had to work, and her two sisters-in-law, the Nurses González and González—Esperanza, male, and Bertha, female—were her supervisors.

152 As a favor to Dolores, González the Elder, Esperanza would often give her a left-over tray of "regular" food, the patient having checked out or on to other resting grounds. Usually I'd have gone home after the ritualistic glass of tea but one day, out of boredom perhaps, most likely out of curiosity, I hung around the surgical floor talking to Dolores, my only friend in all the hospital. I clung to her sense of wonder, her sense of the ludicrous, to her humor in the face of order, for even in that environment of restriction, I felt her still probing the whys and wherefores of science, looking for vestiges of irregularity with immense childlike curiosity.

153 The day of the left-over meal found Dolores and me in the laundry room, sandwiched between bins of feces and urine stained sheets to be laundered. There were also dripping urinals waiting to be washed. Hunched over a tray of fried chicken, mashed potatoes and gravy, lima beans and vanilla ice cream, we devoured crusty morsels of Mr. Smith's fried chicken breasts. The food was good. We fought over the ice cream. I resolved to try a few more meals before the summer ended, perhaps in a more pleasant atmosphere.

154 That day, I lingered at the hospital longer than usual. I helped Dolores with Francisca Pacheco, turning the old woman on her side as we fitted the sheet on the mattress. "Cuidado,no me toquen,"° she cried. When Dolores took her temperature rectally, I left the room, but returned just as quickly, ashamed of my timidity. I was always the passing menu girl, too afraid to linger, too unwilling to see, too busy with summer illusions. Every day I raced to finish the daily menus, punching in my time card, greeting the beginning of what I considered to be my *real* day outside those long and smelly corridors where food and illness intermingled, leaving a sweet thick air of exasperation in my lungs. The "ooooh" of Elizabeth Rainey's anxious flesh.

155 The "ay ay ay" of Great Aunt Eutilia's phantom cries awaited me in my father's room. On the wall the portrait of his hero Napoleon hung, shielded by white sheets. The sun was too bright that summer for delicate fading eyes, the heat too oppressive. The blue fan raced to bring freshness to that acrid tomb full of ghosts.

---

la Llorona the Weeper-Ghost
Cuidado, no me toquen Carfeul, don't touch me

156 I walked home slowly, not stopping at the quiet place. Compadre Regino Suárez was on the roof. The cooler leaked. Impatient with Regino and his hearty wave, his habit of never doing any job thoroughly, I remembered that I'd forgotten my daily iced tea. The sun was hot. All I wanted was to rest in the cool darkness of my purple room.

157 The inside of the house smelled of burnt food and lemons. My mother had left something on the stove again. To counteract the burnt smell she'd placed lemons all over the house. Lemons filled ashtrays and bowls, they lay solidly on tables and rested in hot corners. I looked in the direction of Eutilia's room. Quiet. She was sleeping. She'd been dead five years but, still, the room was hers. She was sleeping peacefully. I smelled the cleansing bitterness of lemons.

158 MRS. DANIELS

159 When I entered rooms and saw sick, dying women in their forties, I always remembered room 210, Mrs. Daniels, the mother of my cousin's future wife.

160 Mrs. Daniels usually lay in bed, whimpering like a little dog, moaning to her husband, who always stood nearby, holding her hand, saying softly, "Now, Martha, Martha. The little girl only wants to get your order."

161 "Send her away, goddammit!"

162 On those days that Mr. Daniels was absent, Mrs. Daniels whined for me to go away. "Leave me alone, can't you see I'm dying," she said and looked toward the wall. She looked so pale, sick, near death to me, but somehow I knew, not really having imagined death without the dying, not having felt the outrage and loathing, I knew and saw her outbursts for what they really were: deep hurts, deep distresses. I saw her need to release them, to fling them at others, dribbling pain/anguish/abuse, trickling away those vast torrential feelings of sorrow and hate and fear, letting them fall wherever they would, on whomever they might. I was her white wall. I was her whipping girl upon whom she spilled her darkened ashes. She cried out obscenely to me, sending me reeling from her room, that room of loathing and dread. That room anxious with worms.

163 Who of us has not heard the angry choked words of crying people, listened, not wanting to hear, then shut our ears, said enough, I don't want to. Who has not seen the fearful tearstreamed faces, known the blank eyes and felt the holding back, and, like smiling thoughtless children, said: "I was in the next room, I couldn't help hearing, I heard, I saw, you didn't know, did you? I know."

164 We rolled up the pain, assigned it a shelf, placed it in the hardened place, along with a certain self-congratulatory sense of wonder at the world's unfortunates like Mrs. Daniels. We were embarrassed to be alive.

165 JUAN MARÍA/THE NOSE

166 "Como se dice° when was the last time you had a bowel movement?" Nurse Luciano asked. She was from Yonkers. a bright newlywed. Erminia, the ward secretary, a tall thin horsey woman with a postured Juárez hairdo of exaggerated sausage ringlets, replied through chapped lips. "Oh, who cares, he's sleeping."

167 "He's from México, huh?" Luciano said with interest.

168 "All illegal alien," Rosario retorted. She was Erminia's sister, the superintendent's secretary, with the look of a badly scarred bulldog. She'd stopped by to invite Erminia to join her for lunch.

169 "So where'd it happen?" Luciano asked.

170 "At the Guadalajara Bar on Main Street," Erminia answered, moistening her purple lips nervously. It was a habit of hers.

171 "Hey, I remember when we used to walk home from school. You remember, Rocío?" Dolores asked, "We'd try to throw each other through the swinging doors. It was real noisy in there."

172 "Father O'Kelley said drink was the defilement of men, the undoing of staunch, god-fearing women," I said.

173 "Our father has one now and then," Rosario replied, "that doesn't mean anything. It's because he was one of those aliens."

174 "Those kind of problems are bad around here I heard," Luciano said, "people sneaking across the border and all."

175 "Hell, you don't know the half of it," Nurse González said as she came up to the desk where we all stood facing the hallway. "It's an epidemic."

176 "I don't know, my mother always had maids, and they were all real nice except the one who stole her wedding rings. We had to track her all the way to Piedras Negras and even then she wouldn't give them up," Erminia interjected.

177 "Still, it doesn't seem human the way they're treated at times."

178 "Some of them, they ain't human."

179 "Still, he was drunk, he wasn't full aware."

180 "Full aware, my ass," retorted Esperanza angrily, "he had enough money to buy booze. If that's not aware, I don't know what aware is. Ain't my goddamn fault the bastard got into a fight and someone bit his nose off. Ain't *my* fault he's here and *we* gotta take care of him. Christ! If *that* isn't aware, I don't know what aware is!"

181 Esperanza González, head surgical floor nurse, the short but highly respected Esperanza of no esperanzas,° the Esperanza of the short-bobbed hair,

---

Como se dice How do you say
Esperanza of no esperanzas Hope of no hopes

the husky deferential voice, the commands, the no-nonsense orders and briskness, Esperanza the future sister-in-law of Dolores, my old friend, Esperanza the dyke, who was later killed in a car accident on the way to somewhere, said: "Now get back to work all of you, we're just here to clean up the mess."

182 Later when Esperanza was killed my aunt said, "How nice. In the paper they called her lover her sister. How nice!"

183 "Hey, Erminia, lunch?" asked Rosario, almost sheepishly. "You hungry?"

184 "Coming, Rosario," yelled Erminia from the back office where she was getting her purse. "Coming!"

185 "God, I'm starving," Rosario said, "can you hear my stomach?"

186 "Go check Mr. Carter's cath, Dolores, will you?" said Esperanza in a softer tone.

187 "Well, I don't know, I just don't know, " Luciano pondered. "It doesn't seem human, does it? I mean how in the world could anyone in their right mind bite off another person's nose? How? You know it, González, you're a tough rooster. If I didn't know you so well already, you'd scare the hell out of me. How long you been a nurse?"

188 "Too long, Luciano. Look, I ain't a new bride, that's liable to make a person soft. Me, I just clean up the mess."

189 "Luciano, what you know about people could be put on the head of a pin. You just leave these alien problems to those of us who were brought up around here and know what's going on. Me, I don't feel one bit sorry for that bastard," Esperanza said firmly. "Christ, Luciano, what do you expect, he don't speak no Engleesh!"

190 "His name is Juan María Mejía," I ventured.

191 Luciano laughed. Esperanza laughed. Dolores went off to Mr. Carter's room, and Rosario chatted noisily with Erminia as they walked toward the cafeteria.

192 "Hey, Rosario," Luciano called out, "what happened to the rings?"

193 It was enchilada day. Trini was very busy.

194 Juan María the Nose was sleeping in the hallway; all the other beds were filled. His hospital gown was awry, the grey sheet folded through sleep-deadened limbs. His hands were tightly clenched. The hospital screen barely concealed his twisted private sleep of legs akimbo, moist armpits and groin. It was a sleep of sleeping off, of hard drunken wanderings, with dreams of a bar, dreams of a fight. He slept the way little boys sleep, carelessly half exposed. I stared at him.

195 Esperanza complained and muttered under her breath, railing at the Anglo sons of bitches and at all the lousy wetbacks, at everyone, male and female, goddamn them and their messes. Esperanza was dark and squat, pura

india° tortured by her very face. Briskly, she ordered Dolores and now me about. I had graduated overnight, as if in a hazy dream, to assistant, but unofficial, ward secretary.

196 I stared across the hallway to Juan María the Nose. He faced the wall, a dangling I.V. at the foot of the bed. Esperanza González, R.N., looked at me.

197 "Well, and *who* are you?"

198 "I'm the menu, I mean, I *was* the menu . . . " I stammered. "I'm helping Erminia."

199 "So get me some cigarettes. Camels. I'll pay you tomorrow when I get paid. "

200 Yes, it was really González, male, who ran the hospital.

201 Arlene returned from the Luray Caverns with a stalactite charm bracelet for me. She announced to Mr. Smith and me that she'd gotten a job with an insurance company.

202 "I'll miss you, Rocío."

203 "Me, too, Arlene." God knows it was the truth. I'd come to depend on her, our talks over tea. No one every complimented me like she did.

204 "You never get angry, do you?" she said admiringly.

205 "Rarely," I said. But inside, I was always angry.

206 "What do you want to do?"

207 "Want to do?"

208 "Yeah."

209 I want to be someone else, somewhere else, someone important and responsible and sexy. I want to be sexy.

210 "I don't know. I'm going to major in drama."

211 "You're sweet," she said. "Everyone likes you. It's in your nature. You're the Florence Nightingale of Altavista Memorial, that's it!"

212 "Oh God, Arlene, I don't want to be a nurse, *ever!* I can't take the smells. No one in our family can stand smells."

213 "You look like that painting. I always did think it looked like you . . . "

214 "You did?"

215 "Yeah."

216 "Come on, you're making me sick, Arlene."

217 "Everyone likes you."

218 "Well . . . "

219 "So keep in touch. I'll see you at the University."

---

pura india pure Indian

220 "Home Ec?"

221 "Biology."

222 We hugged.

223 The weeks progressed. My hours at the hospital grew. I was allowed to check in patients, to take their blood pressures and temperatures. I flipped through the patients' charts, memorizing names, room numbers, types of diet. I fingered the doctors' reports with reverence. Perhaps someday I would begin to write in them as Erminia did: "2:15 p.m., Mrs. Daniels, pulse normal, temp normal, Dr. Blasse checked patient, treatment on schedule, medication given to quiet patient."

224 One day I received a call at the ward desk. It was Mr. Smith.

225 "Ms. Esquibel? Rocío? This is Mr. Smith, you know, down in the cafeteria."

226 "Yes, Mr. Smith! How are you? Is there anything I can do? Are you getting the menus okay? I'm leaving them on top of your desk."

227 "I've been talking to Nurse González, surgical; she says they need you there full time to fill in and could I do without you?"

228 "Oh, I can do both jobs; it doesn't take that long, Mr. Smith."

229 "No, we're going by a new system. Rather, it's the old system. The aides will take the menu orders like they used to before Arlene came. So, you come down and see me, Rocío, have a glass of iced tea. I never see you any more since you moved up in the world. Yeah, I guess you're the last of the menu girls."

230 The summer passed. June, July, August, my birth month. There were serious days, hurried admissions, feverish errands, quick notes jotted in the doctor's charts. I began to work Saturdays. In my eagerness to "advance," I unwittingly had created more work for myself, work I really wasn't skilled to do.

231 My heart reached out to every person, dragged itself through the hallways with the patients, cried when they did, laughed when they did. I had no business in the job. I was too emotional.

232 Now when I walked into a room I knew the patient's history, the cause of illness. I began to study individual cases with great attention, turning to a copy of *The Family Physician*, which had its place among my father's old books in his abandoned study.

233 Gone were the idle hours of sitting in the cafeteria, leisurely drinking iced tea, gone were the removed reflections of the outsider.

234 My walks home were measured, pensive. I hid in my room those long hot nights, nights full of wrestling, injured dreams. Nothing seemed enough.

235 Before I knew it, it was the end of August, close to that autumnal time of setting out. My new life was about to begin. I had made that awesome leap into myself that steamy summer of illness and dread—confronting at every turn, the flesh, its lingering cries.

236 "Ay, Ay, Ay, Ay, Canta y no llores! Porque cantado se alegran, Cielito Lindo, los corazones . . . "° The little thin voice of an old woman sang from one of the back rooms. She pumped the gold pedals with fast furious and fervant feet, she smiled to the wall, its faces, she danced on the ceiling.

237 Let me jump.

238 "Goodbye, Dolores, it was fun."

239 "I'll miss you, Rocío! But you know, gotta save some money. I'll get back to school someday, maybe."

240 "What's wrong, Erminia? You mad?" I asked.

241 "I thought you were gonna stay and help me out here on the floor."

242 "Goddamn right!" complained Esperanza. "Someone told me this was your last day, so why didn't you tell me? Why'd I train you for, so you could leave us? To go to school? What for? So you can get those damned food stamps? It's a disgrace all those wetbacks and healthy college students getting our hard earned tax money. Makes me sick. Christ!" Esperanza shook her head with disgust.

243 "Hey, Erminia, you tell Rosario goodbye for me and Mrs. Luciano, too," I said sadly.

244 "Yeah, okay. They'll be here tomorrow," she answered tonelessly. I wanted to believe she was sad.

245 "I gotta say goodbye to Mr. Smith," I said, as I moved away.

246 "Make him come up and get some sun," González snickered. "Hell no, better not, he might get sunstroke and who'd fix my fried chicken?"

247 I climbed down the steps to the basement, past the cafeteria, past my special table, and into Mr. Smith's office, where he sat, adding numbers.

248 "Miss Esquibel, Rocío!"

249 "This is my last day, Mr. Smith. I wanted to come down and thank you. I'm sorry about . . . "

250 "Oh no, it worked out all right. It's nothing."

251 Did I see, from the corner of my eye, a set of Friday's menus he himself was tabulating—salisbury steak, macaroni and cheese . . .

252 "We'll miss you, Rocío. You were an excellent menu girl."

253 "It's been a wonderful summer."

254 "Do you want some tea?"

255 "No, I really don't have the time."

256 "I'll get . . . "

257 "No, thank you, Mr. Smith, I *really* have to go, but thanks. It's really good tea."

Porque. . . corazones Because when they sing, Beautiful Little Sky, hearts rejoice

258 I extended my hand, and for the first time, we touched. Mr. Smith's eyes seemed fogged, distracted. He stood up and hobbled closer to my side. I took his grave cold hand, shook it softly, and turned to the moist walls. When I closed the door, I saw him in front of me, framed in paper, the darkness of that quiet room. Bless this mess.

259 Eutilia's voice echoed in the small room. Goodbye. Goodbye. And let me jump.

260 I turned away from the faces, the voices, now gone: Father O'Kelley, Elizabeth Rainey, Mrs. Luciano, Arlene Rutschman, Mrs. Daniels, Juan María the Nose, Mr. Samaniego and Donelda, his wife, their grandchildren, Mr. Carter, Earl Ellis, Dolores Casaus, Erminia and her sister, the bulldog. Esperanza González, Francisca Pacheco, Elweena Twinbaum, the silver-haired volunteer whose name I'd learned the week before I left Altavista Memorial. I'd made a list on a menu of all the people I'd worked with. To remember. It seemed right.

261 From the distance I heard Marion Smith's high voice: "Now you come back and see us!"

262 Above the stairs the painting of Florence Nightingale stared solidly into weary soldiers' eyes. Her look encompassed all the great unspeakable sufferings of every war. I thought of Arlene typing insurance premiums.

263 Farther away, from behind and around my head, I heard the irregular but joyful strains of "Cielito Lindo" played on a phantom piano by a disembodied but now peaceful voice that sang with great quivering emotion: De la sierra morena, Cielito Lindo . . . viene bajando . . . °

264 Regino fixed the cooler. I started school. Later that year I was in a car accident. I crashed into a brick wall at the cemetery. I walked to Dolores' house, holding my bleeding face in my hands. Dolores and her father argued all the way to the hospital. I sat quietly in the back seat. It was a lovely morning. So clear. When I woke up I was on the surgical floor. Everyone knew me. I had so many flowers in the room I could hardly breathe. My older sister, Ronelia, thought I'd lost part of my nose in the accident and she returned to the cemetery to look for it. It wasn't there.

265 Mr. Smith came to see me once. I started to cry.

266 "Oh no, no, no, now don't you do that, Rocío. You want some tea?"

267 No one took my menu order. I guess that system had finally died out. I ate the food, whatever it was, walked the hallways in my grey hospital gown slit in the back, railed at the well-being of others, cursed myself for being so stupid. I

De la sierra . . . bajando From the dark mountains, Beautiful Little Sky . . . you are descending

only wanted to he taken home, down the street, past the quiet-talking place, a block away, near the Dairy Queen, to the darkness of my purple room.

268 It was time.

269 PREVIOUS EMPLOYMENT: Altavista Memorial Hospital

270 SUPERVISORS: Mr. Marion Smith, Dietician, and Miss Esperanza González, R.N., Surgical Floor.

271 DATES: June 1966 to August 1966

272 IN A FEW SENTENCES GIVE A BRIEF DESCRIPTION OF YOUR JOB: As Ward Secretary, I was responsible for . . . let me think . . .

—1986

✧ ✧ ✧

Louise Erdrich

(b. 1954)

Fleur

Born in Little Falls, Minnesota, Erdrich grew up in North Dakota. Her father was a teacher with the Bureau of Indian Affairs, and both he and her mother encouraged her to write stories from an early age. Erdrich holds degrees from Dartmouth College and Johns Hopkins University, where she studied creative writing. Her novel *Love Medicine* won the National Book Critics Circle Award for 1984. Much of Erdrich's fiction draws on her childhood on the Great Plains and her mixed cultural heritage (her ancestry is German American and Chippewa). In addition to *Love Medicine* she has published two other novels, *The Beet Queen* (1986) and *Tracks* (1988), which contains other stories about Fleur Pillager; several prize-winning short stories; and a book of poetry. Erdrich and her husband, Michael Dorris, another Native American writer, have appeared in two documentary films shown on PBS. Along with James Welch and Leslie Marmon Silko, Erdrich is redefining earlier definitions of Native American fiction. As the *Columbia Literary History of the United States* says, "These authors have had to resist the formulaic approaches favored by the publishing industry, which has its own opinions about what constitutes the 'proper' form and content of minority fiction."

The first time she drowned in the cold and glassy waters of Lake Turcot, Fleur Pillager was only a girl. Two men saw the boat tip, saw her struggle in the waves. They rowed over to the place she went down, and jumped in. When they dragged her over the gunwales, she was cold to the touch and stiff, so they slapped her face, shook her by the heels, worked her arms back and forth, and pounded her back until she coughed up lake water. She shivered all over like a dog, then took a breath. But it wasn't long afterward that those two men disappeared. The first wandered off, and the other, Jean Hat, got himself run over by a cart.

2 It went to show, my grandma said. It figured to her, all right. By saving Fleur Pillager, those two men had lost themselves.

3 The next time she fell in the lake, Fleur Pillager was twenty years old and no one touched her. She washed onshore, her skin a dull dead gray, but when George Many Women bent to look closer, he saw her chest move. Then her eyes spun open, sharp black riprock, and she looked at him. "You'll take my place," she hissed. Everybody scattered and left her there, so no one knows how she dragged herself home. Soon after that we noticed Many Women changed, grew afraid, wouldn't leave his house, and would not be forced to go near water. For his caution, he lived until the day that his sons brought him a new tin bathtub. Then the first time he used the tub he slipped, got knocked out, and breathed water while his wife stood in the other room frying breakfast.

4 Men stayed clear of Fleur Pillager after the second drowning. Even though she was good-looking, nobody dared to court her because it was clear that Misshepeshu, the waterman, the monster, wanted her for himself. He's a devil, that one, love-hungry with desire and maddened for the touch of young girls, the strong and daring especially, the ones like Fleur.

5 Our mothers warn us that we'll think he's handsome, for he appears with green eyes, copper skin, a mouth tender as a child's. But if you fall into his arms, he sprouts horns, fangs, claws, fins. His feet are joined as one and his skin, brass scales, rings to the touch. You're fascinated, cannot move. He casts a shell necklace at your feet, weeps gleaming chips that harden into mica on your breasts. He holds you under. Then he takes the body of a lion or a fat brown worm. He's made of gold. He's made of beach moss. He's a thing of dry foam, a thing of death by drowning, the death a Chippewa cannot survive.

6 Unless you are Fleur Pillager. We all knew she couldn't swim. After the first time, we thought she'd never go back to Lake Turcot. We thought she'd keep to herself, live quiet, stop killing men off by drowning in the lake. After the first time, we thought she'd keep the good ways. But then, after the second drowning, we knew that we were dealing with something much more serious. She was haywire, out of control. She messed with evil, laughed at the old women's advice, and dressed like a man. She got herself into some half-forgotten medicine, studied ways we shouldn't talk about. Some say she kept the finger

of a child in her pocket and a powder of unborn rabbits in a leather thong around her neck. She laid the heart of an owl on her tongue so she could see at night, and went out, hunting, not even in her own body. We know for sure because the next morning, in the snow or dust, we followed the tracks of her bare feet and saw where they changed, where the claws sprang out, the pad broadened and pressed into the dirt. By night we heard her chuffing cough, the bear cough. By day her silence and the wide grin she threw to bring down our guard made us frightened. Some thought that Fleur Pillager should be driven off the reservation, but not a single person who spoke like this had the nerve. And finally, when people were just about to get together and throw her out, she left on her own and didn't come back all summer. That's what this story is about.

7 During that summer, when she lived a few miles south in Argus, things happened. She almost destroyed that town.

8 When she got down to Argus in the year of 1920, it was just a small grid of six streets on either side of the railroad depot. There were two elevators, one central, the other a few miles west. Two stores competed for the trade of the three hundred citizens, and three churches quarreled with one another for their souls. There was a frame building for Lutherans, a heavy brick one for Episcopalians, and a long narrow shingled Catholic church. This last had a tall slender steeple, twice as high as any building or tree.

9 No doubt, across the low, flat wheat, watching from the road as she came near Argus on foot, Fleur saw that steeple rise, a shadow thin as a needle. Maybe in that raw space it drew her the way a lone tree draws lightning. Maybe, in the end, the Catholics are to blame. For if she hadn't seen that sign of pride, that slim prayer, that marker, maybe she would have kept walking.

10 But Fleur Pillager turned, and the first place she went once she came into town was to the back door of the priest's residence attached to the landmark church. She didn't go there for a handout, although she got that, but to ask for work. She got that too, or the town got her. It's hard to tell which came out worse, her or the men or the town, although the upshot of it all was that Fleur lived.

11 The four men who worked at the butcher's had carved up about a thousand carcasses between them, maybe half of that steers and the other half pigs, sheep, and game animals like deer, elk, and bear. That's not even mentioning the chickens, which were beyond counting. Pete Kozka owned the place, and employed Lily Veddar, Tor Grunewald, and my stepfather, Dutch James, who had brought my mother down from the reservation the year before she disappointed him by dying. Dutch took me out of school to take her place. I kept house half the time and worked the other in the butcher shop, sweeping floors, putting sawdust down, running a hambone across the street to a customer's bean pot or a package of sausage to the corner. I was a good one to have around because

until they needed me, I was invisible. I blended into the stained brown walls, a skinny, big-nosed girl with staring eyes. Because I could fade into a corner or squeeze beneath a shelf, I knew everything, what the men said when no one was around, and what they did to Fleur.

12 Kozka's Meats served farmers for a fifty-mile area, both to slaughter, for it had a stock pen and chute, and to cure the meat by smoking it or spicing it in sausage. The storage locker was a marvel, made of many thicknesses of brick, earth insulation, and Minnesota timber, lined inside with sawdust and vast blocks of ice cut from Lake Turcot, hauled down from home each winter by horse and sledge.

13 A ramshackle board building, part slaughterhouse, part store, was fixed to the low, thick square of the lockers. That's where Fleur worked. Kozka hired her for her strength. She could lift a haunch or carry a pole of sausages without stumbling, and she soon learned cutting from Pete's wife, a string-thin blonde who chain-smoked and handled the razor-sharp knives with nerveless precision, slicing close to her stained fingers. Fleur and Fritzie Kozka worked afternoons, wrapping their cuts in paper, and Fleur hauled the packages to the lockers. The meat was left outside the heavy oak doors that were only opened at 5:00 each afternoon, before the men ate supper.

14 Sometimes Dutch, Tor, and Lily ate at the lockers, and when they did I stayed too, cleaned floors, restoked the fires in the front smokehouses, while the men sat around the squat cast-iron stove spearing slats of herring onto hardtack bread. They played long games of poker or cribbage on a board made from the planed end of a salt crate. They talked and I listened, although there wasn't much to hear since almost nothing ever happened in Argus. Tor was married, Dutch had lost my mother, and Lily read circulars. They mainly discussed about the auctions to come, equipment, or women.

15 Every so often, Pete Kozka came out front to make a whist, leaving Fritzie to smoke cigarettes and fry raised doughnuts in the back room. He sat and played a few rounds but kept his thoughts to himself. Fritzie did not tolerate him talking behind her back, and the one book he read was the New Testament. If he said something, it concerned weather or a surplus of sheep stomachs, a ham that smoked green or the markets for corn and wheat. He had a good-luck talisman, the opal-white lens of a cow's eye. Playing cards, he rubbed it between his fingers. That soft sound and the slap of cards was about the only conversation.

16 Fleur finally gave them a subject.

17 Her cheeks were wide and flat, her hands large, chapped, muscular. Fleur's shoulders were broad as beams, her hips fishlike, slippery, narrow. An old green dress clung to her waist, worn thin where she sat. Her braids were thick like the tails of animals, and swung against her when she moved, deliberately, slowly in her work, held in and half-tamed, but only half. I could tell, but the others never saw. They never looked into her sly brown eyes or noticed

her teeth, strong and curved and very white. Her legs were bare, and since she padded around in beadwork moccasins they never saw that her fifth toes were missing. They never knew she'd drowned. They were blinded, they were stupid, they only saw her in the flesh.

18 And yet it wasn't just that she was a Chippewa, or even that she was a woman, it wasn't that she was good-looking or even that she was alone that made their brains hum. It was how she played cards.

19 Women didn't usually play with men, so the evening that Fleur drew a chair up to the men's table without being so much as asked, there was a shock of surprise.

20 "What's this," said Lily. He was fat, with a snake's cold pale eyes and precious skin, smooth and lily-white, which is how he got his name. Lily had a dog, a stumpy mean little bull of a thing with a belly drum-tight from eating pork rinds. The dog liked to play cards just like Lily, and straddled his barrel thighs through games of stud, rum poker, vingt-un. The dog snapped at Fleur's arm that first night, but cringed back, its snarl frozen, when she took her place.

21 "I thought," she said, her voice soft and stroking, "you might deal me in."

22 There was a space between the heavy bin of spiced flour and the wall where I just fit. I hunkered down there, kept my eyes open, saw her black hair swing over the chair, her feet solid on the wood floor. I couldn't see up on the table where the cards slapped down, so after they were deep in their game I raised myself up in the shadows, and crouched on a sill of wood.

23 I watched Fleur's hands stack and ruffle, divide the cards, spill them to each player in a blur, rake them up and shuffle again. Tor, short and scrappy, shut one eye and squinted the other at Fleur. Dutch screwed his lips around a wet cigar.

24 "Gotta see a man," he mumbled, getting up to go out back to the privy. The others broke, put their cards down, and Fleur sat alone in the lamplight that glowed in a sheen across the push of her breasts. I watched her closely, then she paid me a beam of notice for the first time. She turned, looked straight at me, and grinned the white wolf grin a Pillager turns on its victims, except that she wasn't after me.

25 "Pauline there," she said, "how much money you got?"

26 We'd all been paid for the week that day. Eight cents was in my pocket.

27 "Stake me," she said, holding out her long fingers. I put the coins in her palm and then I melted back to nothing, part of the walls and tables. It was a long time before I understood that the men would not have seen me no matter what I did, how I moved. I wasn't anything like Fleur. My dress hung loose and my back was already curved, an old woman's. Work had roughened me, reading made my eyes sore, caring for my mother before she died had hardened my face. I was not much to look at, so they never saw me.

28 When the men came back and sat around the table, they had drawn together. They shot each other small glances, stuck their tongues in their cheeks, burst out laughing at odd moments, to rattle Fleur. But she never minded. They played their vingt-un, staying even as Fleur slowly gained. Those pennies I had given her drew nickels and attracted dimes until there was a small pile in front of her.

29 Then she hooked them with five-card draw, nothing wild. She dealt, discarded, drew, and then she sighed and her cards gave a little shiver. Tor's eye gleamed, and Dutch straightened in his seat.

30 "I'll pay to see that hand," said Lily Veddar.

31 Fleur showed, and she had nothing there, nothing at all.

32 Tor's thin smile cracked open, and he threw his hand in too.

33 "Well, we know one thing," he said, leaning back in his chair, "the squaw can't bluff."

34 With that I lowered myself into a mound of swept sawdust and slept. I woke up during the night, but none of them had moved yet, so I couldn't either. Still later, the men must have gone out again, or Fritzie come out to break the game, because I was lifted, soothed, cradled in a woman's arms and rocked so quiet that I kept my eyes shut while Fleur rolled me into a closet of grimy ledgers, oiled paper, balls of string, and thick files that fit beneath me like a mattress.

35 The game went on after work the next evening. I got my eight cents back five times over, and Fleur kept the rest of the dollar she'd won for a stake. This time they didn't play so late, but they played regular, and then kept going at it night after night. They played poker now, or variations, for one week straight, and each time Fleur won exactly one dollar, no more and no less, too consistent for luck.

36 By this time, Lily and the other men were so lit with suspense that they got Pete to join the game with them. They concentrated, the fat dog sitting tense in Lily Veddar's lap, Tor suspicious, Dutch stroking his huge square brow, Pete steady. It wasn't that Fleur won that hooked them in so, because she lost hands too. It was rather that she never had a freak hand or even anything above a straight. She only took on her low cards, which didn't sit right. By chance, Fleur should have gotten a full or flush by now. The irritating thing was she beat with pairs and never bluffed, because she couldn't, and still she ended up each night with exactly one dollar. Lily couldn't believe, first of all, that a woman could be smart enough to play cards, but even if she was, that she would then be stupid enough to cheat for a dollar a night. By day I watched him turn the problem over, his hard white face dull, small fingers probing at his knuckles, until he finally thought he had Fleur figured out as a bit-time player, caution her game. Raising the stakes would throw her.

37 More than anything now, he wanted Fleur to come away with something but a dollar. Two bits less or ten more, the sum didn't matter, just so he broke her streak.

38 Night after night she played, won her dollar, and left to stay in a place that just Fritzie and I knew about. Fleur bathed in the slaughtering tub, then slept in the unused brick smokehouse behind the lockers, a windowless place tarred on the inside with scorched fats. When I brushed against her skin I noticed that she smelled of the walls, rich and woody, slightly burnt. Since that night she put me in the closet I was no longer afraid of her, but followed her close, stayed with her, became her moving shadow that the men never noticed, the shadow that could have saved her.

39 August, the month that bears fruit, closed around the shop, and Pete and Fritzie left for Minnesota to escape the heat. Night by night, running, Fleur had won thirty dollars, and only Pete's presence had kept Lily at bay. But Pete was gone now, and one payday, with the heat so bad no one could move but Fleur, the men sat and played and waited while she finished work. The cards sweat, limp in their fingers, the table was slick with grease, and even the walls were warm to the touch. The air was motionless. Fleur was in the next room boiling heads.

40 Her green dress, drenched, wrapped her like a transparent sheet. A skin of lakeweed. Black snarls of veining clung to her arms. Her braids were loose, half-unraveled, tied behind her neck in a thick loop. She stood in steam, turning skulls through a vat with a wooden paddle. When scraps boiled to the surface, she bent with a round tin sieve and scooped them out. She'd filled two dishpans.

41 "Ain't that enough now?" called Lily. "We're waiting." The stump of a dog trembled in his lap, alive with rage. It never smelled me or noticed me above Fleur's smoky skin. The air was heavy in my corner, and pressed me down. Fleur sat with them.

42 "Now what do you say?" Lily asked the dog. It barked. That was the signal for the real game to start.

43 "Let's up the ante," said Lily, who had been stalking this night all month. He had a roll of money in his pocket. Fleur had five bills in her dress. The men had each saved their full pay.

44 "Ante a dollar then," said Fleur, and pitched hers in. She lost, but they let her scrape along, cent by cent. And then she won some. She played unevenly, as if chance was all she had. She reeled them in. The game went on. The dog was stiff now, poised on Lily's knees, a ball of vicious muscle with its yellow eyes slit in concentration. It gave advice, seemed to sniff the lay of Fleur's cards, twitched and nudged. Fleur was up, then down, saved by a scratch. Tor dealt seven cards, three down. The pot grew, round by round, until it held all the money. Nobody

folded. Then it all rode on one last card and they went silent. Fleur picked hers up and blew a long breath. The heat lowered like a bell. Her card shook, but she stayed in.

45 Lily smiled and took the dog's head tenderly between his palms.

46 "Say, Fatso," he said, crooning the words, "you reckon that girl's bluffing?"

47 The dog whined and Lily laughed. "Me too," he said, "let's show." He swept his bills and coins into the pot and then they turned their cards over.

48 Lily looked once, looked again, then he squeezed the dog up like a fist of dough and slammed it on the table.

49 Fleur threw her arms out and drew the money over, grinning that same wolf grin that she'd used on me, the grin that had them. She jammed the bills in her dress, scooped the coins up in waxed white paper that she tied with string.

50 "Let's go another round," said Lily, his voice choked with burrs. But Fleur opened her mouth and yawned, then walked out back to gather slops for the one big hog that was waiting in the stock pen to be killed.

51 The men sat still as rocks, their hands spread on the oiled wood table. Dutch had chewed his cigar to damp shreds. Tor's eye was dull. Lily's gaze was the only one to follow Fleur. I didn't move. I felt them gathering, saw my stepfather's veins, the ones in his forehead that stood out in anger. The dog had rolled off the table and curled in a knot below the counter, where none of the men could touch it.

52 Lily rose and stepped out back to the closet of ledgers where Pete kept his private stock. He brought back a bottle, uncorked and tipped it between his fingers. The lump in his throat moved, then he passed it on. They drank, quickly felt the whiskey's fire, and planned with their eyes things they couldn't say out loud.

53 When they left, I followed. I hid out back in the clutter of broken boards and chicken crates beside the stock pen, where they waited. Fleur could not be seen at first, and then the moon broke and showed her, slipping cautiously along the rough board chute with a bucket in her hand. Her hair fell, wild and coarse, to her waist, and her dress was a floating patch in the dark. She made a pig-calling sound, rang the tin pail lightly against the wood, froze suspiciously. But too late. In the sound of the ring Lily moved, fat and nimble, stepped right behind Fleur and put out his creamy hands. At his first touch, she whirled and doused him with the bucket of sour slops. He pushed her against the big fence and the package of coins split, went clinking and jumping, winked against the wood. Fleur rolled over once and vanished in the yard.

54 The moon fell behind a curtain of ragged clouds, and Lily followed into the dark muck. But he tripped, pitched over the huge flank of the pig, who lay mired to the snout, heavily snoring. I sprang out of the weeds and climbed the side of the pen, stuck like glue. I saw the sow rise to her neat, knobby knees, gain

her balance, and sway, curious, as Lily stumbled forward. Fleur had backed into the angle of rough wood just beyond, and when Lily tried to jostle past, the sow tipped up on her hind legs and struck, quick and hard as a snake. She plunged her head into Lily's thick side and snatched a mouthful of his shirt. She lunged again, caught him lower, so that he grunted in pained surprise. He seemed to ponder, breathing deep. Then he launched his huge body in a swimmer's dive.

55 The sow screamed as his body smacked over hers. She rolled, striking out with her knife-sharp hooves, and Lily gathered himself upon her, took her foot-long face by the ears and scraped her snout and cheeks against the trestles of the pen. He hurled the sow's tight skull against an iron post, but instead of knocking her dead, he merely woke her from her dream.

56 She reared, shrieked, drew him with her so that they posed standing upright. They bowed jerkily to each other, as if to begin. Then his arms swung and flailed. She sank her black fangs into his shoulder, clasping him, dancing him forward and backward through the pen. Their steps picked up pace, went wild. The two dipped as one, box-stepped, tripped each other. She ran her split foot through his hair. He grabbed her kinked tail. They went down and came up, the same shape and then the same color, until the men couldn't tell one from the other in that light and Fleur was able to launch herself over the gates, swing down, hit gravel.

57 The men saw, yelled, and chased her at a dead run to the smokehouse. And Lily too, once the sow gave up in disgust and freed him. That is where I should have gone to Fleur, saved her, thrown myself on Dutch. But I went stiff with fear and couldn't unlatch myself from the trestles or move at all. I closed my eyes and put my head in my arms, tried to hide, so there is nothing to describe but what I couldn't block out, Fleur's hoarse breath, so loud it filled me, her cry in the old language, and my name repeated over and over among the words.

58 The heat was still dense the next morning when I came back to work. Fleur was gone but the men were there, slack-faced, hung over. Lily was paler and softer than ever, as if his flesh had steamed on his bones. They smoked, took pulls off a bottle. It wasn't noon yet. I worked awhile, waiting shop and sharpening steel. But I was sick, I was smothered, I was sweating so hard that my hands slipped on the knives, and I wiped my fingers clean of the greasy touch of the customers' coins. Lily opened his mouth and roared once, not in anger. There was no meaning to the sound. His boxer dog, sprawled limp beside his foot, never lifted its head. Nor did the other men.

59 They didn't notice when I stepped outside, hoping for a clear breath. And then I forget them because I knew that we were all balanced, ready to tip, to fly, to be crushed as soon as the weather broke. The sky was so low that I felt the weight of it like a yoke. Clouds hung down, witch teats, a tornado's green-brown cones, and as I watched one flicked out and became a delicate probing

thumb. Even as I picked up my heels and ran back inside, the wind blew suddenly, cold, and then came rain.

60 Inside, the men had disappeared already and the whole place was trembling as if a huge hand was pinched at the rafters, shaking it. I ran straight through, screaming for Dutch or for any of them, and then I stopped at the heavy doors of the lockers, where they had surely taken shelter. I stood there a moment. Everything went still. Then I heard a cry building in the wind, faint at first, a whistle and then a shrill scream that tore through the walls and gathered around me, spoke plain so I understood that I should move, put my arms out, and slam down the great iron bar that fit across the hasp and lock.

61 Outside, the wind was stronger, like a hand held against me. I struggled forward. The bushes tossed, the awnings flapped off storefronts, the rails of porches rattled. The odd cloud became a fat snout that nosed along the earth and sniffled, jabbed, picked at things, sucked them up, blew them apart, rooted around as if it was following a certain scent, then stopped behind me at the butcher shop and bored down like a drill.

62 I went flying, landed somewhere in a ball. When I opened my eyes and looked, stranger things were happening.

63 A herd of cattle flew through the air like giant birds, dropping dung, their mouths opened in stunned bellows. A candle, still lighted, blew past, and tables, napkins, garden tools, a whole school of drifting eyeglasses, jackets on hangers, hams, a checkerboard, a lampshade, and at last the sow from behind the lockers, on the run, her hooves a blur, set free, swooping, diving, screaming as everything in Argus fell apart and got turned upside down, smashed, and thoroughly wrecked.

64 Days passed before the town went looking for the men. They were bachelors, after all, except for Tor, whose wife had suffered a blow to the head that made her forgetful. Everyone was occupied with digging out, in high relief because even though the Catholic steeple had been torn off like a peaked cap and sent across five fields, those huddled in the cellar were unhurt. Walls had fallen, windows were demolished, but the stores were intact and so were the bankers and shop owners who had taken refuge in their safes or beneath their cash registers. It was a fair-minded disaster, no one could be said to have suffered much more than the next, at least not until Fritzie and Pete came home.

65 Of all the businesses in Argus, Kozka's Meats had suffered worst. The boards of the front building had been split to kindling, piled in a huge pyramid, and the shop equipment was blasted far and wide. Pete paced off the distance the iron bathtub had been flung—a hundred feet. The glass candy case went fifty, and landed without so much as a cracked pane. There were other surprises as well, for the back rooms where Fritzie and Pete lived were undis-

turbed. Fritzie said the dust still coated her china figures, and upon her kitchen table, in the ashtray, perched the last cigarette she'd put out in haste. She lit it up and finished it, looking through the window. From there, she could see that the old smokehouse Fleur had slept in was crushed to a reddish sand and the stock-pens were completely torn apart, the rails stacked helter-skelter. Fritzie asked for Fleur. People shrugged. Then she asked about the others and, suddenly, the town understood that three men were missing.

66 There was a rally of help, a gathering of shovels and volunteers. We passed boards from hand to hand, stacked them, uncovered what lay beneath the pile of jagged splinters. The lockers, full of the meat that was Pete and Fritzie's investment, slowly came into sight, still intact. When enough room was made for a man to stand on the roof, there were calls, a general urge to hack through and see what lay below. But Fritzie shouted that she wouldn't allow it because the meat would spoil. And so the work continued, board by board, until at last the heavy oak doors of the freezer were revealed and people pressed to the entry. Everyone wanted to be the first, but since it was my stepfather lost, I was let go in when Pete and Fritzie wedged through into the sudden icy air.

67 Pete scraped a match on his boot, lit the lamp Fritzie held, and then the three of us stood still in its circle. Light glared off the skinned and hanging carcasses, the crates of wrapped sausages, the bright and cloudy blocks of lake ice, pure as winter. The cold bit into us, pleasant at first, then numbing. We must have stood there a couple of minutes before we saw the men, or more rightly, the humps of fur, the iced and shaggy hides they wore, the bearskins they had taken down and wrapped around themselves. We stepped closer and tilted the lantern beneath the flaps of fur into their faces. The dog was there, perched among them, heavy as a doorstop. The three had hunched around a barrel where the game was still laid out, and a dead lantern and an empty bottle, too. But they had thrown down their last hands and hunkered tight, clutching one another, knuckles raw from beating at the door they had also attacked with hooks. Frost stars gleamed off their eyelashes and the stubble of their beards. Their faces were set in concentration, mouths open as if to speak some careful thought, some agreement they'd come to in each other's arms.

68 Power travels in the bloodlines, handed out before birth. It comes down through the hands, which in the Pillagers were strong and knotted, big, spidery, and rough, with sensitive fingertips good at dealing cards. It comes through the eyes, too, belligerent, darkest brown, the eyes of those in the bear clan, impolite as they gaze directly at a person.

69 In my dreams, I look straight back at Fleur, at the men. I am no longer the watcher on the dark sill, the skinny girl.

70 The blood draws us back, as if it runs through a vein of earth. I've come home and, except for talking to my cousins, live a quiet life. Fleur lives quiet

too, down on Lake Turcot with her boat. Some say she's married to the waterman, Misshepeshu, or that she's living in shame with white men or windigos, or that she's killed them all. I'm about the only one here who ever goes to visit her. Last winter, I went to help out in her cabin when she bore the child, whose green eyes and skin the color of an old penny made more talk, as no one could decide if the child was mixed blood or what, fathered in a smokehouse, or by a man with brass scales, or by the lake. The girl is bold, smiling in her sleep, as if she knows what people wonder, as if she hears the old men talk, turning the story over. It comes up different every time and has no ending, no beginning. They get the middle wrong too. They only know that they don't know anything.

—1986

Index of Critical Terms

Acknowledgments

Chinua Achebe, "Civil Peace" from *Girls at War and Other Stories.* Copyright © 1972, 1973 by Chinua Achebe. Used by permission of Doubleday, a division of Bantam Doubleday Dell Publishing group, Inc. and Harold Ober Associates, Inc.

Margaret Atwood, "Rape Fantasies" from *Dancing Girls and Other Stories.* Copyright © 1977. Reprinted by permission of the Canadian publishers, McClelland and Stewart, Toronto.

Raymond Carver, "Cathedral" from *Cathedral.* Copyright © 1983 by Raymond Carver. Reprinted by permission of Alfred A. Knopf, Inc.

Willa Cather, "Paul's Case" from *Youth and the Bright Medusa* (New York: Alfred A. Knopf, Inc., 1928).

Denise Chávez, "The Last of the Menu Girls," first published in *The Last of the Menu Girls.* (Houston: Arte Público Press, 1986). Reprinted by permission.

John Cheever, "Reunion" from *The Stories of John Cheever.* Copyright.© 1962 by John Cheever. Reprinted by permission of Alfred A. Knopf, Inc.

Anton Chekhov, "The Lady with the Pet Dog" from *The Portable Chekhov,* edited by Avrahm Yarmolinsky. Copyright © 1947, 1968 by Viking Penguin, Inc. Renewed copyright © 1975 by Avrahm Yarmolinsky. Used by permission of Viking Penguin, a division of Penguin Books USA Inc.

Kate Chopin, "The Storm" reprinted by permission of Louisiana State University Press from *The Complete Works of Kate Chopin,* edited by Per Seyersted. Copyright © 1969 by Louisiana State University Press.

Ralph Ellison, "Flying Home." Reprinted by permission of William Morris Agency, Inc., on behalf of the author. Copyright © 1944, (renewed) by Ralph Ellison.

Louise Erdrich, "Fleur" from *Esquire,* August 1986. Copyright © 1986 by Louise Erdrich. Reprinted by permission of the author.

William Faulkner, "A Rose for Emily" from *Collected Stories of William Faulkner.* Copyright © 1930 and renewed 1958 by William Faulkner. Reprinted by permission of Random House, Inc.

Ernest Hemingway, "A Clean, Well-Lighted Place." Reprinted with permission of Charles Scribner's Sons, an imprint of Macmillan Publishing Company, from *Winner Take Nothing* by Ernest Hemingway. Copyright © 1933 by Charles Scribner's Sons; copyright renewed © 1961 by Mary Hemingway.

Shirley Jackson, "The Lottery" from *The Lottery.* Copyright © 1948, 1949 by Shirley Jackson, copyright renewed © 1976, 1977 by Lawrence Hyman, Barry Hyman, Mrs. Sarah Webster, and Mrs. Joanne Shurer. Reprinted by permission of Farrar, Straus and Giroux, Inc.

James Joyce, "The Dead" from *Dubliners.* Copyright 1916 by B. W. Heubsch. Definitive text copyright © 1967 by the Estate of James Joyce. Used by permission of Viking Penguin, a division of Penguin Books USA Inc.

D. H. Lawrence, "The Horse Dealer's Daughter," copyright © 1922 by Thomas B. Seltzer, Inc., renewed © 1950 by Frieda Lawrence, from *Complete Short Stories*

D. H. Lawrence. Used by permission of Viking Penguin, a division of Penguin Books USA Inc.

Doris Lessing, "A Woman on a Roof" from *A Man and Two Women.* Copyright © 1963 by Doris Lessing. Reprinted by permission of Jonathan Clowes Ltd. on behalf of Doris Lessing.

Gabriel García Márquez, "The Handsomest drowned Man in the World" from *Leaf Storm and Other Stories.* English translation copyright © 1970 by Gabriel García Márquez. Reprinted by permission of HarperCollins Publishers.

Bobbie Ann Mason, "Shiloh" from *Shiloh and Other Stories.* Copyright ©1982 by Bobbie Ann Mason. Reprinted by permission of HarperCollins Publishers.

Guy de Maupassant, "The Necklace" from *The Collected Novels and Stories of Guy de Maupassant,* translated by Ernest Boyd. Copyright © 1924 and renewed 1952 by Alfred A. Knopf, Inc. Reprinted by permission of the publisher.

Alice Munro, "Wild Swans" from *The Beggar Maid.* Copyright © 1977, 1978 by Alice Munro. Reprinted by permission of Alfred A. Knopf, Inc. and Virginia Barber.

Joyce Carol Oates, "Where Are You Going, Where Have You Been?" from *The Wheel of Love and Other Stories.* Copyright © 1970 by Joyce Carol Oates. Reprinted by permission of John Hawkins & Associates, Inc.

Flannery O'Connor, "Everything That Rises Must Converge" from *Everything That Rises Must Converge.* Copyright © 1965 by the estate of Mary Flannery O'Connor. Reprinted by permission of Farrar, Straus and Giroux, Inc.

Katherine Ann Porter, "The Jilting of Granny Weatherall" from *Flowering Judas and Other Stories,* copyright © 1930 and renewed 1958 by Katherine Anne Porter, reprinted by permission of Harcourt Brace Jovanovich, Inc.

John Steinbeck, "The Chrysanthemums," copyright © 1937, renewed © 1965 by John Steinbeck, from *The Long Valley* by John Steinbeck. Used by permission of Viking Penguin, a division of Penguin Books USA Inc.

John Updike, "A & P" from *Pigeon Feathers and Other Stories.* Copyright © 1962 by John Updike. Reprinted by permission of Alfred A. Knopf, Inc. Originally appeared in *The New Yorker.*

Alice Walker, "Everyday Use" from *In Love & Trouble, Stories of Black Women,* copyright © 1973 by Alice Walker, reprinted by permission of Harcourt Brace Jovanovich, Inc.

Eudora Welty, "Livvie" from *The Wide Net and Other Stories,* copyright © 1942 and renewed 1970 by Eudora Welty, reprinted by permission of Harcourt Brace Jovanovich, Inc.

Edith Wharton, "Roman Fever" reprinted with permission of Charles Scribner's Sons, an imprint of Macmillan Publishing Company from *Roman Fever and Other Stories* by Edith Wharton. Copyright © 1934 by Liberty Magazine, renewed © 1962 by William R. Tyler.

Richard Wright, "The Man Who Was Almost a Man" from *Eight Men.* Copyright © 1987 by the Estate of Richard Wright. Used by permission of the publisher, Thunder's Mouth Press.